SEARCH for
THE TALI
QANIKKAAQ
ONDAI
THE KARG
MIROMARA
the Freshwaters
S.S. Brittania
the Freshwaters
ATLANTICA
reshwaters
MATALI
CAPE HORN
Achilles
WILLIWAW
SOUTHERN OCEAN

DARK TIDE

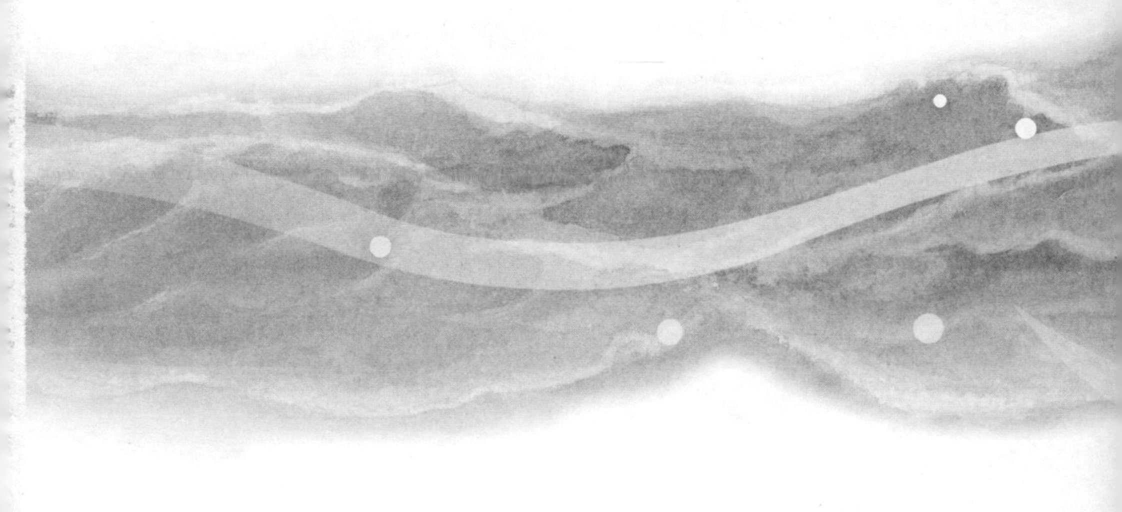

The Waterfire Saga

Deep Blue
Rogue Wave
Dark Tide
Sea Spell

DARK TIDE

JENNIFER DONNELLY

Hodder Children's Books

First published in the US in 2015

First published in Great Britain in 2015 by Hodder Children's Books

10 9 8 7 6 5 4 3 2 1

A Catalogue record for this book is available from the British Library

Typeset in Granjon by Avon DataSet Ltd, Bidford-on-Avon, Warwickshire

ISBN 978 1 444 92361 2

Printed and bound in Great Britain by Clays Ltd, St Ives plc

The paper and board used in this book are made from wood
from responsible sources.

Hodder Children's Books
An imprint of Hachette Children's Group
Part of Hodder & Stoughton
Carmelite House
50 Victoria Embankment
London, EC4Y 0DZ
An Hachette UK company

www.hachette.co.uk

For L.A.M.

There is no way back for me now. I am going to take you on journeys you've never dreamed were possible.

– Alexander McQueen

PROLOGUE

THE MERMAID'S SWORD glinted in the watery twilight of Tanner's Deeps. She held it in front of her, both hands gripping the hilt, as she moved through the deserted village.

Tanner, whoever he was, was long gone. So was everyone else. Yet the mermaid kept her sword raised. Blacktip sharks were known to hunt along the lonely currents that swept through abandoned villages. Predators of another kind prowled them, too – looters who ransacked the houses of the disappeared for anything of value.

The mermaid was travelling back to Ondalina, her arctic home, and had seen many such villages on her way. In the Freshwaters. In Miromara, and here, in Atlantica. All were gutted and ruined. Their mer had been abducted. The few who'd managed to escape told of soldiers in black who'd come for them with weapons and cages. Where the mer had been taken, no one knew.

Satisfied no looters were near, the mermaid sheathed her sword. She was weary and night was coming with its many dangers. A small house, its door off the hinges, was directly in front of her. She entered it cautiously, startling some mackerel.

The downstairs rooms showed signs of violence – an overturned table, smashed plates, toys scattered across the floor. She swam upstairs and found a room that offered her a soft, anemone-filled bed.

Weariness was etched on her face. She craved sleep, but dreaded it, too. Nightmares haunted her. Every time she closed her eyes, she saw it – Abbadon, the monster. She saw it advancing on the others – Ling, Ava, Neela, Becca, and Sera – and tearing them apart.

I should have stayed with them, she thought. I should have helped them.

But they wouldn't have wanted her help. Not once they'd learned the truth.

As she swam towards the bed, something moved behind her. She caught a blur of darkness, a pale face.

There was someone else in the room.

The mermaid spun around with the speed of a tarpon, her heart thumping in her chest, her hand on the hilt of her sword.

There *was* someone else there, she saw, but not in the room. He was inside a mirror that was hanging on a wall.

'Don't be afraid, Astrid Kolfinnsdottir. I would never hurt you,' he said. 'I know your secret. I know how you've suffered. They mock you and call you weak, yet you have the blood of the greatest mage who ever lived running through your veins. Come with me. I'll put an end to the cruel words, the laughter. I'll make you powerful, more powerful than any creature alive.'

The mermaid eyed him warily. He was human. His face was obscured by shadows. But she could see that, at his neck, a flawless black pearl hung from a chain.

'How do you know my name? Who are you?' she demanded.

The man replied by offering his hand. It pushed through the silvered glass and hovered in the water – a question instead of an answer.

The mermaid's fins prickled, but she ignored her fear. Something about him drew her closer, something as powerful as the tides.

She lifted her hand to his. As she did, she glimpsed her own reflection in the glass. And beyond it, the man's face, no longer in the shadows. For an instant, his eyes – as black and bottomless as the Abyss – became her own.

In terror, she slammed her tail fin into the mirror and shattered it. As the pieces rained down, the mermaid bolted from the room.

She swam as fast as she could. Out of the house, away from the village. Into the cold, dark waters of the night.

ONE

SERAFINA DI MERROVINGIA, rightful regina of Miromara, cocked her crossbow.

'Shoot to kill,' she ordered.

Twenty-five Black Fin fighters nodded in unison, then fanned out, their camo blending in with the weedy rock face at the base of Miromara's royal palace. Casting a last glance at the dark waters above her, Sera turned and headed for a tunnel in the rock. Her uncle's soldiers rarely patrolled this lonely part of the palace grounds, but she could afford no surprises tonight.

THE TRAITORS' GATE, read the ancient words carved over the tunnel's entrance. Enemies of Miromara had been brought to the dungeons through this passageway for thousands of years, until it had been permanently locked during an unprecedented era of peace and then forgotten. The irony was not lost on Sera. The real traitors were *inside* the palace – her uncle Vallerio; his new wife, Portia Volnero; and their daughter, Lucia. They'd assassinated

Sera's mother, Regina Isabella, and stolen the throne.

A few yards into the tunnel, darkness gave way to the light of a portable lava globe, hung on the wall by one of the Black Fins. Its glow played over Sera, revealing a mermaid very different from the one who'd lived in the palace not too long ago.

Sera cut a commanding figure now – strong, straight-backed, and sure of herself. Muscles rippled in her arms and tail. Her hair, dyed black, was cut pixie-short so no enemy could grab it and hold her back, as the Mirror Lord once had. As all Black Fins did, she wore a short military jacket of dark blue with black trim to honour Cerulea, the capital of Miromara. A dagger rested at her hip. The doubt and hesitance that had clouded her green eyes were gone; a dangerous new light burned in them.

Up ahead, Sera saw a tall iron gate crusted with barnacles. Four young mermen were furiously sawing at its bars, muscles straining in their backs and arms. Iron repelled magic, so no songspells could be used to break or liquefy the metal.

She lowered her weapon. 'How much longer, Yaz?' she asked one of the mermen.

'Five minutes max,' Yazeed replied. 'We're almost through.'

He was her second-in-command, and this had been his idea. Sera remembered when he and Luca, another fighter, had come swimming into the Black Fins' headquarters at four one morning, whooping and laughing.

'Look what we found!' Yaz had crowed.

He'd unrolled an ancient kelp parchment and placed it on the table in the safe house. Serafina and the rest of the Black Fins had gathered around.

'It's the original building plan for the palace. Complete with the entire network of lava pipes,' Yaz had explained, rubbing his hands together. 'This run of pipe' – he'd pointed to a thick black line drawn in squid ink – 'carried lava from the seam underneath the palace to the west wing. It was supposed to have been removed two centuries ago, when the treasury vaults were moved from the Grande Corrente to the palace.'

Luca had jumped in. 'But it never was!' he said, unrolling a second parchment. 'These are the plans for the relocated treasury vaults. They couldn't place them close to lava pipes because if the pipes broke, the lava would melt the walls, leaving the treasure vulnerable. So a new run of pipe was laid – well below the vaults. The old pipes were only closed off, not demolished.'

'Everything's still there!' Yaz had said gleefully. 'The pipes, the diverter, even the shutoff valve. Only a foot of rock separates the old pipe from the treasury. All we have to do is break the pipe, open the old valve, let the lava burn through the rock—'

'—and we're in the vaults!' Sera had interrupted, excitedly slapping tails with him.

'But how do we get inside the palace in the first place?' Neela – Sera's best friend, Yazeed's sister, and now a Black Fin, too had asked.

'The old Traitors' Gate on the north side of the palace. It's at the bottom of the seamount and it's overgrown by seaweed. It'll give us plenty of cover,' Luca had replied.

Sera had known about the Traitors' Gate, but she'd been amazed to learn about the network of old lava pipes. Clearly she'd missed much during her days as a pampered princess. Songcasting, school and her mother's endless lectures had filled her hours. These things were important, but they didn't get one into the treasury vaults – cunning and daring did.

'When do we go?' Neela had asked.

'As soon as I can get Mahdi to throw a party – a big one, with a lightworks show,' Yaz had replied.

'I don't follow,' Neela had said. 'Why do we need a party? And lightworks?'

'Because when we divert lava off the main line, the pressure in the palace will drop. Any lights on that line will flicker. Lavaplaces will fizzle. Someone's bound to notice and become suspicious.'

'So Mahdi cuts the lights for the show and nobody's the wiser!' Neela had exclaimed.

'Exactly,' Yazeed had said. 'By the time the lightworks are over, the lava's flowing again and we're on our way back to HQ with as much swag as we can carry.'

'Yaz, you're a genius,' Sera had said.

'So true,' Yazeed had agreed. Everyone laughed and then eagerly started planning the heist.

Sera had been so thrilled about their having the building plans that it was only later, as they were heading to their bunks to crash, she had thought to ask Yaz *how* he had got them.

'Luca and I went to the Ostrokon,' Yazeed had replied lightly. 'You can learn a lot there, you know.'

Sera had raised an eyebrow at his joke. Everyone knew that the Ostrokon was one of her favourite places in Cerulea. Before the city had been attacked, she had loved to go there and listen to history conchs, but it wasn't safe now. 'That was risky, Yaz. It's heavily patrolled,' she'd said. She hadn't even wanted to think about what would have happened if they'd been caught. She could not have asked for a better second-in-command. Yaz was smart, brave, and bold – but sometimes he was too bold.

He had grinned. 'Not heavily enough, apparently,' he'd said, continuing to his bunk.

'Hold on a minute,' Sera had said, stopping him. 'I still have a question for you: the old pipes . . . How do you know for sure that they're still there?'

'We checked,' he had admitted with a shrug.

'You *checked*? The pipes are *inside* the palace. And there's a bounty on your head. Just how did you check?'

Yaz had frowned. He'd tapped his chin with his finger. 'Hmm. Well, now that I think about it, we might've crashed a party. Lucia sure loves parties.'

Sera had pressed a palm to her forehead. 'Gods, no. Tell me you didn't.'

Yaz had cast a quick illusio spell. His hair had lightened to blond. His eyes had turned blue. Tattoos, swirling and ornate, had appeared on his face, neck, and chest. He had affected a vapid look and the voice to match it.

'Bro, that's *Bilge* playing! I loooove that band! Hey, did you see the *ballast* on that merl? It's time to get jolly, Roger!'

Sera had shaken her head angrily. He'd gone too far. 'You could've been *captured*, Yazeed. *You*, a leader of the Black Fin resistance. Do you have *any* idea what they would have done to you?'

'But we weren't. And now *we're* going to do some capturing. As in treasure.'

He'd kissed her forehead and flopped into his bunk. As angry as she had been with him, Sera hadn't been able to suppress a triumphant smile. The resistance needed gold – lots of it, and Yazeed had found a way to get it.

'We're in!' he called out now.

Sera turned her attention to the gate. Six bars had been cut away to make a space big enough to swim through. She raced back to the tunnel entrance and whistled. Almost instantly, the camoed fighters were at her side, following her into the tunnel.

Yazeed and his mermen – Luca, Silvio, and Franco – were ready at the gate, carrying pickaxes, weapons, and lava torches. Sera saw the determination on the faces of her comrades, and her heart clenched. Their loyalty, their trust, their willingness to die for the cause was what made the resistance strong.

She knew the mission they were about to undertake was insanely risky; she also knew they had no choice. The Black

Fins were fighting not only for her realm, but for *all* the mer realms. Vallerio and Portia had already taken Miromara and Matali. They wanted Atlantica, Ondalina, Qin, and the Freshwaters, too. The vicious human Rafe Mfeme was helping them in their quest.

Someone else was helping, too, though Sera didn't know who or why. She'd heard this someone else referred to as he, and knew he'd paid for her uncle's invading mercenaries – the death riders. In return, Vallerio and Portia were aiding him in a search for six talismans – powerful objects that had belonged to the mages of Atlantis. Sera had learned that this person, whoever he was, planned to use the talismans to unleash a great evil submerged in the Southern Sea – Abbadon, a monster created by Orfeo, one of the mages. Who *was* the mysterious *he*? And why would her uncle ally with him? Sera didn't know, but she knew that Vallerio and Portia didn't care how many mer were killed, as long as they satisfied their desire for power and wealth. What they didn't seem to realize is that there would be nothing left to rule, nothing left to plunder, if this shadowy *he* got his way. She had to stop him, but to do so, she first had to stop her uncle.

Sera cast one last glance at her fighters.

Fossegrim, the realm's liber magus, had been their leader. After his arrest, Sera had taken over. He was dead – Sera was certain of it – but neither she nor his fighters would forget him.

Words her mother had once spoken echoed in her head. *A ruler's greatest power comes from her heart – from the love she bears her subjects, and the love they bear her.*

The Black Fins were Sera's subjects. They were her brothers and sisters, too. Her family. And she loved them fiercely.

Gods, protect them, she prayed now. *Keep them safe*.

Sera raised her crossbow and addressed her fighters. 'Fast and furious, just as we planned,' she said. 'Watch your own back. Watch each other's backs. No fear, no screwups, no prisoners. Let's *go*.'

TWO

FRANCO WENT FIRST with a lava torch, followed by Serafina, with the others right behind them. They shot through the murky tunnel, its walls furry with algae, not stopping until they entered the palace's enormous lava chamber.

The cavernous space had been hollowed out of the palace's rock foundation. In the centre of it was the channeller – the main pipe that directed lava from a seam deep below the seafloor. As it neared the ceiling, the pipe branched into four tributary pipes that snaked through tunnels in the rock. Each tributary had about four feet of space around it, allowing workers access for maintenance and repairs.

Sera, Yazeed, Luca, and Franco were going to follow the tributary on the west side of the room to the old pipe that ran above the treasury vaults. The rest of the Black Fins would stay where they were and wait for the four to return.

Yaz and Franco put their crossbows down. They were still carrying torches and had pickaxes slung over their backs;

the tributary's tunnel was too narrow to allow the weapons, too.

Sera started for the channeller, her crossbow raised, when Yazeed suddenly grabbed her arm. He pointed wordlessly, but she'd already seen what had spooked him. A watchman had entered the room. He swam to the channeller and bent down to examine a glass-covered dial, his back towards them.

The Black Fins had prepared for all eventualities. Sera nodded at Silvio, her best marksman. He raised his crossbow and a split second later, a dart found his target's neck.

The watchman gave a surprised shout of pain. The dart's tip was filled with weak stingray venom. Full strength, the venom would kill a mer. Diluted, it only put its victim to sleep. Silvio caught the watchman as he fell backwards, his eyes already fluttering closed.

'Nice shot, Sil,' Yaz said, racing by him. Franco and Sera were right behind him.

As two other Black Fins dragged the unconscious merman over to a closet, Silvio cast an illusio spell to transform himself into an exact double of the watchman. He would busy himself checking dials and valves in case Vallerio's soldiers decided to patrol the lava chamber.

Sera, Yaz, Luca, and Franco swam into the west tunnel, hugging their tools and weapons close to their bodies, and followed it upward. Lava globes, spaced ten yards apart, illuminated the tunnel. Each had a hook underneath it to hold maintenance workers' tool bags. Unable to move their tails vigorously for fear of smashing the globes or getting caught on the hooks, the four lost speed. They'd hoped to reach their target destination in five minutes, but it took them nearly ten.

'I see it,' Franco finally said, pointing above them to where the main artery split into two. One section of pipe continued straight up into the palace. Another ran due west above the treasury vaults. 'We're behind,' a tense Yaz said as they reached the join. 'The lightworks show is going to start soon.'

'There's the valve,' Luca said, pointing at a bronze handwheel jutting out just past the join. 'All we have to do is rip a hole in the old pipe, then open it.'

'Easier said than done,' said Yaz, holding his torch up to the tunnel that contained the west-running pipe.

The tunnel snaked horizontally through the rock foundation and was much narrower than what they'd just swum through. Small blue crabs clung to its top; they scuttled away from the torch's light. A thick layer of silt lined its bottom.

Franco was the slimmest of the three mermen. He entered the tunnel's mouth and started to swim through, holding his torch in front of himself. When that didn't work, he crawled . . . until he got stuck.

'I can't move!' he called out. 'Yo, pull me out!'

Yaz and Luca grabbed his tail fin and yanked. He came out covered in silt.

'I'm the smallest. I'll go,' Sera said.

Her nerves were as taut as a bowstring as she entered the tunnel. She was worried about getting stuck in the small space, but excitement overrode her misgivings. They'd made it this far. They might actually *do* this if she could just break the pipe.

Yaz handed her his pickaxe. 'Swim about ten yards in, then rip open a good-sized hole,' he said.

Sera made her way down the passageway on her back, holding the torch and pickaxe on her chest and pushing herself along with her tail. Silt swirled around her, making it nearly impossible to see.

When she got far enough down the tunnel, she waited for the water to clear. There was so little room to manoeuvre that she had to extend both arms above her head and swing the pickaxe from her shoulders without bending her elbows. Within minutes her muscles were screaming. Gritting her teeth against the pain, she forced herself to swing over and over again.

The pipe was made out of goblin-forged steel, strong enough to resist the extreme heat of lava, but it was centuries old and corroded. Finally, just when she thought she couldn't swing the axe even one more time, Sera heard a satisfying metallic screech as its blade punctured the pipe. She gave a victory yell and swung again and again, ripping at the hole's edges until it was big enough. Then, spent and shaking, she wriggled back down the tunnel. As she crawled out, her excitement dimmed. She'd realized they had a problem. A big one.

'I was able to rip the pipe open, but that doesn't change the fact that the tunnel's super narrow,' she informed the others. 'Even if we manage to get into the vault, how are we going to get any treasure out? Most of the fighters won't be able to squeeze through.'

This was the Black Fins' one and only chance to get into the vaults. Their break-in would eventually be discovered and Vallerio would make sure it could never be repeated.

'We'll think of something,' Yaz said. 'We have few weapons, little food, and no medicine. We can't keep fighting without any gold.'

'We need the ochi now,' said Luca. 'It's gotta be close to showtime in the Grand Hall. You ready?'

Sera nodded. An ochi, or spying songspell, was fiendishly difficult to cast and needed all the energy the caster could summon. It required that a gândac, or bug, usually a shell of some sort, be placed near the mer to be spied upon.

It would have been tough to get into the palace to place a gândac, and even if Sera could manage it, Portia had the rooms swept for them regularly. But what Portia didn't know was that a gândac was already in place. It was one of Sera's favourite shells – a large, beautiful nautilus.

When her beloved grandmother had died, a heartbroken Sera had placed the shell, her most prized possession, in the cupped hands of a statue of her grandmother that stood in the Grand Hall. The nautilus had been there for so long, everyone thought it was part of the statue.

Sera closed her eyes now and cast the ochi. As soon as an image of the hall formed in her mind, she launched straight into a convoca spell, so that Yaz, Luca, and Franco could see it, too.

'Got it?' she asked, her voice straining with effort.

The mermen said they did, and Sera focused even harder. A rough eddy of emotion swirled through her heart as the image sharpened. Her mother, Regina Isabella, had died in the Grand Hall, at the foot of her throne, protecting Serafina. It was hallowed ground to Sera, and Lucia had turned it into a nightclub.

Above the guests, jellyfish with huge diaphanous bells and long ruffled tentacles pulsed to the music, turning different colours with every beat. Bright sea lilies decorated the tables. Banded kraits twined in the arms of the huge chandeliers and neon anemones bloomed on the walls.

Lucia was dancing with Mahdi. He had his arm around her waist. She was laughing, her head thrown back, her black hair fanning out in the water like a swath of midnight.

Sera's heart leapt at the sight of the merman she loved. She hadn't so much as glimpsed him since that day in the kolisseo when she'd watched as he'd 'promised' himself to Lucia. Yazeed had forbidden convocas between them. The spells were to be used only when absolutely necessary. Powerful songcasters could break them and listen in. Mahdi sometimes managed to get a conch to the Black Fins' headquarters, but even that was risky. He and Yaz had planned tonight's raid with the help of a palace groom who couriered conchs while exercising hippokamps in the waters outside Cerulea.

The partiers at the palace tonight included Lucia's parents and some of their friends, but they were mostly members of her court – young, gorgeous mermaids and mermen all dressed as colourfully as parrot fish. Lucia didn't tolerate anyone plain or dull.

Breathless and laughing, Mahdi dipped Lucia at the end of the song, and kissed her.

Jealousy seared Serafina's heart. She quickly doused it. Hard lessons had taught her to control her emotions. Mahdi's life depended upon his ability to keep Lucia convinced that he loved her. All their lives did.

As the guests hooted and clapped, Mahdi straightened, grinning, then held up a hand for silence.

Sera drank in every detail of his appearance – his ebony hair, tied back; his white sea-silk shirt and emerald jacket; his shimmering blue tail; his dark, expressive eyes. She longed to touch him, to be with him. To hear him say that he still loved her. Her left hand instinctively went to the ring she wore on her right. The ring Mahdi had given her, carved from a shell.

'I have a little surprise . . .' he began.

Oohs and ahhs went up.

'I've brought the best lightworkers from Matali here to dazzle you with their art. Lightworks, with their rare and sparkling beauty, remind me of the light of *my* life . . . my future wife, Lucia.'

Franco rolled his eyes. Luca acted like he was going to hurl. Yaz smiled grimly and Sera tried to.

Mahdi's performance was a lie. He was *hers*, not Lucia's.

Sera and Mahdi had exchanged their own vows months ago in a secret Promising ceremony. He wanted to defeat Vallerio as much as she did.

As a thumping Matali beat began, lightworkers in bright silks and glittering jewels, their faces painted with swirls of colour, danced into the Grand Hall. Some threw handfuls of pearls high up to the ceiling, where they exploded into shimmering clouds of pink and yellow. Others trailed ribbons of silver and gold waterfire behind them. As they warmed up the guests, six master lightworkers prepared to cast.

'The lights, bro, the *lights*,' Yaz whispered to himself.

As if on cue, Mahdi signalled for the chandeliers to be dimmed. Most of the lighting in the Grand Hall ran directly off the lava lines. A few wall sconces did not; their globes, self-contained and full of bubbling lava, continued to glow faintly.

'We're on,' Yaz said.

Sera ended the convoca and the four snapped into action. Yaz grabbed hold of one side of the handwheel, Franco the other. Sera and Luca swam above them to give them room to work in the confined space. Yaz and Franco counted to three, then threw all their strength against the wheel, but it wouldn't budge. The wheel was green with corrosion and crusted with barnacles. They tried again. Luca took a turn, replacing Franco, but still the valve wouldn't open.

Yaz slapped his tail against the valve's housing. 'We don't have time for this!' he yelled.

'We could scrape some of the barnacles off,' Franco ventured.

He started working at them with the broad edge of the pickaxe. As he did, Sera heard something – tiny voices angrily shouting. She realized that she understood them.

Bending down to the barnacles, she politely asked them to get off the valve. Furious over the assault on their home, they stubbornly refused. Sera then explained that it was their ruler asking them to do so and the survival of the realm depended upon their cooperation. Immediately a staccato of pops was heard as the barnacles released their grip. Some relocated to the new pipe, others to the tunnel walls.

'Since when do you speak Cirrian?' Yaz asked, astonished.

'Since the bloodbind,' Sera replied, silently thanking her friend Ling, an omnivoxa – one who can speak all languages.

Back in the Iele's caves, Sera, Ling, Ava, Becca, and Neela had sworn a blood oath, and in so doing, each had received some of the others' powers. They were sisters now, bound forever by magic and friendship.

Yaz and Franco grasped the handwheel again and put every last ounce of their strength into turning it. For a few seconds, nothing happened; then there was a groan as the ancient valve opened, and a deep rumbling as lava entered the old pipe.

'*Yes!*' Yaz said, tailslapping Franco.

Sera and Luca cheered, but their cheers were cut off as bubbles blasted out of the old tunnel, followed by a rush of sulphur gas. It swirled around the four violently, filling the water with hot, choking fumes.

'Something's wrong,' Yaz said tersely.

'What's hap—' Sera started to say, before a fit of coughing overtook her.

'Oh, my *gods*,' Franco whispered, lurching towards the valve.

Yaz peered down the tunnel. Fear filled his eyes. 'Blowback!' he shouted. 'Close the valve! *Now!*'

THREE

SERA FOLLOWED YAZ'S gaze, horrified. Lava was rapidly filling the tunnel. They'd released too much and now it was flowing in the wrong direction . . . towards them.

'Franco! Grab the handwheel!' she shouted, ripping her jacket off and tying it around the bottom half of her face.

But Franco couldn't hear her; he was limp in the water, overcome by the poisonous gas. Luca was thrashing his tail in pain. He'd been closest to the tunnel and his back had been burned by the superhot bubbles.

'Luca, get Franco out of here! Swim *down*!' Sera shouted, her voice muffled by her jacket. She knew the gases would rise and that clean water was below them.

Luca, shaking with pain, grabbed Franco and swam. Yaz, teeth clenched, was already on the handwheel. Sera joined him. They tried their hardest to turn it, but it didn't move. Yaz and Franco together had barely been able to open the valve, and Sera wasn't as strong as Franco.

She glanced fearfully at the lava again. It was only a foot

away from the lip of the main tunnel. In a few more seconds it would be dripping down into it. She and Yaz would not be able to swim back down the main tunnel and get out, as Luca and Franco hopefully had. They'd have to swim up into the palace and try to escape through a window – if they weren't caught first. The Black Fins' one chance at the vaults would be gone.

Desperation gripped Sera. Without treasure, she'd never be able to take Cerulea back. Lucia would remain upon Miromara's throne. The death riders would continue to raid villages and enslave their inhabitants. Vallerio and Portia would get away with murder, and the mysterious figure for whom they were trying to get the talismans just might succeed in freeing Abbadon.

These things can't happen, Sera thought fiercely. *I won't* let *them happen*.

With a warrior's cry, she threw all her strength against the handwheel. The muscles in her arms shuddered; the cords stood out in her neck. She and Yaz, on opposite sides of the wheel, churned the water white, using the force of their powerful tails as leverage. And finally, with a grudging groan, the wheel turned.

'Keep going, Sera!' Yaz shouted.

Sera did, and a few seconds later, the valve was closed. The flow of lava stopped. Yazeed looked down the old tunnel and shook his head.

'It's over,' he said, his shoulders sagging, defeat in his voice.

'Over?' Sera echoed in disbelief. 'It *can't* be over!' She ripped her jacket away from her face and tied it around her waist.

'It didn't work, Sera,' Yazeed said. 'I can't tell if the lava ate a hole in the wall or not. Even if it did, there's too much of it in the tunnel. We can't swim through lava. We're done.'

Bitter disappointment filled Sera.

'We should go,' Yaz said. 'Get back to the others and—'

His words were cut off by a deafening roar. He grabbed Sera and pushed her against the main tunnel's wall, covering her body with his. A rush of hot water came shooting out of the old tunnel, followed by pieces of rock and a thick cloud of silt.

Sera braced herself for the searing pain. For the suffocating fumes. For the end.

But it didn't come.

The hot water spiralled up. The debris sank. There were no more bubbles. No lava. As Yaz and Sera opened their eyes and waved the silt away, they saw there was no more old tunnel, either – just a gaping hole where it used to be. A soft, golden light emanated from the other side.

'You okay?' Yaz asked.

'Yeah, I think so. How about you?'

But Yaz didn't answer. He was already at the edge of the hole, looking down. Sera joined him, and caught her breath.

Gold glinted up at her. Rubies, emeralds and sapphires sparkled.

Lava globes on the walls of the vaults illuminated

mountains of Miromaran treasure.

'Damn, merl,' Yaz said in a hushed voice. 'We didn't just burn a hole in the wall, we caved it in.'

Sera nodded, her eyes sparkling like the jewels below her. The old pipe, the tunnel it had run through, most of the treasury vault's back wall, and a good part of its ceiling were gone. Lava, still bubbling, covered some of the treasure. They'd have to be careful to avoid it, but there was plenty of treasure left untouched.

An electric thrill ran through Sera as she realized that her fighters could move much faster through this wide space than they could've through the old tunnel – and they could carry more loot, too.

Yaz read her mind. 'We can haul out twice what we'd planned to,' he said excitedly.

'If we don't get caught,' Sera added. She nervously glanced up. 'It'll be a miracle if they didn't hear anything.'

'We'll be okay. Mahdi has drummers up there. Singers, too. And plenty of lightworks explosions. Their noise will cover ours,' Yaz said.

Sera smiled. She reached for a sailcloth sack tucked under her belt, then plunged down into the vaults. 'Come on, Yaz!' she called over her shoulder. 'It's time to rob the robbers!'

FOUR

BIANCA DI REMORA, swathed in bright pink sea silk, fluttered like a butterfly fish around Lucia Volnero.

Bianca's gown was pretty, but not overly so. She'd been wearing a yellow gown earlier, one that had done a better job of showing off her lush, curvy figure. Lucia had thought it quite beautiful and therefore had promptly made her change it. Her courtiers should shine, of course, but only a little. After all, they were merely the setting; *she* was the jewel.

'Those were, like, the best lightworks *ever*,' Bianca gushed. 'And Mahdi did it all for you! He's *sooo* in love.'

'He is, isn't he,' Lucia purred.

She was seated in the centre of the Grand Hall, at the Royal Table. The lightworks show had just ended and Mahdi had swum over to the lightcasters to tell them how pleased he was.

'You should have seen how he was looking at you during the show!' Bianca said. 'Then again, *everyone's* looking at you tonight.'

Of course they are, Lucia thought.

She was wearing a spectacular gown made of thousands of tiny overlapping discs of polished abalone. The shells caught the light as she moved, casting an iridescent shimmer. She wore her long, blue-black hair down. A stunning sapphire, set in a platinum headband, rested just above her widow's peak. It sparkled darkly, like her eyes.

Lucia's gown, her sapphire, her beautiful face – they all turned heads, but she hardly cared. There was only one merman whose gaze she craved – Mahdi's.

She'd wanted him for her own ever since he'd come to Miromara for Serafina's Dokimí. With his long dark hair, his chiselled features and soulful eyes, he was the most handsome merman she'd ever seen. And he was the Emperor of Matali, a large and powerful realm. She deserved no less.

Her eyes sought him out now. He was floating by the throne, laughing with the lightcasters. He was beautifully dressed and so good-looking it made her ache. Watching him, she recalled that he had not looked so good after the fall of Cerulea, when she'd found him in a prison cage.

Captain Markus Traho, commander of the death riders and a merman who served both Vallerio and the terragogg Rafe Mfeme, had killed Mahdi's parents – on her father's orders – and had imprisoned Mahdi. Her father hadn't trusted him. Mahdi's parents had been staunchly loyal to Isabella, and Mahdi himself was rumoured to be a serious partyboy and loyal to no one. Vallerio wanted someone better for his daughter. But Lucia, besotted, had begged for his life and her father had relented.

'I can't say no to you, Lucia,' Vallerio had said. 'I'll spare his life, but before any Promising ceremony occurs, Mahdi must prove his loyalty.'

And he had. By raiding rebel safe houses. By rounding up those unloyal to her. By finding an invaluable object for Traho – a necklace with a blue, tear-shaped diamond in it that Traho had immediately delivered to Mfeme. Why Mfeme wanted it, Lucia didn't know. Nor did she care. All that mattered to her was that Mahdi convinced her father. And eventually, he had.

'I was wrong, Lucia. And, for once, I'm glad about it,' Vallerio had said a few weeks ago. 'My opinion of the boy has changed considerably.'

Lucia had been pleased to hear that – she'd needed her father's consent for the Promising – but even with it, and even with the Promising behind her, there was still an obstacle to her happiness. There was one whose opinion was far more important to her than her father's, her mother's, or any friend's. This one had helped her snare Mahdi – with songspells, potions and enchantments. And this one was still sceptical.

'Be careful, child,' she'd warned. 'The boy professed to be in love with the last principessa, and now he says he's in love with you. It seems he sells his heart to the highest bidder. You may have to pay a very high price for it.'

Those words had tortured Lucia. She told herself they weren't true. They *couldn't* be. Mahdi had Promised himself to her, hadn't he? He gave her expensive gifts. He threw parties celebrating their betrothal. His whispered words made her catch her breath – and his kisses took it away completely.

And yet, she was never entirely sure.

Is he only pretending? she wondered now, her eyes darkening as quickly as her mood had. *Or does he really love me?*

'Mahdi . . .' she said as he returned to their table and sat down next to her.

'What is it, Luce? You look upset. Didn't you like the lightworks?'

'I loved them. I really did.'

'Then what's wrong?' he asked, taking her hand.

'Let's move our wedding day up. I don't want to wait anymore,' Lucia said in a rush.

Mahdi looked surprised. 'There's nothing I'd like more, but we can't.'

Lucia's eyes flashed. 'Why not?' she demanded.

Mahdi cupped her face with his hands. 'I don't want to begin our life together until our realms are secure. It's too dangerous. You remember the invasion of Cerulea, and how its people suffered. We all do.'

Lucia nodded. She remembered it well. Her father had ordered his assassins to kill Regina Isabella, Principe Bastiaan, and many more. But that was a secret, and it had to stay that way.

'Isabella was killed because she was Miromara's regina. Now *you're* the regina, and it would kill *me* if anything ever happened to you. You know that, don't you?' Mahdi asked, his beautiful brown eyes searching hers.

Lucia's angry expression softened. *He's always so protective of me*, she thought. *Like a true love would be*.

'Our day will come. Soon,' he said, his hands still cradling her face. 'Your father, Traho, me . . . we're getting closer to the Black Fins all the time. We'll find them soon and put them down like the dogfish they are. *Then* we'll be married, Luce, and no one will be happier or prouder on that day than me.'

He kissed her then, and the words that the other one had spoken, the words that tormented Lucia, faded from her mind. Mahdi was hers and hers alone. She saw that in his eyes, heard it in his words, and felt it in his touch.

'Excuse me, Your Graces,' a voice said, low and harsh.

Lucia knew who it belonged to – Traho. She turned away from Mahdi and saw that he was at her father's side. He'd swum into the Grand Hall quietly. A compactly built merman with closely cropped brown hair and a cruel face, he was not known for attending parties. Lucia sensed that his sudden appearance at this one did not bode well.

'What is it?' Vallerio asked tersely.

'There's been a break-in. The treasury vaults were breached,' Traho replied, bending low so that only Vallerio, Portia, Lucia and Mahdi could hear him.

'What?' Vallerio said, crashing his fist down on the table. 'How did this happen?'

'An old valve was opened. Lava was released. It destroyed

one of the vault's walls. We're trying to contain the intruders right now, but they're fighting hard.'

'How much treasure was taken?' Portia demanded.

'A substantial amount.'

Vallerio cursed. 'Black Fins?' he asked.

'We think so, sir.'

'It's her, damn her. Serafina,' Vallerio growled.

Lucia's eyes widened. '*Serafina?* But how?'

'Yes, Vallerio, how?' Portia asked, her voice a cool contrast to her husband's angry one. 'Serafina's dead. She fled the palace after Cerulea was invaded and hasn't been seen since. There's no way she could have survived in the open waters for this long.'

'Of course she's dead,' Vallerio said quickly. 'I misspoke in my anger. Traho, follow me to the vaults. Portia, Lucia, Mahdi . . . stay here. Smile. Dance. Act as if nothing's happened. I don't want the guests to find out about this. If word spreads, the Black Fins will use it to their advantage.'

Lucia barely heard her father's instructions. Doubt had crept into her mind, as chilling as a sea fog. Her parents always maintained that Serafina was killed in the attack on Cerulea. Neither had ever publicly voiced any suspicion that she might still be alive. Had they been lying to her? The mere thought made her furious.

If it were true, if Sera was alive and leading the resistance, she was a threat. The mer had loved her. They would fight to the death for her. Lucia had everything she ever wanted now, but Serafina could take it all – Mahdi, her crown, her life.

It can't be true, she quickly told herself. Sera *had* to be dead. There had been no word of her for months. She was weak. She had no survival skills – not a guppy like her, always swimming around with a conch glued to her ear, listening to some dull account of this battle or that treaty.

Lucia took a deep breath. She tried to calm down. Instinctively, she glanced at Mahdi for reassurance.

But Mahdi didn't offer any. He wasn't even looking at her. His eyes followed Vallerio and Traho as they disappeared through a stone archway. There was a look in them that Lucia had never seen before. Raw, naked fear.

Then Bianca called Mahdi's name and started fawning over him, and he was laughing and the look was gone.

But Lucia knew she would always remember it.

Who is he afraid for? she wondered. *Is it me?*

Or Serafina?

FIVE

THE STEEL SPEAR hit the wall only inches above Yazeed's head.

Shrapnel sprayed through the water. One piece tore a gash in Yaz's cheek; another clipped a Black Fin named Sophia, carving a stripe across her forearm.

'Time to make wake, Sera!' Yaz yelled. 'Can't hold them much longer!'

He and Sophia were still inside the Traitors' Gate tunnel. They were shooting at the death riders who were trying to storm through it as Sera attached a huge sailcloth sack filled with treasure to a giant manta ray.

'Sargo's Canyon,' she told the manta in RaySay, as she cinched the sack. 'Hurry!'

This was the last load. The sack was heavy with gold and jewels, but the ray was young and strong. Sera was thankful for that. He would have to swim fast to avoid capture. The creature flapped his huge wings, picked up speed and veered north. He swam low, blending in with the seafloor, invisible to anything swimming above him. Fifty more of his kind were already on their way. Neela was leading them.

'Get out of here,' Sera ordered the six remaining Black Fins fanned out above her. 'Cast your pebbles and haul tail.'

The transparensea pebbles she'd issued to her fighters were poor quality – weak and unreliable – but they were better than nothing. The fighters cast them, shimmered and disappeared. They would follow the ray to Sargo's Canyon, where the treasure would be safely stashed in an abandoned farm house. Sera prayed to the gods that they'd make it.

The heist had been a success. The Black Fins had hauled out twice as much treasure as they'd expected. But they'd been discovered just as the last loads were being carried out through the lava chamber.

A battle had ensued, and three Black Fins had died, including Luca and Franco, along with at least ten enemies. Yaz and Sophia had been able to hold the death riders back at a bend in the tunnel, about ten yards from the Traitors' Gate, while the rest of the Black Fins escaped. Sera didn't allow herself to think about the fighters they'd lost. She would mourn them later, when the mission was over.

'You ready, Sera?' Yaz shouted now.

'All set!' Sera yelled back.

A few seconds later she heard an explosion, and she knew that Yaz and Sophia had set off an ink bomb – a large conch shell packed with squid ink and explosives. It would turn the water in the tunnel as black as night and keep it that way for a good thirty seconds.

'I'll cover you both. *Go!*' Yazeed shouted at Serafina as he and Sophia came hurtling towards her.

As Yaz flattened himself on the seafloor, Sera grabbed her crossbow and streaked away, with Sophia hot on her tail. She put distance between herself and the Traitors' Gate, then pulled her transparensea pebble out of her pocket, ready to cast it. But as she did, a pain – white and blinding – tore through her body. She screamed as she went tumbling through the water. She dropped her bow. The pebble fell out of her hand.

Sera slammed into the seafloor face-first. She righted herself, dazed, and spit out silt. Blood swirled around her. She frantically searched to see where she'd been hit.

Her eyes widened when they found the wound.

'*No!*' she cried.

A spear was buried in her tail.

SIX

TERROR FLOODED THROUGH SERA.

It wasn't the sight of her own blood that scared her, or the cruel silver spear sunk into her flesh. It was the thin white line trailing from the spear – and the death rider at the other end of it. He grinned evilly, then began to reel in the line.

The pain was excruciating. Sera screamed and thrashed against it, which sank the barbed spearhead even deeper into her flesh.

'Sera, *listen* to me!' a voice hissed in her ear. 'Stop thrashing. Pretend you're surrendering.'

Sera whipped her head around. It was Sophia's voice, but there was no Sophia in sight. *She must've cast her pebble*, Sera thought.

'Move closer to him,' Sophia hissed. 'I need slack in the line so he can't feel me cutting it.'

Sera put her hands up and let herself drift. The death rider stopped pulling on the line and started swimming towards her. With his eyes fixed on Sera, he didn't see a loop form in the line, or see that loop go taut.

'I've got one!' he yelled. Two more soldiers rushed towards him.

'Hurry, Soph . . . oh, gods, hurry,' Sera groaned.

'Trying . . . it's thick . . . wait . . . *Got it!*'

Death swims on a fast fin, Tavia, Sera's nursemaid, used to say. It swam so fast to the soldiers, they never saw it coming.

As the two ends of cut line sank to the seafloor, Sophia's knife whizzed through the water and buried itself in the chest of the death rider who'd shot Serafina. Sera dived for her dropped crossbow, grabbed it and fired twice. She'd become an excellent shot; the other two death riders were dead before their bodies hit the silt.

'Let's go. Before their friends come looking for them,' she said to Sophia.

'You can't swim with the spear in you.'

Sera knew what Sophia was saying. 'Do it,' she said, her voice ragged with pain.

'I'll be quick, I swear. I'll—'

'Just *do it*, Soph.'

Sophia cut the line again, as close to the spear's shaft as she could. Then she grabbed Sera's tail with one hand and the shaft with the other. Sera bit back a shriek as Sophia forced the spearhead all the way through her tail and out the other side. The pain bent her double. More blood plumed from the wound. Sophia grabbed Sera's jacket – tied around Sera's waist – and wrapped it around her tail.

'You still with me?' she said.

'Barely,' Sera rasped.

'We've got to get away from here. They're pouring out of the Traitors' Gate. They'll fan out to search the grounds.'

Sera was aware of voices now, and the glow of lava torches.

'Go, Soph. They can't see you. Swim back to the hills.'

'Forget it. I'm not leaving you.'

'That's an ord—'

With a sickening *thuk*, a spearhead sank into the silt only inches from Serafina.

Invisible hands grabbed her. 'Come *on*!' Sophia yelled.

Before the death rider could shoot again, Sera and Sophia were streaking for cover. They sped over coral and seaweed, zigzagging to confuse him. Spears ricocheted off rocks around them, or buried themselves in kelp. The shooter had been joined by others.

'Follow me!' Sera shouted.

The reggia, Merrow's ancient palace, was just ahead. Merrow, the first ruler of the merfolk, had built the reggia four thousand years before. Sera loved the ancient ruins and had often stolen away from her court to explore them. She was hoping to draw the death riders into the ruins after her, lose them in the maze-like interior, then bolt out again.

The shouts behind them grew louder. The spears kept coming. Sera plunged down through the water, shot under a crumbling stone arch and swam through a passageway.

'Sophia?' she called as loudly as she dared. 'Are you there?'

'Right behind you,' came the answer.

Sophia was shimmering. Her transparensea pebble was wearing off. Sera sang a quick illuminata and gathered some moon rays into a ball. She grabbed Sophia's hand and pulled her down a long hallway just as the death riders swam through the arch.

The two mermaids sped from room to room, through tunnels, and across courts. After five minutes of swimming flat-out, they'd lost their pursuers. Sera stopped, panting, to catch her breath.

'Where are we?' Sophia asked, fully visible now.

'Merrow's private wing,' Sera replied. 'We've just come through her apartments. They connect to the stables and an indoor ring that backs onto the kelp forest.'

Merrow had loved to ride, and had gone hunting in the forest almost every morning. The ancient kelp stalks, lovingly tended through the centuries, covered a large swath of seafloor.

'If we can just get into the forest, the kelp will give us cover,' Sera continued. 'We'll be well north of the city by the time we swim out of it.'

'How's your tail?' Sophia asked.

Sera looked at it, grimacing. The makeshift bandage was soaked with blood.

'It hurts, but I'll make it,' she said. 'Let's keep moving.'

No matter how much agony she was in, Sera knew she couldn't allow herself to be caught, not with so much at stake. Hoping that the other Black Fins and the manta rays had made it to safety, she pushed the pain down and started swimming again.

She and Sophia moved warily through the stables. Empty stalls loomed eerily in the weak glow of Sera's illuminata. She was glad when they reached the other side and emerged in the indoor ring.

Its floor was pitted and cracked, its walls colonized by anemones and tube worms. The ring was immense. It was not only wide, but its ceiling was very high, as mer swooped up and down on their mounts when they rode.

'Ugh. Do you smell something?' Sophia suddenly asked, wrinkling her nose. 'Something really bad?'

'Something really dead,' Sera said, her fins prickling.

She held the illuminata at arm's length and turned in a slow, wary circle. Its light glinted off a metallic object in the middle of the ring. It appeared to be a large and deep trough, stabilized with four short metal legs. The two mermaids swam towards it and peered over its edge.

'Whoa!' Sophia said, recoiling. 'That is *so* nasty!'

The smell, up close, was sickening. The sight was even worse.

The trough was full of bones. Sera saw the skulls of large fish, the spines and ribs of smaller ones, and a few terragogg legs – some with shoes still on them. Chunks of flesh and guts, all in various stages of decay, had been mixed with the bones.

'It looks like some kind of feeding trough,' Sera said when she could speak again. 'Though I'd hate to see what it fed.'

'Sera . . . oh, my gods, Sera . . .' Sophia said. She wasn't looking at the trough any more.

'What is it?' Sera asked, turning to her.

'Do. Not. *Move*,' Sophia said, her voice cracking with fear.

'Okay. I'm not moving,' Sera said.

'Look up. Very, very slowly.'

Sera did. And gasped.

Clinging to the ceiling, like demons in a nightmare, were three massive Blackclaw dragons.

SEVEN

SERA'S HEART WAS beating so hard, she thought it would crack her ribs.

Enormous and powerful, with lethal teeth and talons, Blackclaws were one of the fiercest breeds of dragon known to mer.

'The death riders must be stabling them here,' Sera said, anger replacing her fear. She'd had no idea the fragile ruins were being used to house such destructive creatures.

As she and Sophia watched, one of the dragons – the biggest one, a female – scented the water. Her head swayed slowly from side to side. Her yellow eyes narrowed to slits. The spiked frill on her neck stood up.

'It's my wound. She can smell the blood. We're chowder,' Sera said.

'We might be able to make it back to the doorway,' Sophia whispered.

As if sensing her intent, the huge dragon scrabbled across the ceiling towards the entrance.

Sera glanced around wildly, searching for a way out. 'Soph, look!' she said excitedly. 'To the right of the trough!'

'Please don't tell me it's another dragon.'

'There's a crack in the floor! I think we can fit through it!'

Sera slowly swung the illuminata around to her right. Sophia's eyes followed the light. A section of floor had heaved up – probably, Sera reasoned, from the dragons stomping around on it. The broken pieces had been driven into one another like plates of ice on a polar sea. Two of them didn't meet entirely, leaving a space that was small, but maybe just big enough for a mermaid to fit through.

'We don't know what's down there,' Sophia said.

'We know what's up here, though. And it's not good,' Sera said. 'Start moving. Nice and slow.'

Sophia did, and Sera followed. They were only a few feet away from the crack when the big dragon hissed. She crouched, ready to spring, and then the sound of voices coming from the stables stopped her. Her head swivelled towards the noise. That was all the two mermaids needed.

'Forget slow!' Sera said. '*Hurry*, Soph!'

Sophia shot into the crack. Sera was right behind her, still holding her illuminata. She had just enough time to see that they were in some sort of underground room when the big dragon started roaring.

Sera and Sophia peered out of the crack. The death riders, torches blazing, had stopped in the safety of the doorway. The dragon, furious she couldn't get at them, was shrieking now and flapping her enormous wings.

'I think we're safe. For the moment,' Sera said. 'The death riders won't come after us unless they want to get eaten.'

She started to swim away from the crack, intending to explore the space they'd swum into, but Sophia stopped her. 'First, we need to do something about that hole in your tail. Sit.'

Sera didn't argue. She sat down, leaned against a wall, and closed her eyes. Sophia untied the blood-soaked bandage and grimaced at the wound. Fresh blood was leaking from it. The spear had torn Sera's flesh horribly.

'Wow. Gods. This is a *mess*. So's your face. You're as white as a barnacle.'

Sera managed to smile. 'Great bedside manner, Soph.'

Shaking her head, Sophia asked Sera for her dagger, cut the sleeves off her own jacket and used them to fashion a new bandage.

A few minutes later, she said, 'There. Done. Hopefully that will do the trick until we get back to HQ.'

'Thanks,' Sera said. The pain was still bad, but the bleeding had slowed.

'Any idea where we are?' Sophia asked, glancing around.

'Not a clue,' Sera replied.

She rose, held up her illuminata and looked around. The room was hexagonal, and every square inch of it was covered in mosaics. Painted urns stood on the floor. Ancient bronze lava lamps hung from the ceiling.

'I thought you knew everything about the reggia,' Sophia said.

'So did I,' Sera said, her eyes wide, her voice full of wonder.

'I've listened to every conch there is on this place. And no one – no courtier or minister or historian – ever mentioned a room under the stables.'

'Sera . . . those figures,' said Sophia, pointing to one of the six walls. 'They're not gods. And they're not mer.'

Sera swam to one of the walls and gazed up at the intricate mosaic of the man who adorned it. 'They're human,' she said, running her fingertips over the man's sandalled feet.

Each figure had a name above it, written in ancient Mermish. Sera's pulse quickened as she read them aloud. 'Merrow, Nyx, Sycorax, Pyrrha, Navi, Orfeo . . . the Six Who Ruled. This is a tomb, Soph, only it has no bodies in it. I bet Merrow had this built in memory of her fellow mages.'

Sera knew that Merrow was the only one of the Six who had survived the fall of Atlantis. The other mages' bodies were never recovered. As her eyes travelled over the figures, she saw that they were all depicted the same way – gazing out at the viewer, left hand at his or her side, right hand raised to chest height, palm up. Resting on each palm was a different object. Sera gasped as she realized what they were.

'Great Neria, it's all *here* in this room . . .' she whispered, trembling with excitement. 'The answers I've been trying to find ever since I entered the Iele's caves are right in front of me!'

She and Ling had discovered what three of the six talismans were when they'd visited the ruins of Atlantis, but they'd had to flee for their lives before learning about the rest.

'Sera, check this out,' Sophia said. 'Merrow's holding—'

'—a blue diamond,' Sera said.

'And Navi's got—'

'—a moonstone.'

'Orfeo's holding—'

'—a black pearl.'

'How did you know that?' Sophia asked. 'You're not even looking at them.'

Sera didn't answer. She was still gazing at the figure before her – a regal, dark-skinned man with long black braids and blind eyes.

'Nyx has a ruby ring,' she said out loud, wanting to engrave the image into her memory.

She swam to the next wall. A tall, strongly built woman with long red hair and intense blue eyes stared back at her. 'Pyrrha has a gold coin with an image of Neria on it,' she said, her excitement growing.

The mosaic on the next wall featured a slender woman with onyx-black hair and almond-shaped eyes. Sera examined it closely. 'Sycorax has a white . . . is that a puzzle ball? Looks like it has a phoenix on it. Remember that, Sera. You have to *remember*,' she told herself.

'Hey, Sera?' Sophia said. 'What's going on?'

'We know *where* they are. I discovered where Merrow hid them thanks to a conch in the Ostrokon. And now we know *what* they are – *all* of them. We know, and Rafe Mfeme *doesn't*!' Sera said, still staring at Sycorax.

'Um, okay. Which means?' Sophia prompted.

Sera turned to Sophia, her eyes triumphant. 'Which means that maybe, just maybe, we actually can *do* this!'

EIGHT

'WHAT *EXACTLY* ARE you talking about?' Sophia said, her patience with Seraphina's cryptic comments wearing thin. 'Would you *please* tell me?'

Sera struggled with herself. Only a handful of mer knew the enormity of the battle they were fighting. It was safer that way. Spies were everywhere.

'You can trust me. With your life. You know that,' Sophia said, as if sensing the reason behind Sera's hesitation.

It was true. Sophia had proven herself worthy of Sera's trust outside the Traitors' Gate. Also, Sera realized, as regina and leader of the Black Fins, she was currently in a compromised position – badly wounded and a long way from safety. There was still a good chance she'd be captured. If that happened, how would she get the information she'd just learned to Neela, Yaz, and the others? She *had* to rely on Sophia.

Taking a deep breath, Sera started to talk. 'Our fight . . . it's bigger than Miromara. It's as big as all the waters of the world and every creature in them,' she said.

While Sophia listened, wide-eyed, Sera explained that the mage Orfeo had created a monster called Abbadon and had used it to destroy Atlantis. Then she told her that she and five others – Neela, Ava, Astrid, Becca, and Ling – had been summoned by Baba Vrăja, the leader of the Iele, a coven of river witches, and had been given the task of destroying the monster.

'Why you?' Sophia asked.

'Because each of us is a descendant of one of the Six Who Ruled,' Sera explained. 'We have their magic inside us and it gets stronger when we're together. Vrăja hoped it would be strong enough to defeat Abbadon.'

'But why did Orfeo create that thing in the first place? Why did he let it destroy Atlantis?'

'Because he was angry. And sad. And out of his mind,' Sera said. 'His wife, Alma, died, and he couldn't accept her death. He decided to march on the underworld and take her back, but he needed help, so he went to Morsa, the death goddess. He sacrificed people to her.'

'He did *what*?' Sophia said, appalled. 'We never learned that in school!'

'No, we didn't,' Sera said ruefully. 'Merrow didn't want anyone to know the truth; she kept it secret. She thought the mer would be safer that way. I can almost see why. I found the temple where the sacrifices were made. I touched the blood, heard the victims' voices. It was horrible.' She shuddered at the memory.

'Why didn't anyone stop him?' asked Sophia.

'By the time his fellow Atlanteans found out, it was too late. Morsa, the death goddess, had given Orfeo a talisman – a black pearl – that made him very powerful. Ling and I learned this from a vitrina we met in the ruins of Atlantis. She said that Orfeo beseeched Morsa to share the secrets of immortality with him, and that he somehow used them to create Abbadon. The monster was incredibly powerful. All the other mages could do was kill Orfeo, imprison Abbadon, and then sink it in the Southern Sea.'

'*Imprison* Abbadon? Not kill it? You mean it's—'

'—still alive? Yes. But locked away forever. Or so Merrow thought. The prison can only be opened or closed by fitting a certain six talismans into its lock,' Sera said, gesturing at the walls. 'The objects that the mages are holding in these mosaics *are* those talismans. Merrow hid them in different waters to make sure no one could ever use them to free Abbadon. But someone else has been trying to find them. We don't know who, but we're trying to stay ahead of him. So far, we've found two of the talismans – a blue diamond that belonged to Merrow and a moonstone that Navi owned. When we have them all, we can open the prison and try to kill Abbadon.'

'Hold on, Sera . . . you're going to try to kill a monster that the most powerful mages ever couldn't kill? That's insane!'

Sera nodded solemnly. 'Yeah, it probably is.'

'And just *how* are you going to do that?'

Sera sighed. 'I wish I knew. But, according to the Iele, we have to. Before the shadowy *someone* frees it.'

Sophia was quiet when Sera finished. She looked like she was in shock. 'That *is* a big fight,' she finally said. 'The biggest. I mean, as if trying to defeat your uncle and take back Miromara wasn't enough.'

Sera was about to agree when a bolt of pain shot up her tail. Wincing, she bit back a cry. The excitement of finding Merrow's secret rooms and the mosaics they contained had dulled the pain, but now it was coming back with a vengeance.

'What's wrong?' Sophia asked, worried.

'My tail . . .' Sera said.

Sophia took her arm. 'Sit down, Sera. You need to rest.'

Sera spun away. 'No, we've got to get going.'

Sophia started to argue, but Sera cut her off. She turned around and looked deeply into her friend's eyes.

'Soph, I'm still bleeding and the death riders are still out there,' she said. 'I told you about the talismans because I trust you, but for another reason, too: if you make it back to HQ and I don't, you need to tell Neela what we saw here. Promise me. The information can't die with me.'

Sophia shook her head. 'You're going to tell her yourself, Sera, because you're going to make it back. I'm going to *make* you make it,' she said.

'Sophia, listen to me . . .'

'No, Sera, *you* listen. They don't get to do this – Vallerio, Portia, Lucia, Mfeme. They don't—' Her voice broke. She struggled to regain her composure. 'I never told you why I joined the Black Fins. The death riders came to my house. They took my parents. I managed to grab my little brother and hide in our garden. He's safe now, with friends. But my parents are missing. I don't know if I'll ever see them again.'

Sera's heart ached. 'I'm so sorry, Sophia,' she said. She knew the mermaid's pain all too well. She'd lost her own parents to Vallerio and his death riders. Her brother, Desiderio, was missing.

'They don't get to hurt mer and tear families apart all for power and gold,' Sophia continued, her expression grim and determined. 'I'm a Black Fin because I want to do everything I can to stop them. Which means getting you back to HQ. There's got to be a way out besides the crack we swam through. Merrow got in and out of here, after all. I know she was powerful, but even she couldn't swim through stone.'

Sera nodded wearily. 'Let's start looking for it.'

'No, *I'm* going to look for it. *You* are going to *sit down*, close your eyes, and gather your strength.'

Sera protested, but Sophia was firm, so she sat and rested her throbbing tail. Across the room, Merrow's image gazed down at her, and Sera had the unshakable feeling that her ancestor was helping her.

'Thanks for this,' Sera whispered. 'Thanks for the Black Fins and the manta rays. Thanks for getting us into the vaults. And for saving us from the dragons.'

Before she closed her eyes, she thanked her ancestor for one more thing – for the fighter by her side who was brave, loyal, and strong.

For an ally and a friend.

For Sophia.

NINE

WITHOUT ANY WARNING, the trawler's engines stopped. Their deep thrum had been a constant for the past three weeks, and the sudden silence hung ominously in the water.

'Why are we stopping? What's happening?' a mermaid cried out.

Ling, who'd been sitting down, her tail stretched out in front of her, her back against the cold steel of the ship's hull, was instantly alert. *We're here. Wherever here is*, she thought with a sense of dread. *You've got one last chance. It's now or never*.

The mermaid who'd cried out spoke again. '*Please*,' she said, her voice trembling with fear. 'Where are they taking us?'

Ling saw that the mermaid was very close by. Two small children clung to her.

'Shut up, will you? You're making it worse!' a merman yelled.

'Don't shout at her. She's scared,' Ling said.

'We're *all* scared!' the merman shot back.

'But we're not all acting like jerks,' said Ling.

The merman lunged at her, but a chain brought him up short.

'Momma, I'm *hungry*,' one of the mermaid's children said. 'Why did the noise stop? I don't like this!'

'Shh, it's okay,' the mermaid soothed. 'They'll bring us some food soon. It'll be all right.'

But it wouldn't be. In fact, Ling was sure things were about to go from bad to worse. She needed to escape before that happened. She *had* to find a way to tell Sera and the others what she'd learned aboard this ship.

There was only one way out, though – through the door that separated the prisoners' containment area from the rest of the hold. Beyond the door was a water lock. The death riders used it to enter and exit the ship. Ling had watched them operate it when they brought her aboard; she had tried to memorize which buttons they pushed on the control panel. If she could get to it, she might be able to let herself out. But she was shackled to the ship's hull and the guards had the keys. They wore them on rings secured to their belts with a loop and toggle, right next to their speargun holsters.

She'd tried to steal the keys before. Once by pretending to collapse and fall against a guard. Another time by tugging on a guard's arm as she begged for food. The guards were wary of prisoners' tricks, though, and all she ever managed to get for her trouble was a slap.

But now the ship had stopped. Something was going on; she could sense it. Maybe that something would give her the chance she needed.

Ling, together with about three hundred other mer, was imprisoned aboard the *Bedrieër*, an immense trawler. The vessel's hold was filled with salt water, but there were so many mer packed into it that the water had become murky and hard to breathe. The prisoners all had iron collars around their necks to prevent them from songcasting. Some – the ones the death riders thought troublesome – were chained to the wall. Ling's time aboard the ship had taken its toll. Her left eye was badly bruised. Her hair was matted. The cast on her arm was dirty, and the once-bright orange patches on her ivory tail were dull.

The *Bedrieër* belonged to a brutal terragogg named Rafe Iaoro Mfeme. Or so Ling had thought when she'd first been hauled aboard it. She'd entered the waters of Qin and had been making her way home when death riders had surrounded her. After interrogating her on the whereabouts of the talismans – and getting nothing out of her – Mfeme had revealed his true identity.

He was Orfeo, the most powerful mage who'd ever lived.

He'd removed the sunglasses he constantly wore, revealing eyes that were empty, black voids. Ling's blood had run cold at the sight of them. She'd realized that she'd seen him before – in a mirror in Atlantis. He'd tried to crawl out of it, to come after her and Sera, but Sera had broken the mirror before he could.

'You *can't* be Orfeo. It's impossible,' Ling had whispered. 'You're dead. You've been dead for four thousand years!'

Orfeo had laughed. 'Anything is possible, Ling, if you want it badly enough.'

'I don't believe you,' Ling had said.

But as he'd spoken, the rays of the setting sun had glinted off the black pearl he wore around his neck.

The pearl! Ling had thought, remembering that Orfeo's talisman was a black pearl given to him by Morsa. Had he somehow used it to keep himself alive? That was the moment when Ling had believed him, with all her heart, and terror had gripped her – not for herself, but for her friends. They had no idea who Mfeme really was. Desperate to tell them, she'd tried to cast a convoca, but Orfeo had clamped an iron collar around her neck before she'd sung two words of the spell.

'There's no need to warn your friends, Ling,' he'd said as he locked the collar. 'I'm not going to kill them. Not yet. I want them alive so they can keep searching for the rest of the talismans. I thought Vallerio and his henchmen would have found them by now, but they've only obtained one – Merrow's blue diamond.'

Ling's heart had filled with bitter defeat. Orfeo had two talismans – Merrow's and his own. How would she and the other mermaids ever get them away from him?

Orfeo had sat down on the gunwale and looked out over the water. 'A few centuries ago, I almost got the blue diamond myself. I was *so* close, but then the Infanta and her damned hawk . . .' He'd waved the memory away. 'Ah, well. One must be patient. Neela's found her talisman. Ava and Becca will find theirs, I'm sure. Astrid refuses to even look, but then again' – he'd tapped the black pearl – 'she doesn't need to.'

He had shifted his soulless gaze back to Ling. 'And *you*,' he'd said. 'I very much hoped you'd found your talisman, but not to worry. I will. Because there's a pattern, Ling. I can see it now. Merrow disposed of her talisman on the shores of her own realm. And she put it in a very dangerous place – the hands of a human. She put Navi's moonstone in her home waters, in the claws of a dragon queen.'

Ling hadn't wanted to take part in this conversation, but she'd been so upset to learn that Orfeo had two talismans and knew about Neela's, she hadn't been able to stop herself.

'How do you know Neela has the moonstone?' she'd blurted.

'Because Hagarla, the dragon queen, is unhappy that her prized possession was stolen. She wants it back and is offering a fortune to the one who brings it to her. A death rider heard of her offer and told Traho. He reported it to me.'

Orfeo had paused to untie the ropes securing Ling to her chair, then he'd continued. 'Merrow was *such* a fool. Always led by her heart,' he'd said. 'It makes sense that she would've returned our talismans to the waters nearest our original homes. And *that* means' – he'd leaned on the chair's arms, bent down, and looked Ling in the eye – 'that Sycorax's talisman, an ancient puzzle ball, is in Qin. And what's the most hazardous place in Qin?' He'd straightened and clapped his hands. 'The Abyss, of course!'

'The Abyss is endless. You'll never find such a tiny object in such a large area,' Ling had said. She'd seen puzzle balls. They were small, cunningly carved, and contained spheres within spheres. Each sphere had a hole in it. The puzzle was solved when the holes were lined up, allowing one to see the centre of the ball and the surprise it contained.

Orfeo had smiled. 'You're right. I, myself, will not find the puzzle ball, but you might. You'll certainly have every opportunity, where you're going.'

Was that where the Bedrieër *was headed?* Ling had wondered. *To the Abyss?* Why? What could a trawler do there? Submarines couldn't plumb those depths. They were too much even for the mer. Ling's own father, an archaeologist, had died in the Abyss. He'd gone exploring and had never returned. Her family assumed he'd succumbed to depth sickness.

'I'll take *all* the talismans, Ling,' Orfeo had continued, his smile hardening. 'And Vallerio will take the mer realms. He'll unite them into one army. He'll help me free Abbadon, and together we'll march on the underworld. The gods themselves will fight me, but I'll win. I'll take Alma back if I have to destroy the entire world to do it.'

Then he had motioned to two thugs standing nearby. They'd hoisted Ling out of the chair, hauled her off and thrown her into the hold. Ever since, she'd spent her every waking minute looking for a way to escape.

A thunderous noise ripped her out of her thoughts now.

The *Bedrieër* was dropping anchor. All around her, prisoners clutched each other, wild with fear.

'What's happening? Where are we? What are they going to do with us?' panicked voices called out.

The death riders didn't make them wait long for the answers.

TEN

BECCA QUICKFIN looked longingly at the basket of marsh melons on the farmer's stall. Her mouth watered as she thought of cutting one open and scooping out its gooey black flesh.

The melons were expensive, though, and Becca had little currensea left – only a handful of copper cowries and silver drupes. Those coins had to last her; she was still a long way from home and it was hard to swim on an empty stomach. She knew that all too well.

'Four water apples, please,' she said with a sigh, pushing her glasses up on her nose. The frames were made of polished razor clam shells, the lenses of rock crystal. They were heavy and often slipped down.

The farmer picked out some plump blue apples and tumbled them into Becca's bag. She paid him, then swam off to see if she could find some squid eggs to go with them.

The market was set up in a public hall in the centre of a sizeable village, and Becca felt lucky to have happened across it. She'd eaten her last handful of reef olives this morning. It was lunchtime now and her stomach was twisting with hunger.

As she moved through the market, she saw and heard some troubling things. DEATH RIDERS OUT! was scrawled on one wall of the hall, and several of the stalls were empty.

'Where's Pete today?' one farmer shouted to another, as Becca passed by.

'Nothin' to sell! Soldiers came and took his crop!'

Dread, as cold as pack ice, gripped Becca. Traho's reach, it seemed, now extended well into Atlantica. She pushed a strand of auburn hair behind one ear and swam on. She had a plan: ten minutes to shop for food – no more, then a quick swim out of the village to the open water. She felt safer on the back currents. Death riders had tried to capture her and the others back in the Iele's caves. She doubted they'd given up the hunt.

A few minutes later, Becca spotted a pile of squid eggs. 'How much?' she asked the farmer.

'Five drupes per pound. These are first-rate,' he said, proudly hoisting a moplike clump. The egg sacs reminded Becca of fat, fleshy fingers. She loved the way they burst in her mouth when she bit into them. They were more than she could afford, just like the melons, but maybe if she looked hard, she could find a small clump.

'I'll take two bunches,' a brusque voice said from the far end of the stall. 'Wrap them to go.'

Becca recognized that voice. She craned her neck, trying to see past the other shoppers. A mermaid with braided blonde hair and the black and white markings of an orca was drumming her fingers on the stall.

Ugh, Becca thought. *It's Astrid*.

Becca didn't want to deal with her. Though Astrid was from the icy waters of the Arctic, she was a hothead – quick-tempered and rude. Selfish, too, judging by her hasty exit from the Iele's caves. She'd swum out on everyone, leaving them to confront the tough task ahead without her. If Abbadon were freed, it could destroy all the waters of the world. Astrid had a responsibility to help defeat the monster, as they all did. How could she just turn her back on it?

Becca decided to forget about the squid eggs and sneak away before Astrid saw her, but she faced a problem: there was only one way in and out of the market hall and she'd have to swim right by Astrid to get to it.

Maybe if I head in the opposite direction, I can thread my way back to the doorway without her seeing me, she thought.

At that very second, Astrid turned her head, forcing Becca to duck down. When Becca dared, she glanced in Astrid's direction and was horrified to see that the obnoxious merl was swimming right towards her!

Becca squeezed under the stall's table, apologising to the surprised farmer. When she was certain Astrid had passed by, she crawled out, then headed up the aisle Astrid had just swum down.

Becca kept her eyes on the tall doorway, using it to navigate her way through the maze-like market. She had nearly reached it, and was just congratulating herself for having avoided Astrid, when a merman blocked her way. 'Farm-fresh crab eggs! Just harvested!' he bellowed, thrusting a clamshell heaped high with tiny orange spheres at her.

'No, thank you,' Becca said.

She darted to the right, but the merman darted with her. She zipped to the left, but he intercepted her again.

'Come on, Red, buy some eggs. They're on special! Two drupes a pound!'

Becca realized she wasn't getting past him without purchasing some of his wares. 'Half a pound, then,' she said, exasperatedly. 'Can you wrap them *really* fast?'

'Right away!' the merman said. He swam behind his stall and weighed out a half pound of eggs, carefully tapping them out of their container onto his scale, making sure to get the amount just right.

'Here's your money,' Becca said impatiently, handing him some coins.

'Crab eggs are delicious tossed with keel worms. But if you cook 'em, use low heat and don't—'

Becca cut him off. 'Great. Thanks. Gotta go,' she said, reaching for her package. She opened her travelling case and stuffed it inside.

'Becca? Is that you?'

Oh, silt, Becca thought. She turned around. 'Astrid. Hey,' she said, forcing a smile.

Astrid blinked, as if she couldn't believe her eyes. 'What are you doing here? I thought you were with' – she glanced around warily – 'with the others.'

Becca was relieved that Astrid hadn't said more.

'I was,' she replied. 'But we had some, um, unexpected guests. I'm on my way home now.'

Astrid's eyes widened. 'What happened?' she asked quietly.

Becca arched an eyebrow. 'Suddenly you care?'

'Yeah, Becca, I do. A lot.'

'Funny way of showing it,' Becca said, anger flaring inside her.

'The others . . . are they—' Astrid started to ask.

But Becca didn't let her finish. 'Dead? Alive? I have no idea. We were attacked. I don't even know if they made it out of the caves.'

Astrid winced at her sharp tone. 'I'm sorry,' she said.

'You're *sorry*?' Becca echoed, incredulous. 'You know something, Astrid? You don't get to be sorry, and you don't *get* to care. Not after you abandoned us.'

Astrid, who'd been looking at the seafloor, met Becca's gaze. 'But I *am* sorry, and I *do* care,' she said.

Becca was surprised to see a deep sadness in Astrid's eyes. She wondered at it, but she didn't have time to dwell on it. 'Look, I can't hang. I only came here to get some food,' she said. 'Got homicidal maniacs on my tail, you know?'

'There's a rocky valley east of here. It's on the way. My way, at least. Maybe yours, too. We could find an overhang there and eat lunch together,' Astrid ventured. 'You could tell me what happened.'

Becca didn't relish the idea of spending any more time with this merl. She had a plan and she meant to stick to it. 'Sorry. I've got to make wake.'

'Becca . . .'

'Look, Astrid, I can't. Okay? I really have to—'

'Becca, be *quiet*.'

'*What?* Why should I?' Becca asked indignantly. 'I'm not the one—'

'Becca, *please*!' Astrid hissed. She wasn't looking at Becca any more. She was looking past her, through the doorway towards the village square.

Becca turned, following Astrid's gaze, and gasped.

Twenty soldiers dressed in black uniforms were heading for the market.

ELEVEN

BEFORE BECCA EVEN knew what was happening, Astrid had grabbed her hand and pulled her under an empty table.

'Death riders. They found out you were here,' Astrid said, her voice low.

'How?' Becca asked, panicking.

'Someone must've seen you and told them. You don't exactly blend with that red hair.'

'*Me?* What about *you* with the black-and-white tail?'

'Do you want to argue? Or do you want to get out of here?' Astrid asked.

A table went over. The loud crash made both mermaids flinch.

'They're already inside the market hall,' she added grimly. 'Escaping just got a whole lot trickier.'

And then Becca remembered something. 'I have transparensea pebbles!' she whispered. 'Vrăja gave them to me. We can cast them and escape!'

Becca held one out, but Astrid shook her head. 'It won't work on me,' she said.

'Of course it will. They work on everyone!' Becca insisted.

'Not me. Cast one and go, Becca. Hurry!' Astrid urged.

'No. I'm not leaving you.'

Astrid, who was peering out from under the table now, turned back to Becca. Again Becca saw a terrible sadness in her eyes.

'You *should* leave me,' Astrid said.

'Why, because *you* left *us*? Just because *you're* a lumpsucker doesn't mean *I* have to be one!' Becca whispered angrily.

'No! Because I can't help you! Not in the Iele's caves. Not here. All I can do is get you killed!' Astrid whispered back.

'What are you *talking* about? What do you—'

But Becca's questions were cut off by more crashes as crates were upended and baskets dumped out. A farmer protested and was beaten. Becca started to shake. The death riders were swimming through the market, getting closer with every stroke.

'What else have you got in that bag? Anything?' Astrid asked.

Becca could hear fear in her voice now. She rooted through her bag again.

'I have a vial of Moses potion . . .' she said.

'I have no idea what that is,' said Astrid.

'Neither do I. That's it . . . no, wait! There's this . . .' She pulled out a large sea urchin shell. It was packed with squid ink and sealed with kelp paste. Vrăja had given it to her along with the transparensea pebbles and the Moses potion.

Astrid's eyes lit up. 'An ink bomb! *Perfect!*' she whispered as she took it from Becca. She peered out from under the table again. 'I'm going to draw the death riders away from the door. Stay here until the bomb goes off, no matter what you hear me say. Then cast the pearl and swim for the door. Ready?'

Becca wasn't, but she nodded anyway.

Astrid took a deep breath. She swam out of her hiding place and along the floor. When she reached the back of the hall, she rose over the stalls.

'Hey! I surrender, okay?' she shouted. 'Leave these mer alone!' Her hands were raised, but she'd tucked them behind her head to hide the ink bomb.

Becca watched from under the table, her heart in her throat, as the death riders advanced on Astrid.

'Where's the other one?' their sergeant shouted.

'What other one?' Astrid asked, affecting a confused look.

'The other mermaid! We know she's here!'

Astrid shifted her eyes to the ceiling. 'Hurry, Becca! Swim!' she shouted.

Understanding dawned across the sergeant's face. 'She cast a transparensea pearl!' he shouted. 'She's up by the ceiling and heading for the door! Don't let her out!'

Becca stayed put, remembering Astrid's instructions not to move until the bomb went off. The death riders hovering in the doorway swam towards the ceiling, spearguns drawn.

That's when Astrid struck. She hurled the ink bomb to

the floor with all her might. It exploded with a deafening bang, spreading a thick, choking cloud of squid ink through the hall.

Astrid dived to the floor and raced to the exit, streaking past Becca. Becca was on her tail instantly, following her as she zipped past stalls, crates and frightened merfolk.

It was as dark as night inside the hall now, but the ink cloud hadn't drifted all the way down to the ground yet. Becca could just make out where she was going. Astrid veered left, then right, and then the doorway came into view. She put on a burst of speed and streaked through it. Becca was right behind her, and she was almost out when a pair of rough hands grabbed her. She and the death rider tumbled out of the doorway together. In her frightened state, she'd forgotten to cast the transparensea pebble.

'Where are you going? No one leaves!' he barked at her. His eyes roved over her face; they took in her red hair. 'It's *you*!' he said.

'Let me go!' Becca said, struggling to break free.

But the death rider only tightened his grip. He opened his mouth to shout for help . . . and never saw the punch coming.

Astrid slugged him so hard he was out before he even hit the ground.

Becca, wide-eyed, looked from the unconscious merman to Astrid, but the other mermaid was already swimming back to the market hall's doors.

'Give me a hand!' she shouted, swinging one closed.

Becca grabbed the other door and slammed it shut.

Each door had a curved iron handle on it. Astrid unbuckled the sharkskin belt she was wearing, looped it through the handles, and knotted it tightly. A split second later, both mermaids heard thumps and yells as the death riders tried to pound their way out.

'That belt won't hold forever,' Astrid said, backing away. 'Come on, Becca, let's go.'

Becca hesitated. This wasn't part of her plan. Only moments ago, she'd been so angry at Astrid, she'd refused to even swim out of the village with her.

I don't trust her, Becca said to herself. *I don't even* like *her. She's difficult and rude . . .*

. . . *and brave*, a voice inside her countered – a voice that always pointed out things that Becca wished it wouldn't. *She just saved you from being captured*.

'Look, Becca, stay here if you want, but I'm going,' Astrid said, eyeing the doors. The pounding on the other side of them was getting louder. Villagers were starting to gather.

'What happened?' one of them asked. 'What's going on?'

Becca gave Astrid a nod. 'Okay,' she said. 'Let's go.'

The two mermaids took off, streaking down the main current and into the open water, leaving the death riders behind them.

TWELVE

A LEAGUE OUT OF THE VILLAGE, the flat seafloor gave way to the foothills of the Bermuda Rise, a collection of seamounts. Becca and Astrid found a rocky overhang and swooped down to investigate it. Underneath was a spacious sea cave. Once inside, they'd be invisible to anyone swimming above.

'Wait here,' Astrid instructed Becca. She swam in first, her sword out. 'All clear!' she called out after a minute.

Becca joined her and cast an illuminata spell to light the dark cave. Then she put her travelling case down, opened it and dug inside for the sea flax blanket she'd brought with her. It would make a good tablecloth. She snapped the blanket open and was just about to spread it out when she noticed that the cave's floor was covered with silt.

'Astrid, would you mind cleaning the silt away?' Becca asked. 'Otherwise it'll get into our lunch.'

'Sure,' Astrid said, and she started sweeping the silt away with her tail fins.

That's odd, Becca thought. Most mer would toss off a quick canta prax spell to whirl the silt away. Astrid's method was time consuming and made the water in the cave cloudy. When it finally cleared, Becca spread her blanket out.

Astrid dug in her pack and set out the food she'd bought. In addition to the squid eggs, she had a ripe marsh melon, oysters and some silt cherries. Then she sat down.

Becca awkwardly pulled the water apples and crab eggs she'd bought out of her own pack and placed them on the blanket, embarrassed that they were all she had to contribute.

'Oh, wow, water apples. My favourite,' Astrid said, picking one up and biting into it.

Becca knew it wasn't true. If they were Astrid's favourite, she would've bought some. But still, it was a nice thing to say. And – coming from Astrid – a surprising one.

'Have some squid eggs,' Astrid said, offering a clump to Becca.

Becca broke off an egg sac and popped it into her mouth. 'Mmm. *So* good,' she said, sitting down across from Astrid.

'Eat tons. I bought too much and don't want to carry it. I shouldn't shop when I'm hungry,' said Astrid, still munching on the apple.

Becca doubted *that* was true, either. She had the feeling that Astrid knew she didn't have much money and was being careful not to make her feel bad about it.

Becca frowned, perplexed. This considerate Astrid and the Astrid who'd risked her own safety to rescue Becca from the death riders didn't square with the Astrid whom Becca had met in the Iele's caves. Becca wondered if she'd misjudged her. Well, whether she had or hadn't, she definitely owed her a thank-you.

'Hey, Astrid . . .'

'Mmm?' Astrid replied, swallowing a bite of apple.

'Thanks for getting me out of the market. I'm really grateful to you.'

Astrid gave her a rueful smile. 'You shouldn't be. I nearly got you captured.'

'What do you mean?' asked Becca, puzzled.

'If it wasn't for me, you could've got out right away. All you had to do was cast your transparensea pebble.'

Becca remembered how Astrid had refused the pebble. 'I still don't understand why you wouldn't.'

Astrid looked away. 'Like I said, they don't work on me.' Her brusque tone was back.

'But—'

'Tell me about the Iele,' said Astrid, changing the subject. 'What happened? Why aren't you still with them?'

Becca saw that Astrid wasn't going to answer her question, so she answered Astrid's instead. She told her how Markus Traho and his troops had found the Iele's cave, and that she, Sera, Ling, Ava and Neela had narrowly escaped by diving into a mirror that Vrăja kept in the Incantarium.

'So *that's* how you ended up in North Atlantica so quickly,' Astrid said. 'I was wondering how you caught up. It's taken me weeks to swim this far.'

'Vadus was a creepy place. I was scared I'd run into the mirror lord the whole time, but he must've been busy elsewhere. A couple of vitrina showed me a way out . . . after I gave them about a thousand compliments,' Becca said, shivering at the memory of the quicksilver world.

'What about Vrăja? Did she escape, too?' Astrid asked.

'I wish I knew,' Becca replied. 'It's all I've been thinking about ever since I left. I hope to gods she's all right. The others, too. I haven't heard anything for so long. I've tried to convoca them, but I haven't had any luck. Which is really worrying. My magic's grown stronger so I ought to be able to do it.'

Astrid had picked up an egg sac. She lowered it again. 'Your magic grew stronger? Really? How?' she asked, clearly curious.

'We did a bloodbind before we escaped,' Becca explained. 'Ever since, I've been able to understand languages I've never been able to speak, cast awesome illuminatas and do lots of other spells, too. I think it's because I have some of the others' blood in me now.'

'Wow. That's really cool,' Astrid said, a wistful note in her voice.

'Yeah, it is. But if my magic's strong enough to do a decent convoca, why can't I reach the others? What if it's because they can't be reached? Because they've been captured or . . . or worse,' Becca said, her voice fraught with concern.

'Lots of things affect songcasting, Becca. The tides. The moon. The presence or absence of whales. Everyone knows that.' Becca nodded, unconvinced. She worried about her four friends constantly.

Astrid must've seen her feelings on her face, because she said, 'They're smart, Becca. Tough, too. They made it all the way to the River Olt. They can make it home.'

'You almost sound as if you like them,' Becca said, a reproachful note in her voice. She still didn't understand why Astrid had left the Iele's caves, and she still felt angry about it.

'I *do* like them,' Astrid replied. 'I like you, too.'

'Then why didn't you stay with us?' Becca demanded.

'Because.'

Becca snorted. '*Because*? That's so weak, Astrid. What's the real reason?'

'Because I couldn't, all right? Because things are really complicated,' Astrid said testily.

Becca held her hands up. 'Okay, fine. Don't tell me. I really don't care.'

Only a few minutes ago she thought she might've misjudged Astrid. Now she saw that she hadn't. The merl was just as obnoxious as ever.

An awkward silence descended. Becca reached for a cherry. As she did, she saw something crawling on the marsh melon.

'Ugh. Crabs. They've smelled the food,' she said.

A small army of the creatures had invaded the cave. Some were attacking the squid eggs. Others were carrying off a water apple. Becca scolded them, but they paid no attention.

She brushed the one crab off the melon, but a dozen more were scuttling towards the cherries.

'They're getting everywhere!' she exclaimed, picking up the cherries. 'Astrid, can you help me shoo them away?'

Astrid reached for her scabbard, took her sword out, and brandished it. 'I think I'll have some nice, fresh crabmeat with my melon,' she said loudly. The creatures must've understood Mermish, for they scattered.

Again, Becca was puzzled by Astrid's decision not to use magic. *Why didn't she cast a commoveo spell?* she wondered as she put the cherries back down on the blanket. She didn't understand Astrid's weirdness at all.

Then suddenly she did.

Oh, wow, she thought. *That explains everything! Astrid's unwillingness to songcast . . . her interest when I talked about my magic growing stronger . . . her defensiveness . . . They're all part of the same problem.*

Becca reached for her travelling case and started to dig through it, pretending that she was looking for something. She was pretty certain she'd figured out the reason behind Astrid's eccentricity, but she wanted to confirm her suspicions before confronting her.

'I, uh, I just remembered I have some, um . . . candied mussels in my bag. They'd make a nice dessert, don't you think? Could you cast an illuminata for me?' she asked lightly. 'The one I cast earlier isn't strong enough to light up *this* mess.'

'An illuminata? Um, well, I really shouldn't,' Astrid said.

'I've got a cold and my voice is raspy. It would go *way* wrong.'

But Astrid's voice wasn't raspy. And Becca hadn't heard her sniffle once.

I am *right*, she thought. She closed her case and put it aside. 'Astrid . . .' she said gently.

Astrid quickly looked away, but not before Becca glimpsed the desperation in her eyes, and the fear. Becca recognized those emotions. She knew them well. She reached for Astrid's hand.

'What, Becca? For gods' sake, *what*?' Astrid said, knotting her hand into a fist.

'You don't really have a cold, do you?' Becca asked.

Astrid didn't reply, but her eyes filled with tears.

This was bad. Very bad. This was about the worst.

'Oh, Astrid,' she said, her heart aching for this tough, sad, misunderstood mermaid. 'You can't sing.'

THIRTEEN

ASTRID QUICKLY BLINKED away her tears and tried to recover her cool.

'Of *course* I can sing,' she said.

Becca shook her head. 'No, you can't. That's why you left us. Because you wanted to keep it a secret and were afraid we'd find out. Afraid we wouldn't accept you.'

Astrid rolled her eyes. 'Oh, please. Spare me the amateur psych session, would you?' She rose and started stuffing the leftover food into her backpack.

'What are you doing?' asked Becca.

'Packing up. I've got to get going. I've wasted enough time here already.'

Becca was stung by the insult, but she didn't give up. 'So I'm a waste of time, huh? Nice, Astrid. Is that how you cope? By pushing mer away when they come too close? By swimming off when you get scared?'

Astrid snorted. 'I'm not scared of much, Becca. Certainly not of you,' she said.

'You're scared of the truth, though.'

Astrid finished packing. She cinched her backpack. 'It's been real,' she said, turning to swim away. 'Happy travels.'

Becca tried one last time. 'Hey, Astrid? This isn't an attack, okay?' she said. 'It's me being a friend. Or trying.'

Astrid stopped. Her shoulders sagged. She looked like a puffer fish that had suddenly deflated.

'I understand. I really do,' Becca said softly.

Astrid whirled around. 'No, you *don't*,' she said hotly. 'How could you? You're normal, Becca. Your whole life is normal. You have parents who aren't disappointed in you. You go to school and no one makes fun of you. No one talks behind your back. No one thinks you're a joke.'

'Yep,' Becca said brightly. 'That's me, Little Miss Normal.'

'How did you know, anyway?' Astrid asked.

'Well, the fact that you never songcast kind of gave me a clue. And . . .'

'And what?'

'And I always know when someone's hiding something,' Becca said.

'Yeah? How?' Astrid asked sceptically.

'Because I usually *am* that someone,' Becca replied.

'*You?* What are you hiding? A to-do conch? An ebb-and-flow chart?' Astrid joked, poking fun at Becca's tendency to be hyperorganized.

Becca didn't laugh. 'I haven't been straight with you, either,' she admitted, fiddling with the edge of the blanket. 'Or with the others. I'm not in school. I left a year ago to get a job. And I'm not heading home to a nice house with two doting parents.'

'I don't understand,' Astrid said, setting her backpack down. 'At the Iele's you said—'

'I told you a story. About the happy life I wish I had,' Becca confessed, forcing herself to meet Astrid's searching gaze. 'I'm an orphan. My father died of mercury poisoning when I was four. The waters where he grew up were full of it. His health was always bad, and it got worse as he got older. A year after I lost him, I lost my mother to longline hooks. Her body was recovered before the lines were reeled in. That's something, I guess.'

'Becca, I had no idea. I'm so sorry,' Astrid said, sitting back down.

'I didn't have any relatives able to take me in, so I was put in a foster home. It was pretty chaotic. Bigger merkids stole my food, and my stuff. Nobody really cared how I did in school, or if I even went.' She laughed sadly. 'I think that's why I'm so off-the-charts organized. I always had to have a plan – a plan to get to the table first so I'd get *something* to eat. A plan for avoiding barracudas. A plan for getting myself to school on time. I *do* work at Baudel's as a spellbinder – that much is true. The owners are good to me; they let me live in an apartment over the shop. It's small but it's all mine. It has a bedroom, a sitting room, and the tiniest kitchen you've ever seen. But I love it for what it doesn't have . . . barracudas.'

Astrid nodded. Barracudas were killer fish with sharp teeth, but the word was also mer slang for what the terragoggs called bullies. 'I know what you mean,' she said. 'Barracudas don't steal my lunch – they wouldn't dare, me being the admiral's daughter – but they still have their weapons: the jokes, the whispers, the snide remarks.'

'At least you have a family,' Becca said wistfully. 'It must be nice to have parents to turn to.'

Astrid shook her head. 'I wouldn't know. My parents are ashamed of me,' she said miserably. 'No one in the admiral's family is supposed to be anything less than perfect. My parents have tried to keep my problem a secret. Most Ondalinians don't know, but some inside the Citadel do.'

'The what?'

'The Citadel,' Astrid replied. 'That's where Ondalina's admirals live. With their families and the top members of government.'

Becca tilted her head. 'How did it happen?' she asked.

A mermaid who couldn't sing was rare; she'd never met one before.

'I don't know,' Astrid replied. 'I had a singing voice when I was little, but I lost it. It was right after Månenhonnør – Ondalina's moon festival. I was having such a good time – dancing and singing, and eating too many slices of Månenkager. It's a cake made of pressed krill and iced with ground mother-of-pearl. It shines like the moon.'

Becca nodded. She'd heard of Månenkager and knew that right before the cake went into the lava ovens, the baker dropped a silver drupe into the batter. Whoever got the coin in her piece would have good luck for the coming year.

'A few days after the festival, I started losing my ability to sing. Two months later, it was gone completely. My father called in the best doctors in Ondalina. None of them could figure out what had happened, but they all said I was lucky not to have lost my speaking voice, too.' Astrid went silent for a bit, then said, 'I don't *feel* lucky. What good is a mermaid without magic?'

'A *lot* of good,' Becca said fiercely. 'Who saved us from Abbadon, hmm? Wait, I'll give you a hint – it wasn't me. It wasn't Sera, Ling, Ava or Neela, either. It was you. You took it straight to that monster.'

Becca vividly remembered when Vrăja had given them a glimpse of the horrible monster Abbadon. It was so strong and vicious that it had broken through Vrăja's ochi spell – even through waterfire – and attacked them. Astrid had rushed straight at the creature with her sword and had cut off one of its hands, forcing it to retreat.

'Thanks, Becca. That's a nice thing to say. I did help you, but I also left you. Because I was afraid my secret would make me a liability. Like today in the market hall,' Astrid said. 'You need more than a good swordsmer to fight Abbadon. You need a sixth songcaster with some seriously strong magic. I don't have any to give you, and nothing can be done about it.'

How Becca hated those words: *nothing can be done about it*. She'd heard them her entire life.

You're an orphan now, Rebecca, and nothing can be done about it.

It's too bad your doll was stolen, but it's gone. Nothing can be done about it.

I'm sorry you don't have money to go to the kolegio, but you can't go unless you do. That's just the way it is. Nothing can be done about it.

Astrid sat, shoulders slumped, drawing in the silt with her finger. Becca's green eyes narrowed as she watched her. Astrid had magic inside her – dormant, maybe – but it was there. Becca was sure of it. She could see it sparking in the merl's intense ice-blue eyes. She could feel it in her sure, powerful movements. The question was how to get it out of her.

Becca immediately went into problem-solving mode, as she always did when confronted with a challenge. An idea started to form in her mind. Becca was an expert at coming up with strategies. Life was often messy and unpredictable, but a good plan could make it neat and orderly. She would need a few things to carry out this particular plan: a length of bamboo or some sort of water reed. Better yet, whalebone. Some pretty shells, too.

Becca was not only good at making things, she was good at making things better. Life in foster homes had taught her that if she waited for someone else to make things better, she'd be waiting a very long time.

'Hey, we'd better get going,' Becca said. 'Sitting here all day isn't going to get us home.'

Astrid raised an eyebrow. 'That was sudden,' she said.

'Yeah, well. I, um, just realized . . . that we probably

shouldn't hang out here all day,' Becca said. 'You know, death riders and all.'

She rose and grabbed her travel case. Astrid slung her backpack over her shoulder. As they swam out of the cave, Becca spotted something glinting from the seafloor, half in and half out of the silt. She bent down to pick it up.

'What is it?' Astrid asked.

'A piece of sea glass,' Becca replied, showing her her find. It was cobalt blue, polished by sand and surf to a milky opaqueness. 'Pretty, isn't it?'

'Dreaming up a new shade for your Whirlpearl Glitterbombs?' Astrid teased, referring to the line of songpearl cosmetics Becca had mentioned on their way to the Iele's caves.

'No, I just like bright, shiny things,' Becca said airily. 'They inspire me, you know? You never know where your next big idea will come from.'

'For an eyeshadow,' Astrid said. 'Or a lipstick.'

'Or something that just might save the world,' Becca said, pocketing the sea glass.

Astrid laughed.

Becca didn't.

FOURTEEN

'GET UP!' the death rider shouted, slapping an elderly merman with his powerful tail fins.

A dozen soldiers – spearguns drawn – had swum into the Bedrieër's hold. They were herding frightened prisoners out of the ship's containment area and into the water lock.

Ling rose in the water, straining against her chain, trying to see what was happening. She glimpsed a large cage. Prisoners were being forced into it. When the cage was full, a hatch was opened and the cage was lowered into a chamber underneath the ship's hull.

Ling knew that there was another hatch in the chamber. She was certain that the death riders would open it, and then the cage would plummet through the water . . . but why? Where were the prisoners going?

She also knew that the death riders would have to detach the chain that tethered her to the hold's wall if they wanted to put her in that cage. When they did, she might be able to break away.

If she could slip out of the water lock into the death riders' quarters, or the hold's kitchens – someplace, *anyplace*, where she could hide until the rest of the prisoners were gone – she might be able to steal to the water lock and let herself out.

Ling knew her plan was a total long shot. A thousand things could go wrong and probably would, but she had to try.

As she waited and watched, more cages were filled with prisoners and dropped through the water lock. Most of the death riders were grouped around the cage's door, where they were encountering resistance. If she could somehow skirt the door, maybe she could swim off without being noticed.

The guards were moving through the prisoners quickly. In only a few minutes, they would be unchaining her. Her heart thumped in her chest as she watched the frightened mermaid near her, the one with two children, being herded towards the water lock.

Don't give in to fear. Be strong, she told herself. *Weakness is for guppies*.

'You, there! Hands on your head!' a death rider shouted at her.

Ling did as she was told. The death rider opened the padlock on her collar, pulled the chain free of its hasp, then locked the padlock.

'Move!' he yelled, shoving her.

Ling needed time. She swam slowly, her head lowered.

CHAPTER 14

Her hair was hanging over her face, but behind it, her eyes moved rapidly, noting the position of every death rider.

But the death riders were watching her, too. If she didn't find a way to distract them, her plan would never work. Then she spotted the merman – the one who'd yelled at the frightened mermaid earlier. She swam up behind him, placed her hand in the middle of his back, and shoved him. It was an awful thing to do, but she had no choice.

The merman lost his balance and fell against the prisoner ahead of him. Scared and angry, they both lost their tempers. Harsh words were traded, then punches. Two other mermen, caught by the flailing fists and thrashing tails, joined the fight. Instantly, every death rider in both the containment area and the water lock converged on them. A fight could quickly turn into a riot, and they knew it.

Ling didn't waste a second. She ducked behind a sobbing mermaid, darted into the water lock, then disappeared down a narrow hallway. There were doors on both sides of it – some open, some closed. Ling peered around one and saw a small room with two bunks in it.

That's when she heard the voices.

Ling looked down the hallway. It ended in a T. The voices were coming from the passage that led off to the right and were growing louder. *More death riders*, she thought frantically. They'd round the corner any second now.

Ling did the only thing she could think of. She swam into the room.

'Shut the damn door, Arturo,' a sleepy voice said.

'I'm trying to take a nap here.'

Ling didn't utter a sound. She stayed perfectly still, praying that the death rider stretched out on his bunk would fall back asleep.

But he didn't.

He rolled over, opened his eyes, and blinked at her. Surprise chased the weariness from his face. 'You're not Arturo,' he said, sitting up.

Ling panicked. 'Don't turn me in. *Please*,' she begged.

But he was on her before she even finished speaking. He grabbed her good arm, twisted it behind her back, and forced her out of his room.

'Captain! This one was trying to escape!' he shouted, as he pushed her back into the water lock.

An officer turned around. He swore at Ling, then backhanded her across her face. Stars exploded behind her eyes. She felt herself being thrust into the cage.

The soldiers crowded so many more mer in with her that she was nearly crushed against the bars. She felt the cage being lowered into the chamber under the hold. An instant later, it was plummeting through the dark ocean. All around her, prisoners were shrieking and sobbing. Ling closed her eyes, devastated. This was the end, it had to be. She'd failed. Sera and the others wouldn't find out that Orfeo was still alive until it was too late. Too late for them. For the waters. For the entire world.

And then the cage hit the seafloor with a bone-rattling thud. As the silt cleared, Ling opened her eyes.

She had once heard that some terragoggs believed in the existence of a place of eternal suffering called *hell*.

As she looked out through the bars of the cage and saw where they had landed, she believed in it, too.

FIFTEEN

'I STILL DON'T SEE why you made us pick through a cemetery.'

'Go to *sleep*, Astrid,' Becca said, as she sorted through a pile of barnacles, looking for a juicy one. A slender piece of whalebone lay across her lap.

'A *cemetery*!'

'It wasn't an ordinary cemetery. You know that. It was a whalefall. Gods!' Becca huffed.

A whalefall was the hushed, hallowed ground where the remains of dead whales lay. When a whale's life was over, her body sank through the water and came to rest on the seafloor. Her flesh provided sustenance for hungry sea creatures, and her skeleton enhanced the magic of any mer lucky enough to happen across it. Whales were highly magical creatures – so magical, in fact, that some of their powers remained in their bones after death.

Becca and Astrid had been swimming together for three days now. Eventually Astrid would have to veer north to

Ondalina, and Becca would continue west, but they'd decided that until then they were safer together.

Yesterday, they'd come across the remains of a humpback. Becca had been thrilled; she'd tossed away the kelp stalk she'd been carrying around and had swum through the enormous skeleton, hunting for what she needed – a smooth piece of bone: narrow, cylindrical, and about as long as her forearm. While she searched, Astrid kept a lookout.

Half an hour later, Becca had what she wanted and she and Astrid were on their way again. But ever since they'd left the whalefall, Astrid had been jumpy. She'd swum with her sword in her hand, twitching at every change in the current. Becca had tolerated her behaviour, but she was getting fed up now.

An hour ago, they'd made camp for the night under a large coral reef. Becca had cast an illuminata and was working by its light. Astrid announced that she was going to go to sleep. She'd made herself a cozy bed from a few armfuls of seaweed she'd gathered, and had curled up in it, but she was wide awake and driving Becca crazy.

'That place totally gave me the creeps,' she grumbled.

'Yes, you told me that. Twenty times at least,' Becca said, selecting a nice fat barnacle from her pile.

'Bones wherever you look. Scavengers, worms. Places like that draw EisGeists, you know,' Astrid said darkly.

EisGeists were murderous spirits that dwelled in cold waters. Legend had it that Morsa had created them when she was practising necromancy and trying to unlock the secret of immortality. They were botches – tormented, half-souled spectres, neither alive nor dead. Morsa had thrown them into the Arctic Ocean hoping the frigid water would destroy them, but the EisGeists had endured, roaming down into the northern reaches of the Atlantic.

Becca had seen one once and never wanted to see another. It was pale and wraithlike, with long limbs, clawed hands, and white irises. EisGeists fed on bones. They tangled their victims in ropes woven from seaweed and dragged the bodies behind them until the flesh had rotted away.

'Did you *see* any EisGeists?' Becca asked, trying her best to remain patient with Astrid.

'No,' Astrid admitted grudgingly.

'So what are you worried about?'

'They might've seen *us*. They might be following us. I have this feeling. Like we're not alone. I keep *hearing* something, Becca.'

'What?'

'Weird noises . . . voices . . . I don't know.'

'Instead of worrying about nonexistent EisGeists, you should've taken a piece of whalebone for yourself while we were in the whalefall. It augments magic, you know.'

Astrid snorted. 'Like that matters?' she said.

Becca sighed. She was learning that it was not easy to be Astrid's friend. One needed a high tolerance for sarcasm and the ability to resist getting drawn into arguments. She understood now why Astrid was the way she was, but that didn't make it any easier to deal with her.

Returning her attention to her work, Becca squeezed the barnacle she'd chosen. A drop of thick, sticky liquid fell from it onto the whalebone. She quickly pressed a shell into the glue and held it in place for a few seconds. Barnacle glue was fast acting and super strong.

For the past few days, Becca had been working diligently to implement her plan to help Astrid – gathering bits of sea glass and polished shells, and carving the piece of whalebone at night after Astrid was asleep.

Becca glued another shell onto the whalebone. She had made a beautiful design of shells and sea glass, and she was nearly done with her project.

Astrid, watching her, said, 'What are you doing? Why are you still up? You're keeping *me* up. What is that thing, anyway?'

'A murder weapon.' Becca said this through gritted teeth, but she would have shouted it, if she was the shouting type.

'Ha. *So* funny,' Astrid said. She picked up her sword from where it lay on the seafloor beside her and got out of bed.

'You only just settled down. Why can't you relax?'

'Because I hear it again . . . a voice,' Astrid replied.

She swam to the mouth of the cave and looked out into the night waters. As she did, Becca glued the last piece of sea glass into place.

'Becca?'

'Hmmm?' Becca said, inspecting her work.

'Becca?'

'Yes?'

'Becca!'

'Astrid, what do you *want*?' Becca snapped. 'I'm right here. Stop shouting!'

'I didn't shout!' Astrid shouted. '*You* did! You shouted my name.'

Becca put the whalebone down. 'No,' she said slowly, her fins flaring. '*You* shouted *my* name.'

Please . . . can you hear me? Talk to me! Say something! a voice called out.

Astrid raised her sword, ready to attack whoever, or whatever, was outside the cave. Becca swam to her side.

Astrid, is that you? Becca?

Becca gasped. She knew that voice. '*Sera?*' she called out. 'Is that you? Where are you? I can't see you. It's too dark!'

'I'm in your head! I've been songcasting for days . . . trying to get you . . .'

'What is this? What's happening?' Astrid asked uncertainly, her sword still raised.

'It's a convoca!' Becca said excitedly. 'Sit down, Astrid. Close your eyes. It's easier without any distractions.'

'But . . . but how is this happening? I can't songcast,' Astrid said, looking bewildered.

'You don't need to. Sera's doing the casting. All you have to do is listen. Sit down before we lose her!' Becca ordered. She grabbed Astrid's free hand and pulled her to the cave floor.

'No way. I'm not part of this. I left, remember?' Astrid said, breaking free of Becca's grasp. 'I'm useless to them.'

Sera was still calling, but her voice had started to fade. Becca panicked. She couldn't lose her.

'Astrid, can it *not* be about you for once? I need to see if Sera's okay. And the others, too. You're part of this convoca, whether you want to be or not, so stop telling me you're useless and start being use*ful*. If this spell gets messed up because you won't participate, I'm going to be really, *really* angry!'

By the time she finished, Becca was shouting at the top of her lungs.

Astrid blinked and sat down. Then both mermaids closed their eyes.

SIXTEEN

SERA WAS SONGCASTING with all her might. Neela was with her.

Becca could see them inside her head. 'Sera! Neela! You're safe!' she exclaimed. 'You made it out of the Iele's caves!'

Neela nodded but didn't speak, not wanting to break Sera's concentration.

Becca had been so excited to see Sera that she hadn't focused on her friend's appearance. She did now and was amazed by the changes she saw. Sera was wearing camo, and her body was leaner and harder than Becca remembered. But the biggest change was one that Becca couldn't see, only sense: a new sureness. The mermaid she'd met in the River Olt – the one who was hesitant and full of doubt – was gone. A confident leader had taken her place.

As Becca sat, eyes closed, waiting, Astrid appeared in her head, then Ava. Becca felt as if all of them were right next to her, floating in a circle. Happiness flooded through her, but it was quickly replaced by worry when she realized one of them was missing.

'Where's Ling?' she asked.

'I can't reach her . . . I've tried and tried,' Sera said anxiously. 'Something's wrong. She'd answer if she could. I know she would.'

'You've got everyone else now. Talk quickly, Sera, before the songspell fades,' Neela urged.

'Becca, Ava, you still there?' Sera asked.

'Yes!'

'Right here, *querida*!' said Ava.

'Okay, got you!' Sera exclaimed. '*Astrid?* Is that you? I thought I felt you with Becca, but I wasn't sure.'

'Yeah. Hey, Sera. I met up with Becca and—'

'Does that mean you're with us now?' Neela asked hopefully.

Astrid's eyes widened. 'What? *No!* I'm not. I just—'

'Got to interrupt, sorry,' Sera said urgently. 'This convoca's not very strong. I could lose you at any second.' She took a deep breath, then continued. 'I've got news. Lots of it. Neela and I found our talismans.'

'No way!' Becca said. 'Sera, that's amazing!'

'I also found out where the rest of the talismans are and *what* they are.'

'That's *huge*! Good work, *mina*!' Ava said.

'It's a start,' Sera allowed. 'But I'm not going to celebrate until we have all six in our hands. Becs, Pyrrha's talisman is a gold coin with the image of Neria on it. It's at Cape Horn, with a wind spirit called—'

'The Williwaw,' Becca said grimly.

'You've got to be kidding me,' Astrid said.

'Be extremely careful approaching it,' Sera cautioned. 'It can stir up a raging storm in seconds.'

'Or don't approach it all,' Astrid said. 'Just a thought.'

Sera ignored her. 'Ava, Nyx's talisman is a ruby ring in a gold setting. It's in the swamps of the Mississippi, guarded by water spirits called the Okwa Naholo,' she said. 'They are serious bad news.'

'*Bad news?*' Astrid scoffed. 'They're worse than EisGeists! You *know* they are. Everyone does!'

'What about Sycorax's talisman?' Becca asked, dread gnawing at her. 'And what about Ling?'

'Sycorax's is a puzzle ball. It's in the Great Abyss.'

'Which is only, like, a million miles deep,' Astrid pointed out.

'I'm really worried about Ling,' Sera continued. 'She's in trouble. I know it. Ava, can you feel her?'

Ava went quiet for a moment, then shook her head. 'I can't. I'm trying, but I'm getting nothing.'

Sera heaved a troubled sigh.

'There might be a reason, though,' Ava quickly added. 'She might be sheltering in a wrecked ship, one with an iron hull. Or she might be in a place with a lot of mer, where it's not safe to answer.'

Astrid swore, startling everyone. Becca could feel Astrid's anger growing, and the tension building between her and Sera. She remembered how they'd clashed in the Iele's caves, several times. They couldn't even talk, it seemed – not then and not now – without fighting.

'She's *dead*. Face it. The death riders probably got her,' Astrid said. 'I *told* you this would happen, Sera. Back in the River Olt. You're asking too much of them. Will Ling's death stop you? Or are you going to keep on with the insanity until Becca's dead, too? And Ava? And Neela?'

'I'm going to keep on until *Abbadon's* dead,' Sera replied, her voice steely and determined. Then she said, 'I'm glad you're part of this convoca, Astrid. Even if you're still not part of our group. Because I owe you an apology.'

'For what? For getting Ling killed?' Astrid asked. 'Not accepted. Because I liked her. A lot.'

'For accusing Ondalina of attacking Miromara. It wasn't your father; it was my own uncle, Vallerio, who did it in league with one of Miromara's duchessas – Portia Volnero. He sold out his realm and assassinated his regina – his own sister, my mother. He killed my father, too. Maybe my brother as well. No one's seen Desiderio since he left to guard our borders.'

'*Meu Deus!*' Ava exclaimed.

'I didn't know any of this when we met in the Iele's caves, but I do now,' said Sera. 'I shouldn't have made the accusations against your realm. I'm sorry.'

Astrid nodded curtly, and it struck Becca how one might think the balance of power had just tipped in her favour, but it hadn't. Sera had owned a wrong and apologized for it, and she seemed stronger for having done so, not weaker.

'I'm fighting back against my uncle with the help of some brave Miromarans,' Sera continued. 'It's hard. Vallerio wants us dead. We're going to have to leave Miromara, and look for a safe haven . . .' She hesistated, wary, then said, 'Somewhere else. Vallerio's taken over Matali as well as Miromara.'

'And you're telling me this why?' Astrid asked.

'My uncle's searching for the talismans, too. He and Rafe Mfeme are behind the raids on the villages. They're forcing the stolen mer into labour camps and making them search for the talismans. If Vallerio gets them, he'll give them to the one who wants to unleash Abbadon. I still don't know who that person is, but I'm trying to find out. In return, that person will help my uncle take over the other realms. *All* of them, Astrid.'

Sera paused here, to let the weight of her words sink in. Then she said, 'When I was in Cerulea, I spied on Vallerio and Portia and overheard Portia say that the person who wants to free Abbadon has two of the talismans – Merrow's and Orfeo's.'

'But I thought you had Merrow's talisman,' Ava countered.

'I do. Vallerio has what he *thinks* is Merrow's blue diamond, but it's only a fake. I have the real one,' Sera explained. 'Orfeo's talisman is a black pearl that Morsa gave him. I'm praying the pearl Portia mentioned is also a fake and hoping that the real one is still where Merrow hid it – in a maelstrom off the coast of Greenland.'

Astrid laughed harshly. 'Good luck trying to get it.

That maelstrom? It's called the Qanikkaaq. It swallows trawlers whole.'

'I don't need luck, Astrid. I need you,' Sera said. 'I need you to go to the maelstrom, find out if the real pearl's still inside it, and get it out if it is.'

Astrid looked trapped. 'I told you, Sera . . . I can't. I just *can't*,' she said.

Becca knew why. She wished she could tell the others, but she couldn't. It was for Astrid to do, not her.

Sera nodded stoically, but her eyes told a different story. Becca saw the desperation in them. The convoca started to weaken. The image blurred. Voices rose as everyone tried to talk at once, then they faded. Becca heard broken pleas, warnings, and goodbyes.

'. . . anything from Ling, get word to me . . .'

'. . . don't go alone . . .'

'. . . careful! Those waters . . .'

'. . . love you, merl . . .'

And then Sera, Neela and Ava were gone, and it was just Becca and Astrid again. Astrid rose, angrily slapped her tail fin against the cave's wall, then swam outside and stared into the darkness.

Becca joined her. 'I'm not going home,' she said. 'Not now. I'm going straight to Cape Horn. I've got to get that talisman from the Williwaw.' She was quiet for a bit, then added, 'You want to help her, too. I know you do. I saw it in your eyes.'

'I don't know what I want,' Astrid said miserably.

'Then it's a good thing I do,' said Becca.

She swam back to where she'd been sitting, picked up the object she'd been working on, and handed it to Astrid. In Becca's clever hands, the whalebone had become a slim, graceful pipe. It had a tapered mouthpiece and several stops.

Astrid looked at it uncertainly. 'It's beautiful, Becs. It's more than beautiful – it's amazing.' She raised her eyes to Becca's. 'But what am I supposed to do with it?'

Becca smiled. 'Make magic.'

SEVENTEEN

ASTRID EYED THE slender whalebone pipe.

A few minutes before, there had been anger in her eyes. Now they were filled with a mixture of hope and fear.

Becca wasn't surprised to see those emotions together. She knew that sometimes hope was the scariest feeling of all.

'Is this some weird Atlantean custom?' Astrid asked. 'Giving mer instruments they don't know how to play?'

Becca didn't answer. Instead, she hummed a simple canta prax melody – one of the first taught to mer children. It was a camouflage songspell, used by mer to turn themselves bright green so they could blend in with algae or kelp.

'I learned that when I was little. Did you? When you could still sing?' she asked.

Astrid nodded.

'Try it,' Becca said. 'It's not hard to play.'

Astrid shrugged. 'If it'll make you happy.'

She touched the mouthpiece to her lips, placed her fingers over the stops, and sounded a few notes. After a few minutes, she had most of the melody figured out. Taking a deep breath, she played it through, with only a few mistakes.

'Okay, there it is,' she said, glancing at Becca. 'Hey, what's with you?'

Becca was grinning from ear to ear. 'Look at your arms!' she squealed.

Astrid did. They'd turned a muddy shade of olive. So had the rest of her body. It wasn't the bright green of a kelp thicket, but it was a start.

'Oh, my gods!' she yelped, nearly dropping the pipe. 'Did that . . . did I . . .'

'Make magic?' Becca trilled. '*Yes!*'

'But I don't . . . I can't . . .'

'You *do* and you can. Remember how jumpy you were at the whalefall? And ever since? You thought you were hearing EisGeists, but it was Sera trying to convoca us. You might have lost your singing voice, but you still have magic in you, Astrid. You just needed a way to get it out.'

Astrid looked down at the pipe as if she was holding a moray eel in her hands.

She's scared, Becca thought. *Scared that she'll try again and nothing will happen, that this was all a fluke.*

Becca swam to her friend and took her by the shoulders. 'Listen to me. Back in the Incantarium, you were brave for all of us. You saved us from Abbadon. I'm asking you to be brave for yourself now.'

Astrid lifted her eyes to Becca's. The look in them was heartbreakingly vulnerable.

'You can *do* this,' Becca said. She hummed another easy canta prax spell.

Astrid lifted the pipe to her lips and played the tune after only two tries.

'Not bad!' Becca cheered. 'You were supposed to turn purple, but blue's good. Keep going!'

Astrid did. Over the next hour, she turned rocks orange, her hair pink, and put polka dots on a swordfish. She turned Becca's face bright yellow, her tail silver, and made tentacles sprout from her head.

'Okay, okay, that's enough!' Becca finally said. 'It's late. I've got to get some sleep.'

'I'll stay outside the cave so I don't disturb you,' Astrid said. 'I *can't* sleep, Becca. I might never sleep again!' She looked down at the ground, suddenly awkward. 'Thank you for this,' she said, with a shy smile. 'Thank you *so* much.'

Becca waved her thanks away. 'It's nothing.'

'Becca, you're so wrong,' Astrid said. 'It's *everything*.'

Astrid was so excited, and so agreeable for once, that Becca decide to take a chance. 'Will you join us now?' she asked. 'Will you try to get the black pearl?'

Astrid's smile faded.

'I know, Astrid,' Becca said in a rush. 'You're scared. Scared you won't be able to songcast. Scared you'll put us in danger. But we're *all* scared. I'm supposed to be a whizz with waterfire. Sometimes I can call up enough to light up a whole town. Other times, the flames are so tiny they wouldn't heat a pot of sargasso tea. I wonder all the time if my magic will be there when I need it the most.'

'Becca, I can't even turn myself the right shade of green.'

'*Yet*,' Becca said.

Astrid shook her head. She opened her mouth to speak, but Becca cut her off.

'Don't say yes, but don't say no. Can you give me that much?'

Astrid nodded. 'I can.'

Then she swam outside the cave to practise. Becca put her tools away in her travel case, then burrowed down into the pile of seaweed she'd carried in earlier. She was exhausted.

As she closed her eyes, the music Astrid was making floated into the cave. Occasional flashes of light or colour played against its walls. Becca heard her friend whooping and giggling, but she didn't mind.

This is the first time I've ever heard Astrid laugh . . . really *laugh*, she thought. *Happiness. What a lovely sound.*

Becca's eyes closed. As sleep stole over her, she felt pleased that the first part of her plan had worked – that she'd found a way to help Astrid. If only the second part would work now – if only Astrid would help *them*.

Becca drifted off hoping that friendship, some of the most powerful magic there was, had cast its spell over Astrid.

EIGHTEEN

NOTHING, NO NORTHERN river or arctic flow, felt as cold to Serafina as the grey North Sea. Restive winds howled across its waters, whipping up enormous swells. Storms swept in with savage fury.

Even here in Scaghaufen, capital of the Meerteufel sea goblin tribe, with its hot, sulfurous vents and its bubbling lava pits, the cold went right through her.

Sera was in the palace of the Meerteufel's chieftain, Guldemar. The palace was made entirely from slag – the molten waste separated from pure metal when ore was smelted. It loomed up from the seafloor like a black cloud – craggy and misshapen. From its windows, visitors could see the entire goblin city.

The capital's fiery heart was a blast furnace fifty feet high that roared day and night. It was shaped like the head of the first Meerteufel chieftain, Kupfernickel. Lava bubbled in his mad eyes. From his snarling mouth flowed a white-hot stream of slag. Foundries dotted the city. They belched steam and sprayed sparks as molten Kobold steel was cast into weapons and armour. In the distance, mines pitted the seafloor, and slag heaps rose like mountains.

Sera was waiting to be admitted to Guldemar's stateroom. She and her retinue of twenty Black Fins had assembled with ten chests, each filled with gold, silver, and jewels.

The Black Fins were in serious trouble. They'd managed to steal plenty of treasure, and to hide it well, but they'd enraged Vallerio and he'd vowed to kill every last one of them. His forces were moving ever closer to their hideout, making it almost impossible to leave it. Two Black Fins had been captured while trying to gather food. The youngest fighter, a mermaid named Coco, had witnessed it and raced back to headquarters to tell Sera, but there was nothing anyone could do. When the captives had refused to give up any information, even under torture, Vallerio had had them executed. It was only a matter of time until the Black Fins' hideout was discovered, and they needed to be long gone when it was.

Sera wished she could go to the new Duca di Venezia for help, but word had it the palazzo was deserted and the Duca nowhere to be found. She'd sent envoys carrying requests for safe haven to the elder of Qin, the president of Atlantica, and the queen of the Freshwaters – the leaders of every free realm except Ondalina. With tensions running high between Kolfinn and Vallerio, she'd thought it too dangerous.

The envoys had returned empty-handed. The leaders – stunned by Vallerio's invasion of Matali – were playing their cards carefully. They'd been told Serafina was dead, the envoys reported. She would need to prove her identity. Meetings would have to be held. They needed time. But Sera didn't have time. Desperate, she'd decided to seek help from the fractious Meerteufel.

Yazeed swam to her side now. 'Nervous?' he asked her.

'Very,' she admitted.

'Who do the Kobold hate?' he asked.

Sera laughed darkly. 'Everyone.'

'Who do they hate the *most*?'

'Each other,' she replied.

'Exactly. And the enemy of my enemy is my friend. Remember that, Sera.'

Sera nodded, grateful, as always, for Yazeed's counsel.

The Kobold goblins, once a single people, had splintered into several tribes thousands of years ago, and had feuded over lava seams and ore deposits ever since. Many members of the Feuerkumpel tribe were in Cerulea, serving as mercenaries in her uncle's army. The Feuerkumpel and the Meerteufel despised each other. Sera planned to take advantage of that fact now.

Sera heard the sound of footsteps, so alien to mer ears, and then doors to the stateroom swung open. Standing in the entryway was a short, stocky goblin. Like all other sea goblins, he had transparent eyes, holes for nostrils, and gills on his neck, but Meerteufel goblins had two features that distinguished them from other tribes: black-lipped mouths, and horns. One pair of horns curved up from the goblin's temples, the other sprouted downward from his jaw. Sera recognized him. He was Stickstoff, head of the Meerteufel's military.

'*Hövdingen tar emot nu!*' he barked.

Sera understood him. *The Chieftain will see you now!*

Her hand automatically went to her ring – Mahdi's ring. Touching it made her feel like he was near, and that gave her strength. She took a deep breath and led her fighters into the stateroom. Her back was straight, her head was high. She wore no silty camo fatigues now; she'd come before the Meerteufel dressed as the queen she was in a shimmering blue sea-silk gown and long, high-necked black coat. A choker of pearls and sapphires circled her neck. A crown of pure gold adorned her head.

The goblins did not need to know that Neela had made the dress and coat out of draperies she'd found in an abandoned mansion, or that the jewels had been snatched during the Black Fins' raid on Miromara's treasury vaults.

They didn't need to know that Sera, and her Black Fins, were in constant fear for their lives. That they were weak, exhausted and desperate. That these negotiations were their last hope.

Sera was doing what generations of reginas before her had done in times of peril – she was bluffing.

Sera hadn't had the luxury of learning how to rule during peacetime. This was war, and she had to learn fast, while hungry and dirty and scared. Her mother had often told her that ruling was like playing chess, and that she must play the board, not the piece. The last few months had taught Sera the meaning of her mother's words: ruling was a game of moves and countermoves, of feints and ripostes. One had to anticipate her opponent, and think several moves ahead. Sera was now playing a game of life and death. And she was playing to win.

'Approach . . . *regina*,' snarled a goblin voice in Mermish.

It belonged to Guldemar. He was sitting on his throne, which was shaped like a giant sea serpent. Its coiled lower body was the throne's seat, a pair of fins the arms. Its horrible, thick neck stretched up above Guldemar, and its fanged head hung over him like a canopy. Sera knew this was Hafgufa, the kraken. According to ancient North Sea legends, the Meerteufel chieftains could call the creature forth from its lair, deep under the seabed, in times of great trouble.

Fanned out on either side of Guldemar were prominent members of his court: Nok, his wife; Pelf, the keeper of his treasury; and Nörgler, his foreign minister. Stickstoff took his place with them. They regarded the Black Fins with a mixture of suspicion and contempt.

Sera swam to the throne and curtsied deeply to the fearsome leader.

'Greetings, most dread chieftain,' she said, rising. 'You have my gratitude for welcoming me, Miromara's true regina, and my court, into your presence.'

Guldemar chuckled derisively. 'Fine clothing and flowery words do not a regina make,' he said. 'Another sits on the throne of Miromara now and demands that all sovereign realms recognize *her* as ruler. Some say she has a legitimate claim. She, too, is a daughter of the blood – a Merrovingian and your cousin. Your uncle has told the world that Regina Isabella and her unfortunate daughter are dead.'

Sera's blood boiled. How could he even suggest that Lucia's claim was legitimate?

'Lucia Volnero is the daughter of a son, Guldemar. The ruler of Miromara must not only be a daughter of the blood, but a daughter of a daughter.'

'Unless – as I believe the law states – there isn't one,' Stickstoff interjected.

Sera turned to him, eyes blazing. 'But there *is*,' she said. 'She's right before you, and she plans to retake her throne.'

Guldemar flapped a hand at her. 'My sources tell me that the Black Fins are few in number. You have little food or currensea. Your uncle's soldiers hunt for you day and night. You fight bravely, but how long can you *keep* fighting?'

'Not long,' Sera admitted. 'That's why I've come. To propose an alliance.'

Guldemar laughed raucously. His court followed suit. 'And why would the Meerteufel wish to ally themselves with *you*? You have no palace, no throne. You are poor, and the Kobold do not work for free.'

Serafina smiled. She had expected this. 'As long as one is bold, one is never poor,' she said. She nodded at her Black Fins. They swam to her, placed the chests on the floor, and then – at her command – opened them.

Scaghaufen was rich in iron, copper and nickel, but it

lacked precious metals. The Meerteufel adored silver and gold, and they especially loved jewellery.

Guldemar's eyes lit up with greed as they roved over the treasure, then became sly. 'You offer me what I can take,' he said, nodding at the fierce goblin soldiers standing at attention all around the room. 'What's to stop me from ordering them to kill you and your Black Fins and helping myself to these chests?'

'Nothing,' Sera said. 'But if you do, you won't get the rest of my payment – twenty more chests, all as full of treasure as these, delivered to you the day we advance on Cerulea.' She paused to let her words sink in, then said, 'My offer is a good one, Guldemar.'

He held up a hand and inspected his filthy claws. 'A good one for *you*, perhaps.' He sniffed.

'No, for *you*,' Sera shot back, fed up with his coyness. 'While you play games, your enemies the Feuerkumpel, fuelled by my uncle's gold and arrogance, talk openly of attacking your people when they return to the North Sea. They want your lava seams, your furnaces and foundries.'

Guldemar lowered his hand. His eyes met Sera's. Though he tried to hide it, she could see worry flicker in them.

'Help me now,' she urged him, 'and when I take back my throne, not only will I give you the treasure I promised, but as Neria is my witness, I will declare war on the Feuerkumpel traitors. The world will see what becomes of those who betray Miromara.'

'And when your uncle obliterates you – which is the more

likely scenario – what then?' asked Stickstoff.

'The Meerteufel still get the twenty chests of treasure.'

Guldemar stood up. He walked to one of the chests, scooped a handful of gold coins out if it, then let them fall through his fingers. He picked up a silver goblet, studded with gems, and admired it.

'We will give you troops,' he finally said, tossing the goblet back.

Sera's heart leapt, but she kept her face impassive. 'How many?' she asked.

'Ten thousand.'

'Thirty.'

'Twenty. That's my final offer,' Guldemar said. 'Each will be armed with a crossbow and battle-axe.'

Sera pressed for more. 'I also need a place to billet and train the troops you've just given me. I need a safe haven,' she said.

'Take the Kargjord,' Guldermar said.

'*Please*,' drawled Stickstoff, to more laughter from the court.

Sera's heart sank. The Kargjord was a hilly, desolate barrenness at the northernmost reaches of the Meerteufel's realm. The rocks surrounding it were full of iron ore, which wreaked havoc with magic. It was cold, too. Little grew there, so finding food would be difficult. Supplies would have to be bought from the Meerteufel, and Sera knew they'd charge her dearly for them. She also knew it was the Kargjord or nothing.

Curtseying once again, she said, 'I thank you, Guldemar, for the generosity and loyalty you have shown Miromara.'

Guldemar clapped loudly. Instantly, servants appeared carrying jugs and platters. As was goblin custom, the negotiations were concluded by pouring *räkä*, a thick, frothy drink made from fermented snail slime, and passing goblin delicacies: *sej*, pickled squid eyes; *smagfuld*, blackened cod tongues; and *sprøde*, the wrinkled toes of drowned terragoggs.

Guldemar enlivened the celebrations by grabbing several pieces of jewellery out of a chest and making his courtiers fight for them. He thought it great fun to pit soldiers, ministers, even his wife and her ladies against each other.

Sera had no taste for bloodsport. She took her leave and motioned for her fighters to follow. Guldemar barely noticed. He was too busy applauding Nok, who'd just beaten Pelf's wife silly over an emerald ring.

As the stateroom doors slammed behind them, Sera's shoulders sagged with relief. She'd secured the troops and weapons she so desperately needed, and a safe haven, too. She would send word to her fighters who were still in Miromara to head for the Kargjord right away.

Today's success marked a new phase in the resistance. With the goblin allies they would no longer be guerilla fighters, sabotaging the death riders' barracks, raiding the treasury at night. They'd be a full-on military force.

'Nice work,' Yaz whispered to her, as they swam down the hallway to the palace rooms in which they were staying. 'You got what you wanted.'

Sera laughed joylessly. 'Did I?' she said. 'We've got twenty thousand troops now. And I have no idea how to feed them, or where to house them in that godsforsaken Kargjord.' She shook her head, wondering why every time she met one challenge, a bigger one took its place. 'I don't know how to do this, Yaz.'

Yazeed patted her on the back. 'What else is new, Sera? You'll figure it out. You always do.'

'I'd better,' Sera said tiredly. She shook her head. 'Did I get enough troops? Enough weapons?' she wondered out loud. 'My mother would have demanded more. She would have known how to handle Guldemar better. My mother—'

'—would be very proud of you,' Yazeed finished.

Sera nodded, a lump in her throat. 'Thanks, Yaz,' she said, when she could speak again.

'Come on, merl. No time for tears,' Yaz said. 'You've got to get out of that dress. And we've got to get out of this ugly-wrasse palace. It's time to head to the Kargjord. We've got a war to win.'

NINETEEN

LUCIA VOLNERO REGARDED herself in a mirror in her mother's sitting room. A vitrina flitted into view within the mirror's silvery depths. Lucia waved it away.

'I leave for Ondalina tomorrow,' Portia said, tucking a sheaf of kelp parchments into her bag. 'The signs are fortuitous, Lucia. The gods are favouring us. My spies tell me that Kolfinn and his advisors are angry about Vallerio's claim that Ondalina attacked Miromara – and worried. They fear we'll attack in retaliation. Which is exactly what we want them to think.'

Lucia barely heard her. Foreign relations, espionage, military strategy – these were her parents' concerns. She was fighting a different kind of battle – a battle for Mahdi's heart. And beauty was the weapon she would use to win it.

She shook her head now, watching with satisfaction as her long, silky hair moved fetchingly about her shoulders. Her brows were perfectly arched. The shimmering grey shadow she'd chosen for her eyes emphasized their indigo depths. Her lips sparkled silver thanks to a dusting of ground mother-of-pearl. The dress she was wearing, also a deep grey, showed off her slender figure. A crown of diamonds graced her head. More diamonds sparkled at her ears and neck.

Lucia knew she would turn every head in the palace at dinner tonight. Just as she always did. So why was she nervous? Why was she worried? Why did the same agonizing doubts always crowd in upon her?

'Lucia? Are you listening? This is important. *Pay attention*,' Portia scolded. 'Our accusation that Ondalina was behind the attacks on Cerulea is utter nonsense, of course, but Kolfinn doesn't know that,' she continued. 'We've put him on the defensive and made him eager for an alliance. Rylka, his own commodora, has seen to that for us. Hand me that bracelet, will you please? Lucia? *Lucia!*' Portia said impatiently. 'Have you heard *anything* I've said?'

Lucia tore her eyes from her reflection and fetched her mother the ruby bracelet she was pointing at.

Portia frowned as she took it. 'You're worrying about something. Stop it. It's making lines on your forehead. What's bothering you?'

'The fact that I haven't seen Serafina's dead body,' Lucia replied.

'You don't need to,' Portia reassured her. 'She was so incompetent she could barely survive inside the palace. I'm sure she didn't last long outside of it.'

'She escaped from Traho, though,' Lucia countered. 'She made it to the Iele's caves. *He* said so.'

She shuddered now to think of that *he* – the terragogg Rafe Mfeme. She'd met him months ago. He'd taken her hand and kissed it. His lips were like ice on her skin. The cold spread throughout her body like a sea mist, seeping into her bones, chilling her insides.

He'd smiled at her and, in a voice so low only she could hear him, said, 'Beauty and ruthlessness in equal measure. You'll go far, my dear. Very far.'

Mfeme had somehow found out where Sera and her friends had gone. Neela, Mahdi's treacherous cousin, was among them. So was Admiral Kolfinn's daughter, Astrid. And three other mermaids from foreign realms who were of no rank or importance. Why these six had travelled to the Iele's caves together, Lucia didn't know, but whatever the reason, it couldn't be good. Mfeme had told Vallerio where the six were, and Vallerio had sent Traho after them. They'd come so close to catching them.

'Yes, Serafina *did* escape from the Iele's caves,' Portia allowed now, 'but she hasn't been seen since. Do stop fretting about her, Lucia. She's dead, and soon the rest of the Black Fins will be, too. Would you fetch me the necklace that matches the bracelet, please? It's in the vault in my bedroom.'

Lucia swam to the bedroom, hoping her mother was right about the merls. She hated Serafina. Just as she'd hated Isabella, and Isabella's mother, Artemesia.

Because of Artemesia, Lucia had grown up without her father, without a proper family. Because of Artemesia, she and her mother had been mocked and shamed.

The Volneros have traitors in their family, Artemesia had said when her son, Vallerio, had asked her permission to marry Portia. *Their line is tainted*.

A union between a member of the royal family and a Volnero was out of the question, she'd decreed. Vallerio could father no Volnero children.

What Artemesia hadn't known, though, is that there was already a Volnero child on the way when she'd made her decree – Lucia.

Breaking a regina's decree was treason and punishable by death, and both Vallerio and Portia knew it. Heartbroken and desperate, Portia had quickly married another man, one who looked like Vallerio, in order to keep her secret safe. When he'd committed suicide by drinking poison, there had been whispers of foul play, but nothing had ever been proved.

After her husband had died, Portia had left Cerulea to live at her country estate twenty leagues outside of the city. Vallerio had visited whenever he could. Lucia hadn't known who he was, not at first. She'd thought he was just a friend of her mother's.

Then, when she'd turned thirteen, Lucia had been summoned by Isabella to attend the principessa and learn the ways of the court, as a future duchessa must. Vallerio had sat down with Lucia before she left for the palace. He'd revealed that he was her real father, and stressed that she must never, ever tell a soul.

'One day, we will swim together as a family,' he'd

promised. 'One day all the water realms, and everyone in them, will know that you are my daughter. Until then, keep our secret safe. No one must guess the truth. Our lives depend upon it.'

Lucia had gone to court as planned. She'd become one of Serafina's ladies-in-waiting. She'd shown due respect to the regina, and she'd treated her father with the same distant deference everyone else showed him. She'd curtseyed and smiled, but all the while hatred had burned inside her.

Poor Lucia, merfolk said. *Such a pretty little thing. How sad for her to have no father.*

It was all she could do not to shout out, 'I do have a father! He's Vallerio, the high commander, the most powerful merman in the realm!'

Instead, she'd bit her tongue until it bled, and she'd smiled. She'd smiled as she watched Serafina ride hippokamps with *her* father, Principe Bastiaan. She'd smiled when she'd seen the dresses and jewels Bastiaan had given her. She'd smiled as she'd watched him twirl Serafina across the dance floor at state dinners.

As she'd got older, Lucia had heard the whispers. From behind a painted sea fan. Or a heavily jewelled hand. Confided over a cup of sargasso tea.

There goes the widowed duchessa. Pity she never remarried. Her first husband was a total nobody. Then again, she was lucky she found anyone *to marry her. Tainted blood, don't you know. Lucia will have to marry beneath her too. These things aren't forgotten.*

And they weren't. The words varied, but their meaning was always the same: her mother's Volnero blood, the same blood that flowed in Lucia's veins, wasn't good enough for the royal family. Or any noble family.

Now, thanks to her father and his soldiers, those who'd mocked and denied her were dead. Now her tainted blood was good enough – good enough to put her on the throne of Miromara. Good enough, even, to make her an empress. She and Mahdi would have children one day, and those children would rule not only Miromara and Matali, but all the waters of the world.

Her father had already given her Miromara and Matali. Ondalina was next. The three other realms – Atlantica, Qin, and the Freshwaters – would fall, too. No one would stop Vallerio from taking them, and no one would stop her from taking Mahdi . . . as long as Serafina was dead.

But *was* she?

After the treasury vaults were robbed, Lucia had worried anew that Serafina might still be alive. In the fighting that had followed the break-in, three Black Fin mermen had been killed. Another – a mermaid – had been wounded, but had managed to escape. The death riders who'd pursued her reported that she had short black hair and was a highly skilled fighter. That certainly didn't describe Serafina.

But still, Lucia worried. She wanted a corpse. Nothing less would make her happy.

Lucia removed the ruby necklace from her mother's safe and returned to the sitting room. As she handed it to Portia, they both heard a knock from behind the lavaplace.

The sound startled Lucia, but Portia was unperturbed. She swam to the mantel – a solid piece of lapis lazuli, beautifully carved with sea nymphs and fishes – and pressed a stone dolphin. An instant later, a mica-covered panel to the left of the lavaplace silently swung open. Lucia was intrigued. She hadn't known there was a secret entry to her mother's rooms and wondered if there were other passageways in the palace.

Before she could ask, an eel-like merman swam into the room. He wore a black sharkskin jacket. His hands were covered with silver rings. A large moray was draped across his shoulders like a shawl. It rested its fearsome head on his raised forearm.

'Your Grace,' he said, bowing first to Lucia, then to Portia.

'You have news?' Portia asked briskly.

The man gave her an oily smile. 'Indeed I do,' he said.

'Come in,' Portia said impatiently. She turned to Lucia, and adopted a formal tone. 'Your Highness, I present your loyal subject, Baco Goga. Captain Traho hasn't been able to turn a member of the resistance,' she explained. 'Without a spy in their midst we have no hope of defeating them. I hired Baco in the hopes that he would succeed where Traho failed.' She gave the merman a barracuda's smile. 'I hope he has not disappointed me.'

'Baco Goga never disappoints,' the merman said, in his strange singsong voice. 'I turned a Black Fin. One who is highly placed.'

'How?' Portia asked.

Baco flapped a hand dismissively. 'There are always ways,' he said.

'What did he say?' Lucia demanded.

'How do you know it's a he?' asked Baco, raising an eyebrow.

Lucia felt that he was teasing her, playing with her. She didn't like it. She didn't like him.

'*She*, then,' Lucia said, wishing he would tell them what he knew and leave. Quickly.

Baco laughed. 'This . . . *mer* tells me that the Black Fins were headquartered in the Azzuros until very recently,' he said.

Portia's expression darkened. 'I don't care where they *were*. Tell me where they *are*!' she insisted. 'Why else am I paying you?'

The moray eel's long dorsal fin flared at her tone. The creature lifted its head off Baco's arm.

'Easy, my Tiberius,' Baco soothed. 'We're in the palace now. We must remember our manners.'

The eel put its head back down, but eyed Portia sullenly. Baco's eyes were still on Lucia.

'Baco is happy to oblige,' he continued. 'Baco is always happy to oblige the beautiful regina.'

Lucia forced herself not to look away from his creeping gaze. 'The Black Fins are in the North Sea, Your Graces. In the Kargjord,' Baco said.

Portia went rigid. 'They're in *Kobold* waters?'

Baco nodded. 'They've made an alliance with Guldemar, the Meerteufel chieftain. He gave them troops, weapons, and safe haven in exchange for treasure. Ten chests, with twenty more to come.'

Portia's cheeks flushed with fury. She swam back and forth in the room, her hands clenched into fists. Then she whirled around and smashed a table with her tail fins.

'Treasure *stolen* from the regina's vaults!' she hissed. 'I'll send troops. I'll annihilate the Black Fins, and the goblins, too!'

'Be careful, Your Grace,' Baco cautioned. 'Guldemar's waters are well defended, the Kargjord included, and there's nothing he loves more than a fight. Think hard before you send your troops there.'

Portia's eyes narrowed. 'I pay you for information, not instruction,' she said. 'Get out!'

The moray unwound itself from Baco's shoulders and circled him protectively.

'As you wish, Your Grace,' Baco said slyly. 'But what a shame it would be for me to leave before I've shared the rest of my information.'

'Tell us. *Now*,' Lucia ordered.

Baco smiled. 'I've learned the identity of the Black Fins' leader,' he said, drawing out his words.

He's enjoying this, she thought. *Why?* And then she realized, with a sickening certainty, that she knew why. She knew exactly what he was going to say.

'It's the prin— Ah! Forgive me, my regina, I meant the

former principessa. Serafina. You thought she was dead, I believe? I'm so sorry to disappoint you, but she's very much alive.'

TWENTY

ASTRID LIFTED HER face to the sky and smiled as the snow kissed her cheeks.

Her eyes drank in the colours of home – the soft grey of an arctic gull's wing. The clear blue heart of an ice floe. The crystalline white of a million snowflakes. To Astrid, these shades of pale were the most beautiful colours in the world.

She'd surfaced a moment ago, eager to hear a guillemot's cry, a seal's bark, the silence of snowflakes falling on water, before descending to the Citadel.

In the distance, she could see icebergs drifting, secret and mute. To the goggs, they were places where no one and nothing lived – which is just as the Ondalinians wanted it. But under the surface, there was movement and life, colour and sound. The massive bergs, weighing millions of tons, contained floating mer cities.

Ondalina was the northernmost realm, and most mer found it forbidding, but Astrid loved it. The cold made her heart beat faster. It cleared her mind. She could think straight among the glaciers, the pack ice, the snow.

And she desperately needed to think. She and Becca had parted company a week ago, when they reached the current that Becca would follow south to Cape Horn.

'Becca, I can't—' Astrid had begun. She meant to finish by saying 'thank you enough for the whalebone pipe,' but Becca, misunderstanding, had cut her off.

'You're not allowed to say no, remember?' she'd scolded. Then she'd hugged Astrid tightly. 'I'll miss you,' she'd added. 'And I'm still hoping that you'll join us. Think about it, Astrid. Please. We need you.'

Becca wants me with them, even though she knows I can't sing, Astrid thought now, still unable to fathom it. Becca actually believed Astrid could make the group stronger. Here, in Ondalina, a mermaid who couldn't sing would be shunned as a weakling.

Sera wants me with them, too, Astrid thought. *But she* doesn't *know the truth about me. If she did, she might change her mind.*

All the way home, Astrid had asked herself, 'What do *you* want?'

She still didn't know the answer.

Part of her wanted to join her new friends. She wanted to help them fight Abbadon. But part of her was scared. If she joined them, she'd have to tell them the truth about herself, and that went against everything Astrid had been taught.

Openness wasn't the Ondalinian way. Life was harsh in the Arctic. Bitter cold stalked the mer constantly. Food was scarce. Predators were everywhere. Ondalinians prized toughness, hunting prowess and the ability to hide – to hide yourself, your home and, above all, your weaknesses.

Ondalinian camouflage spells were known throughout the merworld to be the best. Children learned them while they were still in the cradle. When a merbaby was born, well-wishers didn't say, *Congratulations!* Instead they said, *Hide it!*

Becca had asked Astrid to think about joining them, and Astrid was. She knew she'd soon have to stop thinking, though, and make a decision.

But there was another thing Astrid had to think about – her father. Eyvör, her mother, always told her to listen to her instincts. And right now, Astrid's were telling her – loudly and clearly – that the things she'd learned during her journey to the Iele's caves and back were connected to the bad things that had happened to her father. What she didn't know was *how*.

Before she'd set off for the River Olt, someone had placed a sea burr under Kolfinn's saddle, causing his hippokamp to rear and throw him into a wall. He'd broken several ribs. Then someone had slipped poison from a medusa anemone into his food, making him very sick. He'd mostly recovered, but the poison had left him weak.

Both the burr and the anemone were found only in Miromaran waters. In the Iele's caves, Sera had vehemently denied that her mother had had anything to do with the attempts on Kolfinn's life. Astrid hadn't believed her then, but she did now. Sera, she'd learned, was many things, but she wasn't a liar. Yet *someone* had attempted to assassinate Kolfinn.

Was it Vallerio? Astrid wondered now. According to Sera, he'd ordered Isabella's assassination and had decimated his city in order to place his daughter on Miromara's throne. If he could murder his own sister in his quest for power, he'd have no qualms about poisoning a merman he barely knew.

But if Vallerio *had* made attempts on Kolfinn's life, how had he done it? Security around her father was impenetrable. He was constantly surrounded by his guards. How could an assassin have slipped through them?

The answers to these questions eluded Astrid. She knew the best thing to do was to go to Kolfinn and tell him where she'd been and what she'd learned. He would know what to make of it all. Before she could tell him anything, though, she had to find him. He could be in the council chamber of the admiral's palace, or in any number of ministry buildings. Her mother, however, was only ever in one place – the stables. A seasoned rider and celebrated hunter, Eyvör spent a good part of each day with her hippokamps. Astrid decided to go there first. Eyvör would know where Kolfinn was.

Astrid felt a deep relief at the thought of her father being well again and back in command. The waters were growing more dangerous, and the balance of power between the mer realms more unstable, with every passing minute. Ondalina needed a strong hand at her helm, now more than ever.

With a last glance at the sky and the snow, Astrid dived and headed for home.

Thank gods, she thought as she sped towards the Citadel, *that Ondalina has Kolfinn*.

TWENTY-ONE

THE CITADEL HAD been built thousands of years ago, using a method that was still followed today.

Carvers had selected an enormous iceberg, calculated the midpoint of its submerged section, then tunnelled inside it. They'd hollowed out the ice around the centre point, creating the huge public square where the admiral's palace was located, and where he addressed his mer and paraded his troops.

The carvers then cut concentric rings in the berg, working outward from its centre. Passageways were cut between the rings, allowing inhabitants to move freely throughout the berg. Dwellings were sculpted into the ice that remained – mansions and palaces that were as finely detailed as anything in the great gogg cities of Saint Petersburg, Prague and Paris.

Though much of the Citadel was contained within the iceberg, farmhouses, stables and the sprawling market quarter were located along the berg's craggy bottom, allowing hunters to come and go with their hippokamps, farm animals to roam and merchants to drive their carts into the market.

It was to the admiral's stables that Astrid now swam. Since they'd been sculpted at the bottom of the iceberg, their roofs were attached to the berg and their lower floors, trimmed with decorative carving, hung down into the water.

Astrid swooped inside the main building. She passed hippokamp stalls, and then the tack room. The stables were illuminated by lava globes suspended from the ceiling. Lava could not be piped into an iceberg, so Ondalinians imported lava globes.

'Astrid Kolfinnsdottir? Is that you? Where have you been all this time?' a voice asked.

It belonged to Sanni, the head groom. She'd swum out of the tack room, still holding a silver bit she was polishing.

Astrid stopped and turned around. 'Hi, Sanni. I've been hunting,' she fibbed. It was the excuse she'd come up with to explain her absence. 'Where's Eyvör?'

Ondalinian children called their parents by their first names. Ondalinians, no matter their age, shuddered at words like *Mummy* and *Daddy* and thought mer who used them were ridiculous.

'In the ring. With Prince Ludovico,' Sanni replied.

'Kolfinn's not with them, is he?' Astrid asked.

Sanni stopped polishing. '*Kolfinn?*' she said. 'Astrid, you . . . you don't know?' she asked, her eyes widening.

'Know what?'

'The admiral, he . . . he's not here,' Sanni said, clearly uncomfortable.

'Any idea where he is?'

Sanni didn't respond. She was polishing again, furiously.

'Sanni?' Astrid pressed, vexed by the groom's silence. 'Is something wrong?'

'Go and see your mother,' Sanni said. She turned away then, but not before Astrid saw a glimmer of tears in her eyes. An Ondalinian *never* shed tears publicly.

Fear took root in Astrid. 'What is it? What's going on?' she asked.

Sanni shook her head and swam back into the tack room.

Astrid's fear blossomed. She sped through the stables to the indoor ring, desperate to find out what had happened to her father. Eyvör was in the centre of it, her hands on her hips, her brow furrowed. Tall, blonde and muscular, she was wearing a long walrus-skin coat and a necklace made from the claws of a polar bear that had been foolish enough to attack her. Near her, a groom was leading a hippokamp in a circle. Astrid recognized the animal: Blixt, Eyvör's favourite mount.

Eyvör was talking with a distinctive-looking merman. His hair was black with a white streak in it; his eyes were blue. He was Principe Ludovico di Merrovingia, younger brother to Vallerio and the late Regina Isabella. Astrid knew him well.

Ondalina and Miromara had once battled each other in the War of Reykjanes Ridge. A condition of the peace treaty was the permutavi – which decreed that the ruling families must exchange a child when that child came of age. It was thought the realms were less likely to attack each other that way.

Ludovico had been exchanged with Sigurlin, Kolfinn's sister, who lived on an estate in rural Miromara with her family. Astrid was supposed to have been exchanged with Sera's brother, Desiderio, but Kolfinn had refused to send her. He knew her disability would become known were she to move to Miromara and he didn't want that to happen.

Ludo, as he was known, was a breeder of hippokamps. He also trained the orcas used by Ondalina's military. He and Eyvör were close friends.

Although right now, they were having a heated argument.

'Rylka's the acting admiral. Talk to *her*, Ludo,' Eyvör said.

Astrid, who'd been about to swim closer, was so stunned she couldn't move. Rylka was Kolfinn's commodora, the second most powerful mer in Ondalina. Astrid couldn't stand her, or her son Tauno. They both knew her secret and treated her dismissively because of it. *Why had Rylka been made acting admiral?* she wondered.

'I *tried* to talk to Rylka,' Ludo said angrily. 'I can't get in to see her. And even if I could, it wouldn't do much good. This insanity is all her doing. Why is he in prison, Eyvör? Why can't I see him?'

Astrid remembered Sanni's refusal to say anything about Kolfinn. She put that together with Eyvör saying that Rylka had been made acting admiral and jumped to a terrible conclusion.

'Eyvör, Ludo . . . what's going on? Is Kolfinn in prison?' she blurted out.

Blixt startled at the sound of her voice.

Eyvör did, too. She turned around. 'Astrid, you're back. I'm glad,' she said evenly. 'Was the hunting good?'

'Eyvör . . . who *cares* about the hunting?' Astrid asked, upset but trying not to show it. 'Why is Rylka acting admiral? Why is Kolfinn in prison?'

'Don't be ridiculous. Kolfinn's not in prison,' Eyvör said, rubbing her left temple. She turned to the groom. 'Keep leading Blixt around,' she instructed.

Astrid exhaled, relieved, but something was still very wrong, she could feel it. Eyvör looked exhausted. Ludo looked like he was going to explode.

'Well, *someone's* in prison,' she said. 'I wish one of you would tell me who.'

'It's my nephew, Desiderio,' Ludo said. 'He's been thrown into a dungeon cell and I'm not allowed to see him.'

'Desiderio?' Astrid echoed. 'But I thought—'

. . . *he was dead. That's what Sera thinks*, she was about to say. *She said he was sent to defend Miromara's western borders and never came back.*

But she stopped herself. She'd told Eyvör she was going hunting. If Eyvör learned where she'd really gone, she'd demand an explanation, and Astrid didn't want to give her one. Not until she'd learned more.

'I mean, what's Desiderio doing all the way up here?'

'He's been accused of masterminding a plot to assassinate Kolfinn,' Eyvör said.

Astrid couldn't believe what she'd just heard. She'd racked her brains trying to figure out who'd tried to kill her father. Now Eyvör was saying it was *Desiderio*?

'But he *didn't* do it,' Ludo insisted. 'I know him. And I know . . . *knew* . . . my sister. Neither of them would *ever* do such a thing.'

'Then why is he in prison?' Astrid asked.

'Because Rylka says he *did* do it,' Eyvör explained. 'She and her soldiers found him one league south of the Citadel riding hard with a thousand troops at his back. She says he set up a hidden camp in Ondalina from which he sent assassins to the Citadel. On Isabella's orders. When they failed to kill Kolfinn, he took the job upon himself.'

'And what does Desiderio say?' Ludo asked hotly. '*Nothing!* Because he's not allowed to speak! And nobody's allowed to speak to him!'

'Rylka says it's for his own good, Ludo. She says that there have been death threats made against him and the only way she can guarantee his safety is by keeping him isolated,' said Eyvör. Astrid could see she was struggling to keep her emotion under control.

'I don't *care* what Rylka says!' Ludo shouted. 'The boy's facing execution. He needs a lawyer. He has the right to defend himself!'

At that moment, Blixt stumbled. He lifted one of his

hooves and curled it under. His long serpent's tail thrashed to and fro.

Ludo swore. 'Stop!' he yelled at the groom. 'Keep him still.' He hurried over to inspect the hoof, then said, 'It's founder. Ice the foot immediately.'

'Tell Sanni to cut his sea straw, too,' Eyvör instructed, watching as the groom led Blixt away.

Astrid could hear worry in her mother's voice, but she heard something else, too, something deeper. What was it? Founder was serious, but Eyvör had dealt with it before. Neither animal ailments nor arguments were normally enough to upset her.

As Astrid was puzzling over her mother's odd behaviour, Ludo spoke again.

'The boy's my *nephew*, Eyvör. My flesh and blood.'

'I'll do whatever I can,' Eyvör said, her voice cracking.

'Whatever you can? That's not enough! Rylka's going to execute him without a tribunal and you don't even *care*!'

Eyvör whirled on him, her eyes blazing, her composure gone. 'I *do* care, damn it!' she shouted. 'But I happen to have other concerns at the moment! My husband is *dying*, Ludo!'

'*What* . . .' Astrid tried to speak but couldn't. She squeezed her hands into fists and tried again. 'Eyvör, *what* did you say?' Her voice was barely a whisper.

Ludo looked from mother to daughter, an expression of disbelief on his face. 'You haven't *told* her? She doesn't *know*?' he asked.

Eyvör looked at the floor.

'You Ondalinians. I'll *never* understand you.' Ludo had learned the ways of his adopted realm, but in his heart he was still Miromaran and showed his emotion instead of hiding it. 'I'll leave you,' he said. 'Astrid, I'm sorry.'

Astrid didn't even hear him. Her eyes, wide with shock, were on her mother.

'Kolfinn is very sick, Astrid,' Eyvör said, when Ludo was gone.

'I-I don't understand,' Astrid said, completely bewildered. 'When I left, he was better.'

'It was a show of strength,' Eyvör explained. 'He wanted everyone to think he was recovering. Especially his enemies. His doctors kept the truth a secret to buy some time.'

Astrid felt as if she was going to come apart. A maelstrom of emotion whirled inside her, its gyre widening. Grief overwhelmed her. Anger, too. This secret should not have been kept – not from her.

'How long does he have?' she asked.

'The poison has damaged his heart. It's . . .' Eyvör's face crumpled, but she regained control. 'Not long.'

'I need to see him,' Astrid demanded. '*Now*.'

'That's not a good idea. He's in the hospital. He's very weak.'

'He's my *father*, Eyvör!' Astrid shouted. 'Can I at least say *hello*?'

Eyvör shook her head sorrowfully. 'Oh, Astrid,' she said, her voice finally breaking. 'It's not *hello*. It's goodbye.'

TWENTY-TWO

'A COWRIE FOR YOUR THOUGHTS,' Sophia said.

Sera, who'd been staring up at the pale moon through Miromara's blue waters, turned to her, a wistful smile on her face.

'I was thinking about a princess,' she said.

'A friend?'

Sera laughed. 'Far from it. A shipwreck ghost. An infant of Spain. Her name was Maria Theresa. She had Merrow's talisman. She gave it to me. And almost killed me.'

'*Why?*'

'Because she wanted to go home,' Sera said. 'She'd haunted her sunken ship for four hundred years. You'd think she would have forgotten the place where she was born, but no.'

'She must've missed her palace and the life she'd had there,' Sophia said.

Sera shook her head. 'It was the warm winds of her realm that she longed for. Jasmine. Oranges. The blue sky. I didn't understand then, but I do now. I don't miss the palace, either. Or my gowns and jewels. But I'll miss the way the moon shines down on Miromara, the sight of bluefin tuna slicing through the water, and the scent of water apples on the current. *So* much.'

'You'll be back, Sera. I know you will,' Sophia said, determination in her voice. 'That's what we're fighting for. To put the rightful regina back on the throne. To take back our city, and our realm.'

Sera nodded, moved by her friend's loyalty. 'How are they doing?' she asked, nodding at a deserted farmhouse a few yards away.

'They're packing up the last load. Yazeed started out with the first group of rays. Neela and Silvio are leading the second. I'm taking the third.'

'Any sign of death riders?'

'None.'

'Good,' Sera said, relieved.

Sera, Sophia and the rest of the Black Fins were in Sargo's Canyon. With the help of the same manta rays who'd carried the loot away from the palace, they were moving the treasure from its hiding place to the Black Fins' new headquarters in the Kargjord.

It was a long trip. The rays would stop to rest along the way, but Sera knew it would still be hard going. She knew, too, that getting everyone out of Miromara to a safer place was the right thing to do, but it didn't make saying goodbye to all the things she loved any easier.

A whistle sounded in the darkness.

'That's my signal,' said Sophia. 'Gotta go.'

She and Sera embraced, and then Sera was alone. She'd told the others she would catch up. There was one last goodbye to say.

Will he come? she wondered.

The farm at Sargo's Canyon had been abandoned decades ago. The branches of its untended water apple trees had become gnarled and entwined. They made excellent cover.

Sera swam under them now, to an overgrown stone pavilion in the centre of the orchard, hoping against hope that he'd be there. A groom had helped them arrange a meeting by passing their conchs back and forth. They'd agreed that if anything seemed off, they would forsake the plan. Though Sera constantly longed to see him, his safety was her chief concern.

She sang a few notes of the mer Promising ceremony now. It was their agreed upon code. But she got no response.

Maybe he's late, she thought, trying to keep her hopes up. *Maybe it was impossible for him to get out of the palace*.

She waited a few minutes, then sang again. Still no reply. Sera was crushed. It had been so long since she'd seen him, since she'd heard his voice and felt his touch. She hungered for time together, a few precious minutes. But it wasn't to be. He wasn't coming. She started back through the orchard.

And that's when she heard it – a voice in the darkness, singing softly.

'Mahdi!' she cried, turning around.

She raced to the pavilion. Her breath caught. He was *there*, waiting for her. She gazed at the face she loved so much. It looked older to her. Weary and careworn. But his beautiful dark eyes shone with love.

'Sera? Is that you?' he asked, his handsome face breaking into a smile.

Sera nodded tearfully, then threw herself into his arms. The two of them embraced, whirling around and around in circles.

'Let me look at you,' Mahdi said as they stopped. 'You're *so* beautiful, Sera. Gods, how I've missed you.'

He took her face in his hands and kissed her so passionately, with such longing, that it made her tail fins curl. Then he held her close, his forehead touching hers.

'I can't stay long,' he whispered. 'There's a party going on, and I was able to sneak away, but I have to get back before I'm missed.'

'How did you get out of the palace?' she asked.

'A transparensea pearl and a window. I've got another pearl to get me back in. Listen, Sera, before I go, there are things I need to tell you,' he said. 'Something's afin. Something big.'

'What is it?' Sera asked, breaking their embrace.

'I wish I knew,' Mahdi replied. 'But Vallerio and Traho are spending a lot of time behind closed doors with a merman named Baco Goga. They're plotting something, I'm sure of it.'

Sera's fins prickled. 'Baco's bad news. He's the one

who sold us – Neela and me – to Traho.'

'I think he's a spy. But I don't know who he's spying on.'

'Not us. We would have seen him.'

Mahdi looked unconvinced. 'Keep your eyes peeled for him. Tell the others to do the same.'

'I will,' Sera said.

'There's more. Portia Volnero's about to leave for Ondalina. It's Vallerio's next target. And then there's Lucia. I pay one of her ladies-in-waiting to keep an eye out for me. She told me Lucia's been sneaking out of the palace at night, but she doesn't know where she goes.'

'It can't be good,' Sera said grimly.

'I'll pass on any info that I learn,' Mahdi said.

'How?' Sera asked. 'Your groom won't be able to get to us any more. We'll be too far away from each other.'

'There's a farmer. Her name's Allegra. She delivers produce to the palace kitchens. She has a network of family between Miromara and the North Sea. They're willing to pass conchs back and forth between us.'

Sera took his hand and squeezed it. 'That's good news,' she said, pleased at the thought of being able to stay in touch with him somehow. She hated that they never had time to talk about all the silly things two mer in love talked about, but the exchange of information crucial to the resistance was what mattered – not the way the moonglow glinted in his amazing eyes or how the dark waters seemed to deepen the blue of his tail. Maybe one day, when all of this was behind them, there would be time for that.

As Mahdi took her other hand, Sera thought of something else she needed to know.

'Have you heard anything from Duca Armando's son?' she asked. 'The palazzo's empty. And no one can find him.'

'No, I don't know where he is. The Praedatori have scattered. Vallerio has branded them traitors; he wants their heads.'

'Make sure my uncle doesn't brand you a traitor, Mahdi. I worry about you so much. Be careful. Promise me you will.'

'Don't worry about me. I'm fine. You're in a lot more danger than I am.'

Sera shook her head. 'I'm surrounded by friends and fellow fighters,' she said. 'You're surrounded by cold-blooded killers. If they ever find out where your loyalties really lie . . .'

'They *won't*,' Mahdi said. 'I've won them over.'

'You do have irresistible charm,' Sera teased, smiling.

He pulled her close and kissed her one last time. 'I've got to go,' he whispered.

Sera nodded and released him. 'Goodbye, Mahdi,' she said. Tears blurred her vision. She hastily wiped them away. Reginas didn't cry. Not for themselves.

'Goodbye, Sera. Please stay safe,' he said. 'You have my heart and my soul. You *are* my heart and soul. Never forget that.'

Sera watched him swim back into the orchard and fade into the trees. And then he was gone.

'Will I ever see him again?' she whispered to the ancient trees. 'Will I ever return to Miromara?'

She took a deep breath, pulling the waters of home deep into her lungs, imprinting the scent of water apples, the glow of the moon and the warmth of Mahdi's touch in her heart, where she would keep them always. No matter what happened.

Then she turned away and began the long journey north.

TWENTY-THREE

MASSIVE IRON GATES, twenty feet high and encrusted with ice, protected the passages that led to the Citadel's interior.

Astrid, swimming fast, approached the entrance now. In the glow of the large lava globe that hung above it, she could see two creatures, both nearly as tall as the gates. They looked like ice come to life. Their bodies and limbs were as solid as a glacier. Their long hair and the beards on their broad faces were like the spikes of an icefall. Pale blue light glowed in their eyes.

They were members of the Fryst, a clan of giant ice trolls. Their kind had protected the Citadel ever since it was built.

As Astrid neared them, the Fryst advanced menacingly. One raised a club made of a boulder lashed to ship's timbers. Then he recognized Astrid and called out a greeting. The trolls' language was all groans and creaks – the sound pack ice makes as it moves over the sea. Astrid called back and the Fryst waved her through.

She continued on, speeding through labyrinthine passageways, past the modest dwellings of the Citadel's poorer citizens, the graceful mansions of its more prosperous ones, and the palaces of the military elite until she finally arrived at the towering admiral's palace.

Soldiers nodded solemnly to her as she entered the palace and sped to the west wing, which contained offices on its top level, dungeons in the bottom and a private hospital. When she reached the hospital's spacious foyer, she spotted Kolfinn's doctor. Together they swam to Kolfinn's room.

'Your father is not the merman he once was,' the doctor cautioned as he led her through the hospital corridors. 'The poison has ravaged his system.'

'Why haven't you stopped it?' Astrid asked angrily.

'We've tried. We've given him every antidote we know, but nothing's worked. The poison may be a new formulation. Or he may be unusually susceptible to it.'

The doctor stopped at a chamber flanked by guards. He put his hand on the knob.

'Prepare yourself, Astrid,' he said as he opened the door.

Astrid thought she had, but nothing could have readied her for the sight that greeted her. Kolfinn's body was wasted, his face now just thin, sallow skin stretched over a skull. His hair was stringy and dull.

Where was her strong father, with his powerful black-and-white tail; his riveting ice-blue eyes; his long, thick locks, the colour of the winter sun? Where was Ondalina's fierce admiral with his black tattoos – the mark of his rank –

circling his thickly muscled arms?

He was dying, Eyvör said. But he *couldn't* be. He was the admiral. He'd kept Ondalina safe for two decades. He'd kept *her* safe. It was hard enough being a mermaid who couldn't sing *with* a powerful father to protect her. What would her life be like without him?

Kolfinn was propped up in his bed, his eyes closed. As Astrid's gaze swept over him, it came to rest on three jagged stripes across his chest. Scars inflicted by a mother polar bear.

Astrid remembered all too well how he got them. As a child, she had once strayed too close to a pair of cubs on an ice floe. She could still hear the mother's roar, see her bared teeth, as the animal charged straight at her. Having no magic to call on, Astrid hadn't been able to defend herself. She couldn't cast so much as a camo spell.

Then there had been a black-and-white blur in the water, and Kolfinn emerged, spear in his hands. When he put himself between Astrid and the bear, the creature swiped her mark into his flesh with her claws. Kolfinn didn't kill her, though he could have. She was a mother protecting her young, like he was doing. He'd just driven her off and scooped up a sobbing Astrid.

He still protected her now. From whispers and glances. Laughter. Cruel remarks. It was how he showed his love. Astrid loved him, too, though she sometimes feared him and often disappointed him.

The doctor left, to give them privacy, and closed the door behind him. Astrid leaned against it, hands behind her back, afraid to move or speak, afraid to make the spectre she saw before her real.

Kolfinn opened his eyes. 'Astrid?' he said weakly. 'Come closer.' He patted the edge of his bed. She put down her pack and sword and swam over to him. 'I'm glad you're home,' Kolfinn said. 'We need to talk. I haven't got much longer.'

Sorrow, as swift and lethal as a spear, pierced Astrid's heart. 'Kolfinn, *no*. You'll get better,' she said, her voice breaking.

Displeasure surfaced in her father's eyes like an orca's fin knifing through water. 'I expect better of you, Astrid,' he admonished. 'Soft displays are for our southern cousins. We of the northern seas have no use for such foolishness.'

Astrid nodded. She swallowed her tears.

'When I die, Ragnar will become admiral, as you know. Rylka, whom I've appointed acting admiral, will oversee the transition.'

Ragnar was Astrid's brother. He was twenty, older than Astrid by three years. Rylka, the realm's commodora, was officially in charge of the realm's military. Unofficially, she was Ondalina's spymaster. Nothing happened anywhere in the realm without Rylka getting word of it.

'Why does Ragnar need Rylka? He's strong,' Astrid said. 'He'll make a good admiral.'

'He *is* strong, but he's inexperienced. Rylka will guide him,' Kolfinn said. 'I'm fearful both for Ragnar's ascension and for the security of the realm. We're on the verge of war with Miromara.'

Astrid's stomach lurched at that. '*War?* Why?'

'The Miromarans have been trying to kill me. Shortly, they'll succeed,' he said wryly. 'What's more, Vallerio has accused Ondalina of invading Cerulea and killing Isabella, Bastiaan, and Serafina. He's wrong, of course, but we can't convince him otherwise. He's taken over Matali and he'll have that realm's military might behind him if he attacks us. We can't hope to fight off a force of that size.'

It's time to tell him where I've been and what I've learned, Astrid thought, shoring up her nerve. She took a deep breath, then plunged in.

'Kolfinn, you'll never convince Vallerio. Because he's not wrong, he's lying. Serafina's not dead. Isabella and Bastiaan are, and he's the one who killed them.'

Kolfinn paled, obviously alarmed by this news. 'How do you know that?'

'Serafina told me.'

Kolfinn's eyes narrowed. 'You've been with Serafina? I thought you went hunting.'

Astrid nodded guiltily. 'I *did*. Sort of. But, um, for answers instead of animals.'

She told him everything that had happened – from the first time Vrăja had summoned her, to fighting Abbadon in the Iele's caves, to her trip through Atlantica with Becca.

When she finished, Kolfinn, who'd sat forward so he could hear her every word, flopped back against his pillow, stunned.

'Astrid, I find all this almost impossible to believe,' he said.

'I don't blame you,' she said. Then she touched her fingers to her chest, to the place over her heart, and pulled a bloodsong. It showed her and the five other mermaids fighting Abbadon. She pulled another that showed Sera during the convoca, telling Astrid and Becca about Vallerio's treachery.

As the blood faded into the water, Kolfinn's expression hardened. 'Vallerio murdered his own sister,' he said. 'The danger we face is even greater than I thought. A merman capable of such an act is capable of anything.'

'Kolfinn, the Iele summoned me to help fight Abbadon,' Astrid said. 'Sera and the others have asked me to join them.' She hesitated, working up her courage, then said, 'I want to go.'

Kolfinn shook his head. 'Absolutely not. It's far too dangerous. I forbid it.'

'But they need my help! They can't fight Abbadon without me!'

'A monster in a cage on the other side of the world troubles me less than the monster in Miromara,' Kolfinn said. 'And what good would you be to those other mermaids? You can't songcast.'

His blunt words cut her, but Astrid pressed on. 'There's something else I need to tell you . . . I can make magic again.'

Kolfinn's eyes widened. 'You can? *How?* When did this happen?'

Astrid didn't reply. Instead, she pulled the whalebone pipe out of her backpack. Taking a deep breath, she played a canta prax spell and mottled the room in shades of purple.

'See?' she said excitedly, expecting her father to be pleased.

But he wasn't. Far from it. Scorn thinned his lips.

'A *pipe?*' he said. 'Pipes are for children. No admiral's daughter is going to be seen casting songspells with a *pipe*.'

Astrid shrank under his disdainful tone. She tried to protest, but he spoke over her.

'Do you understand what's at stake? Nothing less than the survival of our realm. An envoy is en route from Miromara to Ondalina as we speak, led by Portia Volnero. Miromara calls us aggressors and demands our surrender. Portia will offer us terms. If we refuse, she'll declare war. All we have for a bargaining chip is Desiderio and his soldiers. They were captured—'

'Eyvör told me,' Astrid said, to save him the explanation.

'Rylka wanted to execute him, but I stopped her,' he continued. 'He's only valuable to us alive.'

He tried to sit forward again. Astrid could see that he was racked by pain. *How did it happen?* she wondered for the hundredth time. *How did an assassin get close enough to him to poison his food?*

'Lie still, Kolfinn,' she said anxiously. 'You're using up your strength.'

'I *can't* lie still!' Kolfinn shouted.

Astrid heard the desperate anger of a dying merman in his voice and it terrified her.

'I *have* to put things in order,' he insisted. 'I have to keep you and Ragnar safe. I doubt I'll be alive to meet with Portia.

Ragnar will be the one to do it. I *must* ensure his success. You need to do your part, too. There will be challenges to your brother's authority from outside Ondalina. There can be no challenges within it.'

Astrid understood what her father was saying. 'You mean my secret can't get out,' she said bitterly.

'If our enemies learn that you can't songcast, they may think your disability was inherited and that Ragnar's magic is also compromised. I've instructed Rylka to punish any who speak of it. I wish to the gods you had not told that mermaid – Becca – your secret. She may tell others.'

'Are you *that* ashamed of me?' Astrid asked, her head bowed, her voice barely a whisper.

Kolfinn winced. Pain filled his eyes. 'I'm that *afraid* for you, Astrid,' he replied. 'Your disability is a sign of weakness, and weakness can't be tolerated – not in a member of the ruling family. You know how precarious our lives are. Never more so than now, with Miromara circling. Survival is what matters. And in Ondalina, only the strong survive.'

A heavy silence descended. Astrid, her jaw clenched, rose from the bed and swam across the room to the window. She was hurt and angry, but another emotion was rising in her, too – defiance.

He only sees what I'm not, not what I am, she thought. *I'm not weak, I'm strong. Stronger than he knows. And the future of this realm might depend on me in ways he doesn't know.*

Kolfinn was the first to speak. In a conciliatory tone, he said, 'You'll be safe after I'm gone. I've made sure of it.

Commodora Rylka, always loyal to me, has offered her son Tauno in marriage.'

Astrid, lost in her thoughts, didn't take in his meaning. She turned back to him and asked, 'Why? To form an alliance with another realm? Who'd Rylka find to marry that lumpsucker? Some poor fool from Atlantica?'

Kolfinn's eyes darkened. They locked once more on his daughter's.

'No, Astrid. *You*.'

TWENTY-FOUR

ASTRID WAS SPEECHLESS. She tried to talk, but had no breath. It was as if she'd had the water knocked out of her.

Kolfinn took her silence for acquiescence.

'There will be an official Promising tomorrow, and then the marriage contract will be signed. I want everything taken care of before I die.'

Astrid's breath came rushing back. 'No!' she shouted. 'I won't do it!'

'Astrid—'

'I'm only seventeen! I don't want to get married to *anyone*! Especially not to Tauno!'

'Why not? He's a good leader. A strong merman. He'll protect you.'

'He's a barracuda! He beats his hippokamps. I've seen him! And . . . and . . .'

Kolfinn raised an eyebrow. 'And what?'

'He's *stupid*! He never paid attention in class. He sat in the back with his dumb friends and shot iceballs at everyone,' said Astrid.

'That was years ago,' said Kolfinn dismissively. 'I'm sure he's grown up since then.'

'I *won't* do it,' Astrid declared. 'Better *udstødt* than married to Tauno.'

Udstødt were Ondalina's outcast. Their numbers were made up of criminals and loners. They lived in the southernmost part of the realm, in broken off pieces of icebergs.

'It's your *duty* to marry. You *know* that,' Kolfinn said. 'If something happened to your brother, or the sons he'll someday have, your future sons would rule Ondalina.' He shook his head. 'You've spent too much time in southern waters. That explains your ridiculous behaviour. *Värme gör oss dumma*,' he said, in Ondalinian mer.

Astrid knew the expression. All Ondalinians did. *Heat makes us stupid*.

'I'm *not* marrying Tauno,' Astrid insisted. 'You can't—'

Kolfinn cut her off. 'Good gods, child! Are you actually going to make me say it?' he thundered.

'Say what?' Astrid thundered back.

'You have no choice! Tauno's the only one who wants you!'

Astrid felt as if she'd been slapped. She floated perfectly still, utterly humiliated.

'Who wants a mermaid without magic?' Kolfinn continued. 'Who, in these waters, would risk having children who couldn't songcast? How would such children defend themselves? How would they contribute to our society?'

'You're *wrong*, Kolfinn,' Astrid said defiantly, thinking of Becca and Sera. 'My friends want me.'

'*Friends?*' Kolfinn echoed scornfully. 'Rulers have no friends. Rulers have realms.' In a tone that brooked no further discussion, he added, 'I'll have my advisors bring the requisite documents to my bedside tomorrow at noon. Tauno will be here. Rylka, too. Make sure *you* are.'

Noon, Astrid thought. It was seven o'clock now. In seventeen hours she would be back here, signing her name to a marriage contract. With Tauno, a merman she despised. The thought filled her with revulsion.

'What we do, we do for Ondalina,' Kolfinn said, as if reading her mind.

Astrid nodded. She dutifully kissed her father's withered cheek, slung her sword and her pack over her back, and left his room.

She swam out of the hospital, and then down the Hall of Elders, an arched passageway that led through the palace to her family's private apartments. The hall was empty. On either side of it, life-size statues of Ondalina's past admirals stood. Astrid's head was high and her gaze cold as she glided by them, but inside her emotions burned like waterfire.

Part of her desperately wanted to swim away. Now, before it was too late. But another part refused to desert her family or her realm. She told herself that she would face tomorrow, and her Promising, the same way she'd faced every other hard thing in her life – by encasing her heart in ice. She had no choice. It was the only way. For her and for Ondalina. Kolfinn had said so.

Astrid stopped dead. Her anguished eyes swept over the statues, over their silent, stony faces. 'But is it?' she asked them.

The statues didn't answer. They just stared through unseeing eyes as Astrid struggled to make sense of her warring feelings.

Staying here and promising herself to that squid Tauno, watching as her realm capitulated to Miromara's demands, and knowing that all the while Abbadon grew stronger . . . how would doing these things help Ondalina?

As she continued to gaze at the admirals – some who'd ruled hundreds of years ago, some thousands – Astrid realized that their ways, and her father's, were the old ways. Their strength had come from hiding. From camouflaging. From keeping secrets in, and keeping others out.

That had been Merrow's tactic, too. According to Vrăja, Merrow had hidden many truths – the truth about Atlantis's destruction, the truth about Abbadon – to protect the mer. Instead she'd put them in terrible danger.

'Kolfinn's way, Merrow's way . . . they aren't *my* way,' Astrid whispered.

She had embarked on a different current the moment she'd set off for the Iele's caves. Meeting Vrăja, learning the truth of the mer's origins, spending time with Sera and the others, had all carried her further down that new current. Was she going to turn back now?

'There has to be *another* way,' she said. She had less than a day to find it.

TWENTY-FIVE

'MACAPÁ, AT LAST, BABY!' Ava said wearily but happily to her pet piranha. '*Meu deus*, I thought we'd never get home.'

Ava couldn't see her home, but she could hear it, smell it and feel it.

She heard the sounds of children playing. Someone singing a lullaby. Dishes clattering. Mothers yelling. The spicy smell of mud peppers wafted by, followed by the sour tang of marshfruit. She felt the warmth of Macapá's waters, and its mer.

She'd lost her sight at the age of six – young, but old enough to allow her to remember how the village looked.

Its dwellings were made from the empty shells of giant river mussels, tethered to the riverbed by ropes made of tree roots. Round holes were cut into the shells' walls for both doors and windows, and the windows were framed by brightly painted shutters, which were closed at night and opened in the morning. Glass was costly and Macapá was a poor village. Tiny snail shells, threaded on river vines, dangled in doorways to keep the pesky purple, blue and orange discus fish out. Caimans floated on the river's surface, their bellies like pale clouds drifting by. Anacondas slithered across the river's muddy bed.

Ava couldn't wait to be inside her house. She missed the sound of her mother singing, the taste of her father's spicy salamander stew and the comfort of her own bed. As she and Baby made their way down the narrow, crowded current that flowed through Macapá, Baby snapped constantly, annoying everyone around him.

'Stop it, *louco*, or I'll put you back on your leash!' Ava scolded.

She was exhausted. The trip from the River Olt was long, and it had been made even longer by the need to stay off the main currents in order to avoid Traho and his death riders. Both she and Baby were thin. They needed rest and home cooking. Ava was sure they would get plenty of both. When she felt strong again, she would set off for the swamps of the Mississippi to look for Nyx's ruby ring.

Her parents had been unhappy when she'd sat them down at the kitchen table and told them she intended to travel halfway around the world, to a cold, dark river in the Carpathian Mountains. But when she'd explained why, they'd understood.

The gods took your sight for a reason, her father always told her.

'Maybe now they'll tell you why,' her mother had said.

Like all the villagers of Macapá, Ava lived close to her gods. They weren't distant figures to be worshipped once a week in cold stone temples, but living deities to be loved, invoked, and sometimes even scolded. No bride-to-be would think of marrying without asking the sea goddess Neria's blessing. A new business venture required an offering to Ploutos, the god of money. And if Ava's father's salamander stew turned out bitter, the first one he blamed was Estia, the kitchen god.

Ava had waited most of her life to learn why she had lost her sight.

All the way to the Olt, and all the way back again, she'd hoped the gods would reveal their intentions, but they'd remained silent. She'd learned about Orfeo, and the talismans, and a murderous creature called Abbadon that she would have to help defeat – but how, exactly, was her blindness supposed to help her fight a monster powerful enough to destroy an entire island?

Five mages of Atlantis, with strong magic and full vision, hadn't been able to kill Abbadon. What chance did she have?

Throughout her journey home Ava had cajoled and begged the gods, hoping for an answer.

In the Canary Islands, where she'd come out of the mirror realm, she'd surfaced and called out to the sky god. *Why did you take my vision, Cassio? Can I have a hint? Just a tiny little clue? I hate to bother you, but I kind of have to save the world and I can't even see it.*

On her way through the Cape Verde Basin, she'd chided

the god of healing. *You think this is funny, Eveksion? When Abbadon figures out that I can't get him in my sights – because I don't have any sight – he's going to rip my head off. Even you won't be able to fix that.*

In the Gambia Plain, she'd tried to engage the twin gods of the tides. *Hey, Trykel and Spume, here's a riddle for you: what do you get when you send a blind mermaid to fight a monster with twelve hands? Answer: splattered.*

And one night, in the Doldrums, hiding out from death riders in a cave while hungry, alone and scared, she'd cried out to the sea goddess herself. *Neria, please, tell me the reason. This is life-or-death, you know? Maybe that's not a huge deal if you're immortal, but I don't want my friends to die.*

But the gods had kept their silence.

Ava wasn't far from home now. She felt the current bend to the left and dip down, and she knew her house was only about twenty yards away.

She could already hear her mother fuss over her as she swam through the door, and feel her father's strong arms around her as he swept her up in a hug.

He would be so happy to see her. She knew exactly what he would say. He'd missed her. He'd been so worried. He loved her. And she was too skinny.

He would tell her, *These peppers are so darn hot, they must've been planted by Helios himself! I'm going to take them right back to the grocer and tell him to stick them in his ear!*

'Wait . . . *what*?' Ava said out loud.

Her father's voice . . . it was so loud, so clear. It was as if he was not in her imagination, but floating right next to her.

Ava stopped short, in an alley. Her hands went to her head. She was having a vision – one so intense, it made her dizzy. Her ability to see with her mind's eye had only grown stronger since she'd travelled to the Iele's caves and met the other five mermaids.

She saw her father and mother sitting at the kitchen table. Her father was chopping peppers. Her mother was knitting. Usually they talked or sang while they worked. But they were quiet, and their faces were grim.

Something's weird, Ava thought. *Something's wrong*.

'Ay, Mami, these peppers are burning my hands,' her father said. He looked up from his chopping board then, and stared directly at Ava. 'They're so hot, they're *dangerous*. They have to go.' He rose then and turned towards the garbage can near the kitchen door. Ava watched him and saw that two death riders were positioned on either side of the door. One had a crossbow trained on her mother. The other was holding a net.

Ava gasped. Baby, hearing the fear in her voice, growled low in his throat. He circled her defensively. Death riders were waiting to ambush her. The crossbow was to prevent her parents from songcasting a convoca to warn Ava. Her father must've suspected that she was near, though. He knew she could sense things, and see things in her mind.

The vision cleared and Ava was left leaning on the alley wall, her heart pounding. What if there were more death riders lurking in the current outside her house? Hiding on the roof? Or the neighbour's balcony? She had to get out of there. Fast.

Ava was numb with weariness. She had little food and even less money. She yearned for her parents. She needed their comfort, advice and protection. But they needed protection themselves.

There was nothing to do but leave. Eventually, the death riders would realize she wasn't coming home, give up and leave her parents alone.

Bitter tears welled in her eyes. 'Mami, Papi . . . I love you,' she whispered.

There was only one place for her to go now . . . to the swamps of the Mississippi, where the Okwa Naholo were holding Nyx's talisman. She couldn't go home again. Not for a long time. Not until this was over.

Ava pulled the scarf that was wrapped around her neck up over her head. Then she turned and quickly swam away, just another mermaid on Macapá's bustling current.

TWENTY-SIX

SWIMMING WITH HER head down through the Hall of Elders, Astrid almost didn't see Rylka and Tauno until it was too late. They had just rounded a bend in the corridor and were coming towards her. Their heads were lowered, too; they were deep in conversation.

Astrid panicked. Tauno was the very last mer she wanted to see right now, and Rylka was a close second. Desperate to avoid them, she ducked behind one of the statues in the hall and hunched down. Her hair plumed out around her. She twisted it together and stuffed it down the back of her vest. As they drew nearer, she made herself as small as she could, hoping they would quickly pass by.

But they didn't. Rylka stopped Tauno right in front of the statue Astrid was hiding behind. Astrid could see them both. Rylka was wearing her black commodora's jacket, with its crossed polar bear claws at the collar. She wore her dark blonde hair cropped close to her head, as most Ondalinian soldiers did. Her amber eyes were piercing. Tauno's colouring was the same as his mother's. Three vertical orca teeth at his collar indicated his major's rank. He was tall and broad-shouldered. His face was broad and handsome – or it would have been, if not for his habitual sneer.

Astrid had grown up with him. He'd been the sort of merboy who liked to hide an elderly merman's glasses. Tie shells to the tail of a dogfish. Make fun of a mermaid who stuttered. He was not the sort of merboy she was going to marry.

Rylka straightened her son's collar now. She brushed at his jacket. 'You smell like a hippokamp. There's silt all over you,' she said disapprovingly.

'What do you expect, Rylka? I just got back from manoeuvres,' Tauno said sullenly.

'The admiral himself has summoned you. At least fasten your jacket,' Rylka scolded, working a rounded piece of whalebone through a buttonhole.

'Why *did* he summon me? The messenger wouldn't tell me.'

Rylka glanced up and down the hall, making sure they were alone, then she said, 'Because he wants you to marry his daughter.'

Tauno laughed in disbelief. '*Astrid?*'

'Does Kolfinn have another daughter I'm not aware of?'

'Holy silt . . . you're serious.' Tauno held up his hands and took a stroke backwards. 'Forget it, Rylka. I'm not marrying her. She's a freaky freakin' freak!'

You're quite the wordsmith, Tauno. In addition to your many other wonderful qualities, Astrid said to herself.

'You *will* marry her,' Rylka insisted.

'I won't. I'm out of here,' Tauno said, turning to swim back down the corridor.

Looks like my father was wrong, Astrid thought bitterly. No one *wants me. Not even Tauno.*

'Move a fin, and I'll have your sorry tail thrown into the brig.' Rylka's voice was quiet and low, and all the more menacing for it.

Tauno faced her. 'You would, wouldn't you? You'd lock up your own son.'

'I'd court-martial any soldier who disobeyed an order,' Rylka said.

'Is that what this is? I'm being *ordered* to marry Astrid? By Kolfinn?'

'Kolfinn will ask you. *I'm* the one ordering you.'

Tauno swore. He shook his head angrily.

'Stop arguing with me for five seconds and *listen*, Tauno. Things are about to change. For Ondalina. For all of us,' said Rylka.

Tauno's eyes narrowed. 'What do you mean?'

'Portia Volnero is travelling to the Citadel. Kolfinn will be dead by the time she arrives. She's going to offer Ragnar a deal.'

'How do you know what Portia's going to do?' Tauno asked.

'Because I've been in contact with her. She approached me months ago. I know the terms of her deal. She's going to tell

Ragnar that Ondalina's attack on Miromara was an act of war and that he must surrender. Either he accepts Lucia Volnero as the new ruler of Ondalina or Miromara obliterates our entire realm. I will advise Ragnar to accept her terms.'

Astrid stifled a gasp. Kolfinn believed Rylka was loyal to him, but she'd been secretly allying herself with Portia Volnero!

Tauno snorted. 'That doesn't sound like much of a deal.'

'For Ragnar, no,' Rylka allowed. 'For you, it could be a very good deal.'

'How so?'

'Ragnar will never accept Portia's offer. He'll insist that Ondalina didn't attack Miromara, and then he'll fight because he's his father's son. During the ensuing battle, he'll be killed.'

'You don't know that,' Tauno said.

'Yes, I do. Because I'll see to it,' Rylka said. 'Friendly fire and enemy fire can be so difficult to tell apart.'

Astrid started to tremble. She leaned against the statue to steady herself, unable to believe what she'd just heard – Rylka plotting to *murder* Ragnar, Astrid's own brother.

'Ragnar has no sons yet, so when he dies, Astrid will become admiral,' Rylka continued. 'However, shortly after she's sworn in, she'll have a hunting accident. So tragic. But everyone knows how dangerous hunting is, and you – her faithful husband – warned her to be careful *so* many times.'

Tauno's eyes lit up. 'And then *I* become admiral,' he said excitedly.

'Exactly,' Rylka purred.

A violent fury rose in Astrid. Rylka was going to murder her and Ragnar, and hand Ondalina to Portia Volnero – all to make her own son admiral! It was all she could do not to rush out and confront them both. But she stopped herself. They weren't finished talking and she wanted to hear everything they had to say.

'Astrid will leave behind no children – it was too early in the marriage,' Rylka continued. 'And when an admiral has no heirs, the admiralship passes to a spouse, as decreed by Ondalinian law. Then you can marry whomever you like and rule Ondalina as a vassal of Miromara,' she said, sounding quite pleased with herself.

How clever you are, Astrid thought. *You have it all figured out, don't you?*

Tauno's expression darkened. 'I don't like the vassal part,' he said. 'Ondalina is nobody's vassal.'

'Ondalina has no choice,' said Rylka. 'If we resist, our people will be slaughtered, our cities and towns destroyed – and for what? Miromara will win in the end. We'd be fools to decline Portia's offer.'

You're a fool to believe a word Portia says, Astrid thought.

She'd seen the raided villages. She'd listened to Sera explain where the stolen merfolk had been taken – and why. And she knew that as soon as Ondalina capitulated, its mer, too, would be herded into prison camps and forced to search for the talismans.

'Come on, Tauno,' Rylka said, patting him on the chest,

'it's time to grant Kolfinn's dying wish.'

'Wait, Rylka . . .'

Rylka raised a perfectly arched eyebrow.

'How can you be so sure that Kolfinn's dying?' Tauno asked. 'He rallied before; he might do so again. Especially now that we've caught Desiderio. He's the one who sent assassins to poison Kolfinn.'

Rylka reached into her breast pocket and pulled out a tiny glass vial. Its liquid contents were an inky blue. 'Somehow, I don't think Kolfinn will rally,' she said.

'What is that?' Tauno asked.

'Poison derived from the Medusa anemone. From the beginning, Kolfinn suspected that Miromara had a hand in his poisoning. He was half right. Portia supplied the poison. The assassin, however' – she paused to smile – 'was home-grown.'

Astrid was out of her hiding place in an instant, driven by an uncontrollable rage. Her sword was in her hand.

All this time Rylka had insisted that the Miromarans had poisoned Kolfinn, but it was she – Kolfinn's own commodore – who'd done it, a mermaid sworn to protect him.

'Traitor!' Astrid shouted. 'My father trusted you!' She swung the flat of her sword into Rylka's arm as hard as she could, knocking the vial out of her hand. Astrid lunged for it. Her fingers closed around it. 'How *could* you? I just saw him. He told me you were loyal to him!' she spat, gripping the vial with one hand, keeping her sword trained on Rylka and Tauno with the other.

'Look out, Astrid!' Rylka shouted, her eyes on the vial.

Astrid followed her gaze and saw that what she thought was a vial was actually a poisonous sea krait writhing in her fist. It bared its fangs. Instinctively, Astrid dropped the venomous creature before it could strike.

She realized too late that it was only an illusio spell. Rylka had enchanted the vial so it would look like a deadly snake to anyone who snatched it from her. Astrid lunged for the vial, taking her attention off Tauno for a split second. Which was all he needed.

A seasoned fighter, Tauno twisted his powerful tail around and slammed it into Astrid's back, knocking the sword out of her hand. Before she'd even recovered from the blow he'd grabbed her arms. She tried to break free, but Tauno shook her so hard, he dazed her.

'Good work, Tauno!' Rylka said. 'Keep her there. I'm going to fetch a guard.'

'But she'll tell them what she heard!' Tauno protested. 'She'll tell them you poisoned Kolfinn.'

'She won't get the chance. She just said she was with her father. I'll tell the guards that we saw her come out of his room with something in her hand. We were suspicious, so we followed her and asked what it was. She refused to show it to us. She tried to put it in her satchel, but dropped it instead. I grabbed it and knew immediately that it was poison.'

'No!' Astrid shouted, trying to shake Tauno off.

Rylka smiled her cold killer's smile. 'I'll have to admit I was wrong. How I hate that,' she said. 'It wasn't a Miromaran assassin who poisoned Kolfinn. It was his own daughter. She fed him the Medusa venom weeks ago, but didn't give him enough to kill him. So tonight she tried to finish the job.'

Rylka picked up the vial. As she started down the hall, bellowing for Kolfinn's guards, Astrid once again tried to break free.

'Stop it or I'll break your arms,' Tauno threatened.

Astrid knew she had to escape. She had to get to her father. If Rylka succeeded with her lie, the guards would lock Astrid up. And then Rylka would be free to administer the fatal dose. But Tauno's grip was brutal. Astrid felt like she was caught in a polar bear's jaws.

A polar bear.

Astrid heard her father's voice in her head. She was a child again and he was soothing her after he'd rescued her from the mother bear.

If a bear ever gets hold of you, don't struggle, Astrid. Go limp in its jaws. Make it think you're dead. It'll stop shaking you and relax its grip. When it does, you've got a weapon: surprise. Use it.

If surprise works on a polar bear, it'll work on Tauno, Astrid thought. *He's ten times stupider*.

Astrid went limp. She hung her head and pretended to cry. Tauno, used to bullying mer into submission, must've figured she'd given up. He relaxed his grip.

An instant later, using Tauno's arms for leverage, Astrid pushed off the floor with her strong tail, flipped up and over in the water, and brought her tail fins crashing down on his head.

Tauno gave a surprised grunt of pain. He let go of her. Astrid shot off down the hallway.

He bellowed for Rylka. After a few seconds, she rejoined him and they both chased after Astrid. Within moments, they'd gained on her.

'Tackle her, Tauno, and make sure she doesn't get up again!' Rylka shouted.

Astrid put on a desperate burst of speed. Up ahead, only about ten yards away, the hallway split into three. The centre part continued on to her family's apartments. The tunnel to the left led to the Hall of Justice, and the one on the right led to the dungeons. Two soldiers were stationed at the fork.

'Guards! Stop her!' Rylka shouted. 'She tried to murder the admiral! *Stop her!*'

The guards snapped into action. They blocked the centre passage, obviously thinking Astrid would make for home. She knew she had only one chance to evade capture. She feinted left. Both guards moved to intercept her. A split second later, she swerved sharply to the right and swam down the passageway to the dungeons, her black-and-white tail a blur in the water. Astrid, fit and swift from her trip to the River Olt, spiralled through the hallway at a dizzying speed, putting distance between herself and her pursuers.

Her heart was pounding. Her muscles were straining. Her lungs were working to pull water in and push it out again, giving her the oxygen she needed to keep moving.

She didn't know what she would do when she got to the dungeons. All she knew was that she was swimming.

For her life.

And her father's.

TWENTY-SEVEN

THE PASSAGEWAY to Ondalina's dungeons plunged deep into the base of the Citadel.

The waters grew colder. The ice became dark and opaque. There were few lava globes to light Astrid's way; they were too costly to be squandered on prisoners.

Astrid hoped to lose her pursuers in the dungeons' mazelike tunnels. She and Ragnar used to swim down here on dares when they were little. They never got further than the gate – the guard wouldn't let them through it. She'd looked through the bars, though, and knew that the single passageway split just beyond them. She'd been told that countless smaller corridors – all lined with cells – snaked off the main passageways and there was an exit at the other end of the dungeons. With any luck, she could reach it before Rylka and Tauno caught up to her.

But first she had to get past the guard.

She saw him now as she rounded a curve. He was sitting in a small office to the left of the gate, listening to a conch.

He rose at Astrid's approach and swam out to meet her.

Astrid said the first thing that popped into her frantic mind. 'I'm here to inspect the dungeons. On my father's – Admiral Kolfinn's – orders. I've just come from his bedside. Rumours of a breakout are circling through the Citadel. One of the prisoners has threatened the admiral's life.'

The urgency in her voice was real, even if her words were a lie. The guard heard it, but he was uncertain about Astrid's request. She could see it in his face.

'I haven't heard any rumours,' he said.

'You need to open the gate and let me in,' Astrid said calmly. 'Right *now*.'

Voices echoed down the passageway. Terror clutched at Astrid's heart. She kept it hidden.

'That's the commodora,' she said. 'She's right behind me. Perhaps you'd like to explain to her your refusal to follow the admiral's orders?'

The guard blanched, clearly unwilling to cross Rylka. He fumbled for the large iron ring dangling from his belt, then inserted a long skeleton key into the gate's lock.

Astrid's heart was beating so hard now, she could barely breathe. She heard fins beating the water, and then Tauno came hurtling around the curve with Rylka right behind him.

'You there, stop her! That's an order!' Rylka shouted.

They were only yards away. Astrid had a heartbeat in which to get her next move right.

As the guard pulled the key out of the lock, she struck. Whipping her powerful tail around, she caught him broadside. The impact sent him sprawling into the wall. He hit it hard, then sank to the floor with a groan, dropping the key ring.

Astrid snatched it up and was through the doorway in a flash. 'I'm sorry,' she said as she pulled the gate closed. She jammed the key into the lock and tried to turn it, but it wouldn't budge. A whimper of fear escaped her. 'Come on . . . come on . . .' she pleaded.

She wriggled the key and tried again, and this time it turned. Just as the lock's bolt shot home, Tauno slammed into the gate. He thrust an arm through the bars.

He can't get the key ring! Astrid yanked the key out of the lock with her right hand and tossed it behind her. Tauno swore and grabbed her left arm, his fingers digging into her flesh.

'I've got her, Rylka! Find another key!' he bellowed.

Rylka swam into the guards' office and proceeded to ransack it.

Tauno thrust his other arm through the bars, trying to get a better grip on her. His body was pressed up against the bars. His face was jammed between two of them.

Astrid saw her chance and took it. She cocked her arm, then drove the heel of her hand though the gap in the bars, straight into Tauno's nose. He let go of her and fell backwards, blood gushing from his nostrils.

Astrid grabbed the key ring and swam flat out. Dead ahead, the tunnel split into three, as the one in the Hall of Elders did. Speeding down the middle passage, she barely registered that there were cell doors on either side of her or that there were prisoners behind them. She was focused on one thing only: getting out.

The tunnel got smaller. It veered left, then right. Astrid swam with arms over her head, palms together, to reduce drag. She rounded bend after bend, hoping each time that the exit would appear in front of her, but it didn't. Her breath was coming harder; she was tiring. A sharp hairpin turn loomed in front of her. She rounded it, then stopped short, skidding through the water.

A guard – an elderly merman, stooped and shuffling – was a few yards ahead of her, pushing a cart that held a large black pot and two stacks of bowls. Luckily, his back was to her. Beyond him, maybe twenty yards away, was another gate, much like the one at the dungeons' entrance. The exit, she was sure. One of the keys might open it. If only she could get there! But she feared there wasn't enough room in the cramped tunnel to allow her to get past the guard. She would have to wait until he went inside a cell, then swoop by.

The guard unlocked a door now and pushed it open.

'Prisoner up!' he shouted.

Astrid heard a chain dragging. The guard slowly ladled slop into a bowl.

Come on! Hurry up! she silently urged him, nervously glancing back the way she'd come. She didn't dare retrace her strokes – what if she swam straight into Rylka and Tauno? She flattened herself against the ceiling, ready to inch by the guard. Why was he taking so long?

Finally he put his ladle down. 'Hands on your—' he started to yell. The rest of his command was drowned out by shouting. It was Rylka.

'Come out, Astrid Kolfinnsdottir! I have prison guards searching every tunnel!'

Astrid moved along the ceiling towards the gate as fast as she dared.

The guard turned and squinted down the tunnel. 'What in the gods' names is going on?' he asked cantankerously. He banged the bowl on his cart, then passed right underneath Astrid, missing her by only a scale's breadth.

Astrid was about to try for the gate when Rylka shouted again, from much closer, just on the other side of the bend. Astrid was hopeful that one of the keys on the ring would open it, but which one? And how long would it take to try them all?

She didn't have time to find out. If she allowed herself to be captured, her father would die. Moving swiftly, she ripped a walrus-tooth button off her vest, threw it down the hallway, and ducked into the open cell. Chest heaving, she swam up above the doorway and pressed herself against the wall.

A prisoner, his hands on his head, an iron collar around his neck, floated in the centre of the cell. He looked at Astrid, surprise on his face. She held a finger to her lips, then mouthed one word: *please*.

The prisoner dropped his gaze and looked straight ahead.

'You there!' Astrid heard Rylka call. 'Have you seen the admiral's daughter?'

'The *admiral's daughter?*' the guard echoed, in a tone that suggested Rylka might be crazy. 'Here in the dungeons? There's no one down here but me and the prisoners!'

'She's wanted for poisoning her father,' Rylka said, swimming into the cell. 'If you see her, apprehend her immediately.'

My gods, if she looks up . . . Astrid thought, squeezing her eyes shut.

'Ah, it's *you*,' Rylka said.

Despair engulfed Astrid. She opened her eyes. It was over. Her father would pay the price.

But as she looked down, she saw that Rylka was speaking to the prisoner, not her.

'You have no right to keep me here,' he said. 'I've done nothing wrong. I have a right to counsel. To a trial. I have—'

Rylka cut him off. 'There won't *be* any trial. Not in your lifetime.'

She glanced at the bowl of food on the cart. 'Don't waste food on this one,' she told the elderly guard. 'We don't need him any more, and Miromara doesn't want him. There's no reason to keep him alive.'

Another prison guard was floating near the doorway. 'Commodora!' he said, holding something out to her. 'We found this on the floor a few feet down the hallway.'

The walrus-tooth button.

Rylka scowled. 'It's hers,' she said. 'She must have let herself out. Tauno, swim to the hospital in case she tries to get to her father. I'll go through the gate and try to catch up with her. Out of my way, you stupid old fool,' she added, shoving the elderly guard.

The cell door slammed shut. The key turned in the lock. The guard moved off, pushing his food cart.

Astrid's entire body was trembling. She sank through the dusky water until she was sitting on the floor, still clutching the key ring. The prisoner remained where he was.

The two looked at each other. Astrid took in the merman's copper-coloured hair, his emerald-green eyes. She'd never seen his face before, yet she knew it. It was the spitting image of his sister's. But thinner and marked with bruises.

Neither Astrid nor the prisoner said a word until the guard had finished his rounds, wheeled his cart past the cell door, and made his way back down the winding corridor. When they could no longer hear him grumbling, the prisoner spoke.

'Quite a place, this Ondalina,' he said. 'You must be Astrid. I'm Desiderio. Pleasure to meet you.'

TWENTY-EIGHT

LUCIA CAST A GLANCE around the VIP room of the Depth Charge, a nightclub in the heart of the Lagoon, near the terragogg city of Venice. It was empty except for herself and Mahdi. And that was exactly what she wanted.

Music blared from the next room. Throughout the club, bioluminescents – tiny shrimps, squids and frilly jellies – filled the darkness with a bewitching blue light. Neon angelfish darted between the glowing creatures, their scales flashing pink, green and orange.

Lucia, dressed in a clingy, low-cut purple gown, was perched on a long banquette made of three giant clams. The creatures inside the open shells, mottled bright blue and yellow, were so soft to sit on. Or sleep on. As Mahdi was doing now.

He was stretched out across the banquette, his head in Lucia's lap, his tail fins hanging off the edge. Lucia stroked his lustrous black hair.

Most of the club kids had already left. Lucia's courtiers

remained, as did her personal guards. They would have to leave soon, too, before the waters lightened. It was much easier to sneak out of the palace – and back in again – with her mother en route to Ondalina and her father and Traho occupied with constant closed-door meetings. Still, Lucia didn't want to be spotted by some gossipy minister or tattling noble.

The Lagoon was forbidden because it was full of spies, informants and criminals, but the danger didn't worry Lucia; that's what guards were for. Her concern was privacy. The Depth Charge's VIP room offered it and the palace did not. Lucia needed to be away from prying eyes tonight.

She gazed at Mahdi while he slept, tracing the outline of his jaw with a crimson-tipped finger. A fierce possessiveness gripped her. She wanted him to love her as much as she loved him. She *needed* him to. She would not suffer her mother's fate – being denied the merman she loved, becoming a figure of pity and scorn.

Most of the time Lucia believed that Mahdi *did* love her, but sometimes she would catch him staring off into the distance, unaware that she was watching him, with an expression of such deep longing on his face that it made her catch her breath.

She *had* to know if he still cared for Serafina, and there was only one way to find out. Being careful not to wake him, she lifted Mahdi's head off her lap and slid to the edge of the banquette. He stirred and rolled onto his back but didn't wake. She rose and was about to swim to the door to lock it, when it opened.

'Hey, Luce, you coming out to dance?' Bianca asked loudly, swimming inside in a swirl of orange sea silk. She spotted Mahdi asleep on the banquette. 'Oops! Sorry!' she whispered. 'Wow, how can he be asleep? It's sooo noisy in here. Being emperor must be *really* tiring!'

'Don't be stupid,' Lucia said. 'No one could fall asleep in here. I drugged him. I poured a somna potion into his drink.'

Bianca's eyes widened. 'Where did you get it?'

Lucia smiled.

'*Her?*' Bianca said, shocked. She lowered her voice. 'Luce, you *said* you were done with her. It's canta malus. If anyone finds out you're using darksong—'

'No one will. Unless *you* tell them.'

Bianca was quick to reassure her. 'I won't. Of course I won't. But why do you want Mahdi to be asleep? Aren't we heading back to the palace soon?'

'Lock the door,' Lucia ordered.

Bianca did as she was told. Lucia swam over to the banquette and sat down next to Mahdi. Bianca cast a regretful glance at the door, as if wishing she was still on the other side. Then she joined her friend. As she did, Lucia began to songcast.

'A stealing songspell?' Bianca asked, with a nervous giggle. 'What are you going to do? Boost Mahdi's wallet?'

Klepo, thief god, hear my plea,
A robber's skills I ask of thee.

Grant me cover, grant me stealth,
Not for gain, or goods, or wealth,
But for secrets the heart does keep,
Buried in bloodsong, dark and deep.
Love, false or true, I must reveal,
It's the truth I wish to steal.

Bianca's silly chatter stopped abruptly as she saw Lucia press her hand to Mahdi's chest, then violently yank it back. Skeins of blood were entwined in her fingers. He groaned in pain. His eyes fluttered open.

Lucia panicked. *If he wakes up* . . . she thought. *If he realizes what I'm doing* . . . But he didn't. His eyes closed again. Relief washed over her. The somna potion was strong.

'Oh, my gods, Lucia . . . *don't*!' Bianca said, horrified. 'That's against the law! It's worse than canta malus – it's canta sangua – blood magic!'

Lucia ignored her. She knew that pulling someone else's bloodsongs was wrong, that it was a heinous violation of both body and soul, but she didn't care.

She swirled her hand through the blood now, avidly watching the images coalesce. She saw Mahdi riding his hippokamp. Talking with Traho. Commanding death riders. None of those memories was what she wanted. Impatiently, she waved the blood away and pulled more.

'Lucia, be careful,' Bianca warned. 'You'll *hurt* him.'

Lucia paid her no heed. She pulled another skein of blood, and then another. Mahdi's face turned a pale, sickly shade, but she kept on drawing out his memories until finally she saw what she was after.

She watched Mahdi kiss Sera in a safe house.

She watched him take Sera's hand in a room in a farmhouse.

She watched him Promise himself to Sera in an official ceremony in the farmhouse's garden.

And then she could watch no more.

She rose, her hands clenched, her eyes dark with malice. Jealousy shrivelled her heart. Rage turned it black. Mahdi was a traitor. He had betrayed Miromara and Matali. Worse, he had betrayed *her*.

She picked up an empty glass and hurled it against a wall, shattering it. She toppled a table. And then another. Then she remembered the dagger hidden in a pocket of her dress. She pulled it out, trembling with fury, and advanced on the defenceless Mahdi.

Bianca, wide-eyed, swam in front of her. 'Lucia, no! *Wait!*' she frantically pleaded.

Lucia glared at her. 'For *what*?' she asked venomously.

'What if this is all a mistake? What if this *isn't* Mahdi? The real Mahdi, I mean.'

Lucia's eyes narrowed. 'What do you mean?'

'Sera must've enchanted him somehow. So she could use him to advance the Black Fins' cause.'

Lucia thought about this, then slowly nodded. 'You're right. That's exactly what happened. That explains everything. Mahdi would *never* prefer Sera to me.'

'Of course he wouldn't. How could he?' Bianca said soothingly.

'She used darksong on him to make him *believe* that he loves her. To make him spy for her. She'll stop at nothing to take my throne,' Lucia said.

Bianca glanced nervously at the blade Lucia was still clutching. 'Put that away,' she said. 'You don't want to cut yourself.'

Lucia looked at the dagger as if she had no idea how it had got there. She put it in her pocket, then turned back to Mahdi. 'I have to break the songspell,' she said. 'I have to free him.'

'How?' Bianca asked. 'It's super hard to undo someone else's songspell. You have to figure out exactly which spell was used, then invent a counter-melody and—'

'There's another way,' Lucia said impatiently. 'It's much quicker.'

'What is it?'

Lucia remembered Baco Goga's report about the location of the Black Fins, and their leader. Her father said he would attack them. He was gathering intelligence. He was making a plan.

He was taking too long.

'Lucia, what's the other way?' Bianca asked again.

Lucia smiled. 'Kill the songcaster.'

TWENTY-NINE

ASTRID, HER EYES on Desiderio, flattened herself against the cell door.

His face darkened. 'Oh, right, I forgot. I'm an assassin. Don't worry, I won't murder *you*,' he said caustically. 'I can't. See?'

As he started towards her, the heavy chain attached to his collar pulled taut and stopped him. Droplets of blood fell onto his bare chest. The iron collar – designed to prevent both escape and songspells – was biting into his skin.

Astrid's mind raced. Her parents had told her that Desiderio was a spy, that he'd tried to kill Kolfinn and that he'd been arrested with his troops near Ondalina. She knew now who was really trying to kill her father, but that didn't mean that Desiderio wasn't a spy, and that he wasn't here on Vallerio's orders. She would have to proceed cautiously.

'You're *accused* of being an assassin,' she said.

'From what I just heard, so are you,' Desiderio shot back.

'Something tells me there's no truth to *that* claim, either.'

He swam unsteadily to a narrow cot pushed against the far wall. He sat down, leaned back and closed his eyes. Another drop of blood fell onto his chest.

He's seriously hungry, Astrid thought. *And probably in pain, too. Torture? Starvation? This is not how Ondalina treats its prisoners*. She put down the key ring, took off her pack, and started digging through it. 'What happened with you and your troops outside the Citadel?' she asked.

'Does it matter?' Desiderio replied wearily.

'Yeah, it does.'

She found what she was after – a packet wrapped in kelp leaves. It was a little crushed, but she doubted Desiderio would mind. She was about to toss it to him when they heard the sound of tapping, iron on ice.

Desiderio's eyes flew open. 'The guards,' he whispered. 'They swim by every hour until midnight and tap their nightsticks on the doors. You have to show yourself. Get back up above the door. *Hurry!*'

Astrid scrambled up. She got herself to the ceiling just as the guard tapped on Desiderio's door. He rose to attention. The guard peered in through the barred window, then moved on.

Astrid sank back down to the floor. He could have turned her in just then. Or earlier, when Rylka was in his cell. Many prisoners would have, to gain favour.

'Here,' she said, tossing him the packet.

Desiderio caught it and looked at her.

'Squid eggs.' She'd bought them a few leagues outside of Ondalina.

'Thank you,' Desiderio said, tearing the packet open.

Its contents were gone in seconds. When he finished eating, he folded the kelp-leaf wrapper and tucked it under his mattress.

A soldier's trick, Astrid thought admiringly. Kelp leaves weren't the tastiest things – they were used mostly for parchment and wrapping material – but they were edible in a pinch.

Desiderio had a bit more energy now. 'You wanted my story,' he said. 'So here it is: I was sent with four regiments to defend Miromara's western border. This was months ago. My mother and uncle were worried about an attack. With good cause, it turned out. We were ambushed a week after we arrived.'

'By whom?'

'Ondalinians.'

Anger flared in Astrid again at learning that Rylka was using her father's soldiers to attack without cause.

'They came at night,' Desiderio continued. 'It was wholesale slaughter. I lost two-thirds of my troops. The survivors were rounded up. Our hippokamps and weapons were confiscated and we were forced to swim north. More soldiers died along the way. As we neared the Citadel, Rylka rode out to meet us. She accused me of conspiring to attack the Citadel and of trying to assassinate Kolfinn. I said I'd done no such thing, that we – my soldiers and I – had been attacked.

A merman came at me then . . . with three orca teeth on his uniform—'

'Tauno,' Astrid said.

'He hit me in the face with the butt of his crossbow. I blacked out. When I woke up, I was in here.'

Astrid studied his face, looking for a twitch, listening for a false note in his voice, anything that might indicate that he was lying. She saw nothing.

Desiderio studied hers in return. 'I'm telling you the truth,' he said. 'I'll prove it.'

He rose from his cot, touched his fingers to the place over his heart and drew a bloodsong. Blood was impervious to magic; it could not be altered. He could pull bloodsongs even though he wore an iron collar.

Desiderio winced in pain as the crimson skeins plumed through the water. Old memories were the easiest to pull. Ripened by time, they could be plucked like heavy fruit. New memories were more resistant. Their sharp edges snagged.

Astrid watched as sounds and images coalesced inside the bloodsong. She saw Desiderio's border encampment with its tents and lava fires burning brightly in the darkness. Then she heard the sound of hippokamps charging. There were shouts and screams. And later, as the rays of the morning sun penetrated the waters, there were bodies. So many of them. She watched the rest of the bloodsong with a mixture of sorrow and anger. It was all exactly as Desiderio had said.

'I'm sorry,' Astrid said as the bloodsong faded. 'Sorry that this happened. Sorry for being suspicious of you.'

'Why did she do it?' he asked, his voice ragged. Pulling bloodsongs had weakened him even more. 'Why did she accuse me of plotting to attack Ondalina, when Ondalinian soldiers attacked me?'

'She's trying to stir up fear of Miromara in my father and brother. So she can convince them to accept Portia Volnero's deal.'

'Portia Volnero?' Desiderio echoed, confused. 'Why is *she* brokering a deal with Ondalina?'

'Because she and Vallerio are bent on world domination,' Astrid said acidly. 'Now that Lucia's the regina—'

Desiderio stopped her. 'Wait . . . *what* did you say? Lucia's not Miromara's regina, my mother is.'

'No, *Lucia* is. Ever since Cerulea was attacked and . . .' Astrid's words fell away as Desiderio's confusion deepened. Understanding dawned on her. 'Oh, gods. You don't know,' she said. 'No one told you. I'm sorry. I'm so, so sorry.'

'*Tell me*, Astrid, please,' Desiderio said, his eyes huge in his face, his voice barely a whisper.

'I will,' Astrid said. Her heart ached for him, and for all the pain she was about to cause him. 'But I think you'd better sit down first.'

THIRTY

'STOP IT, DESIDERIO. *Stop* it!' Astrid begged.

He was pulling against his chain, trying to free himself. Twisting and flailing with all his might.

'Stop. *Please*.'

If Desiderio heard her, he gave no sign of it.

Astrid had told him everything. He'd crumpled when he learned of his parents' deaths. His grief had turned to fury when he found out how they died, and that fury only increased when Astrid told him what had happened to Sera, and how she was now leading the resistance.

When Astrid finished talking, Desiderio had started tugging desperately at his chain, trying to rip it out of the wall. He didn't seem to know her any more, or himself.

Astrid watched him, looking for her chance. Every few seconds, he would stop thrashing and be still, his chest working to draw breath. She tensed. When he stopped again, she sprang. 'Look at me, Desiderio . . . *look at me*!' she hissed, grabbing his arms and holding them fast.

His eyes were wild. She could feel him straining to break her grip.

'Desiderio . . .' She took his face between her hands now. 'I *said*, look. At. *Me*.'

Their faces were only inches apart now. He raised his eyes to hers. The anguish in their depths was terrible to see.

'I'm not going to tell you it'll be all right. Because it won't be,' Astrid said. 'Not for a long time. Maybe not ever. But choking yourself to death in a dungeon cell won't bring your parents back. It won't help Sera. It won't stop Vallerio or Rylka. Do you understand?'

Desiderio slowly nodded. The crazed look in his eyes receded.

'Okay. Good,' Astrid said, releasing him. 'What we have to do now is get ourselves out of here and get to my father. I have to protect him from Rylka. And he has to protect *you* from Rylka.'

Desiderio shook his head as if he hadn't heard her correctly. '*Get ourselves out of here*?' he repeated. 'Have you somehow missed the fact that I'm chained to the *wall* of a *cell* in a *dungeon*?'

Astrid picked up the iron key ring she'd placed on the cell's floor earlier. 'I bet one of these will open your collar,' she said, swimming back to him.

She tried one key after another in the collar's lock. On her fifth try, it opened. She pulled it off and tossed it aside, wincing at how it had rubbed his skin raw.

'Now one of these other keys will open the gate at the far

end of this corridor. I'm sure of it. If we can just get to there, we're free. I'm betting another key will open the door to this cell.'

'Maybe it will,' Desiderio said. 'But that doesn't help us. The lock's on the outside.'

Astrid looked at the door and frowned, thwarted. Of course. The door was never meant to be opened from the inside.

'You could pretend you're ill,' she suggested. 'And tell the guard you need a doctor.'

Desiderio shook his head. 'That won't work, either. Rylka told the guards to starve me to death. They won't open my cell door again until it's time to carry my body out.'

Astrid knew he was right. 'I've got to show myself then,' she said. 'A guard would definitely open the door if he saw me in here. Rylka's probably promised a big reward to anyone who captures me. I'll lure him in—'

'And I'll attack,' Desiderio started to say, some spirit coming back into his eyes. 'I'll make it look like I'm still shackled—'

'—and grab him when he turns his back,' Astrid finished.

They sat down, tails tucked under them, and hastily sketched a diagram in the silt on the cell floor. Warriors both, they were trained to examine their strategies and look for any weaknesses.

'A lot can go wrong. It's a risky plan,' Desiderio said when they'd finished.

'You have a better one?' Astrid asked.

Before he could answer, they heard the sound of tapping again. An hour had passed. The guard was back on his rounds.

'Ready?' Astrid whispered.

Desiderio nodded. He picked up the iron collar and closed it around his neck, wincing as he did. He threaded the padlock through the collar's hasp, so it would look right to the guard, but didn't close it. Then he lay facedown on the floor and became perfectly still.

Astrid took a deep breath. She arranged her face into an expression of fear. It wasn't hard to do. The tap, when it came, nearly made her jump out of her skin.

'Prisoner 592, show yourself,' the guard droned, peering into the small window.

Astrid swam into view. 'The prisoner's dead. I killed him,' she said. 'I'm Astrid Kolfinnsdottir. You've got to help me.'

THIRTY-ONE

THE GUARD HESITATED. Astrid could see indecision in his small, unintelligent eyes. He glanced down the corridor.

If he goes for backup, we're done for, she thought. She and Desiderio could overpower one guard, but not several.

'I've got currensea on me,' she said, desperate to sway him. She dug in her backpack and pulled out a sharkskin pouch. 'A hundred trocii. It's yours.'

It was a lie – the pouch contained only a few trocii – but it worked. She could read the guard's intentions on his face. He would take her money, and then he'd turn her over to Rylka and pocket whatever reward *she'd* offered, too.

The guard nodded at Desiderio. 'How did you kill him?' he asked warily.

Astrid hadn't anticipated that. She thought fast. 'I stabbed him in the chest with a dagger,' she said.

'Hand it over.'

Astrid pulled her bone-handled dagger out of her satchel and pushed it through the bars in the door's small window. The guard took it.

'Now the money.'

Astrid hadn't seen that coming, either. He wasn't going to help her. He was going to take her money, leave her in the cell, and fetch Rylka.

'No,' she said. 'You open the door and get me out of here, then you get the money.'

'Don't make me come in there or you'll be sorry,' the guard threatened.

'We had a deal,' Astrid said.

'The deal is you give me the money. Or else,' the guard said, brandishing his club.

Astrid feigned fear. She backed away from the door to Desiderio's cot. *Come on . . . come on*, she silently urged him. Everything depended on getting him inside the cell.

The guard jammed his key into the lock.

Astrid's pulse quickened. 'That's it,' she said under her breath. 'Keep coming, lumpsucker . . .'

He'd got her dagger off her. He believed Desiderio was dead. And he was greedy. With any luck, all those things would blind him to the fact that Desiderio's chest was moving ever so slightly.

'Give me the money. Now,' the guard said, advancing on Astrid.

Before he even knew what had hit him, Des looped his chain around the guard's neck and pulled it tight. The guard thrashed his tail. His face turned bright red as he gasped for water.

'Stop struggling or I'll choke the life out of you,' Desiderio said.

The guard kept fighting. He was bigger than Desiderio, but Des had better leverage. He pulled the chain tighter and the guard's face deepened to blue.

'*Stop*,' Des ordered, and finally the guard gave up. 'Hands behind your back.'

Working quickly, he unwound the chain, clapped the iron collar around the guard's neck, and locked it. He used the laces from Astrid's vest to bind the guard's hands and the merman's own belt to gag him.

'Let's go,' he said to Astrid when he finished.

They hurried out of the cell. Des pulled the door closed behind them and locked it, then they sped to the far end of the corridor and the exit gate. They had to try several keys in the gate's lock, but soon had it open. They swam through, locked it again and raced up the tunnel.

'Where does this lead?' Des asked.

'I'm not sure. Back to the hospital, I hope,' Astrid replied.

The tunnel ended at a pair of locked iron doors. Once again they had the right key. Astrid pushed one of the doors open and cautiously peeked out.

She immediately knew where she was. She recognized the antique arms and armour decorating the wall and the quotations from Ondalina's chief justices incised above the doorways.

'The Hall of Justice,' she said.

'Is that good?'

'It's not far from the hospital, but we'll have to be careful.'

Desiderio swam out of the tunnel and joined her.

'We're lucky it's nighttime. Usually, the hall's packed,' Astrid explained. 'We just need to find the passageway that leads us to the—'

Her words were cut off by a rumbling noise. It was the sound of voices singing, mer and Fryst – all so low and sombre, they sounded as if they were coming from the centre of the earth.

'It's a dirge,' Desiderio said. 'Somebody died. Somebody major, judging from the number of lamenters.'

Astrid knew that dirges for heads of state were sung by hundreds. Her whole body went cold. With a terrible dread, she listened for the name of the one being lamented.

The time and tide of life has ceased
A stalwart soul now begs release
A warrior prince both brave and true
Returns now to the vast deep blue
Wind and waves, his body take
While we our lamentations make
Horok, come at our behest
Take brave Kolfinn to his rest

'No!' Astrid cried out. 'Oh, gods . . . *no*.'

She was too late. Rylka had got to her father before she

could. She'd given him a lethal dose of poison.

Astrid tried to swim down the hall, swim away from the tearing pain, but she faltered and caught herself against the wall.

A strong pair of hands lifted her up. 'Lean on me,' Desiderio said.

But Astrid pushed him away. She bent double, her chest heaving. The pain was going to overwhelm her if she didn't find a way to stop it. And she *had* to stop it. Desiderio's life – and her own – depended on it. Closing her eyes, she pictured the blue arctic water of Ondalina flowing into her, swirling all around her heart – and hardening into ice. That was the way she always stopped pain.

But this time it didn't work.

She straightened. The emotion was too much. Grief and rage tore through her like a hurricane.

'I'm going after Rylka,' she said. 'She killed my father and she's going to pay.'

'Astrid, no. That's suicide.'

But Astrid didn't listen. She swam up to a pair of crossed sabres on the wall and yanked one free.

Des swam up to her, holding his hands out. 'Astrid, put the sword down,' he said.

'You need to get out of my way, Desiderio,' she said menacingly.

But he didn't budge. 'Earlier tonight, Rylka accused you of poisoning your father. He just *died*. If she finds you, you'll be charged with murder.'

His words pierced through the hurricane howl inside her. If that were to happen, she realized, even Ragnar couldn't help her. The law was the law.

'She'll lock you up in a dungeon cell. Like she did to me,' Desiderio continued. 'She'll turn everyone against you. We can't stay here. Neither of us.'

'What are you saying? That I should just turn tail and *leave*? Abandon Ondalina? Do nothing about my father's death?' she asked, her voice shaking.

Slowly, carefully, Des pushed the tip of Astrid's sword down. Then he took it from her. Her hands dropped to her sides.

'What I'm saying is this: your father was a warrior. Your brother is. *You are*. And a good warrior knows when to lose a battle so she can live to fight the war.'

Astrid clenched her hands. Her mind started to clear. She remembered the terrible pain Desiderio had been in only hours ago when she told him what had happened to his parents. He'd managed to put it aside, and she had to do the same.

'We're going to get out of here now, okay?' he said. 'We're going to go to the Kargjord.'

'The Kargjord? Why?' Astrid asked, alarmed. Everything was happening so fast. Part of her wanted to join the others, but part of her was still scared.

'Because that's where Sera is. I need to be with her. To help her fight. And so do you. Didn't you tell me that the witch – Vrăja – wanted you all together? Didn't she say you were stronger that way?'

'Yes, but . . .'

'But what?'

Astrid couldn't tell him the truth. He wasn't Becca. He wouldn't understand.

'Okay,' she said softly.

'Good. We're going. So you need to *focus* now, Astrid. Because I don't know my way around the Citadel and you do.'

'Yes. Right. *Focus*,' Astrid said. 'We've got to swim out of here. As fast as we can.'

Desiderio shook his head. 'You're not focusing. We can't just swim out of here. We have no food. No animals. No weapons. Except this old sabre. Rylka's troops would catch us in no time.'

Astrid nodded. Desiderio was right. They had nothing. Even her sword was gone. Tauno had knocked it out of her hands and she'd forgotten to take her dagger back from the guard in the dungeons.

'We need hippokamps,' she said. 'That's the most important thing. And I think I know how to get them.'

'How?'

'Your uncle Ludo,' Astrid said. 'I was with him earlier today. He was desperate to see you. I know he'd help us.'

'Do you know the way to his house?'

'I do, but it's a good distance from here.'

'It would be safer if we camoed, then,' said Desiderio. 'We need to make ourselves white, blue and grey. Like the ice.'

'A camo?' Astrid echoed, panicking. 'I can't . . . I – I . . .'

'I know. You're too upset to cast. You'd probably turn yourself orange,' he said. 'I'll do it.'

He took the other sabre down from the wall and handed it to her. 'It's better than nothing,' he said. Then he sang a quick canta prax spell and seconds later, they both blended in perfectly with the walls.

'Ready?' he asked.

Astrid nodded. She set off out of the Hall of Justice for the network of tunnels that would get them to Ludo's house. Des followed her.

As they swam, she was haunted by images of her father. She remembered how wasted he'd looked in his hospital bed, and she remembered his last words to her.

What we do, we do for Ondalina.

They were different in many ways, she and Kolfinn. But in their love for their realm, they were united. Her father had fought for Ondalina his entire life. He had never stopped. Now, she would carry on that fight.

Kolfinn was dead. His ways, the old ways, were over.

Astrid was about to set off on a new current, the current that Vrăja had ordained.

She knew it would be hard.

She knew it would be frightening.

And only the gods knew where it would lead.

THIRTY-TWO

'ATTEN*TION*!' A HARSH voice bellowed.

Ling was out of her bunk before her eyes were even open. She'd only been at the camp for a week, but already she knew to move fast at Selection. Anyone who didn't was docked an entire day's rations.

She took her place with the other prisoners who lived in Barracks Five. Thin and sickly, they all floated in a single line in front of their bunks – hands at their sides, eyes straight ahead. Ling was near the far end.

Two death riders flanked the open barracks door. Their commanding officer – Sergeant Feng – came through it now, a crop in his hand. Tall and brisk, with hard eyes, he swam down the line of prisoners, looking them over as if he were inspecting sea cows.

He prodded one merman with his crop. Lifted the chin of another. 'You,' he said to a third.

Fear filled the eyes of each prisoner as Feng approached. It turned to relief if he passed them by, horror if he didn't.

All were quiet as he moved down the line. Except for one mermaid who dared speak after she was selected.

'Please, sir . . . I have a child here. Her father's dead. There's no one—'

The sergeant swung his crop so quickly the mermaid never saw the blow coming. The pain silenced her. Tears in her eyes, a crimson welt rising across her cheek, she took her place with the other Selects outside the barracks.

Three more mermaids were chosen. Five mermen. The sergeant had almost finished the Selection when he stopped in front of Ling. He eyed her grubby cast, then moved on.

Ling's wrist had been broken when she was captured in a net lowered by one of Rafe Mfeme's trawlers. The cast was the only thing keeping her alive. Without it, she would already have been selected.

The sergeant picked two more mermen, then turned and addressed the remaining prisoners. 'The rest of you, work hard, and you, too, may soon be selected!' he said. Then he and his soldiers swam through the doorway and disappeared.

Ling heard mer exhaling all around her. A few were crying, upset at the loss of a friend or bunkmate. The death riders said it was an honour to be among the Selects, that only the strongest and bravest qualified. But Ling – and everyone else in the barracks – knew differently.

'Guess we live to see another day at Happy Hills,' whispered Ling's bunkmate, Tung-Mei. She'd arrived at the camp three days ago.

Ling smiled sourly at the nickname the prisoners had

given the labour camp located in a shallow valley near the Great Abyss.

'I'll see you later, Ling . . . if neither of us gets beaten to death today. Gotta go, before they dock my breakfast,' Tung-Mei said.

She darted through the doorway and disappeared into the crowd of prisoners hurrying to their jobs. The waters weren't even light yet, but prisoners were made to work for two hours before rations were handed out. No one wanted to be late. They got little enough food as it was, and being deprived of breakfast meant gnawing hunger until noon.

Ling wasn't far behind her friend. She swam out of the barracks and joined the surge of prisoners. They all wore the same uniforms – a baggy grey tunic and an iron collar. They worked in them and slept in them.

She saw the Selects being herded towards the Edge. Some were dull-eyed and resigned. Others called out desperately to friends, asking them to tell a husband, a wife, a parent or child, that they loved them. Others resisted and were beaten.

Ling's heart would have broken if it were not already in pieces from witnessing the same scene morning after morning.

She tore her eyes away and hurried to the munitions warehouse. She wasn't Select material, not with her damaged wrist, but she could count out arrows and spears with her good hand and load them into crates. That was the job she'd been given. The crates were shipped out daily. Ling didn't know where they went, or why, but she was sure their purpose wasn't good. She'd overheard two guards saying that the elder, Qin's ruler, was too busy dealing with the plastic the goggs had dumped into his waters – and the suffering it was causing the ocean creatures – to notice the movements of some wooden crates through his realm.

Tung-Mei worked in the infirmary. She'd seen the Selects who made it back. Sometimes they could still talk. A few had told her what had been done to them, and she'd told Ling.

They were taken to the edge of the Abyss. Each Select's collar was fastened to an iron chain attached to an individual lava globe. Also attached to the globe was a flexible metal filament line. The lines were very long and were wound on giant spools. Once a Select was leashed in this way, he or she was ordered to swim down into the Abyss, to the very end of the filament's length, and then give three sharp tugs on the iron chain. To discourage a Select from simply gathering the filament in her hands and swimming only a short distance into the Abyss, electric eels were twined around the filament back at the top. They sent a current down the line, shocking anyone who touched it. The glass lava globe acted both as a source of light and a current breaker, preventing the mermaid or merman attached to it from being electrocuted.

At the end of twelve hours, the electric eels were removed and the soldiers stationed at the edge of the Abyss wound the filament back onto the spools. The prisoners came up with it.

Half were usually dead from depth sickness by then, and the rest wished they were. Survivors came up disoriented and trembling, with excruciating headaches. Their faces and hands were blue, and they were usually coughing up blood.

The extreme depth – with its higher pressure and lower levels of oxygen – destroyed lungs and caused brain swelling. The living were hauled off to the infirmary, where they lasted for an hour or two.

Tung-Mei had asked one survivor why they'd been sent down into the Abyss. He'd said they were to look for a white ball.

'So much suffering, so many deaths . . . for a *white ball*?' she'd said.

But Ling knew it was no ordinary white ball. It was Sycorax's talisman – the puzzle ball. Orfeo had told her about it. He wanted it found and didn't care how many were sacrificed for his mad quest.

Ling knew that she would be sacrificed soon, too. She would die here. Her body would be thrown into the cart that came into the camp every evening to collect the dead. Then it would be dumped into a mass grave.

Ling was strong and not afraid to die. She knew that a death from depth sickness was not an easy one, but she would face it bravely. What tortured her, though, was the thought of dying before she could tell Sera what she'd learned aboard Rafe Mfeme's ship.

Ling was an omnivoxa, a mermaid who could speak all creatures' tongues. For her, the most awful part of her imprisonment – worse than the beatings and the hunger and the fear – was being unable to communicate. Her friends had no idea who they were dealing with, no idea of the danger they were in.

When she'd first arrived at the camp, Ling had hoped she'd be able to escape, but it was surrounded by a living fence of sea wasps – giant, bioluminescent jellyfish with long, lethal tentacles. They opened only enough to allow in cages containing new prisoners, food and munitions deliveries, and the death cart.

Ling saw a merman try to escape on her second day in the camp. He'd just been selected. Desperate, he tried to swim between two of the venomous sea wasps. In the blink of an eye, one of the wasps wound a thick, fleshy tentacle around his body. He was dead within seconds.

When she realized that she couldn't escape, Ling looked everywhere for a courier – a small fish, a tiny octopus, or even a young hawksbill turtle – that she could send to Serafina with a message. But the sea wasps kept sea creatures out as effectively as they kept prisoners in.

As Ling approached the munitions warehouse now, a mermaid ahead of her faltered in the water and fell to the mud. The guard prodded the emaciated woman with his spear. She winced, tried to push herself up with her arms, and collapsed again.

Ling felt a hand on her back. It shoved her forward.

'You!' a death rider behind her barked. 'Take her to the infirmary!'

Ling bent down to help the fallen mermaid. 'Can you swim?' she whispered.

The woman shook her head.

'You've *got* to. I'll help you.

'Leave me. Let me die. I don't have any strength left.'

'No,' Ling said firmly. 'Put your arm around my neck. I've got enough strength for both of us.'

The mermaid did so and Ling lifted her.

'There we go . . . That's it, one stroke at a time . . . It's not much further,' Ling coaxed.

The infirmary was only about thirty yards away. If she could just get the mermaid there and hand her off to one of the workers, she might still be able to make it to the munitions warehouse in time for her morning rations. She was so hungry, it hurt.

Flimsy and spare, the infirmary was run by prisoners who had been doctors and nurses before they were taken. Medical knowledge was valuable. Prisoners who had it were sometimes permanently exempted from Selection. Ling hoped Tung-Mei would be. She'd been studying medicine at the University of Qin and was stolen from her village while on break visiting her parents. Through the infirmary's open double doors Ling spotted her bunkmate rushing from patient to patient.

The survivors from the night shift had just arrived. Ling saw mermaids and mermen bleeding and thrashing as they struggled to pull oxygen into their lungs. She knew they didn't have long. All Tung-Mei could do was ease their suffering, not stop it.

'What happened?' she asked, as Ling approached her with the sickly mermaid.

'She collapsed.'

'Anything broken or bleeding?' Tung-Mei asked briskly.

Ling shook her head.

'Take her to the back. Find her a cot. This area's for critical patients only,' Tung-Mei ordered.

Ling nodded and swam to where her friend had pointed. The mermaid's head was lolling now. She was only half-conscious. There were no empty cots.

A merman was bent over another patient, taking her pulse. Ling waited until he was finished, then said, 'This mermaid's sick and I can't find a cot. Where should I put her?'

'You'll have to lay her on the floor,' the merman said.

He rose and turned to her, and as he did, Ling gasped. For a few seconds she felt as if she might collapse herself.

She was looking at a face she knew so well, but never expected to see again. The face of a dead man. A ghost.

The face of Shan Lu Chi.

Her father.

THIRTY-THREE

THE MERMAN WENT pale. His eyes widened. '*Ling?*' he whispered.

Speechless, Ling nodded.

Her father enveloped her in a fierce embrace. And for a moment, in his arms, Ling was no longer in the hellish labour camp, she was in a place of love and light. She was home.

All too soon, however, he released her. And the love that had lit up his face was immediately replaced by other emotions: fear and sorrow. Ling understood. She was so happy to see him, so amazed that he was alive, but she was devastated, too, to know he was in this horrible place.

'How long have you been here?' he asked. 'Your brothers . . . your mother . . . are they—'

Ling shook her head. 'They're not here. I wasn't taken from our village. I was picked up in the waters of East Matali. On my way home. Three weeks ago.'

'*East Matali*? What were you doing there?'

'It's a long story, Dad. What are *you* doing *here*?' asked

Ling. 'We thought you were dead!'

'You two!' a voice shouted. 'Why are you talking instead of working?' He narrowed his eyes. 'And you' – he pointed at Ling – 'you don't belong here.'

It was a guard. He'd just swum into the infirmary. Ling and her father immediately stood at attention, eyes straight ahead, as they were required to do when being addressed by a death rider.

'She brought a patient in, sir,' Shan said. 'I asked her to stay and help me. We're overwhelmed. Several prisoners have died from purple fever. The bodies remain contagious after death. We need to get them into the death cart and out of the camp as quickly as possible.'

The guard recoiled at the word contagious. He put a hand over his nose and mouth. 'Be quick about it!' he ordered, backing away. Then he hurried out of the infirmary.

Ling looked at her father fearfully. He had aged greatly since she'd last seen him. His black hair was shot through with grey now, and his strong shoulders were stooped. Had he been exposed to the deadly disease? Had she?

'There's no such thing as purple fever. I made it up,' he said quietly. 'The death riders are as stupid as they are brutal.'

'Why are you working in the infirmary?' Ling asked. He was an archaeologist, not a medical doctor. He studied ancient mer civilizations.

'When the death riders took me, they went through my things. They saw my ID, with the title of doctor on it, and assumed I was a physician. That misunderstanding keeps me alive.' He cast a worried glance in the direction of the infirmary's door. 'Can you cope with dead bodies? Not contagious – victims of depth sickness. I've got at least ten to deal with. Probably more before the morning's out. We can talk as we load.'

'I can manage,' Ling said, sounding braver than she felt. She'd never touched a corpse before.

'Are you sure?' her father asked, nodding at the cast on her wrist.

'The wrist's pretty much healed,' Ling said. 'But no one needs to know that.'

Shan smiled wanly. 'Looks like we've both found a survival tactic,' he said. 'At least for the time being.'

He motioned Ling over to a cot occupied by a young merman. His skin was grey. His eyes were open, but unseeing. Shan Lu Chi reached into the pocket of his own tunic and pulled out a smooth white pebble. He gently opened the dead merman's mouth, placed the pebble on his tongue, and closed it again.

'I haven't got any pearls. But if I see a nice pebble, I pick it up,' he explained. 'I'm hoping Horok understands.'

Ling knew that a pearl, placed in the mouth of the dead, caught the mer's soul and held it until Horok, the great coelacanth, took the pearl and carried the precious soul safely to the underworld.

'I'll get the top half, you get the bottom,' Shan said.

Ling took hold of the merman's tail, hooking her good arm underneath it, placing her bad one on top to steady the body. His flesh was cold to the touch and just beginning to stiffen. Ling thought she'd feel horror at the task, but all she felt was sorrow.

Together, she and her father carried the body out of the back of the infirmary, where the death cart was waiting. Its driver, an old merman who had a farm nearby, was nowhere to be seen. The two ancient hippokamps that pulled it were munching quietly, their noses in their feedbags.

'The guards never come back here. They hate the death cart,' Shan explained as they laid the body in the cart. 'The driver's probably in the sergeant's office. It's Moonday – the day he gets paid. This is our best chance to talk.'

He took Ling by the shoulders. 'I still can't believe it's you. I longed to see you again someday, Ling. But not here.' His eyes filled with tears; his voice broke.

Ling curled a hand around her father's wrist. 'It's okay, Dad.'

He shook his head. 'No, it's not. Seeing your child in a place like this is definitely not okay. Your brothers . . . they're well?'

'Yun and Ryu are good. At least, they were when I left.'

'And your mother?'

Ling's gaze shifted to the ground. Thoughts of her silent, sad mother always hurt her.

'Ling? What's wrong?'

'She hasn't spoken since you disappeared, Dad. Not once,' Ling explained. 'I've tried to get her to talk. So have my grandmothers, and all ten aunts. No one can get through to her. Most have given up. Aunt Xia keeps trying, but even she's getting frustrated. Grandma Wen says everyone's being too kind, and that all this babying is only encouraging weakness, that it's time to get tough. It makes me sad, but I get angry, too. We fought before I left. At least, *I* fought. Mum didn't say a word.'

'Why won't she speak?'

'Because her heart is broken. She thinks you're *dead*, Dad. We all do. Or *did*. How did you get here?' Ling asked.

'I went to explore the Abyss,' Shan began.

Ling nodded, remembering that day. It was the last time anyone had seen him. When evening came and he still hadn't returned home, his three brothers went to search for him. All they found was the seaflax bag he used to hold his ancient treasures. Ling had known, from the expressions on their faces when they returned, that the worst had happened. The grief she'd felt was searing.

'I dived deep that day and while I was down I found the usual – bones and fossils,' Shan explained. 'But then I came upon something really amazing: an ancient puzzle ball carved from white coral.'

Ling's pulse quickened. Her father had discovered Sycorax's talisman. 'It's the white ball the death riders are searching for.'

Shan nodded. 'It was decorated with a phoenix and covered with writing,' he said. 'The characters were from an ancient language that terragoggs from China spoke. I couldn't translate much, but I did make out the word Atlantis.'

'Dad, where is it?' Ling asked. *Please*, she thought, *please tell me it's somewhere safe*.

Shan was about to answer when a harsh shout was heard. It came from the infirmary, but his eyes took on a wary look nonetheless. 'We need to make sure we're seen working. Come on,' he said, tugging on Ling's sleeve.

They swam back inside. Shan slipped another pebble into the mouth of another dead prisoner, then he and Ling carried the body to the death cart. Shan continued speaking as they worked, making sure to keep his voice low so that only Ling could hear him.

'When I ascended from the Abyss, mermen were waiting for me,' he explained. 'Their leader wanted to know if I'd found anything. I told them I hadn't, but he didn't believe me. He told his men to search me. Something inside told me not to let them get the puzzle ball, so I pulled it out of my bag and threw it back.'

Threw it back? No! was Ling's first reaction. He'd had it in his bag, and now it was back in the Abyss. But better that, she knew, than for it to be in Orfeo's hands.

'I didn't know it then,' Shan continued, 'but the mermen who stopped me were death riders. They beat me silly for throwing the puzzle ball back and brought me here. I wish I knew why they want it so badly.'

'Because it's an incredibly powerful magical talisman that belonged to Sycorax, one of the six mages of Atlantis,' Ling said.

Shan looked stunned. 'How do you know that?' he asked.

Ling glanced around to make sure no guards were nearby. 'Because the Iele summoned me to the River Olt. So I went. And found out that everything we know about Atlantis is nothing but some serious spin perpetrated by Merrow.' She looked at her father again. 'Um, Dad? Close your mouth, okay? In case a guard sees you,' she said.

Shan did so, and Ling, talking fast, told him everything that had happened since she'd left her village – ending with her arrival at the camp.

Shan was stunned when she finished. 'That was a truly insane thing to do, Ling. And a truly brave one,' he finally said. 'So Rafe Mfeme is Orfeo? Mfeme the terragogg? Ling, are you *sure*?'

'Positive,' Ling said, shuddering at the memory of Orfeo's empty, soulless eyes. 'And Vallerio's in league with him. Orfeo's helping him take over the mer realms one by one. When Vallerio's got them all, he's going to combine their armies, help Orfeo free Abbadon, and then they'll attack the underworld. If that happens, the gods themselves will fight against Orfeo. But Orfeo doesn't care if he destroys the mer realms, the terragogg realms, the entire world, as long as he gets his wife back. If we don't get the talismans before he does, we're goners.'

Shan nodded. The dazed expression on his face receded and a determined one took its place.

'That can't happen,' he said. 'You have to escape. You have to find the puzzle ball and get back to your friends.'

'That's a great idea, Dad,' said Ling. 'But there's a slight problem . . . there's no way out of here.'

Shan looked at the bodies they'd just carried out. They were lying three deep in the rickety death cart.

Then he looked at his daughter.

'Actually, Ling,' he said, 'there is.'

THIRTY-FOUR

ASTRID FLATTENED HERSELF against a wall of ice and peered around a corner.

Lights were on in the upper floor of the house that Ludovico di Merrovingia shared with his family. Huge, with a circular courtyard, an ornate facade, and sprawling stables, the house was located on the outskirts of the Citadel at the bottom of the iceberg.

The dimly lit passageway that ran through this part of the Citadel was empty, but Astrid was still wary. As soon as it was discovered that Desiderio had escaped from the dungeons, Rylka's guards would be visiting Ludo's house. Maybe they were already there.

'Any sign of life?' Desiderio whispered.

'Someone's home. Hopefully just your uncle,' Astrid said, tightly gripping the old sabre she was still carrying.

She and Desiderio swam swiftly out of the alleyway, through Ludo's courtyard, to his front door. Des lifted the heavy doorknocker and banged it down twice. Astrid winced at the noise it made.

A few seconds later, the door opened. Astrid expected to see a servant, but it was Ludo himself.

'Thank the gods,' he said, when he saw his nephew. He ushered Desiderio and Astrid inside and locked the door behind them. Then he hugged his nephew tightly.

'I didn't know who I'd see when I opened the door, you or Rylka,' he said.

'You heard already?' Desiderio said.

'Yes,' Ludo said. 'The entire Citadel's in an uproar. You' – he nodded at Astrid – 'are accused by Rylka of murdering your father. If we could just get to the palace and sit down to talk with Ragnar present, we could put an end to these wild accusations and—'

Astrid cut him off. 'Rylka wouldn't let that happen. Vallerio wants to take over Ondalina and she's going to hand it to him. In exchange, Tauno gets to rule Ondalina.'

'*What?*' Ludo said, stunned.

Astrid explained Rylka's scheme. 'But Desiderio and I just wrecked her Plan A,' she finished, 'so she's working on Plan B: executing us. She'll never allow us to get near Ragnar. I'm sure her soldiers have orders to shoot us on sight.'

'That's why we're here, Uncle Ludo,' Desiderio said. 'We need currensea and supplies. We're going to head to the Kargjord. Serafina's there. She's building up an army against Vallerio.'

'Sera's *alive*?' Ludo said. Tears of happiness shone in his eyes. 'I thought she was dead, Des, and that you soon would be. And now you've both been given back to me.' He pulled his nephew into another embrace.

'Look, this isn't the time or the place for a family reunion,' Astrid said urgently. 'We've got to go. But before we do, can you do something for me?'

She looked around Ludo's foyer for what she needed. Her eyes travelled over fine furniture, portraits, swords mounted on the walls, and finally came to rest on a glass urn filled with shells. She ripped its lid off and dumped out its contents.

'What are you doing?' Ludo asked.

Astrid didn't answer. She took a few seconds to steel herself against the pain, then touched her fingers to her chest and drew a handful of bloodsongs, all at once. None of the memories was old; all were painful to pull.

Astrid whirled the red skeins together before they could fade in the water, and stuffed them into the urn. Gasping with pain, she clapped on the lid and held the urn up to the light so she could see what she had. Then she swore under her breath. They weren't all there.

She touched her chest again and wrenched out more bloodsongs – one from the River Olt, another from the convoca with Sera. The pain was awful. By the time she'd added those memories to the ones already in the urn, her face was white.

So was Ludo's.

He'd seen the bloodsongs, too. He'd seen Serafina tell Astrid and the other mermaids in the convoca that it was Vallerio who'd had Isabella assassinated.

'My brother . . . *our* brother,' he said in a broken voice. 'How could he do it? How could he *kill* our sister?' He faltered and had to steady himself against a wall.

Des took his arm and led him into a nearby chair. 'Easy, Uncle Ludo,' he said. 'Take a deep breath.'

Astrid set the urn on a table. 'I'm sorry you had to find out about Vallerio like this,' she said, bending down to him.

Ludo made a visible effort to collect himself, then patted her hand. 'You owe me no apologies, Astrid. You saved my nephew's life.'

'Can you get the urn to Eyvör?' Astrid asked. 'Have her send for Ragnar. The bloodsongs will show them the truth.'

Ludo nodded. A bit of colour had come back into his cheeks. He rose, pulling Astrid up with him. 'I'll get the urn to Eyvör,' he said, carefully stowing it in a cabinet. 'I'll deal with that viper, Vallerio, too. But first, I've got to get you both out of here.' There was a closet off the foyer. He yanked its door open and said, 'Find warm things for the trip. Take whatever you need. I'll be right back.'

He hurried off down a hallway, disappearing through a pair of double doors. A few minutes later, as Astrid and Des were buttoning up some seal-fur parkas, he returned with a bulging pair of panniers.

'I've stuffed them with everything I could find in our kitchen. You should be good for a week. There's currensea in there, too, as well as a compass, a map and two daggers.' He handed the bags to Astrid, then swam to a wall and took down two swords sheathed in scabbards. 'You'll need these, also,' he said, giving them to Desiderio. 'You couldn't fight off a guppy with those things,' he added, nodding at the antique sabres Astrid and Des still carried.

'Thank you, Uncle Ludo. Can you spare us two hippokamps?' asked Desiderio. 'We've got to put some serious distance between ourselves and Rylka.'

Ludo shook his head. 'All I've got right now are foals and their mothers, and a lame gelding.'

Astrid's heart sank. They didn't have a prayer of outswimming Rylka's soldiers without good strong animals under them.

'But I do have Elskan. I was supposed to deliver her to the palace tomorrow. She's fast as lightning,' Ludo said, smiling grimly. 'And every bit as deadly.'

'*Elskan?*' Astrid said, her eyes widening with alarm. 'You mean—'

Ludo nodded. 'The same Elskan your father bought for your mother before he got sick.' He put his hands on his hips and looked Astrid up and down. 'You're pretty good on a hippokamp,' he said. 'Think you can handle an orca?'

THIRTY-FIVE

THE YOUNG KILLER whale spun around furiously, slamming her powerful tail into the front of her stall.

'Nobody rides these things, Ludo,' Astrid said, nervously eyeing her. 'Nobody but lunatics. And my mother.'

'You're a good rider, Astrid. I've seen you. Almost as good as Eyvör.'

'*Almost* won't count for much when I'm dead,' Astrid said.

'The important thing is to let her know who's in charge,' Ludo counselled.

'I think she already knows who's in charge. And it's not me,' Astrid said.

'Shh, orca. Good girl, Elskan. Good girl,' Ludo said soothingly. He made a series of clicking noises to calm the creature.

Elskan eyed him. She clicked back, bobbing her head up and down a few times, then suddenly spun around and slammed her tail into the wall again, opening a crack in it.

Ludo shook his head. 'She's a fifteen year old,' he said.

'And she acts like it.'

On the way to the stables, Ludo had told Astrid and Desiderio that Elskan was fourteen feet long and weighed two and a half tons.

'Here,' he said now, handing Astrid a metal pail. 'Give her a taste of seal. It'll distract her while I tack her up.'

He took a bridle fitted with a silver bit from a hook and looped it over his shoulder. Next he lifted a double-seat saddle, a saddle pad and a girth strap from a nearby rack.

'Ready?' he asked Astrid.

Astrid nodded. Her mouth had gone dry.

Ludo opened the stall door and swam inside. Astrid took a deep breath and followed him.

'Um, nice knowing you both,' Des said, as he closed the door after them.

Neither Ludo nor Astrid acknowledged the joke. They were focused on the orca.

Elskan, scenting a snack, turned to them and opened her very large mouth. Her sharp, conical teeth glinted in the lava light. Each one was three inches long. Astrid tossed her a bloody chunk of meat. Elskan swallowed it in one gulp, then bobbed her head for more.

For a moment Astrid forgot her fear, awestruck by the creature's beauty. 'She's magnificent, Ludo,' she said. 'No wonder Eyvör had to have her.'

Elskan swam up to Astrid. She sniffed her, then nosed the bucket. Astrid tossed her another chunk of meat.

Astrid loved the challenge of mastering her mother's

spirited mounts. She couldn't songcast, but magic didn't matter in the hunt. Courage and strength did, and those she had in abundance. Streaking through the water on a hippokamp like Blixt, Astrid felt powerful and in control. What would Elskan be like?

'She's super smooth if you handle her well,' Ludo said. He'd placed the saddle on the orca's back, just in front of her dorsal fin, and was now buckling the girth.

'And if you don't?' Astrid asked.

'She'll kill you,' Ludo replied simply. 'She works well off your tail. Don't yank on her mouth. Ride with a loop in the rein and give her her head.'

'So she can bite off mine,' Astrid muttered.

'Don't forget to give her plenty of chances to get air,' Ludo instructed. 'Untack her at night and let her roam. When you get to the border, take the saddle and bit off her, give her a slap on the tail, and tell her to go home. She'll know what to do,' he said.

He looped the reins over the whale's head, eased the bit into her mouth and fastened the bridle. Then he attached the panniers to the saddle. When he was satisfied that every piece of tack was secure, he pulled the reins back over Elskan's head and handed them to Astrid.

'Your orca,' he said.

Astrid took a deep breath, then led Elskan out of her stall, through the stables, to a pair of large iron doors. She knew they led directly to the open water.

'Once I open these, she's out of here,' Ludo cautioned. 'So

get on and get ready.'

'Uncle Ludo . . .' Desiderio said.

Ludo turned to him.

'What will you say when Rylka learns that we're gone, and Elskan is, too? You need to stay out of the dungeons. You need to get Astrid's bloodsongs to Ragnar.'

'I'll tell her you held a speargun on me.'

'Are you sure you'll be all right?' Astrid asked, knowing full well how Rylka treated anyone who crossed her.

'Don't worry about me,' Ludo said. 'Get yourselves to the Kargjord. Help Sera.'

'Uncle Ludo . . .'

'Yes, Desiderio?'

'Thank you.'

Ludo nodded.

'Come on, Desiderio,' Astrid called. She was already in the saddle, Elskan's reins in her hands.

The orca, sensing the open water, started to rear.

'Let's *go*,' Astrid said, trying to keep her under control.

Desiderio swam up to Astrid and settled himself behind her.

'What do I hold on to?' he asked.

'Me,' Astrid said. 'Ready?'

'No,' Des replied, wrapping his arms around her waist.

The sensation of a handsome merman's arms around her was new and disconcerting. She didn't need to be disconcerted right now. Not with two and a half tons of killer whale at the end of her reins.

And then a sudden pounding, loud and ferocious, erased all thoughts of Desiderio.

'Ludovico di Merrovingia! Open up!'

Astrid's head whipped around. Tauno was on the other side of the stables' front doors. Luckily, Ludo had locked them after the three of them had swum inside.

Elskan, spooked by the loud noise, started to spin in circles.

'Let us out! *Now*, Ludo!' Astrid shouted.

'Astrid Kolfinnsdottir, we know you're in there! You're under arrest!' Tauno ordered.

Ludo gave the outside doors a shove and they swung open. Elskan whinnied and shot through them.

'Hang on, Des!' Astrid shouted.

And then the world turned into a blur as Astrid learned what it felt like to ride a bolt of lightning.

THIRTY-SIX

LING COUGHED. She took a deep breath and coughed again, wheezing for effect. Then she returned to her task – counting out arrow shafts and putting them in boxes.

She passed a full box to the prisoner across from her – Bai – whose job it was to fletch the shafts with gull feathers.

As she reached for another box, Ling hacked again. She shook her head and wiped her brow with the back of her hand.

'The current here is so warm tonight,' she whispered, even though it wasn't.

Bai's eyes darted from the arrow in his hands to Ling's face. Worry creased his brow.

Ling counted out more arrows. She coughed again, grimacing this time, then pretended to steady herself against the work table.

'Bai . . . help me,' she whispered. 'The room's spinning!'

Before Bai could react, she slumped to the floor where she lay gasping. Then she stopped breathing, hoping her face would turn a sickly shade of violet-blue. It did.

'Purple fever!' Bai shouted, backing away from her.

'Purple fever! Purple fever!' Panicked whispers spread through the warehouse like a red tide. Prisoners seated near Ling shot away and huddled at a distance.

A guard pushed his way through them. 'What's going on?' he demanded.

One of the prisoners pointed at Ling, now writhing on the warehouse floor.

The guard swam to her. He whacked her hard with his tail fins. Ling groaned in pain. That wasn't an act; the slap really hurt. What she did next, however, was. She pushed herself off the floor and made as if she was trying to get up, but sank again, and faked another coughing fit.

'It's purple fever, sir,' a prisoner said fearfully.

'Get her to the infirmary!' the guard ordered. When no one swam forward to do so, he grabbed two mermen by their necks and shoved them towards Ling. 'Get her out of here!' he shouted.

The mermen picked Ling up by her arms and dragged her out of the warehouse. Ling let her body go limp and her head loll. She closed her eyes. That way no one could see the triumph in them.

So far, the plan was working. Her father had said he was going to start a rumour about purple fever. He would falsely diagnose it in every patient with weakness or a temperature. Judging from the reaction her performance just received, the rumour had spread. The prisoners, and the guards, were all terrified of catching the dread disease.

Ling's coworkers brought her to the door of the infirmary, dumped her there, and sped back to the warehouse.

Ling moaned loudly. A few seconds later, Tung-Mei was at her side.

'Oh, Ling, not you!' she exclaimed sorrowfully.

Ling nodded. 'I feel like I'm burning up. Please help me, Tung-Mei,' she rasped. She wished she could tell her friend the truth, but for Tung-Mei's own safety, the less she knew, the better.

'Shan!' Tung-Mei shouted. 'Come quick. We've got another fever patient!'

Ling gave no sign of knowing her father, and he was equally blank-faced as he wound her arm around his neck and helped her to the rear of the infirmary.

'I'm sorry, but all of our cots are full. I'm going to have to put you over here,' he said, propping Ling up against the back wall, away from everyone else. That was part of the plan, too. They could talk here without being overheard.

'The cart's here,' her father whispered tersely, as he pretended to examine her. 'I'm going to load some bodies, then I'll come for you. Lie down and close your eyes. Don't move.'

Ling nodded. Her father moved off to another patient, and she slowly lowered herself to the floor. The infirmary was so busy, no patient or guard would take any notice of one more prisoner quietly succumbing to fever. This was the easy part. As Ling lay there, she ran through the rest of the plan she and her father had devised.

'The cart driver comes at seven in the morning and again in the evening to haul away the dead. The death riders on gate duty are supposed to search the cart, and sometimes they do, but mostly they only glance at it,' her father had told her. 'If someone could fake being dead—'

Ling had cut him off. 'You want me to ride out of here in the death cart. Hidden among the bodies,' she had said. She'd shuddered at the thought, but had pushed her fear aside. She *had* to get away.

Shan had nodded. 'Fake purple fever this coming Moonday evening. Right before dinner rations. You'll 'die' just as the cart's arriving. The driver will leave the cart to get his pay. By the time we're done loading bodies, it's usually eight o'clock. The dusk will give you cover. Wait until the cart passes through the gate. After fifteen minutes or so, you should be well into the hills. You can climb out then and swim off without being seen. It's risky, but it's the only way.'

'I can't swim off,' Ling had said, shaking her head. 'I need to get to Sera and the others, but I have to find the puzzle ball first, while I'm still at the Abyss. It can't fall into Orfeo's hands. But how? The death riders are at the edge of it night and day. One of the Selects told Tung-Mei they've got the whole place lit up. They'll see me.'

Shan had smiled. 'No, they won't. The death riders are looking in the area where I threw the talisman. What they haven't figured out is that the Abyss has a slight current. I'd estimate that by now the talisman will have travelled about two leagues east. Another thing the death riders don't know is how to speak with the creatures of the Abyss. But you do. Talk to them, Ling. One of them may've seen the puzzle ball. It could've landed on a ledge or in a hollow.'

'That's the best-case scenario,' Ling had said. 'It also could've fallen far into the Abyss. It could *still* be falling. Finding it will be like trying to find a minnow in a kelp forest.'

'You've got to try,' Shan had said.

'No, Dad,' Ling had said solemnly. 'I've got to succeed.'

She'd spent a tense week waiting for today, hoping every morning at the Selection that Sergeant Feng wouldn't suddenly decide that her cast should come off, hoping that nothing would happen to her father.

'Look dead,' Shan whispered now. Ling closed her eyes and let her body go limp. She felt her father unlock the iron collar around her neck and heard a clink as he tossed it onto an evergrowing pile. With a glance around to make sure no one was watching him, he quickly cut her cast away with a small surgical saw. When they'd made their plan, Ling had asked him to get it off her before he carried her to the death cart. She knew it would only slow her down. A flex of her fingers brought pain, but not too much. Hopefully her bones had healed. Finally, Shan picked her up.

'Another one?' a voice shouted as Shan swam out of the infirmary.

Ling felt her father freeze. No one else was supposed to be near the cart. If whoever this was – a guard, another prisoner – took hold of her, he'd soon realize she was warm and very much alive.

'I'm afraid so. Purple fever. Keep back, Zhen,' Ling's father warned.

Zhen. That was the driver. Ling felt relief wash over her.

'You don't have to tell me, doc,' Zhen said. 'I don't want any part of it.'

It was hard to tell, but it sounded like – judging by the distance of the driver's voice, and the snorts and whinnies of his hippokamps – that Zhen was in front of his cart.

'You're not leaving yet, are you? I have more bodies to load,' Shan lied. His voice was steady, but Ling – who knew it so well – could hear the strain in it.

'No, not yet. Gotta see the sarge. You've plenty of time to pile 'em high.'

Zhen swam off. Shan exhaled loudly. Ling risked opening an eye. Her father's face was white.

'Ling, maybe this isn't—' he started to say.

She cut him off. 'I can do this, Dad,' she said. She was determined to escape. Her friends, their quest, the fate of all the mer realms depended on her.

Her father searched her face, then nodded. 'Yes,' he said. 'I believe you can.'

Shan had left a space for her in the back of the cart. She instinctively shut her eyes as he gently laid her down between two cold bodies. Then, remembering that this might be her last glimpse of her father, she opened them to find him ripping out stitches at the edge of his tunic. He removed something small and gold – his wedding ring. He pulled a spool of surgical thread and a needle from his pocket. Then he turned up the edge of Ling's tunic, held the ring against the cloth, and quickly stitched it into place.

'Give it to your mother,' he instructed as he sewed. 'Tell her I love her even more now than I did the day she put this ring on my hand. Tell her I look forward to the day when this is over, and she can put it on my hand once again.'

Ling couldn't speak. There was a lump in her throat.

'Tell your brothers to behave themselves, and Ling . . .'

'Yeah, Dad?'

'You're very strong and that's good. But never mistake kindness for weakness, no matter what Grandma Wen says.'

Ling nodded. At that moment, she didn't feel strong and she hated herself for it. She tried for a brave smile, but instead, her face crumpled. She threw her arms around her father's neck and hugged him tightly. A sob escaped her, and then another.

'Shh, *bao bei*, shh. The dead don't cry,' he whispered.

'Come with me, Dad,' Ling said.

'It's too dangerous. Zhen always checks with me before he leaves to make sure he's got all the bodies. He'd think it was strange if I wasn't here.' Shan kissed his daughter's cheek, then released her. 'Are you ready?'

'Yes,' Ling said, wiping her eyes.

'Okay, then. Now I have to' – he swallowed with difficulty – 'I have to cover you with more bodies before Zhen comes back.'

Fear made Ling's mouth go dry too. She tried to imagine herself elsewhere. Anywhere but here.

Her father worked all around her first. When he started to ease a body directly on top of her, he lost his nerve.

'Do it,' Ling said, finding her strength again.

He nodded, and lowered the body. Suddenly Ling was completely surrounded. Her back was pressed against a merman's cold, stiff chest. Her arms were pinned down by more dead flesh. The back of a lifeless young mermaid's head covered Ling's face. She could see the merl's slender, pale neck. For a second, hysteria seized her. She wanted to scream and crawl out from the corpses. Instead, she dug her nails into her palms and the pain brought her back to her senses.

'Lie perfectly still,' her father whispered.

'I will, Dad. *Go*.'

Shan swam down off the cart and closed the back.

'That the last of 'em, doc?' a voice called out.

'That's it,' Shan replied.

'Poor slobs,' Zhen said. 'Well, at least they're free of this place. Night, Shan.'

'Good night . . .' Shan said.

As the death cart lurched forward, Shan spoke again, but in a voice so low and soft that only Ling could hear it.

'. . . and godspeed.'

THIRTY-SEVEN

LING FELT THE DEATH CART SLOW.

'Stop, Zhen,' a lazy voice drawled.

'Why? You searching the cart tonight?' the driver asked.

'Not me. We got orders not to touch any fever bodies.'

Ling, who'd been rigid with fear, relaxed. The guards were no longer searching the carts. Thank the gods. Any second now, Zhen would crack his whip, and they'd be moving through the gates.

'So can I go?' Zhen asked impatiently. 'I want to dump these stiffs and get home. My wife's got a bowl of whelk stew waiting for me.'

'Hang on a minute, will you? We got a new system,' the death rider said.

'What is it? You poke 'em with spears or something?'

'No,' the guard said. 'We use the sea wasps.'

'Ha!' said Zhen. 'That'll make sure there're no live ones.'

Ling's blood turned to ice in her veins. Sea wasp venom was one of the most lethal substances known to mer.

If a tentacle found her, she wouldn't last for more than a few seconds.

'Pull up here, Zhen. Right at the gate,' the guard said.

The cart lurched forward.

It was over. She was truly dead. She'd never find the puzzle ball, or help Sera and the others defeat Abbadon. She'd never get her father's ring to her mother. Instead, she'd end up dumped in a common grave. No one would ever know what had become of her.

'I'm sorry, Sera,' she whispered. 'I'm sorry, Mum and Dad.'

She lay perfectly still, hands clenched, waiting for the pain. There was a body on top of her, and it was dark out, but the sea wasps were giving off so much light that Ling could see the faces of the dead on either side of her. Suddenly a movement to her right caught her eye. She held her breath. A tentacle – blue and quick – came towards her. It wound around the neck of the dead merman next to her, snaked over his face, and then stopped only inches from her own.

Another tentacle slithered over the head of the mermaid on top of her. A third coiled around the neck of the merman on her left.

Then a whistle was heard, and the tentacles were gone.

'Go on, Zhen. You're good,' the guard shouted. 'If anything *was* alive in there, it's dead now!'

Ling exhaled. It was over. By some miracle, the tentacles had missed her. She'd survived.

And then everything went white.

The pain slammed into her as a tentacle slid across the bottom of her tail. Ling felt as if she'd bitten into an electric eel. She clamped down on a scream, gritting her teeth so hard, the cords stood out in her neck.

'Hey, Bella! Back in line!' the guard shouted. 'Swear to gods, Zhen, these things are so damn mean, they'll sting anything – a dead mer, a rock, even each other – just for the fun of it.'

As quickly as it had come, the tentacle was gone again. But the pain was not.

Ling's heartbeat was a crazy staccato. Lights flashed behind her eyes. She dimly heard the guard wave the driver on. The cart lurched forward and picked up speed. She tried to remember how long she was supposed to wait . . . fifteen minutes? Fifteen seconds? She couldn't think straight. It was as if the pain had shorted all the circuits in her brain. She started to convulse. The lights in her head turned into visions. On one side of her, the dead merman started to laugh. Snakes started twining through the hair of the mermaid above her. Terrified, Ling pushed her away. She pushed so hard, she flipped the body onto its side.

Have to get out! Ling's mind screamed. She struggled to sit up, then pulled her tail free. Crawling over the bodies, she made her way to the edge of the cart, then tumbled over the side. She hit the seafloor with a thud and lay on her back, chest heaving, hands scrabbling in the silt.

Sight and sound blurred together inside her head,

then broke apart.

Ling groaned in pain, then lost consciousness.

Only twenty yards from the camp.

THIRTY-EIGHT

'I DON'T LIKE THIS, LUCIA,' Bianca di Remora said, eyeing the decayed hulk looming above them.

HMS BRITANNIA was written on the ship's prow. Rust had devoured some of the letters. 'Then go back,' Lucia said crisply.

'And let you board a ghost ship alone? No way. We're *both* going back. We shouldn't have even come here. If anyone ever found out that we did . . .'

But Lucia wasn't listening; she'd already started for the top deck. She'd come to see Kharis and nothing was going to stop her. Bianca, fretting ever since they'd snuck out of the palace, trailed Lucia, wringing her hands.

Vallerio *still* hadn't attacked the Black Fins. *Soon*, he'd said, when Lucia had asked him why not. *I can't send my troops to the Kargjord right now. I have other tasks for them.* He'd refused to tell her what those tasks were, so Lucia had devised her own plan for dealing with Serafina. And Kharis, a servant of the death goddess Morsa, had something for her

– something she desperately needed in order to set that plan in motion.

Figures flitted inside the ship. Lucia glimpsed them as she swam past portholes to the aft deck. She heard laughter. Glasses clinking. A piano playing.

The *Britannia* had been a luxury ocean liner. A storm had taken her down in the Adriatic Sea in the summer of 1926. Nearly a thousand had perished, passengers and crew.

Humans who died under the water became ghosts. Their bodies decomposed, but their souls lived on trapped beneath the waves – restless and hungry. The *Britannia* pulsed with the force of its ghost passengers' longing. Lucia could hear it in the mournful groaning of the ship's hull. She could feel it in the shuddering of its deck.

The *Britannia* hadn't broken up as she'd sunk, but had settled in one piece on the seafloor, listing slightly to her port side. Her smokestacks still stood, as did the pilothouse. Lifeboats remained in position.

On the top deck, crabs scuttled over upended deck chairs. Tiny fish darted in and out of a woman's shoe. Anemones clustered on hats, books, a pair of binoculars.

Other creatures lived on the decks, too, growling deep in their decayed throats, staggering on their tattered legs, swivelling their eyeless heads.

Rotters.

Bianca grabbed Lucia's arm. 'What are they?' she asked, terrified. 'They look like dead terragoggs.'

'They are,' Lucia said. 'They died in the *Britannia*'s wreck, too. The priestess uses them for protection. They kill anyone – human or mer – who tries to board the ship.'

Unlike ghosts, rotters possessed no soul. They were merely the decaying bodies of humans who'd died on the surface of the water. Their souls had been released at death, and their bodies had sunk to the seafloor. Practitioners of darksong knew how to reanimate the bodies and make them do their bidding.

The rotters lumbered towards Lucia and Bianca now, their hands swiping at the water. Bianca screamed. She tried to pull Lucia away, but Lucia shook her off.

'I am Lucia, regina of Miromara. Take me to Kharis,' she ordered.

The rotters stopped their attack. Their growls became sullen. They turned and headed for an arched doorway.

'Ghosts shun rotters. They think they're disgusting,' Lucia said, following them.

'I can't imagine why,' said Bianca, her voice trembling.

'We need to stay close to them. They'll keep us safe.'

'How do you know all this?' Bianca asked, hurrying to keep up with her.

'I've come here before,' Lucia replied. 'Many times.'

'*Alone?*' Bianca asked, looking at her with a mixture of disbelief and awe.

Lucia nodded. Temples to Morsa, the scavenger goddess of death, were outlawed, but a few still existed – if one knew where to look. A couple of doubloons placed in the right hands bought names and locations. The priestess Kharis had chosen the ghost ship because she knew that fear of its inhabitants would allow her to do her dark work without interference by the authorities.

Lucia knew the way to Kharis's altar, but she allowed the rotters to lead her. They took her down a grand staircase that led into an enormous ballroom. Gleaming mahogany banisters swept down either side of the staircase, and it was lined with bronze statues of sea nymphs. High above it, electric chandeliers hung from the gilded ceiling.

At the ballroom's far end, a ghost orchestra played. Revellers danced and laughed. Women with bobbed hair wore sparkly sleeveless dresses. Diamonds dangled from their ears and glinted on their hands. Their cheeks were powdered and pale; their lips painted vermilion.

Men wore tuxedoes. Their short hair was slicked back off their foreheads. They all looked just as they had in the seconds before the storm-tossed sea sent a rogue wave hurtling at their ship.

Bianca stopped at the top of the stairs as the rotters lurched down it. 'Look at them all,' she whispered, fearfully eyeing the shipwreck ghosts. 'We'll never get through.'

'Stay here if you like,' Lucia said. She'd inserted herself into the middle of the rotters for safety, and Bianca had no choice but to do the same.

The ghosts sensed the mermaids immediately. The music stopped playing. The revellers stopped dancing. Lucia knew it was the ghosts' energy that kept the ship alive and the ballroom looking exactly as it had.

As the two mermaids crossed the dance floor, the ghosts strained towards them. Only the rotters, growling and swatting, kept them away. Lucia could feel the ghosts' hunger. They were greedy for the life that surged in her veins.

The mermaids exited the ballroom and moved down panelled hallways, past lounges with silk wall coverings and electric lamps, through a pair of swinging doors and into the ship's enormous kitchens, where chefs brandished gleaming cleavers and waiters walked with trays on their shoulders. A maître d' with a pencil-thin moustache eyed them ravenously.

'How much further?' Bianca asked weakly as they left the kitchen and swam down another long hallway.

'Just through here,' Lucia replied, pointing ahead.

The rotters pushed open a pair of tall wooden doors and the mermaids emerged in the ship's theatre. Passengers had come here for concerts, plays, and silent movies.

Gold-fringed red velvet curtains hung across an elevated stage. On them had been painted an image of Morsa. The goddess had a skull for a face, a woman's torso and the lower body of a serpent. A crown of black scorpions, tails poised to strike, adorned her head. Waterfire burned in bronze cauldrons, set on either side of the goddess. In front of her, a mermaid wearing crimson sea-silk robes was chanting. When she finished, she turned around, as if she'd known Lucia and Bianca had entered the room.

Lucia dipped her head. 'Greetings, Priestess,' she said.

Kharis, kohl-eyed, her hair moving around her head like dozens of black sea snakes, returned Lucia's bow. 'Your

Grace,' she said. 'I am honoured by your visit. Have you come to admire my work?'

'I have. And to further it,' Lucia replied.

She opened the bag she'd brought with her and pulled out its contents one by one.

'A lock of Mahdi's hair,' she said, handing Kharis a glossy black twist she'd clipped from his head before leaving the Depth Charge. Next came a small crystal scent bottle filled with a dark crimson liquid. 'A vial of his blood,' she said. She'd also thought to capture a bloodsong she'd pulled at the nightclub, knowing well the sort of ingredients Kharis's magic required. 'And finally, a possession of Serafina's – her jacket.'

'Well done!' Kharis said, taking the objects. 'Would you like to see my creation?'

Lucia nodded.

Kharis sang a strange songspell in a minor key that Lucia had never heard before. An instant later, the red curtains parted and a merman swam into the centre of the stage.

Lucia caught her breath.

Bianca shook her head. She looked at the figure as if her eyes were playing tricks on her. 'Mahdi?' she said uncertainly. 'How did *you* get here?'

THIRTY-NINE

LUCIA SWAM AROUND Kharis's creation. 'He's perfect,' she purred, her eyes sparkling darkly. 'Absolutely *perfect*!'

'Of course he is.' Kharis sniffed. 'I made him and the goddess blessed him.'

'Mahdi? *Mahdi?*' Bianca said, swimming up to the stage.

'It's not the real Mahdi. It's a maligno, my dear,' Kharis said.

Bianca turned to her. 'A *what*?'

'A clay merman. Animated by blood magic and Lucia's to command as she pleases.'

Bianca's eyes widened. She backed away from the creature. 'To command? Command how?' She looked at her friend. 'What are you going to do, Lucia?'

'Kill Serafina,' Lucia replied, her gaze still on the maligno. She shifted it to Kharis. 'Why is he still here? Why hasn't he gone after her?'

'Ah, Your Grace,' Kharis said, her voice low and silky,

'the darkest of songspells carries a very high price.'

Lucia spun around. Her eyes hardened. 'I've given you a great deal of gold already, Kharis,' she said coldly. 'What more do you want?'

'It is not what *I* want, Your Grace, but what the goddess demands,' Kharis said, gesturing to the image of Morsa. 'The price of death is death.'

Lucia had visited Kharis many times, and had never felt afraid – until now. She knew what Kharis was asking, but how could she do it? That's what others were for – Traho and his soldiers, Baco Goga, her father's assassins.

Bianca understood what Kharis was asking, too. Her horror was written on her face. She hurried to Lucia.

'Luce, *no*,' she said, desperation in her voice. 'You can't. It's *murder*. The goddess will take her victim's life, and then she'll take your soul. We need to get out of here. *Please!*'

Bianca grabbed her hand, and Lucia – dazed by Kharis's request – let herself be led away.

'Death for death, Your Grace, or I must return your handsome Mahdi to the bed of clay from which I took him,' Kharis said.

. . . your handsome Mahdi . . .

The words echoed in Lucia's mind. But he wasn't hers, no matter how much she wanted him to be, because Serafina had tricked Mahdi into Promising himself to *her*. Promising vows were binding. If anyone who'd been Promised to one mer tried to marry another, the notes of his or her marriage songspell would fall flat.

Lucia knew that as long as Sera was alive, Mahdi would never be hers.

'Your Grace . . .' Kharis said.

Lucia stopped dead. '*No*,' she said.

Bianca let out a ragged sigh of relief. 'Thank gods you've come to your senses. Come on, Luce,' she said, tugging on her hand. 'Let's get back to the palace.'

But Bianca misunderstood.

Lucia stopped. She cocked her head and gazed at her friend. *This is what little fish are for*, a voice inside her said. *To feed big fish*.

'Bring me a sacrifice for the goddess, Your Grace,' Kharis demanded. 'Before the moon wanes.'

Lucia smiled. She tightened her grip on Bianca's hand.

'Not to worry, Kharis,' she said, her eyes glittering darkly. 'I already have.'

FORTY

CONSCIOUSNESS CAME SLOWLY. And painfully.

Ling felt as if she was crawling out of a deep, dark pit. Every bone ached; every muscle throbbed. She knew her body was reacting to the sea wasp venom.

Her eyes were badly swollen. It was hard to breathe, too. It felt as if something was sitting on her chest.

Ling tried to raise her hands, gritting her teeth against the pain, but she couldn't do that, either. Her arms were pinned to the ground.

That's when she realized that something was on top of her. Something smooth, warm, and very much alive. It was pressing down on her, squeezing the water from her lungs.

'I – I . . . can't breathe . . . Get off . . .' she moaned, struggling against the weight.

'*Get off?!* That's the thanks I get?' an indignant voice asked in RaySay.

Ling stopped struggling. She forced her eyes open. Another pair of eyes, widely spaced and unamused, was looking down at her. Below them, two rows of gills opened and closed rhythmically. Ling realized she was underneath a giant manta ray.

'I saved your life, rude little merl. The least you could do is say thank you.'

'Th-thank you,' Ling rasped. 'Where am I?'

'Far too close to the camp from which you tried to escape,' the ray replied.

'But how—' Ling's words were cut off by a violent bout of coughing. The spasm left her gasping for breath.

'Close your mouth, mermaid, and *listen*,' the ray said. 'Listening is more important than talking.'

Ling did as she was told and the ray continued.

'Last night your father called me through the sea wasp fence. He begged me to follow the cart, to make sure you were all right. He, unlike you, is gracious and polite. He helped my daughter once, by untangling her from fishing line, so I agreed to help his. I saw you crawl out of the cart and fall to the ground. Luckily, the guard did not. I hid you all night, but we have to go now. It's nearly dawn and the waters are lightening. I'll swim down the current and into the hills. You swim directly under me so no one can see you.'

The ray rose slightly as she spoke, giving Ling room to move. Ling tried to swim, but couldn't. The base of her tail, where the sea wasp had stung her, was twice its normal size. She couldn't even feel her tail fins.

'I can't move my tail,' she said, panic rising in her. If the ray swam off, she'd be exposed.

The ray huffed water through her gills, irritated. 'Take hold of me, then. I'll carry you as far as I can,' she said.

With effort, Ling hooked her hands over the tops of the manta's wings. The ray silently glided off with Ling hanging on underneath. Only a creature with the eyesight of an osprey would have been able to see Ling's hands, and the guard on duty was no such creature.

The ray swam for what felt like forever to Ling. She stopped when they reached a range of craggy, coral-covered hills.

'This is where I leave you,' she said. 'We're well away from the camp now and there's an old eel cave directly below us. You can hole up in there until you're better. Or dead.'

Rays, Ling knew, were not known for their subtlety. She released the strong, graceful creature. 'Thank you,' she said. 'You saved my life.'

The ray looked at her with a pitying expression, then glided off. 'No food, no currensea, no weapons and a bad case of venom sickness,' she said, her voice trailing away. 'I'm not sure *I'd* be saying thank you. Good luck, mermaid. You're going to need it.'

FORTY-ONE

SERA, HER ELBOWS on the makeshift table in the Black Fins' command cave, massaged her temples. A stocky merman, Antonio, the camp's cook, floated before her. He was furious.

'The goblins are starting trouble. *Again*,' he complained. 'They're angry about the flatworm stew. I've been serving it for three days straight. I don't have a choice; it's all we've got. At breakfast, one of them said he'd cut my head off and eat *that* if I served stew again. You've got to *do* something.'

Sera rued the day she'd agreed to do business with Meerteufel traders. The shipments from Scaghaufen were always late and the quality poor.

'I'll send out hunting parties, Antonio,' she said. 'It will keep the goblins busy, and I'm sure they'll bag some conger eels. You can cook those.'

Antonio nodded and thanked Sera. After he left, Sera listened to Yazeed detail problems with the plans for the infirmary she wanted built. Then Neela reported that another group of civilians had arrived that morning – refugees from Miromara – but there was nowhere to put them. A goblin came in to tell her there weren't enough tables in the mess hall.

The Black Fins had arrived in the Kargjord two weeks ago. The goblin fighters Guldemar had promised had begun to report for duty, too. Soon they would begin military drills, and Sera would have to oversee them. Children like the mermaid Coco, and the ones who arrived daily with their refugee parents, needed a school to attend. Many needed medical attention. And then there were the daunting tasks of housing and feeding everyone.

Running a large camp was overwhelming. Before Sera could solve one problem, ten more cropped up. Operating on little food, and even less sleep, she often sent prayers to the twin gods of the tides, Trykel and Spume, asking them to turn their forces in her favour. She wondered now if they ever would.

As Sera was suggesting to the goblin – his name was Garstig – that perhaps he and his fellow soldiers could *build* some tables, a mermaid appeared in the cave's entrance, accompanied by a Black Fin. She looked exhausted. Her clothing was covered in silt. She carried a messenger bag slung over her shoulder. She had short brown hair. Her grey eyes darted warily. Her hands, clutching the strap of her bag, looked strong and rough.

'Why is she here?' Yaz asked the Black Fin. His eyes travelled to her bag. 'Has she been searched?'

'I went through her bag. Patted her down. She doesn't have any weapons. She says she has to see Sera. Says it's life or death,' the Black Fin replied.

'I have something for her,' the mermaid said. 'From Miromara. My name is Daniella. My cousin is Allegra. She's a farmer from outside Cerulea.'

'Clear the cave,' Sera ordered.

Yaz raised an eyebrow.

'Just do it,' Sera said.

A minute later the only ones left in the cave were Sera, Yazeed, Neela, Sophia, and Daniella.

'Mahdi sent her,' Sera explained to the others. 'Her cousin Allegra delivers her farm's produce to the palace in Cerulea and receives conchs from him. Allegra has family members in the waters between Miromara and the North Sea. Each one carries the conch part of the way. Daniella was the courier for the last leg of the journey.'

Daniella nodded. 'My farm's just south of Scaghaufen,' she said, pulling a conch from her bag. She handed it to Sera.

'Thank you. You took a huge risk coming here and I'm very grateful,' Sera said. 'Please eat something and rest before you return home.'

Daniella nodded and swam out of the cave.

Sera placed the conch on the table, then cast an amplo spell so that everyone could hear the message it contained.

A voice started to speak – a merman's. He didn't address anyone by name, nor did he give his. Names were dangerous. They could get someone killed. Sera felt a deep relief upon hearing the voice – because it meant Mahdi was alive – or at least he had been when he'd made the recording. But she felt fearful, too, because his tone was urgent and his message grim.

'My suspicions have been confirmed,' he said. 'Vallerio *has* been plotting a move – a big one. He's sent death riders after two of the talismans – Nyx's ruby ring and Pyrrha's gold coin. Soldiers left today – Tidesday – for the Mississippi; more are leaving for Cape Horn tomorrow. Mfeme's transporting them in two of his ships. Get your operatives out of there immediately. I'll send another message as soon as I know more. Stay safe, all of you.'

The message ended. Everyone was silent. Sera, furious, rose and swam around the cave.

'How does my uncle *always* know things he can't *possibly* know?' she asked. '*No one* knows the locations of the talismans. No one but us.'

'Correction: no one *knew* the locations but us,' Yaz said.

'Why is Vallerio going to the Mississippi and Cape Horn?' Neela asked. 'Why not the Abyss, where Sycorax's puzzle ball is?'

It was Sophia who voiced the terrible thing they were all thinking. 'Maybe he already has the puzzle ball.'

Sera's heart sank at this possibility. How would they defeat Abbadon without *all* the talismans? And it seemed that Vallerio was about to close in on two more. Mahdi said the death riders had set off on Tidesday – that was already four days ago. 'We've got to do a convoca. Now. Ava and Becca are in serious danger,' she said, sitting back down.

'It's too risky,' Yaz said. 'The moon's waning. The Karg's bad for casting. Songspells don't carry properly here because of the iron in the rocks. Someone could listen in.'

'I don't have a choice, Yaz,' Sera countered. 'They could be swimming straight into a trap.'

Yaz ran a hand through his hair. 'Okay,' he finally said. 'Give it everything you've got.'

Sera, Yaz, Neela, and Sophia all joined hands. Sera found that her convocas were tighter and stronger if she cast them as part of a circle. She sang the words of the songspell.

I send my voice
Throughout the waters,
Trying to summon
Merrow's daughters.
Our minds are one,
Our hearts bloodbound.
Great Neria, help them
hear this sound.

But nothing happened.

'Come *on*, Ava,' she whispered. 'Where *are* you, Becca?'

She cast again but still couldn't get her friends. On her third try, she got a choppy image.

'Becca!' she shouted.

'Sera, Neela? Is that you?' Becca asked blearily. She'd been asleep.

'Yes!' Sera said. 'Hold on . . . I'm trying to get Ava . . .'

On her fifth attempt, she succeeded. She was overjoyed to see Ava, but her happiness turned to alarm as she noted how gaunt her friend looked.

'Ava, where are you? Is Baby with you?'

'He's here, *querida*,' Ava said.

'Good,' Sera said, glad to hear it. That nasty little piranha was Ava's fierce defender.

'I'm at . . . off the . . .' The sound crackled. Ava faded, then came back.

'Listen, I have to be quick,' Sera said. 'I just received bad news. Vallerio found out where Nyx's ring is and Pyrrha's coin. He sent troops to get them.'

'*What?* How did he find out?' Becca asked.

'I have no idea,' Sera replied. 'I *do* know that the death riders left Cerulea several days ago. They're on board Mfeme's ships, which means they're moving fast.'

'How long until they get to Cape Horn?' Becca asked.

Sera looked at Yaz.

'Five days max,' he said.

'I can beat them,' Becca said.

'Becca, what if you're wrong? What if they capture you?'

'I can *do* this, Sera. I . . .'

Becca faded out, then came back.

'Be careful, Becca. *Please*,' Sera begged.

'I will . . . soon . . . okay? Signing off.'

And then she was gone. Ava's image was fading, too.

'Ava, where are you?' Sera asked.

'In the mouth of the Mississippi. I've still got a ways to go to reach the Okwa Naholos' swamp.'

'Not good,' Yaz said. 'By my calculations, the death riders will get there in six days themselves, maybe five if they push hard. Get her out of there, Sera.'

'Ava, did you hear Yazeed?' Sera shouted. Ava was blurring.

'No! What did he say?'

'He said you need to get out of there!' Sera yelled.

Ava snorted. 'And let Traho get that sick ruby ring? I don't think so, *gatinha*. It'll look way better on me than it would on him!'

'Ava, it's *too* risky!'

'How many days have I got?'

'Six, then. But you also need time to get out of the swamp.'

Ava shook her head. '*Sixteen?* What are you worried about? That's plenty of time!'

'Not *sixteen*, Ava! *Six!*' Sera yelled frantically.

'Lost you, *mina* . . . Don't worry . . . can make it . . .'

The convoca faded. Ava was gone.

'Oh, gods,' Sera said, her voice breaking. 'She's chum.'

Sera was silent for a moment, as she tried to regain control of her emotions. Her mind worked its way back to the question she'd asked before.

'How did Vallerio find out? *How?* Of everyone in this camp, only we know the location of the talismans. I've kept it that way on purpose.'

'Maybe somebody cast an ochi on us,' Yaz ventured.

Sera shook her head. 'There's no way. This cave is swept for gândacs every day.'

'According to Mahdi, Baco Goga was seen around the palace,' Yaz reminded her. 'You told us so yourself.'

'Yes, but he wasn't seen *here*,' Sera said.

'He could have turned someone in the camp. That someone may have overheard one of us and reported the info to Baco.'

The mere thought of a spy in their midst sent a shiver through Sera.

Yaz saw it. 'Where's your jacket?' he asked.

'I have no idea. I've been looking for it for days,' Sera said distractedly.

Sophia unbuttoned her jacket now and handed it to Sera. Both mermaids had acquired new jackets after using their old ones to bandage Sera's tail, but it seemed Sera had lost hers.

'I can't take that, Soph,' Sera said.

'Actually, you can,' Sophia replied. 'We can't afford for you to get sick.'

'Thank you,' Sera said, shrugging into the garment. 'I don't know how Vallerio's getting his information, but he can't be allowed to capture Ava and Becca.'

'How do we stop him?' Neela asked.

Sera had an idea. 'We've got troops now, so let's use them,' she said. 'We don't have a super trawler to get our soldiers where they need to go, but we can cast velo spells. And enlist the help of whales, too. In a battle of goblins against death riders, I'd back the goblins any day.'

'This is a real long shot. You know that, right?' Yazeed said.

Sera laughed wearily. 'What *isn't* a long shot, Yaz? I am. You are. This entire camp is. I'm getting used to making long shots work. We've *got* to protect Ava and Becca,' she said.

As Neela and Sophia started to work out how many goblins should be sent to the Mississippi and Cape Horn, Yaz consulted maps to determine the quickest routes.

Sera started out for the munitions cave. Her troops would need crossbows and arrows and she wanted to see how many of each had arrived.

As she swam, worried for her friends but emboldened by her plans, she met the truth head-on. There was no point in waiting for the fickle gods Trykel and Spume to help her. If she wanted the tide to turn, she'd have to turn it herself.

FORTY-TWO

'YOU LOVE HER, don't you?' Des asked Astrid, his eyes crinkling as he smiled.

Astrid, watching Elskan charge off after a school of herring, laughed. 'I guess so. As much as I can love a headstrong, wilful, bad-tempered beast.'

'I think that's *why* you love her. She's strong, spirited and does pretty much as she pleases.' He gave Astrid a sidelong glance. 'Kind of like someone else I know.'

Astrid rolled her eyes. She and Des had been travelling together for three days now and they'd developed an easy, teasing way with each other.

And they had plenty to tease about. They'd both almost fallen off when Elskan had bolted out of Ludo's stable. They'd both been bucked off on several occasions. And Elskan had nipped each of them countless times. Des was missing a few scales on his backside thanks to the orca.

But Des wasn't just a joker. He was sober and serious when he needed to be, and an exceedingly capable soldier.

He knew how to find food or trap it, how to hide all traces of a campsite, and how to cast a superfast camo spell. He knew when schools of haddock or cod were approaching and always made sure he and Astrid got off Elskan when they did so the orca could chase down a meal.

He was sensitive, too. He seemed to know when to give her space to mourn her father. And Astrid did the same for him, allowing him privacy when he became quiet, guessing that he was thinking about his parents.

Nights were the hardest. That was when thoughts and memories crowded in. She and Des would untack Elskan, allow her to hunt – as they'd done just now – and give her a rubdown when she returned. Then they'd set up camp, eat and sleep.

Except that Astrid usually couldn't sleep. She'd sit up and watch fish swim to the surface to feed, let a little blue crab crawl up her arm or gaze at a lion's mane jellyfish drifting by, all the while thinking about Kolfinn and how Rylka had murdered him. And her heart would ache with sorrow and burn with fury.

She admired Des – he was Des to her now – and respected him, and wished to the gods she could tell him her secret. It was hard to keep trying to hide it. She had to constantly invent excuses to explain why she didn't songcast an illuminata or a camo spell when they needed one.

But she was afraid to reveal the truth. She knew the day was coming when she'd *have* to tell him – and Sera, Neela and everyone else – and she dreaded it. What if Kolfinn had been right? What if *no one* wanted a mermaid without magic?

'Elskan's hungry tonight,' Des said now, pulling Astrid out of her thoughts.

'So am I,' Astrid said. 'We only have a few bunches of squid eggs left. I hope the foraging's decent here.'

About half an hour ago, they'd found a large metal shipping container lying on the seafloor broken in two, its colourful but inedible contents spilling out, and had decided to shelter inside it for the night. Sunken containers weren't uncommon. Rough seas sometimes knocked them off the decks of ships.

Tomorrow morning they'd resume their journey to the Kargjord. Only they were making one stop on the way – at the Qanikkaaq. Sera had asked her to get the black pearl, hoping that Vallerio or Mfeme hadn't beaten them to it, and Astrid had refused. But that was before Kolfinn had been murdered. Before she'd become an outlaw. Before Des. Before she'd decided to follow the current Vrăja had set out for her.

Without the black pearl there was no defeating Abbadon. And Astrid knew now that killing the monster, and besting those who were trying to free it, was the only way to save Ondalina. She'd told Des what she wanted to do and he'd immediately offered to help.

'I saw what I think was a water apple orchard a little ways back. Just before we stopped to untack Elskan,' he said now. 'Want to go see if I'm right?'

Astrid nodded. She started to follow him, then halted and frowned.

'What's wrong?'

'I – I don't know. Do you hear something?'

Des listened, then shook his head. 'Do you?'

'It sounds like a voice.'

Des's hand went to the hilt of his sword. He turned in a slow circle, a wary look on his face. 'I don't see anyone,' he said.

'I don't, either,' said Astrid. She heard the noise again. 'I think it's in my head, Des.'

'Is it a convoca?'

'I think so. This happened to me once before, when I was with Becca. I thought I was losing my mind, but it turned out to be your sister. That might be what I'm hearing now.'

'Where were you the last time it happened?

'In Atlantica.'

'No, I mean were you near anything that enhances magic? On the surface, in moonlight? Near whalefall?'

Astrid snapped her fingers. 'Yes, I was! I was in a whale cemetery.'

'Maybe we're close to one,' Des said, looking around. 'Forget the water apples for now.' He nodded at a hill ahead. 'Let's see what's behind that.'

'Hang on a sec,' Astrid said. 'Speaking of whales . . . where did Elskan go?'

Des pointed up above them. The orca was breaching. As she hit the water, then dived, Astrid cupped her hands around her mouth.

'Elskan!' she shouted. 'ELSKAN!'

The orca rolled over like a big black-and-white barrel. With her belly facing the surface, she peered down at Astrid.

'Don't. Go. *Far!*'

Elskan snorted. She righted herself, flipped her tail and sped off.

'Unbelievable,' Astrid said, shaking her head.

'She'll be back,' Des said.

The two mer swam towards the craggy seamount, crested the top and dived down.

'Look,' Des said, pointing to his right. 'Over there.'

'Good eyes,' Astrid said. About seventy yards away was the corpse of a large humpback. Scavengers – fish, crabs and worms – were picking it clean.

Astrid and Des sped towards the whalefall, but as they drew close, Astrid realized that something else was crouched over the carcass – something pale and wraithlike.

Her heart lurched. She grabbed Des's arm, stopping him short.

'Why are we—' he started to say.

Astrid shook her head. She held a finger to her lips and tried to back away quietly, pulling him with her. But it was too late.

The creature looked up. Its white eyes fastened on them. Using its long, clawed hands, it scrabbled over the rotting whale towards them. Ragged seaweed ropes that were entangled with the bodies of dead mer and drowned terragoggs trailed after it.

'What the—' Des started to say.

'It's an EisGeist,' Astrid replied, pulling her sword from its scabbard. 'Get ready for a fight.'

FORTY-THREE

THE SPECTRE SCUTTLED closer. Its grey hair floated crazily around its head. Its white lips curled into a snarl, revealing teeth as jagged and sharp as shards of glass.

'Don't let it near you, Des!'

'As if!' Des said, holding his sword out in front of him.

'It strangles its victims and drags them around until they rot. It eats bones.'

'Astrid, I *so* don't care! Just tell me how to kill it!' Des shouted, saucer-eyed.

'You *can't* kill it! It's a spirit,' Astrid shouted back.

'Great! That's just *great*! What do I do?'

'I'll draw it to me. When I do, cut the seaweed. Make like you're going to steal its swag.'

Des eyed a dead gogg in a wetsuit. 'Ugh, really?'

'It'll try to knot the ropes back together. When it does, we bolt.'

Astrid advanced on the EisGeist. It crouched low, ready to spring at her.

Astrid . . .

That wasn't Des. It was another voice. Inside Astrid's head. It was stronger now, because she was so close to whalebones.

'You have *got* to be joking,' she said.

Astrid, it's me . . .

'Yeah, I *know*. Not now, Sera, okay? I'm right in the middle of something!'

'What did you say?' Des shouted. He was close to the EisGeist now.

'Nothing. Cut the ropes!'

The EisGeist, clever and quick, wheeled around and advanced on Des. It had purposely let him come close so it could attack him.

'Hey! HEY!' Astrid shouted. She rushed at the creature, hacking at it with her sword. The blade went right through it, but the ghost must've felt something because it turned, growling, and rushed at her.

'The *ropes*, Des! Cut the ropes,' Astrid shouted.

'I can't! I think they're enchanted!' Des yelled.

Astrid . . . are you there?

'Not NOW, Sera,' Astrid said, through gritted teeth. The EisGeist wheeled around and moved towards Des. Astrid saw her opening and attacked, but the ghost was only feinting. It turned suddenly, wrapped its hands around the hilt of Astrid's sword and wrenched it away from her. Then it thrust the blade at her, missing her head by a hairsbreadth.

Astrid tried to get away from it, but the ghost had

forced her up against an outcropping of rock. She had nowhere to go.

The EisGeist raised the sword over its head, ready to bring the blade down on Astrid, but before it could, there was a black-and-white blur in the water. Elskan slammed into the spectre, knocking the sword out of its hands.

The ghost screeched and spun around. It swiped at Elskan. Its long claws raked gashes in the orca's side. She roared in pain, turned in the water and charged again.

'Elskan, the ropes!' Astrid shouted.

At the last second, Elskan swerved from the ghost to the seaweed. She opened her mouth wide and bit down hard on the thick ropes, cutting them in two. The EisGeist's enchantment was no match for the whale's magic and her lethally sharp teeth.

Des was right behind the whale. He grabbed the ends of the ropes that were attached to the treasure, twisted them together, and whistled for Elskan. She turned and sped back.

The EisGeist, unaware it had been separated from its hoard, was scurrying towards Astrid once again.

'Go, Elskan! Fast as you can, girl! Dump it and come back!' Des told the whale.

The ghost lunged at Astrid, ready to grab her by the throat, but Elskan shook the ropes, rattling the bones caught up in it.

The EisGeist turned and snarled. Elskan backed up slowly, luring the spectre away from Astrid. The orca shook the ropes again, then streaked away.

Shrieking with rage, the EisGeist rushed after the whale. It was fast, but Elskan was faster.

'Is it gone?' Astrid asked Des, panting.

ASTRID!

Astrid winced. Her hands went to her ears. 'Do you *always* have to be so loud?'

Desiderio blinked. 'I didn't even say anything.'

'Not you . . .'

What's happening? Are you all right? Sera asked anxiously.

'We just fought off an EisGeist,' Astrid replied.

'Yeah, I know that. I was here,' Des said.

Are you all right? Is there someone with you?

'I'm . . . uh . . . I'm not familiar with the songspell for convocas,' Astrid said, desperately hoping Sera wouldn't ask her to songcast. 'Is there some way of including a mer who's nearby?' She glanced at Des.

Take her hands. Sometimes that works, Sera advised.

'It's a he.'

She offered her hands to Des. He gave her a quizzical look, but took them. A warmth flooded through her at his touch.

She told herself it was just the convoca and closed her eyes. Des did the same. They immediately saw each other in the convoca. So did Sera.

'Des!' Sera cried. Her hands flew to her mouth. Neela and Yazeed flickered and faded. Sera quickly grabbed for them again.

'Hey, little sister. Is that you?' Des said. He was trying to sound cool, but Astrid could hear the emotion in his voice.

Sera tried to answer him, but she was overcome by tears. When she could finally speak again, she said, 'I was so worried, Des.'

'Astrid got me out of the Citadel's dungeons. She saved my life.'

'Th-thank you, Astrid,' Sera said, her voice hitching. 'Thank you so much.'

'Her own life's in danger now,' said Desiderio. 'She can't go home. Rylka wants her dead.'

'That's wonderful!' said Sera.

'Yeah, it . . . Wait – *what?*' Astrid said, scowling.

'Since you can't stay in Ondalina, you'll have to come here. Join us, Astrid,' Sera urged.

'It just so happens that I'm on my way,' Astrid said, pleased that Sera still wanted her. 'Des and I both.'

'I'm so happy to hear that!' Sera said. 'Where are you? When will you be here?'

'We're in the Greenland Sea. We should be there in three or four days. We're going to the Qanikkaaq first.'

Sera's smile dropped away. 'No! Don't! Just come to the Karg,' she pleaded.

Astrid blinked. 'Did I just hear you correctly?' she asked. 'The last time we talked, you begged me to go to the Qanikkaaq!'

'Now I'm begging you not to. Vallerio's sent death riders to the Mississippi and Cape Horn. That's why I convoca'd you. In case you changed your mind about the Qanikkaaq.

I'm scared he might send death riders to the maelstrom, too. You and Des could be taken.'

'What else is new, Sera?' Astrid said.

'We'll be okay,' Des assured his sister. 'We'll keep an eye out for Vallerio's soldiers. Astrid told me about the talismans and everything else. We're close to the Qanikkaaq now. We might not get another chance to see if the pearl's still there.'

Sera nodded unhappily. 'Be careful, both of you. Please,' she said. 'Astrid, I know how good you are with your sword, but use your magic, too, okay? You're going to need everything you've got.'

Astrid looked away. Tell her, a voice inside her urged. *Tell her now before you get yourself killed. And Des, too.*

But Astrid couldn't make the words come. She was too afraid. And even if she could, it was too late. The convoca was over. Sera was gone. Astrid released Des's hand.

'Sera's right,' Des said thoughtfully. 'We'll need every bit of magic we can muster to deal with the Qanikkaaq,' Des said. 'It's the biggest, ugliest maelstrom in all the waters. How's your stilo spell? Can you throw a decent frag?'

'I've got to find Elskan,' Astrid said briskly.

'I'll go with you.'

'It's okay. I've got it.'

Des looked puzzled by her suddenly curt tone. 'Hey, Astrid, what's up?'

'Nothing. I'm cool.'

'Yeah, I'll say. Like, icy cool.' Des gave her a look, but then softened. 'Are you worried about the maelstrom? Is that it? I'm not going to let you do this alone. I'll help you. We're in this together.'

Astrid couldn't look at him. 'Sure, Des,' she said. 'Thanks.'

Des nodded. Then he started off after Elskan.

He didn't see the sadness in Astrid's eyes, or hear her as she softly said, 'Yeah, Des, together. Until you find out the truth.'

FORTY-FOUR

'ASTRID KOLFINNSDOTTIR . . .'

'Mmmpff,' Astrid said, turning over in her sleep.

'Wake up.'

'Leave me alone . . . tired . . .'

'Time grows short.'

Astrid sat up, angry to be woken by yet another convoca. 'Argh! Ever hear of *boundaries*, Sera? It's got to be three in the morning! What do you want *now*?'

But Sera didn't answer her.

Astrid looked uneasily around the metal shipping container. It was full of gogg furniture, clothing and trinkets. Both she and Des had found mattresses. Des was sleeping soundly on his. Outside, Elskan was munching contentedly on some seal bones.

Something moved behind Astrid. She saw it out of the corner of her eye. In a flash she was out of bed and reaching for the dagger she kept tucked in her belt.

'There's no need to be frightened,' the voice said.

'I mean you no harm.'

A silvery light shone from the very back of the container. It hadn't been there when she and Des had settled down for the night. Astrid swam towards it now, her dagger in her hand. As she drew closer, she realized that the light was coming from a mirror. It was long and wide, and half-hidden behind a sofa.

A man was standing in the mirror. A human dressed in black and wearing sunglasses. He'd spoken to her once before, inside an abandoned house in a raided village.

'What do you want?' she asked him.

'You.'

'Who *are* you?' Astrid demanded.

The man replied with a question of his own.

'Where are you going, Astrid? To your *friends*?' His tone was mocking. 'Do you really think it will be different with them? What can you offer them? More importantly, what can they offer you? But I can offer you so much, child. If only you would let me.'

He walked up to the glass and pressed his palm against it.

Astrid backed away, worried that he meant to climb through from Vadus, the mirror realm. But he remained where he was, perfectly still, a half smile on his lips.

Slowly, Astrid moved towards him. She didn't understand why.

'Blood is strong, child. Stronger than the tides. Deeper than the sea itself,' the man said.

Astrid raised her hand and pressed it to the glass, her palm to his. As she did, she felt a jolt, as if an electric current was moving through her. She saw herself not as she was – weary and silt-streaked – but in a gown of black sea silk, wearing a crown of polished jet, her white-blonde hair swirling about her shoulders.

She was songcasting.

She was *singing*.

The man's fingers interlaced with her own. His grip was cold and strong. 'I have waited for you. For centuries.'

'No,' Astrid said. '*No*.'

She jerked her hand away as if she'd been burned. She was frightened – of herself. The image she'd seen of herself songcasting . . . she wanted it so badly, she'd nearly dived headlong into the mirror realm and into the presence of a man she didn't even know.

'Who *are* you?' she asked again.

'The blood knows. The blood calls.'

He smiled, and with a slight bow of his head, turned and walked back into the quicksilver world, down a long hall full of mirrors.

Astrid watched him until he disappeared.

'This isn't real,' she said out loud. 'It's only a dream.'

As she continued to gaze into the mirror, Vadus dimmed. She saw only her reflection now – the ice-blue eyes, the blonde braids, the strong nose and full mouth.

'It's only a dream,' she said again.

Then she lay back down on her mattress, stared into the darkness and tried her best to believe it.

FORTY-FIVE

Farewell and adieu to you, fair Spanish Ladies,
Farewell and adieu to you, ladies of Spain,
For we're under orders
For to sail to old England . . .

BECCA, HIDING IN a thicket of kelp, watched the dead sailors gathered around the wreck of the *Achilles*. She put her travelling case down. A silvery, sullen-faced codfish circled it.

'There must be hundreds of them,' Becca whispered. The ghosts were all wearing the clothing of their various times and singing an old naval ballad. Brass lanterns full of moon jellies illuminated them.

Some sported leather doublets laced across their chests. Others wore white tunics with squared collars. Peacoats. Yellow raincoats and rubber boots. Many had single gold hoops in their left earlobes – a badge of honour indicating that the bearer had survived an eastbound run around Cape Horn.

They were shipwreck ghosts. The Williwaw, a wind spirit who lived in a sea cave at the cape, had sent them to their deaths, whipping up fierce storms that destroyed their ships. Yet the sailors bore the spirit no ill will and in fact served him by guarding the underwater entrance to his lair. They'd known the risks of a seaman's life, and the alternative to a watery grave – being buried topside in the cold, hard ground – held no appeal.

They spent their deaths much as they'd spent their lives – telling stories of seas they'd sailed and ships they'd loved. They played cards. Threw dice. Laughed and fought. They made music with accordions and fiddles. Danced hornpipes. The ghosts were merry, loud – and lethal to any mer who came too close.

Becca had been sternly warned to stay well away from them – and the Williwaw – by the owner of a bubble tea shop in a nearby village.

'The Williwaw's deadly,' the merman had said, after Becca had asked him how to find the spirit's lair. 'It's like a giant bird of prey, vicious and territorial. It spends a good deal of time building up its nest. That's why it sinks ships, so it can carry off their rigging and timber and bring it back to its cave. Few have got close to it. If it doesn't kill you, its shipwreck ghosts will. Best to give up this foolish idea.'

'I take your point,' Becca had said, 'but giving up's not an option. The Williwaw has something I need.'

Once the merman saw that he couldn't dissuade her, he had told her more.

'The creature lives in a sea cave inside a rock formation off the cape. Half the cave's submerged, half of it's dry. It flies in and out through an opening above the waterline. Its nest sits on a broad ledge.'

Becca's heart had sunk at that. 'I can't fly,' she had said. 'Is there any other way to get inside the cave?'

'There is – for any mer brave enough to attempt it. Through the *Achilles*.'

'What is it and how do I get to it?' Becca had asked excitedly.

'It's a brigantine that went down in 1793. The captain's name was Maffeio Aermore,' the merman had explained. 'Stories about him persist to this day. Mer who saw his ship go down said he must've been insane, because he steered for the rocks that shelter the Williwaw's cave. The spirit saw the ship coming and sank it. The crew was lost, though some say the captain survived. Hard to believe, if you ask me.'

'Why would a captain sail straight into rocks?' Becca had asked, mystified.

'Ask his crew. You'll be swimming right by them,' the merman had joked.

'What do I do when I find the *Achilles*?'

'You have to swim through the wreck, then through a crack in the base of the rock. It leads to a tunnel. Follow it and you'll find yourself inside the cave,' the merman had said. 'Only a handful have managed it. They all cast transparensea pearls to get past the ghosts. That's the only way. But it's no guarantee. Even if you're invisible, you still make vibrations in the water and the ghosts can feel them. That's about all I can tell you. Good luck.'

The bubble tea seller had given Becca good directions, and she'd found the *Achilles* without much trouble.

As she peered out of the kelp thicket now, she could even see a way into the wreck – through a jagged hole in its hull.

'First thing I have to do,' she whispered, 'is sneak past the ghosts.'

She shuddered to think what would happen if she didn't succeed. The ghosts were jolly with one another, but if they sensed a soul nearby – mer or human – they instantly turned savage. They craved the rush of blood through the veins, the beating of a brave heart. Becca knew they would converge on her, and the touch of so many would drain the life from her body in an instant.

But hopefully that wouldn't happen.

Because Becca, as usual, had a plan.

FORTY-SIX

'*ALL* THE SQUID. NOW,' the codfish said.

'No. I've explained the deal,' Becca said firmly. 'Half of the squid now, half when you get me back out.'

The cod shook his head stubbornly.

'Okay, then. No squid. Ever. Does *that* work for you?' Becca asked huffily.

The cod glowered. He jutted his jaw.

Becca opened her travelling case and pulled out one of two bags of fresh squid she'd bought in the village. She popped a squid into her mouth and ate it.

'Mmm. So good,' she said, savouring it. 'Sweet and chewy.'

'Okay, mermaid,' the cod said. 'Half now, half later. Stop eating my squid.'

Becca had come across the large fish on her way out of the village, and he'd given her an idea. The bubble tea seller had said that she'd need to make herself invisible, but that she'd still create movement the ghosts could sense. The large cod could cover her. If they swam into the wreck together, the ghosts would think that the fish was the one making vibrations.

Becca knew that cod loved squid, so she'd hurried back to the village and bought some. Then she'd got the cod to agree, and they'd made their way to the *Achilles*.

Becca held out one bag of squid to him now, her eyes on the wreck.

'Here, let me grab that with my hands. Oh, wait a minute . . . I don't have any!' the cod said. 'So *not* funny, merjerk.'

Becca hastily apologized. Acting like another sea creature had hands was bad form. She opened the bag and dumped out the squid for him.

'I didn't mean to be rude. Really,' she said. 'A few hundred shipwreck ghosts are kind of distracting.'

The cod snorted. 'You mer think you're so apex with your opposable thumbs, don't you? Hey, if a great white shows up, maybe you can thumb wrestle him. Me, I'll be swimming for it.'

Cod, Becca knew, were super touchy about their place in the food chain. She didn't hold it against him. Tuna and swordfish were the same way. Creatures hunted to the brink of extinction had a right to be prickly.

When the cod had finished eating, Becca said, 'Are you ready?'

He nodded.

'Okay,' Becca said, slipping the second bag of squid into a pocket, 'here we go. I lead, you follow. Stick close.'

She closed her travelling case and tucked it next to a rock.

It would be safe there. Then she reached into another pocket and pulled out the transparensea pebble that Vrăja had given her. She cast it and immediately became invisible.

Summoning all her courage, Becca swam out from the kelp and headed for the Achilles. The ghosts were still singing and dancing. Becca swam between two English sailors who, judging from their clothes, had died centuries ago. They were playing chess.

'You feel something?' one asked, as she passed them by.

'Aye, Jackie! Look out, it's yer wife! She's brandishing a rolling pin!' the other said.

Jackie jumped. He spun around, panic-stricken, then laughed when he saw the cod. 'Naw, that's not me wife,' he said. 'That fish is ten times prettier!'

Yes! Becca thought excitedly. Her plan was working.

She glided past a Spanish sailor wearing a uniform last seen when Ferdinand V ruled. He was fencing with the blue-blazered owner of a yacht who looked like he'd drowned a week ago. The Spaniard, too, swiftly spun around as Becca swam by, cutlass raised, only to relax when he saw the cod.

She moved past more ghosts, careful to stay out of reach, until finally she reached the ship's hull. The hole was in the starboard bow. Becca carefully swam through it and made her way down the hold.

The inside of the ship was murky and filled with more ghosts. As she reached the stern, she spotted what she was searching for. There was another opening there, much larger than the one in the bow, and beyond it rose the rocky base of the Williwaw's lair. Becca could just make out the crack, jagged and wide, that the bubble tea seller had told her about.

Fear raised the scales along the back of her tail. She had no idea what she was swimming into, if the Williwaw was in its cave, where Pyrrha's gold coin might be, or even how long the transparensea pebble would last. She squeezed through the crack and found the passageway. It was dark, but Becca didn't dare cast an illuminata for fear it would be seen, so she had to feel her way along the walls. Creatures of the darkness – soft, slimy, and sightless – moved under her hands. After she'd been swimming down the passageway for five minutes or so, it started to angle up. The waters around her grew lighter.

A few seconds later, Becca surfaced in a soaring space. She tilted her head back and saw that the cave was conical in shape and the top had a large opening that let in air and light.

On a large, broad ledge just above the waterline, sat an enormous nest. It was made of ship's timbers, splintered masts, whalebone, human bones, sailcloth, rigging, pieces of fibreglass and shredded life jackets.

The nest was empty. The cave was empty. Becca was alone.

She heaved a sigh of relief, almost unable to believe her luck. But her relief quickly turned to discouragement as she realized Pyrrha's coin was nowhere to be seen. She'd thought the Williwaw might have a chest, or a special niche where he kept his treasures, but no. The small coin was probably somewhere in that giant nest, and it would take her ages to search it.

The cod poked his nose out of the water. 'Can I have the rest of my squid now?' he asked.

'Not until we leave,' Becca said.

The fish dived. He swam around in circles under the surface, grumbling.

Becca stuck her face in the water. 'Maybe you could *help* me?' she said. 'I need to find a gold coin, very old, with an image of Neria on it.'

'Maybe,' the cod said. 'Wouldn't count on it, though.'

Becca sighed and regarded the nest again. She knew she had to get herself inside it, but how?

She put her hands on the ledge, ready to boost herself up, but her arms were shaking so badly, she couldn't. Becca didn't like leaving the water, and a tail was not much good when it came to climbing. She also didn't like not having a plan.

This is impossible, she thought. *I can't do it*.

She was going to submerge again and try to work up her courage when her eye fell on the scar on one of her palms. It was from the bloodbind. The cut she'd made had been painful and deep, but the scar tissue had closed it and made her skin stronger than before.

Just as the bloodbind had made *her* stronger.

Sera, Neela, Ling and Ava – their blood surged through her. Her friends, her sisters, were with her. She might be scared, but she *wasn't* alone.

Becca's arms stopped shaking. She boosted herself up onto the ledge, then carefully worked her way up the side of the nest, using her hands to pull herself and her tail to push. She knew her next move. That was something. It wasn't a plan, exactly, but maybe it was the start of one.

Half an hour later, she was at the top of the structure, her tail fins planted on a broken mast. She heaved herself over the edge of the nest, landing with a *whump*.

The fall knocked her glasses down her nose. She pushed them back up, then started to search, pulling up the boat cushions and tattered spinnakers that padded the nest. There were hollows underneath, but they contained nothing. Becca soon saw that every component of the nest served the purpose of strengthening it. Nothing was merely decorative.

Why would a coin even be *in here?* she wondered, losing hope.

As she continued to search, she noticed that one of her hands had started to shimmer. The transparensea pebble was wearing off.

She'd just picked up the edge of a sail when she felt it – a vibration. It was coming from the rock itself. The very walls of the cave were shaking.

Something was coming. Something big.

The cod poked its head out of the water. 'I think we've got company,' he said. 'It's the Williwaw. It'll kill you for sure when it finds you in its cave. So can I have my squid now?'

Becca didn't answer him. She was leaning on the edge of the nest, looking out of the hole in the cave's wall.

The vibrations increased. The water below her started to swirl and bubble. And then it came into view, a creature unlike any she'd seen before.

Becca blinked.

And bit back a scream.

FORTY-SEVEN

THE WILLIWAW WAS a parched and tattered thing, death in a handful of dust.

It was a whale washed up on a beach and left to the merciless sun. A broken-winged gull hobbling across the hot sand. A deer collapsing at a dry riverbed.

The top half of its head was a bird skull, bleached white, with a sharp ebony beak, and the bottom half was human, with a wide jaw, and a grey bottom lip. Its feet and hands were tipped with talons. Bones showed through tears in the dry, leathery skin stretched over its manlike body. Trinkets dangled from golden chains around its neck. A pair of black wings sprouted from its back. Each flap brought the creature closer.

'I need to think. Come up with some ideas. I need a *plan*.' Becca was babbling with fear.

'*Plan?*' the cod scoffed. 'You need a *miracle*!'

Becca knew she had to act. Fast. If she didn't, the Williwaw would kill her. But she couldn't move. She was frozen.

The Williwaw drew nearer. Becca squinted. Her glasses were strong and allowed her to make out the treasures around its neck. Gems. Teeth. Bones. And a locket – an ancient gold locket on an ancient gold chain.

It was hanging open and it held a coin.

That's Pyrrha's coin! It has to be! Becca thought. *I bet Merrow put it in that locket, and then put the chain over the Williwaw's head to make sure no one could ever get it.*

Getting it from the spirit would be all but impossible. Calculations would have to be made. It would take time.

But Becca didn't have time. Despair gripped her. She'd never be able to get the coin from the creature. She and the others would fail in their task and Abbadon would rise again.

The sound of rushing wind grew louder.

The cod glanced nervously at the opening. 'Time to improvise, sister,' he said.

'I – I can't improvise. I don't know how. It's not in my comfort zone.'

'What about death? Is death in your comfort zone?' the cod asked.

An image swam before her eyes, of the monster killing one of the Iele. Abbadon would kill her friends, and so many others. Unless she got the coin.

In that instant, Becca's paralysis broke.

She looked at her hands. One was still shimmering, but not much. *I'm still mostly invisible. The cod's still here. And I'm crafty. In more ways than one. I can* do *this*, she told herself.

She looked at the Williwaw again, only yards away now,

and knew she had about sixty seconds.

'Fish!' she hissed. 'Do you still want the squid?'

'What do you think?'

'Then do *exactly* what I say.'

FORTY-EIGHT

THE WILLIWAW SPOKE as it flew into the cave. To Becca, its voice sounded like the vengeful howl of a gale one second, the mad shriek of a hurricane the next. It hovered over another ledge, where it tossed its latest gleanings – driftwood, a fishing pole, an oar – then flew up to its nest. Becca's heart thumped with fear. She was sitting on the far edge of the nest, her back against the cave wall, her tail pulled up under her. She could see the spirit's terrible talons, curved and sharp, as it raked through padding, plumping it up. After a moment, it turned away from her, faced the front of its nest and settled. It folded its wings along its back and started to preen them.

Where's that fish? Becca wondered anxiously, praying that the cod hadn't changed its mind. Mer could breathe air for a little while but it was difficult, and Becca's lungs were beginning to feel the strain.

As if on cue, the fish poked his head out of the water.

'Hail, great Williwaw!' he said.

The Williwaw leaned forward menacingly. 'What do you want, fish?'

'The ghosts sent me. There's a bit of a fracas going on at the *Achilles*, and they told me to give you a heads-up.'

The wind spirit spoke to the fish in its own language, just as Becca had done. She was able to understand everything they said. *So far, so good*, she thought. The cod was saying exactly what she'd told it to.

'What do you mean there's a *fracas*?' the Williwaw asked.

'Seems that Cassio, the sky god—'

'I *know* who Cassio is,' the Williwaw said.

'Right. Well, Cassio's got a thing for Neféli, a cloud nymph. She saw your locket yesterday when you were flying around, and she wants it. So Cassio sent some heavies to get it. Trykel and Spume are down below, battling the ghosts. Looks like they'll be coming in through that crack in the rock any second. And Zephyros is planning to attack from the air. I'm sure he'll be popping through there' – the cod nodded at the opening the Williwaw had flown through – 'pretty soon. So you might want to take the locket off and hide it. Just a suggestion.'

Good job! Becca said silently. Trykel and Spume, the gods of the tides, and Zephyros, Cassio's son, were more powerful than the Williwaw. The wind spirit was sure to be alarmed.

But it wasn't. Instead, it laughed.

'You want me to take off the locket so you can get it,' it said. 'Do you think I'm stupid?'

'Stupid? No. Paranoid? Maybe,' the cod said.

The Williwaw jumped onto the edge of its nest and snapped its fearsome beak in anger.

'Chill, Will. As I'm sure you can see, I'm a *fish*. I don't have legs or wings or a hovercraft. So there's no way *I'm* getting into your nest to steal the locket. I don't even have a neck, so what good is it to me? *Don't* hide the locket. I really don't care. The ghosts told me to warn you, and I did. So I'm out of here.'

The cod flipped its tail and dived, but Becca knew it wasn't finished yet. She'd told it to swim in circles just below the surface to stir up the water and make the Williwaw think Trykel and Spume were coming.

At first nothing happened. But then the water started to swirl, and bubbles rose. The Williwaw saw it and screeched. It tore the locket from its neck, dug up the padding in its nest, and hid the locket under it. Then it climbed back on the edge, its back to Becca once more, its sharp eyes darting between the churning water and the entrance high above it.

Slowly, taking care not to make any noise, Becca slid off her perch. Her lungs felt like they were on fire. Her heart was pounding. It hurt to put her weight on her tail fins. Both hands were shimmering now.

The Williwaw was muttering anxiously to itself, making enough noise to cover the creaks and pops that Becca was causing. Never taking her eyes off the creature, she pulled up the padding, thrust her hand into the hollow under it, and retrieved the locket.

It seemed to glow even brighter in her hand. She could

feel its power. Excitement coursed through her. She had Pyrrha's talisman at last! But fear quickly edged out her excitement. She was even more scared now that she possessed the coin. Because it was hers to lose.

She slipped it into her pocket, then picked up a piece of driftwood. All she had to do was throw the wood at the cave's skyward entrance. She hoped the noise would trick the Williwaw into thinking that Zephyros was approaching and cause it to fly up to intercept him.

When it did, Becca would heave herself over the front of the nest. From there she'd be able to clear the rock ledge and make a clean dive into the water. By the time the Williwaw discovered its locket had been stolen, she would be streaking out of the *Achilles* and heading for deep water. The wind spirit could not touch her there.

Becca swallowed, shoring up her courage for this last move. The seat-of-the-tail actions she'd taken so far had worked.

And they might have continued to if the Williwaw had not, at that instant, turned around.

FORTY-NINE

BECCA KNEW SHE had a split second in which to live or die.

The wind spirit's bright raptor's eyes travelled from the piece of driftwood she was holding down the length of her now-visible body.

Then it opened its murderous beak and lunged.

Without thinking, Becca dived straight off the side of the nest, not knowing where the rock ledge was. A jutting edge caught her as she plummeted into the water, tearing a gash across her right hip.

She ignored the red-hot pain and greedily sucked water into her parched lungs. The fall had knocked her glasses off. Frantically feeling around for them, she finally found them on the cave's floor and put them back on. Even underwater, she could hear the Williwaw's shrieking tempest that now filled the cave.

A grey face loomed out of the murk. 'Pay up,' the cod said. Becca dug in her pocket and pulled out the last bag of squid.

She tore it open, scattered its contents and bolted off. She didn't ask the cod to get her back through the wreck; he could no longer fool the ghosts now that she was visible.

'Thank you!' she called over her shoulder, but the cod's mouth was too full to reply.

Becca raced through the narrow passageway that led back to the *Achilles*. The tunnel was as dark as before and she crashed into a wall twice, but she kept going. Behind her, the water whirled and surged, boiling with the force of the Williwaw's rage.

After a few minutes the passage opened up, and Becca found herself inside the wreck. Speed and surprise would be her only defence now. Swimming with all her might, Becca shot through the wreck's hold, out of the hole in its hull – and straight into a dozen ghosts playing a game of ninepin.

The ghost about to bowl – a Dutch captain – was so surprised, he sent his ball hurtling through the belly of his first mate.

'What have we here?' drawled a bearded sailor.

The ghosts' smiles were sinister, their eyes ravenous. One rushed at her. She dodged him, but his fingers scraped her arm. She gasped, feeling like she'd fallen into an icy pool. More ghosts advanced. Becca wanted to make for deeper water, but the ghosts forced her to swim up.

Becca's tail whipped through the water as she pushed herself towards the surface. The ghosts followed. Their human legs were not as powerful in the water as a mermaid's tail, but that didn't stop them. Becca tried to outpace them. If she could get just get high enough, she could veer off and leave them in her wake.

But the ghosts weren't letting her.

Becca stopped swimming for a few seconds and looked down. The ghosts were fanning out around her like a net. Dread filled her as she realized that they *meant* to drive her to the surface, where the Williwaw was undoubtedly waiting.

Becca swam higher still, but as she rose, the sea became choppy. Waves were swirling and rolling on the surface. The undertow caught her and dragged her along, thrusting her ever upward.

Her head broke the surface. A storm, more powerful and terrifying than any she'd ever seen, was raging. The skies were black. Lightning ripped through them, followed by deafening thunder. A pelting rain stung her face. The Williwaw was flying over the water, shrieking and pushing up monster waves.

When it saw Becca, it flew straight at her. Becca dived in time, but the waves grabbed her, turned her head over tail, and spat her back up.

Again the Williwaw attacked and again Becca dived. She didn't know where the ghosts were any more. Tossed and tumbled, she barely knew where *she* was.

She fought the storm-racked seas, struggling to stay submerged, but then a rogue wave, frothing and furious, lifted her up and hurtled her towards the treacherous coast.

Her eyes trained on the skies and the terrible creature soaring through them, Becca never saw the rocks, jagged and tall, until the second she slammed into them.

And then she saw nothing at all.

FIFTY

'WE'RE SUPPOSED TO find a pearl,' Desiderio said flatly. 'One black pearl . . . in *that*?'

Astrid nodded, wordless and wide-eyed. She'd heard tales of the Qanikkaaq, but she'd never seen the maelstrom for herself.

It was staggeringly immense and whirling furiously. Looking up through the water, Astrid and Des could see that its funnel-like mouth, raised to the surface, was swallowing everything around it. Its eyes, two bright spots on the waves, shone with a gluttonous glee.

As Astrid watched it, wondering how she was going to even get near it, she saw objects of all shapes and sizes spin by: wooden rowboats, plastic bottles, buoys, kayaks, fishing nets, fishermen, orange life jackets, a couple of yachts.

She had an idea about how to approach the maelstrom, but would it work? Or would she find herself spinning around helplessly inside it, just another piece of debris?

Two days ago, before she and Des had left the shelter of

the shipping container, Astrid had gone on a treasure hunt. She'd raided the container, opening boxes and crates, and taking anything interesting and shiny she came across. Stuffing it all in the large duffel bag she'd found, she had swum to Desiderio, who was busy cleaning Elskan's tack.

'What do you think?' she'd asked, holding up a pair of neon-green sneakers.

Des had frowned, confused. 'You're not going all Hans Christian Andersen on me, are you?' he'd asked.

Astrid had laughed. That gogg fairy tale was well known among the mer – as the most ridiculous story they'd ever heard. Who would ever want to trade fins and a tail for feet?

'No, I'm finding things to offer to the Qanikkaaq,' she'd said, holding up strings of shiny Mardi Gras beads and a plastic silver trophy. 'I'm hoping it will do a trade with me.'

'A magical black pearl from a goddess . . . for a bunch of gogg junk?' Des had asked sceptically.

'I was going to phrase the offer a bit differently,' Astrid had said. 'How about: all of these rare and precious sparkling treasures for one dull little pearl? I'm hoping the Qanikkaaq is a more-is-more kind of a guy.'

'Or a total idiot,' Desiderio had said.

Now it was time to try out her idea. Floating here watching the maelstrom spin wasn't getting them any closer to finding out if the black pearl was still inside it. Astrid was nervous, but trying not to show it. Her plan was sound and it risked only her safety, not Desiderio's. But would it be effective? Without magic, Astrid had to rely on strength and cunning. She had plenty of both, but would they be enough to outwit the maelstrom?

'Do you have the rope?' she asked Des.

'Yup,' he replied. 'You sure about this?'

'Not at all,' Astrid said.

'Let me do it.'

'No, Des. It's for me to do,' she said. This was her quest and the dangers were for her to face.

Des nodded. He'd searched the container too and had turned up a coil of strong nylon rope. He was carrying it over one shoulder. He shrugged it off now, knotted a loop into one end, and handed it to Astrid. While she put her arms through it and pulled it down around her waist, Desiderio made another loop in the other end of the rope. That one went over Elskan's head.

The orca was hovering nearby, eyeing the Qanikkaaq uncertainly. The duffel bag full of gogg plunder was attached to her saddle. Astrid swam over to Elskan and unhooked it.

'Ready?' Desiderio asked tensely.

Astrid said she was, and Desiderio led Elskan forward to take the slack out of the rope.

'Greetings, mighty Qanikkaaq!' she shouted as she neared the maelstrom, unsure exactly how to address it.

The maelstrom slowed its spinning. It tilted its giant face down to look at Astrid. As it did, the surface waters became calm.

'Why have you interrupted my meal, mermaid?' the Qanikkaaq asked, glowering.

'I beg your pardon, Your . . . *Maelstromness*,' Astrid said. 'I'm searching for a black pearl. And I thought a magnificent whirlpool such as yourself must have one.'

'*Whirlpool?*' the Qanikkaaq said, clearly offended.

'I meant, powerful, amazing, super-impressive vortex of doom,' Astrid hastily said.

Desiderio's eyebrows shot up. *Vortex of doom?* he mouthed.

The Qanikkaaq was somewhat mollified. 'And if I had such a pearl, why would I give it to you?' it asked.

'Because I will give you ten times as much treasure in return,' Astrid replied.

The Qanikkaaq was pleased. It chuckled – a low, deep, gurgling sound. 'Come closer, mermaid. Show me what you have.'

'Astrid, be careful,' Desiderio warned.

'I've got this, Des,' Astrid said. She moved towards the maelstrom. The Qanikkaaq's eyes fastened on her bag. Astrid took out the silver trophy and tossed it to the creature. It greedily sucked the trinket in. She tossed a handful of Mardi Gras beads next, a ball covered in tiny squares of mirror glass, and then the neon sneakers.

'That's just the beginning, great Qanikkaaq,' she said. 'There's plenty more where that came from, and it's all yours if you give me the pearl.'

'I can't hear you very well,' the Qanikkaaq said. 'I am very old and my ears are not what they used to be. Come closer.'

Astrid knew what the maelstrom was up to – it wanted to swallow her – but she inched forward, playing along.

'I'm sure you can hear me now,' she said, tossing it a plastic tiara. 'So . . . how about that pearl?'

Currents from the Qanikkaaq were swirling around her now, tossing her hair, plucking at her clothing.

'I would oblige you, mermaid, but your request comes too late.'

No! Astrid thought, her hopes crushed. Were Vallerio and Portia right? Did the mysterious *he* really have the black pearl?

'What do you mean, Qanikkaaq?' she asked, leaning in closer.

'I had such a pearl once. A mermaid threw it to me.'

Merrow, Astrid thought.

'But I swallowed a large school of tuna later,' the maelstrom continued, 'and one of the fish survived inside me. It ate the pearl. Then this tuna, a clever fish, found a way to escape. It swam up my gullet and bit the inside of my mouth. I yelled, of course – tuna have sharp teeth – and stopped swirling, and as I did, the tuna jumped out and swam away. However, that fish wasn't *quite* as clever as it thought it was. A nearby fisherman caught it in his net. And when he cut the tuna open to clean it, he found the pearl.'

Astrid, riveted by the Qanikkaaq's story, moved closer. She wanted to find out every detail about the pearl, so she could tell Sera and the others. Des called out another warning, but she barely heard him.

'What happened next?' she asked.

'From what I've been told, a young Viking warrior who

had heard of the pearl's beauty bought it from the fisherman.'

Astrid's fins began to prickle.

'The pearl must have been magical,' the Qanikkaaq said. 'From the day the young warrior acquired it, his power grew. He became a ruthless chieftain, feared by all. He conquered Greenland, Iceland, and Scandinavia – plundering those lands, and their waters, for treasure. His changed his name to Feimor Fa Eaemor – Feimor, son of Chaos.'

'What did he look like?' Astrid asked, dreading the answer.

'Like many of the Norsemen. Blond. Bronzed by the sun, weathered by the sea.'

A chill ran through Astrid. Like the man in the mirror, she thought – the one who she was still trying to convince herself was only a dream.

'They say that his eyes held evil in them and none dared to look into them,' the Qanikkaaq said.

Astrid remembered that the man in the mirror wore dark sunglasses – even though it wasn't sunny in Vadus. And he had a black pearl strung on his neck.

Could they be one and the same person? she wondered. *Could his pearl be the one I'm trying to find? How, though? It's impossible. Feimor has been dead for probably eight hundred years. And his pearl would have been buried with him.*

The Vikings had been a seafaring people, and they and the mer had been friends. Ondalinians were familiar with the Viking sagas and Astrid knew that chieftains were buried with their valuables.

Distracted by her thoughts, she didn't realize that the Qanikkaaq's currents had pulled her a good deal closer. Nor did Desiderio, who'd turned his attention to an agitated Elskan.

The Qanikkaaq realized, though. It smacked its lips and then it struck, surging towards Astrid with its hungry maw wide open.

Astrid screamed and tried to swim away, but the maelstrom pulled her closer.

Desiderio turned around and saw what was happening. 'Grab the rope, Astrid!' he shouted.

Astrid did so and Des slapped Elskan's flank. The orca shot off, and the rope tightened with a *twang*. It jerked Astrid forwards with a wrenching force. And yet, as strong as Elskan's pull was, it wasn't powerful enough to break Astrid free of the maelstrom.

She could feel herself being sucked backwards, and she could see the fear on Desiderio's face. She knew it mirrored her own.

'Cast a songspell, Astrid!' he shouted. 'Try a commoveo! A stilo!'

'I can't sing, Des!' Astrid yelled back.

Des swore. He slapped Elskan's flank again. 'Get up, Elskan!' he ordered. 'Get up, girl!'

The orca pulled with all her might, but still she couldn't yank Astrid free. Astrid, terrified, felt her tail fins disappearing into the Qanikkaaq's mouth. It would take her. And Elskan, too. It would whirl them around inside itself and break them into bits.

Desiderio left the orca and sped to Astrid. He grabbed her hands and heaved, but it was no use. She was slipping further into the maelstrom.

'Cut the line, Des!' she yelled. 'Cut me loose before it takes you and Elskan!'

Desiderio shook his head. Still gripping her hands, he cast a commoveo songspell and used it to push against the maelstrom. To no avail. Half of Astrid's tail was now inside it.

He cast again, this time using a stilo to call up spiked balls of water. He launched one after the other, hitting the maelstrom in its face.

And then he launched one straight into its mouth.

The Qanikkaaq gagged. It stopped spinning and started coughing.

Astrid found herself flying through the water at a dizzying speed. Elskan, who'd been trying her best to bolt off, suddenly found that she could. She streaked through the water dragging Astrid behind her. Des had fallen away.

Unable to breathe, barely able to see because of the water rushing into her face, Astrid pulled herself up the rope hand over hand and climbed onto Elskan's back. After a minute or so she was able to calm the frightened animal and get her to stop. She wheeled her around and doubled back.

She found Des where she'd left him, bent over and panting. The Qanikkaaq had returned to the surface.

Des straightened as he heard Elskan's fins. He was angry.

Astrid could see his emotion on his face. *So much for that friendship*, she thought. *He probably won't want anything to do with me now*. Kolfinn's words came back to her: *Who wants a mermaid without magic?*

'Why didn't you say something?' Des asked.

Astrid didn't answer. She dismounted from Elskan, her eyes downcast.

'By not telling me you can't sing, you almost got us both killed,' Des said. 'I wasted precious time shouting at you to songcast instead of doing it myself.'

'I guess you'll be going now,' Astrid said miserably. 'Take the food. I can find more.'

'Astrid, what are you talking about? I thought we were going to the Karg together.'

Astrid shook her head. 'You should go to the Karg alone, Des. It's okay, really. Most mer don't want to be around me once they know. I'm seen as a liability. Like I was just now.'

Des was quiet for a few seconds, then he asked her a question. 'Is that why Kolfinn didn't go through with the permutavi?'

Astrid, still looking down, nodded. 'He didn't want my secret to get out. He didn't want anyone to know that a member of the admiral's family was weak and defective.'

'That's awful, Astrid,' Des said, still angry.

Astrid thought he meant her father's attempts to cover up her disability, and her own attempts to do the same.

'I'm sorry, Des. I should've been straight with you,' she said.

'No, I meant the way your father treated you,' said Des, his voice softening. 'He shouldn't have done it. He had no right. There's nothing wrong with you. Nothing at all. You're not weak – you're strong. One of the strongest merls I've ever met.'

Astrid looked up at Desiderio uncertainly, wondering if he was teasing her, but she saw no maliciousness in his eyes, only kindness.

'Look, Astrid. I'm sorry, too. I shouldn't have yelled,' he said. 'The only reason I did is that I was scared.'

'Scared?' she echoed. 'Of what?'

'Scared you were going to be sucked inside the maelstrom,' Des replied. 'Scared I'd lose you.'

Astrid looked away again. She could hardly believe what she was hearing. She could hardly believe what was happening.

'Why don't you let me decide if I want to be around you, okay?' he said. 'Because I do. A lot.'

Astrid raised her eyes to his once more. They were warm and smiling, and she felt as if she was falling into their green depths like a stone into calm seas. And then Des took her face into his hands and kissed her. It was fierce and gentle all at the same time and it took her breath away.

She looked at him as he broke the kiss, scared he would do it again, scared he wouldn't.

'A *lot*,' Des said once more, and then, suddenly shy, he swam off to deal with Elskan.

FIFTY-ONE

'IT'S BEEN TWO whole days, Marco,' a worried voice said.

'I know that, Elisabetta. She took a hard blow to her head, but her breathing's good and her colour's improving,' said another.

They were speaking Italian, a terragogg language. Becca was surprised to find that she understood it. *The bloodbind*, she thought. She could follow most of the words, but she had no idea to whom they were directed. The voices seemed so far away. She felt like she was drifting on the surface of the sea. Waves were rocking her gently. She wanted to keep drifting, but she knew she couldn't. She had to open her eyes. She had to keep swimming. There was a reason she had to, but she couldn't remember what it was.

'What if there's a brain bleed? What if there's a hairline fracture? What if—'

'What if you made us some coffee, Little Miss Sunshine?'

Who has a brain bleed? Becca wondered. *What's coffee?*

She opened her eyes. And immediately wished she hadn't. The light sent a bolt of pain straight through her brain. She waited for the agony to subside, then tried again.

Her vision was blurry. Little by little it cleared. As it did, she saw that a face was hanging over her – the most gorgeous face she'd ever seen. Two warm brown eyes, filled with worry, stared at her. The mouth, generous and full-lipped, was frowning, but suddenly broke into a broad, beautiful smile.

It was a man's face.

Wait, Becca's aching brain said. *A man's face? A* man's*?!*

She realized with horror that it was a terragogg who was staring at her. Terrified, she twisted and tried to swim away from him, but she couldn't, because she was inside some sort of shallow tank. Crazed with fear, she started to thrash against it.

'Listen! Please listen to me!' the man pleaded, in Mermish now. 'It's okay. You're safe here. No one's going to hurt you.'

Becca, her heart pounding, swam to the back of the tank. She grabbed the edge and tried to pull herself over it, but her hands slipped. She gave the side another frantic whack with her tail, but it was pointless. The tank was strong and she was weak.

'You've got to stop doing that. You'll rip your stitches out. You've already torn some bandages off,' said the man.

Becca turned to face the man. As she did, her hand went to her temple. The pain in her head was blinding now.

'What are you going to do with me?' she asked, her voice ragged.

'Redo the bandages you wrecked, give you some moon jelly soup and get you to the Karg. Unless you manage to kill yourself first.'

Becca blinked. 'Who are you?' she asked.

The man smiled. 'Marco Contorini, the duca di Venezia.'

FIFTY-TWO

'YOU'RE *NOT* THE DUCA,' Becca said, eyeing the terragogg warily. 'Duca Armando was killed by Rafe Mfeme and his men.'

Marco nodded. 'Yes, he was,' he said, sadness filling his beautiful eyes. 'I'm his son. I've inherited his title and the duties that come with it.'

'You're his son?' Becca asked. 'So you're . . .' The words wouldn't come. It was so hard to think, to remember.

'Head of the Praedatori and the Wave Warriors,' Marco finished. He smiled. 'At least, I'm *trying* to be. What I really am is a student at the University of Milan. Double major – marine biology and filmmaking. I had to leave my studies when my father was killed, and take over his operations.'

'In Venice . . . the palazzo . . .' Becca said. She'd never been there, but knew about it from Sera's stories.

'No, the palazzo's too dangerous for me now. I've had to lock it up and leave it. Rafe Mfeme's men are after me.

With the help of the Wave Warriors, I've managed to stay ahead of them.'

A female terragogg entered the room just then, carrying two mugs.

'Becca, you're awake!' she said, grinning. She put the mugs down.

'This is my sister, Elisabetta,' Marco said. 'She's a student, too. Environmental law.'

'How do you know my name? Where am I? How did I get here?' Becca asked, still wary. Her knowledge of terragoggs was limited to the awful way they treated the seas and their creatures.

'All in good time. First, you need to eat,' Elisabetta said. 'You were badly banged up and you lost a good deal of blood. You need to build up your strength. Can you manage some moon jelly soup?'

Becca realized that she was, in fact, very hungry. 'I suppose I could try . . .' she replied, still leery of the two humans.

'Good, I'll get it for you. Marco will answer your questions.'

'Do you mind if I answer them while I fix that bandage?' Marco asked, nodding at Becca's right arm.

'I – I guess not,' Becca said.

She followed his gaze to her arm and gasped. The bandage was mostly off. Under it was a deep gash, neatly stitched, that ran from her elbow to her wrist. She looked the rest of her body over and saw more bruises and scrapes, and another terrible wound across her right hip.

'You put your arm up just before you crashed into a very large rock. Your head still hit, but not as hard as it would have if you hadn't cushioned your impact,' Marco said.

Becca's hand instinctively went to her scalp. Her fingers touched a bandage.

'More stitches, I'm afraid,' Marco said. 'It's a miracle you didn't fracture your skull. You're lucky to be alive.'

'Do you have a mirror?' Becca asked.

Marco winced. 'If you really want one.'

'I do,' Becca said. *I think*, she added silently.

Marco found a hand mirror and gave it to her. As he gathered bandages, a scissors, and waterproof tape, Becca grimaced at her reflection. The right side of her face was covered with scrapes and her right eye was blackened. The bandage on her head was angled like a cockeyed hat.

She handed the mirror back. The marks on her were not pretty, but they would heal and fade. Something else was bothering her a lot more than her cuts.

'How did you find me?' she asked, still suspicious.

'We were looking for you.'

'But who—'

'Mahdi. The Praedatori are scattered now, but he managed to get word to one of them – Nero – and Nero got word to me,' Marco explained, taking the old bandage off Becca's arm.

Becca felt much better knowing that these goggs were connected to Mahdi.

'I travelled to Cape Horn right away and asked the head of the Warriors in America to get to the Mississippi,' Marco continued, wrapping a fresh bandage around Becca's arm. 'She's been looking for Ava for the past two days.'

'But she hasn't found her,' Becca said dully.

'Not yet,' Marco said. 'But we're still hopeful. We didn't find you right away, either. We circled the waters near the Williwaw's cave for a couple of days, searching for you. When a bad storm came up out of nowhere, we thought it might be the wind spirit's doing and that you might be coming up. That's how he works – getting the ghosts to drive intruders to the surface, then bashing them against the rocks.'

'He sure bashed me,' Becca said, flinching at the memory of the impact.

'El got the boat close to the rocks, and I brought you in with a net. You were out cold. Soon as I had you on board, El gunned it. This is a speedboat. It does eighty knots on smooth seas; fifty in rough ones. We were knocked about a bit, but she got us out of the storm.'

Becca watched Marco expertly cover her new bandage with tape. 'You're pretty good at this,' she said. 'Do you make a habit of rescuing mermaids?'

He smiled. 'Not many mermaids, I admit. But this boat – it's called the *Marlin* – is fitted with a saltwater tank to transport sick and wounded sea creatures. We try to do our part, though it's getting harder, with—'

'Here you go,' Elisabetta interrupted as she returned with a mug of soup. 'Drink this down. It'll do you good.'

'Thank you,' Becca said, taking the mug. She felt reassured enough to try it.

'I hope you like it,' Elisabetta said, frowning. 'I'm not quite sure how moon jelly soup should taste.'

Becca took a sip. 'It's delicious,' she said. 'But I meant thank you for more than the soup. Thank you for saving my life.'

'You're welcome,' Elisabetta said with a shrug. 'Part of the job.'

'You made the Williwaw pretty angry,' Marco said. 'Did you get what you were after?'

Becca hesitated. It wasn't safe to say too much about the talismans.

'It's okay, Becca. Mahdi told Nero about the talismans, and Nero told me. He trusts us. And we trust him,' Marco said.

Becca instinctively reached for her pocket – and realized with a start that she wasn't wearing her jacket. She looked around anxiously.

Marco must've understood what she was searching for, because he lifted something from the bench behind him. He motioned for Becca to give him her mug, and in exchange he handed her the jacket.

It dawned on Becca that he and Elisabetta could easily have helped themselves to the locket if they'd wanted to.

But it was still in the pocket. 'Yes,' she said with immense relief. 'I got it.'

'That's great news!' Marco said excitedly.

'And bad news, too,' said Elisabetta.

'How so?' Becca asked, draping her jacket over the side

of her tank. Marco handed her mug back.

'When we picked you up, the death riders were only three leagues from the *Achilles*,' Elisabetta explained. 'I'm sure that by now they've staked out the wreck and spied on the ghosts. They'll have heard them talking about a mermaid who took something from the Williwaw and was rescued by humans in a boat. Vallerio will be informed. He'll get word to Rafe Mfeme, and as soon as he does, Mfeme will be after us. If he's not already. He has speed boats, too.'

Marco smiled at his sister. 'But his drivers aren't as crazy as you,' he said.

Elisabetta laughed. 'Still, I'm not taking any chances. We're only in the southern Atlantic and we need to get all the way to the North Sea. Boats will meet us along the way so we can refuel, but we've got to keep going.' She gave her brother a look. 'Okay, Marco?'

'Okay,' Marco said. Elisabetta headed topside. Marco turned to Becca. 'I made her stop and cut the engines so she could eat something and rest. But she's right. Mfeme could show up at any minute. It's best to keep moving.'

They both heard a deep thrum as Elisabetta started the *Marlin*'s engines. She opened the throttle and a second later, they were off.

'I should leave you,' Marco said, 'and let you get some rest too. El forgot her coffee mug. I'm going to bring it to her.'

'What's coffee?'

'The drink of the gods. To terraggogs, at least,' Marco joked. 'And nothing you should try if you want to get some sleep.' He smiled, then added, 'It's *okay* to sleep, you know. You're safe now.'

Becca nodded. Her eyes felt so heavy. Her body was aching and exhausted.

You're safe now.

As she looked into his kind eyes, Becca believed, for the first time in many months, that she was.

FIFTY-THREE

THE DARKNESS WAS a living thing, watchful and crouching, all eyes and teeth.

Creatures moved about in it, seeing but unseen. Ling could feel them. She was in the Abyss, about two leagues from the prison camp, where her father had told her the puzzle ball might have drifted.

She held a fat moon jelly in her hand. It was her only source of light. She couldn't cast the most basic illuminata. She couldn't cast *anything*. The sea wasp's venom had sickened her so badly, she'd lost most of her magic. Even her omnivoxa powers were weak. She could speak only a handful of simple languages. Ling shone the moon jelly's glow over the Abyss's jagged south side, looking for Sycorax's ancient talisman. She moved back and forth along a section of wall and, finding nothing, descended further.

As she did, a sharp pain stabbed at her brain.

Depth sickness, she thought. *It's starting*.

She wasn't surprised. She'd been searching for ten hours

straight. She knew the symptoms – headache and nausea, followed by disorientation. Then things got really bad. Victims struggled for oxygen. They coughed blood and became uncoordinated. A brain bleed usually finished them off. Either that or suffocation.

After Ling and the manta ray had parted company, she had crawled into a cave and stayed there for two days – sick and shivering – waiting for the swelling in her tail to go down. On the third day, hunger had driven her out to forage. She'd found fish eggs and some bitter seaweed that she'd choked down. The food gave her energy and strength. On the fourth day, she set off in pursuit of the puzzle ball.

Ling knew she was lucky to be alive. She didn't feel lucky, though. She had no idea how long it would take her to regain her magical powers. What if they never came back? That thought was so terrifying, she couldn't bear to dwell on it.

She kept moving down the south wall of the Abyss now, sweeping her tail fins over clusters of tube worms to see if the puzzle ball had landed in their midst, peering into small caves and niches.

A wave of dizziness washed over her. She closed her eyes until it passed, then started laughing. She was searching for a *ball*, no bigger than the palm of her hand . . . in the *Great Abyss*!

'I've lost my mind,' she said out loud.

The puzzle ball could have landed on any one of a million ledges that lined both sides of the Abyss. It could be buried in thick silt or wedged into a crack. Or it could be leagues below her, and still falling. Legend had it that the Abyss was bottomless.

'This is totally insane,' she said out loud, still laughing. 'It's impossible!'

She laughed so hard she started to struggle for breath – which made her realize that her depth sickness was getting worse.

'You're becoming hysterical,' she told herself. 'Knock it off. *Right now*.'

Ling was strong; she knew she was. And strong mer didn't lose it. They didn't come apart. They got the job done. She descended again. A small hollow lay in a rock below her. Holding the jelly in one hand, she grasped the edge of the cavity with the other and peered into it.

She didn't even have time to scream as a bony face with gaping jaws lunged at her. The giant fangtooth's sharp teeth missed her face by a hairsbreadth. Panicking, Ling raised both hands to protect herself from the fish and dropped the moon jelly. The current carried it away. The fangtooth shot towards it.

'*No!*' Ling cried.

But it was too late. The fish snapped its jaws shut on the tasty jelly and swallowed it whole.

Ling didn't know what the fangtooth did next, or where it went, because she couldn't see *anything*. The water around her was still and silent, the darkness overwhelming. It felt to Ling as if it was swallowing her whole, the way the fangtooth had devoured the jelly.

All she could hear was the sound of her own breathing, rapid and shallow. Dizziness gripped her again. It was so bad this time that she became violently ill. When the racking spasms finally subsided, she realized she had no choice but to ascend. Her breathing was too ragged; it had to normalize. She had to find another source of light.

She swam upwards, but after taking a few strokes, she realized the water was getting colder, not warmer. Was she swimming down instead of up?

Dizziness struck again. Ling swam in the direction of the wall, hands outstretched. If she could find it, she could steady herself against it and hopefully beat back the spinning in her head. But the wall was nowhere to be found. Ling was flailing in the black depths now, completely disoriented.

And then she saw a light.

'Oh, thank gods!' she said, swimming towards it. 'Hey!' she shouted. 'Wait! I'm over here.'

The light glowed more brightly. It came towards her. Ling put on a burst of speed, rushing to meet it.

And then she stopped short, unable to believe what she was seeing.

A man was carrying the light. A human. He had blond hair and empty eyes. He wore a black pearl at his throat.

'Hello again, Ling,' he said.

'*No!*' Ling cried.

It was a face from her nightmares. The face of a monster.

Orfeo.

FIFTY-FOUR

'NO,' LING WHISPERED. 'It can't be.'

Orfeo was here with her in the Abyss.

Crying out in fear, she turned and bolted away from him – only to be brought up short by the appearance of someone even more terrifying.

Morsa.

The goddess was swimming towards Ling, her serpent's tail twining in the water, her lipless mouth twisted into a smile. The scorpions wreathing her head raised their venomous stingers.

'Have you brought me a sacrifice, Orfeo?' she asked in a dry, dusty voice. 'You are ever my faithful servant.'

Ling screamed. She tried to swim away from Morsa, away from Orfeo, but wherever she went, they were there, reaching for her.

Whimpering, she closed her eyes and curled into a ball, waiting to feel Orfeo's rough hand clamp down on her, or Morsa's lethal sting.

But she felt nothing.

Slowly, she opened her eyes. Both Orfeo and Morsa were gone.

'They were never here,' she said to herself. 'You're hallucinating.'

Ling knew she had to ascend. Now. If only she could find a creature that wasn't a predator, one that could tell her which way to go. She needed help but was afraid to call out for it. What if her pleas summoned another fangtooth . . . or something worse?

I'm going to die down here, she thought. *Totally alone*.

Ling thought of Serafina and the others, waiting for her, depending on her. She thought of her father in the prison camp. His hopes were pinned on her, too. She thought of her brothers. Would their village be raided next? Would they be hauled off to a labour camp?

And then she thought of her mother. Not being able to say goodbye to her hurt the most.

Ling had parted from her on bad terms, angry at her silence. But now she realized that the way she felt here in the Abyss – scared, alone and desperate – was how her mother felt every single day of her life.

Ling valued toughness and strength – in herself and others – but she saw now that even the strong couldn't be strong all the time. Everyone was frightened or lonely or heartbroken sometimes, and when they were, they needed others to be strong for them.

For the first time, Ling understood.

She took a deep breath, then shouted at the top of her lungs, 'Please, is anyone here? *Anyone?* Can somebody *help* me? I was looking for a puzzle ball, but now I'm totally lost and I'm sick and I'm scared and I need to get *out* of here!'

No one answered her.

Not at first.

But then Ling heard something. A few seconds later, she saw something, way below her.

A strange creature, with a slender, spiralling body and thousands of glowing tentacles, rose up from the depths. More creatures, just like the first, followed it.

Ling had seen the things in the night skies, things the goggs called *fireworks*. These creatures looked like that, like shining bursts of light in the darkness. They spoke as they rose, and their language sounded like music, mysterious and beautiful.

'Look!' the creatures said. 'Look! Look! Look!'

I must be hallucinating again, Ling thought.

More creatures came. Their light illuminated the dark water. Ling saw that she was very near the wall.

'Are you real?' Ling asked.

'Look!' the creatures said. 'Look! Look!'

Ling did so. Though her head was pounding and she felt sickeningly dizzy, she swam back and forth, searching in cracks and crevices. As her body cried out for oxygen, she dug through silt-filled depressions, waved aside a school of tiny needlenose fish, parted a thicket of ribbon worms.

And then, finally, she saw it. It was only a few feet away, resting on a ledge.

A small white ball.

Ling tried to swim to it, but a fit of coughing, painful and harsh, overtook her. She spat out a mouthful of blood. She tried again, and this time she made it, smiling as she picked up the talisman. It was carved of coral and contained spheres within spheres. A phoenix decorated the outermost one.

Closing her hand around the precious object, Ling tried to swim up, but failed. Her strength was gone. Another fit of coughing gripped her. When it subsided, she could barely breathe.

The strange light-filled creatures began to descend again.

'No!' she rasped. 'Stay! Please! I need you. I can't die here. Please help me.'

As the words left her lips, another fangtooth loomed out of the darkness. It was twice as large as the one that had attacked her. Its teeth were six inches long.

Ling closed her eyes and waited for death.

But it didn't come. The fangtooth swooped down behind her and grabbed hold of her tunic with his fearsome teeth. Ling felt herself being lifted off the ledge and carried upward.

An anglerfish appeared, too. A thin, fleshy stalk protruded from its forehead, and a blue light glowed at the end. It started for the surface, lighting the way, and the fangtooth followed. As they ascended, the tightness in Ling's chest eased. Her dizziness faded. She gripped the talisman tightly.

Half an hour later, she was back at the edge of the Abyss. Lights glowed in the distance. Ling knew they were from the labour camp. She needed to make wake and get far away from it.

'Thank you,' she said to the fangtooth and the angler. She was so overcome with emotion – gratitude, relief, awe – that, for once, she felt tongue-tied. 'You . . . you saved my life.'

'We know why they're searching for the white ball. We hear them talking,' the fangtooth said, nodding at the camp. 'They mustn't win. Go, mermaid. Save many more lives.'

Ling nodded. She watched the two fish return to the deep, then started her long journey. She would travel to Miromara, to find Sera. To prepare for the coming war.

But she would make one stop first. To give her strength to one who needed it. To set things right.

Ling turned and headed for home.

FIFTY-FIVE

'MARCO, ARE YOU *sure* you're not really a merman disguised as a human?' Becca teased.

They were in the ocean, swimming. Marco, floating on his back, raised his feet and wiggled his toes. Becca saw webbing between them.

'*Wow*,' she said, laughing.

'It's a genetic mutation,' he said. 'All the males in the Contorini line have it.'

He dived under the water, came up a foot in front of Becca, and splashed her.

'Really?' Becca said, giving him a look. She raised her tail fins and slapped them down, nearly drowning him.

He shook the water off his face and they swam together. He insisted that they anchor the boat for an hour every day at noon, so he could make lunch, Elisabetta could nap, and Becca could swim.

'You need to move,' he'd told her. 'You need to work all the sore bits, or everything will cramp up.'

Becca left the boat through a small water lock in its hull, directly underneath the saltwater tank. Today, Marco had pulled off his T-shirt and jumped in with her, bronze and bare-chested. Becca marvelled at how strong and graceful he was in the water. She had no idea humans could be those things.

The wind had picked up now and the waves were choppy, but even so it felt wonderful to Becca to move through the ocean after being in the *Marlin*'s small tank. It was even better since Marco had joined her.

They talked as they swam. Becca had known Marco for only four days, yet she felt like she'd known him her entire life. They never ran out of things to say to each other.

'Any word on Ava?' she asked.

'Nothing,' he said. 'The American Wave Warriors reached the Mississippi, but they haven't found her yet. The swamps are enormous, and she could be anywhere. I know their leader, Allie Edmonds. She won't give up.'

'And Ling?'

Marco shook his head.

Becca's heart felt heavy. She feared the worst. She tried to convoca all her friends whenever she got back into the ocean, but she never had any success. The spell was insanely hard and tended to work best when several mer were casting it together.

'We *have* heard that Astrid's okay,' Marco said. 'And that she's making her way to the Karg with Desiderio, Sera's brother.'

'Some good news! *Finally*,' Becca said, encouraged.

'We'll get you to the Karg, too,' Marco said. 'Don't doubt that for a minute.'

'I can't thank you both enough for all that you've done for me already,' Becca said.

Marco shrugged. 'You don't need to thank us. It's what we do.'

'I *do* need to thank you,' Becca insisted. 'I wouldn't be here without you.'

Marco turned to look at her. 'I don't even want to think about that.'

His gaze, suddenly intense, held Becca's as he spoke. For a second, she thought she saw something in it – something more than friendly concern. She quickly looked away, feeling flustered and self-conscious.

'What will you do?' she asked, changing the subject. 'After you get me to the Karg, I mean.'

'Head back to the Pacific,' Marco replied. 'We were helping marine animals there. The elder of Qin and his forces are overwhelmed. It's a bad scene, Becca. Birds are swallowing pieces of plastic they mistake for fish. It makes their stomachs rupture. Dolphins are getting tangled in fishing nets and drowning. Turtles eat plastic bags that they think are jellyfish. The bags block their intestines and they starve.'

Marco's eyes hardened as he spoke. Becca could hear the anger, and the sadness, in his voice.

'People don't get it. Because most of them don't see ocean pollution. If anyone dumped garbage in the Alps, on the Serengeti, or in the Grand Canyon, there would be hell to pay.'

A sea turtle swam close by them. Marco reached out his hand, skimming it over the graceful creature's shell.

'Isn't her life worth more than a plastic bag?' he asked, watching the turtle swim off.

'Yes, it is,' Becca said softly.

'The waters of the world contain million of species we haven't even identified yet. *Millions*. There are plains, mountains, and trenches under the seas we haven't mapped. And we're *destroying* them . . .'

He shook his head, unable to finish. When he got his emotions under control again, he said, 'Elisabetta graduates from law school next year. Then she can continue our father's work – taking marine polluters to court. I graduate in three years – if I can ever get back to school – and then I'll do my part to document the damage, make people sit up and take notice. Maybe my generation can achieve what my father's couldn't. I hope so. It's the only chance the ocean's got.'

Becca was moved by Marco's passion – and surprised by it. She'd had no idea that there were terragoggs who cared so deeply for the seas and their creatures. Nor had she any idea that she could care for a terragogg.

As a friend, she hastily told herself. *And why wouldn't I? He saved my life, and he and Elisabetta have been so kind to me*.

The waves had carried them back to the boat. Becca heard footsteps on deck and looked up. Elisabetta was standing in the bow, binoculars raised to her eyes.

'See anything, El?' Marco shouted to her.

'A manta ray and a school of sea bass,' she shouted back.

Marco spotted the ray about twenty yards away.

'Come on, let's race. Last one to the ray is a rotten squid egg!' Marco said.

They dived. Becca streaked to the manta, certain she'd reach it first, but Marco was right behind her. The ray saw them coming. In no mood for their games, he flipped his tail at them and sped off.

Becca laughed. Then she remembered that Marco was human, not mer, and looked at him, worried that he might need to surface. He understood the concern in her eyes, shook his head, and gave her a thumbs-up.

A movement to her right caught Becca's attention. Something loomed towards them out of the depths. It looked as if a seamount had broken off from the ocean's floor and was floating by.

Becca grabbed Marco's hand. She pointed with her other hand. Marco's eyes grew huge in his face as he followed her gaze. He grinned from ear to ear.

The blue whale was so magnificent and her song so beautiful, that Becca's heart swelled. She felt Marco's hand tighten on hers and knew he felt the same way. She turned to him, but Marco wasn't looking at the whale any more, he was looking at her. He was still holding her hand and was floating close to her now.

Becca suddenly felt like she couldn't breathe, but in a good way. Then she saw that Marco looked like he couldn't breathe, either – but in a bad way. She sped to the surface, pulling him after her. Their heads broke the water and Marco inhaled a gulp of air.

As soon as he caught his breath, he took both of her hands in his, and said, 'Becca, I need to tell you something—'

His eyes had that same intense look they'd had earlier. And Becca once again felt that his gaze held something more than friendship. Her heart started to race. Because she felt something more than friendship, too, but she didn't want to. She knew that anything more than friendship between a human and a mer was a bad idea. A *very* bad idea.

'What is it, Marco?' she asked, almost fearfully.

'I think—'

But the rest of his answer was cut off by shouting, urgent and fearful. 'Marco! Becca! Back in the boat *now*!'

Elisabetta was running to the captain's chair.

'Two speedboats off the starboard bow. Mfeme's!' she yelled.

'Go, Becca! Hurry!' Marco said, pushing her towards the boat.

Becca dived, swam under the boat, then shot onto the narrow platform hanging down from the hull. She positioned herself just as Marco had taught her to and pressed a green button. The platform was pulled up inside the boat, sealing the hull. Becca slid open another hatch above her, hoisted herself into the saltwater tank, and slid the hatch closed.

'She's in!' Marco shouted. 'Go, El!'

Elisabetta tore off. The seas were choppy and the boat

smacked against the waves.

'Marco, it's me they want,' Becca said. 'Open the hatch. I'll swim out and disappear.'

'No way. That's exactly what they're hoping for,' said Marco. 'I'd bet any amount of money they have death riders on board their boats ready to swim after you.'

As they spoke, they heard Elisabetta open the throttle.

'She's trying to outrun them,' Marco said.

Becca crouched down in the tank. Its clear sides allowed her to see the ocean out of a window. The wind had grown stronger and the waves had risen higher.

Marco poked his head out of the hatch and swore. 'It's no good,' he told Becca anxiously, as he returned to the tank. 'They're blocking us. They're trying to cut us off.'

'Hang on, everyone!' Becca heard Elisabetta yell. 'It's about to get bumpy!'

The engines were roaring now. The *Marlin* was going much faster than it should in rough seas.

'Marco, what's happening?' Becca asked fearfully, gripping both sides of the tank. Water was sloshing over them now. 'Where are Mfeme's boats?'

He popped his head out of the hatch again. 'Dead ahead and broadside!' he shouted.

'*Dead ahead and broadside?* But we must be going eighty knots!' Becca exclaimed.

'El's going to try to jump them. The waves will give us lift. If we make the jump at full speed, we can escape,' Marco yelled.

'And if we *don't* make the jump?' Becca yelled back.

Marco didn't answer right away. Then he turned back to her and said, 'We're dead meat.'

FIFTY-SIX

'MARCO, Becca, brace yourselves!' Elisabetta shouted.

Marco sat down sideways in his chair and threw an arm around its back. Becca gripped one side of the tank with both hands. She heard the engines scream as Elisabetta pushed the throttle all the way open.

The *Marlin* rose straight up the side of a giant roller. The powerful wave caught it, heaved it up its crest, and launched it – straight over Mfeme's boats. As it crashed back down in the water, its propellors caught and the *Marlin* shot off.

Marco ran up on the deck. A few seconds later, Becca heard him hooting and laughing.

'Way to go, El!' he whooped.

'What's happening?' Becca shouted.

Marco jumped back down belowdecks. His cheeks were flushed, his eyes sparkling.

'Mfeme's two captains tried to follow,' he explained, 'but before they could turn themselves around, another roller caught them broadside. It capsized one and flooded the other. They're sinking!'

Becca went limp with relief. Racing for the boat and then being convinced she was about to die in a fiery wreck had wiped everything from her mind. Now that she could think straight, what Marco had said to her before Elisabetta turned the *Marlin* into a flying fish came flooding back.

'Marco?'

'Hmm?' he said. He'd walked to the window and was looking out of it now.

'You were going to tell me something earlier. Before Elisabetta shouted for us to get back in the boat. What was it?'

Becca was nervous about what he might say, but she wanted to know. She *had* to know. If he was feeling what she was feeling, then there was trouble ahead for both of them. Such relationships had been attempted on occasion. They never ended well. *Surf and turf*, the mer called them. Becca could hear the scornful jokes already.

Marco turned to her. Though he was tanned, Becca saw a flush creep into his cheeks. He ran a hand through his hair. 'Earlier? Hmm. I forget,' he said. 'Maybe . . . um . . . probably that I think we'll make the Karg soon. Yeah, that was it. In three or four days, tops. Good news, right?' he said, smiling brightly.

Becca nodded. 'Very,' she replied, smiling back just as brightly.

She was wrong. Marco didn't have feelings for her.

Thank the gods.

'Well, I . . . um . . . I should check on El. Make sure everything's okay topside.'

'You probably should,' Becca agreed.

He climbed up the ladder and disappeared.

Becca watched him go, feeling relieved.

And foolishly, maddeningly, sad.

FIFTY-SEVEN

LUCIA TOOK A DEEP BREATH, then pressed the carved dolphin on the mantel in her mother's sitting room. As she did, a secret door to the left of the lavaplace clicked open.

Silently, she thanked the odious Baco Goga for revealing the door and the network of tunnels it led to. She'd made very good use of them in her mother's absence.

Holding a lava torch aloft, she swam into the passageway, closed the door and started down the tunnel. She carried clothing folded over her arm – Mahdi's clothing. She'd stolen it from his room just today, while he was out. A few trocii slipped into a maid's hand had bought her access.

She wished she had company for her journey through the tunnels, but now that Bianca was gone, there was no one she could trust with her secret. Guilt, cold and nauseating, clutched at her at the memory of her friend. Lucia had turned her over to Kharis with barely a backwards glance. Sometimes, in her nightmares, she still heard Bianca's screams.

Lucia shook off the guilt. The regina mattered far more

than any of her subjects. The ruler's happiness was of paramount importance to the realm. Surely, in her last moments, Bianca had been glad to know that she'd fulfilled her duty.

'A little fish gone, that's all. A very little fish. And there are so many more of them in the sea,' Lucia said aloud, pushing all thoughts of Bianca from her mind. She had more important things to focus on now.

The tunnel walls were thickly furred with pale seaweeds, white anemones and other things that thrived in the dark. They reached for Lucia as she swam by. In one tunnel bones littered the floor – mer bones. Lucia glanced down at a skull and tried not to imagine her own bones mouldering here – which could happen if she lost her way. There were no other living souls down here to hear a call for help.

About an hour later, she arrived at her destination – the maze of cave-like rooms under the Kolisseo, a large open-water amphitheatre outside the palace walls. As Lucia moved through the labyrinth to the centremost room, creatures slithered and scuttled away from the light of her torch. She heard a deep, heavy groan – as if an entire scrap heap of metal had suddenly come to life, and then what sounded like sledgehammers striking stone.

'Who comesssss to disssturb Alítheia?' a voice hissed. 'Your bonessss ssshe will eat, intruder. Your blood ssshe will drink.'

Lucia stopped, paralyzed by the anarachna's voice. She hated the creature and feared her, but she needed her, too.

Alítheia's den was the only place in all of Cerulea where no one dared to go – no one but Lucia.

Alítheia was a giant bronze spider. Murderously violent, she killed all mer who came near her – except for the Merrovingian reginas. Alítheia had been created by Merrow and the gods to ensure no imposters ever sat on Miromara's throne. Swallowing her fear, Lucia swam on. 'Alítheia, this is Lucia, your regina! I hope you've guarded my possession well!'

Lucia heard an ear-splitting roar, and then a pounding, and knew the anarachna was furious. 'No bonesss for Alítheia!' the creature howled.

'You'll have your bones, spider,' Lucia said, entering the den. 'My father's dungeons are full of traitors.'

Alítheia scuttled up to Lucia. She was massive, with tapered legs that ended in dagger-sharp points, eight black eyes and long, curved fangs. Lucia raised her lava globe high, lest the spider forget herself. The only thing in the world Alítheia feared was lava.

'Where is my maligno?' Lucia demanded.

The anarachna pointed at the back of its den. 'No bonesss, no blood in it. No heart, no sssoul in it,' she said contemptuously.

Lucia swam to the maligno, past cocoons spun of bronze filament that were suspended from the ceiling. Most of them dangled motionlessly, but some were still moving.

Kharis had delivered her creation to Lucia three nights before. Alítheia's den was the ideal hiding place for it.

'How perfect you are,' Lucia crooned to it now, running a crimson-tipped finger over its cheek. 'No one would ever be able to tell the difference between you and the real Mahdi.'

The maligno stared ahead expressionlessly.

'Take these and put them on,' Lucia instructed, handing it the clothing she'd brought.

The maligno nodded, pulled off the tunic Kharis had dressed it in, and donned Mahdi's white shirt and black jacket.

Lucia buttoned up the jacket, then smiled, satisfied. 'Soon now,' she whispered to the maligno. Then she turned to the spider. 'Goodbye, Alítheia,' she said. 'Continue to guard my possession and I'll reward you well.'

'When bonesss? When blood?' Alítheia asked sullenly.

'Not much longer,' Lucia replied, swimming out of the cave. 'Not long at all.'

FIFTY-EIGHT

THE SMALL VILLAGE of Qīngshuǐ was quiet, deserted. Moonlight shone down on it, illuminating narrow currents and humble dwellings.

Ling could see her home, built high on a soaring rock face like all the others, and she longed to rush to it. But she was well versed now in the ways of the death riders, so she stayed where she was, hidden at the base of the rock for an hour, watching.

When she was certain there were no soldiers waiting to ambush her, she swam up, past the homes of her neighbours, to her own. No lights were glowing in any of the windows. It was after midnight. Everyone was asleep.

Quietly, she entered the back door of her house. The structure was long, narrow and attached to the rock face like a barnacle. It contained not only her immediate family, but also her two grandmothers and many aunts, uncles and cousins.

Ling paused in the kitchen for a moment, inhaling the

familiar scent of home – her mother's perfume, the mouthwatering aroma of the pearl cakes her grandmother Wen always made and Lātà and Zàng, her brothers' lazy dogfish. They were snoring in a corner of the kitchen now. Each one opened an eye, looked her over, then went back to sleep.

Ling had taken a risk in coming here, but she had no choice. She needed to change her prison tunic for some real clothing, stock up on food and currensea and get some medicine. She'd left the Abyss two days ago and had not yet regained her magic. The effects of depth sickness were still plaguing her, causing her to swim slowly, and she needed to purge the sea wasp's poison from her system so she could songcast again.

And there was one more thing she had to do – the most important thing: speak with her sad, silent mother.

Ling made her way to her room, sliding the bamboo door open and closing it again behind her. Her bed looked so soft and inviting, it was all she could do not to flop down on it and sleep for a week. But she couldn't; she had to get to Sera.

Moving quickly, Ling opened her closet door and pulled a backpack off her shelf. She stuffed a change of clothing and a warm jacket into it. The rest of the space in her pack was for food. She planned to travel back currents – the lonelier, the better. She could not afford to be seen.

Once Orfeo found out she'd escaped from the labour camp, he'd have every death rider in the sea after her. The last thing he'd want would be for her to make it to Sera and tell her who Rafe Mfeme really was.

She changed into fresh clothing, first removing the puzzle ball from the pocket of her horrible prison tunic and placing it in the bottom of her pack. Then she cut her father's wedding ring out of the tunic's hem. She almost threw the uniform in the garbage, but thought better of it, instead stashing it in her pack's outer pocket. As soon as she came across a lava seam, she'd toss it in.

She made her way back to the kitchen, selected foods that would travel well and loaded them into her backpack. Next she opened her family's medicine cabinet and searched for something that would heal her. She found creams for cuts and rashes, tonics for fatigue, syrups for coughs and sore throats, but nothing to counteract venom. Moving bottles aside, she spotted her grandmother Wen's special elixir. Ling had no idea what was in it – Wen guarded the recipe closely – but it always made her feel better when she was sick. She uncapped the bottle, took a slug, recapped it and put it in her pack. Leaving her pack on the counter, she swam to her mother's room, patting her father's ring in her pocket.

Zhu was sleeping, but she stirred as Ling opened her door.

'Mum? Mum, wake up, it's me,' she whispered.

Zhu's eyes opened, then widened. She sat bolt upright in her bed, pulled Ling to her and held her tightly. Ling could feel her crying. Ling's anger towards her mother had drained from her heart in the Abyss. There she had experienced what it felt like to be frightened and weak, to have to rely on others. Even the strongest needed help sometimes.

Ling was glad the anger was gone. It made room for other things. Better things.

'It's okay, Mum,' she said. 'I'm here. I'm fine. I wanted to tell you I'm sorry. Sorry for yelling. Sorry for being angry. I didn't understand, but now I do. I think you stopped talking because no one would listen. I have something for you, Mum.'

Her mother released her and Ling pulled her father's wedding ring out of her pocket. She placed it in her mother's hand.

Her mother blinked at it.

'He's alive, Mum.'

Zhu looked at Ling uncomprehendingly.

'Dad. He's alive. He's in a prison camp at the edge of the Abyss.'

Zhu's eyes grew large with fear.

'Do you know about the death riders?' asked Ling. 'Have you seen them?'

Zhu shook her head.

'They're soldiers, Mum, working for a terrible man. They're stealing villagers and forcing them to search for a very important object.' Ling lowered her voice instinctively. 'Dad found that object and refused to hand it over. When they tried to take it, he chucked it back into the Abyss.'

Ling wasn't sure, but it sounded as though her mother might have laughed a little.

'I ran afoul of them, too. Big-time. And I ended up in the

same camp. Dad got me out. He gave this to me and told me to bring it to you.'

Zhu's hand trembled as she gingerly picked up the ring.

'He says he wants you to keep it safe until he gets home. Then you can put it on his hand again, just as you did on the day of your Promising.'

Fresh tears welled in her mother's eyes. She shook her head, overcome.

'This all started with the dreams I was having. About the river witches. Do you remember when I told you about them? You thought they were just nightmares.'

Zhu nodded slowly.

'Grandma Wen told me that the Iele were summoning me and I needed to go. I found out that things are really bad, Mum. These prison camps, they're horrible places, but they're only the beginning. There's a great evil threatening us. The river witches have called on me – and five others – to fight it.'

Zhu pulled on Ling's arm, as if to hold her back.

'There's a reason I was called, Mum. I can't tell you any more, because I want to keep you and the family safe. The death riders will come searching for me. If they do, no one can know I was here. They can't find out about Dad, either. Hide his wedding ring in case the death riders search the house. I've got to go now.'

Zhu shook her head vehemently and started to get out of bed.

Ling held her back and hugged her again. 'The longer I

stay, the more dangerous it is – for me, you, everyone.'

Zhu wiped her eyes and coughed.

At least, Ling thought it was a cough. But no, it was a word, spoken in a voice raspy from disuse.

'Ling,' her mother said.

Ling was overwhelmed by the sound. She longed to stay and talk with her forever.

'I . . . I'm sorry.'

'Oh, Mum. You don't need to apologize. I understand now,' Ling said. 'Just don't give up on us, okay?'

'I love you,' her mother croaked. 'Please . . . be careful.'

'I love you, too, Mum. I'll be back. And Dad will, too. One day, we'll all be together again.'

Ling kissed her mother's cheek. Then, before she could change her mind, she went to the kitchen, grabbed her backpack and swam out of her house, wishing she could believe her own words.

FIFTY-NINE

'ARE YOU *SURE* you have enough food?' Elisabetta asked Becca.

Becca looked at her over the top of her eyeglasses. 'Are you *serious*? You've packed so much for me, I can barely carry it. And if I run out, which I won't, I have currensea.'

The *Marlin* was bobbing in the grey waters of the North Sea. It had been three days since Becca, Marco, and Elisabetta had evaded Mfeme's boats.

'We're five leagues west of the camp,' Elisabetta said. 'We don't dare drop you any closer. The Meerteufel subscribe to the shoot-first-ask-questions-later school of defence,' she added wryly. 'Approach the camp from the seafloor, and you won't spook them. You have transparensea pearls in case of death riders, and—'

Becca threw her arms around Elisabetta, cutting her off. 'Stop worrying, El. I'll be fine. I'm almost there,' she said, hugging her tightly.

Elisabetta hugged her back, then held her by the shoulders.

'Be careful,' she said.

'I will. Thank you, El. I'd be chum if it wasn't for you and Marco. And who knows what would've become of the talisman. I owe you everything.'

'No, Becca, we owe *you* everything,' said Elisabetta. 'You and your friends. Stop them – Vallerio, Traho, Mfeme. Stop them before it's too late.'

Marco came below decks. He handed Elisabetta a pair of binoculars. 'An oil tanker and two shipping vessels. That's all. No sign of Mfeme's goons.'

'Good. The sooner we get out of here, the better,' Elisabetta said.

She glanced at her brother as she took the binoculars from him. She could see, as Becca could, that his mouth was smiling, but his eyes were not.

'I'll . . . uh, say my final goodbye now, Becca. Because I . . . um . . . I need to check . . . the engine,' Elisabetta said awkwardly. She gave Becca a final wave, then climbed up the ladder.

'That was strange,' Becca said as she watched her go.

Marco looked at the floor. 'No, not really,' he said. 'She knows.'

'Knows what?' Becca asked.

He raised his eyes to hers. 'That I have feelings for you.'

Becca caught her breath. She thought she'd only imagined Marco's interest in her. She'd put her feelings for him aside. It was so much safer that way. Falling for a terragogg was *never* part of the plan.

'I kind of lied the other day,' Marco continued, all in a rush. 'When you asked me what I was going to tell you before Mfeme's men chased us. I lost my nerve, I guess. What I wanted to say was that I . . . I think I've fallen in love with you, Becca.'

'Marco, you know I'm a mermaid, right?'

He smiled. 'I hadn't noticed.'

'And you're a human. And no matter what we feel—'

'So you feel the same way?' he asked hopefully.

Becca didn't answer the question. She finished her sentence. 'It's impossible.'

'Everything's impossible, Becca,' Marco said, taking her hand. 'Getting the talismans is impossible. Defeating Abbadon is impossible. Stopping finners and super trawlers and polluters is impossible. Our feelings are impossible—'

'Marco, I—'

'What? You don't have feelings for me? Just tell me so and I'll shut up.'

Becca averted her eyes and didn't say a word.

'A lot of things in this world are impossible until someone *makes* them possible,' Marco finished softly.

Becca couldn't speak. Her practical head was warring with her rebel heart.

'We're very stupid, Marco,' she finally said.

He winced. 'Love is never stupid, Becca.'

'Then I must be.'

'I'm sorry you feel that way,' Marco said, clearly wounded by her words.

'I didn't mean to be harsh. But this hurts,' Becca said. 'As wonderful as the last days have been, I almost wish they'd never happened, because it's so hard to let go of them now. And of you.'

'Then don't.'

'How can I not? I'm *leaving*, Marco. I'm joining my friends to take on death riders, dictators and a homicidal monster. The odds aren't in my favour, you know? Chances are, I'm not coming back.'

Becca's meaning lay heavily in the air between them.

Marco fell silent. Becca did, too. She didn't know what else to say.

Becca was an expert at making things work. As an orphan, she'd had to be. She'd had to make lousy foster homes work. Meagre meals. Secondhand clothing. But no matter how many times she turned her feelings for Marco over in her head, looking at them from different angles, trying to make *them* work, she couldn't.

'Marco, I – I've got to go,' she said, picking up her travelling case.

Marco nodded. 'I'll see you again someday,' he said. 'In another place. A better one . . . I – I love you, Becca.'

Tears filled her eyes. 'Don't *say* that. Not now. It's not *fair*!'

'No, it's not,' Marco agreed. 'But it's true.'

Becca hit the button that allowed her to enter the water lock. The hatch opened. She glanced back once before leaving.

'Goodbye, Marco,' she said.

And then she was gone. She buttoned her jacket up around her neck as she descended, unused to the cold after spending a week in the saltwater tank.

Marco's words rang in her ears . . . *I love you, Becca*.

She hadn't responded, because there'd been no point. It was over before it had even started. It was time to be practical, just as she'd always been. It was time to listen to her head.

But as she swam away, deeper and deeper into the sea, she stopped and looked back. She could just make out the tapered hull of the *Marlin*, silhouetted on the surface of the water. She thought she saw something else, too – on the starboard bow. A shadow. Marco's shadow.

Becca's heart clenched, and she confessed to the sea what she could not say to him.

'I love you, too, Marco. I wish to the gods I didn't.'

SIXTY

SERA HELD UP her crossbow and took aim.

The conger eel was magnificent. She guessed it was about seven feet long and weighed close to two hundred pounds. She didn't want to shoot it, but she had no choice. The goblins were watching.

She prayed to the gods for a clean kill, then let her arrow fly. The eel never knew what hit it. It died instantly, sinking slowly to the mud.

Sera wanted to cry. Instead, she turned around to face the goblins, smiling triumphantly. 'Tonight my brave warriors will feast!' she shouted in the goblins' own tongue.

A cheer went up, loud and guttural. The Meerteufel were pleased with the kill and Sera was relieved. She'd told Antonio, the cook, that she would address the food shortage and she had. Not only did the hunts bring much-needed food to the camp, they channelled the goblins' energy in a constructive way.

That was one problem solved, but there were always

more. They were still short on weapons and barracks space, as well as food. Not all the fighters that Guldemar had promised her had arrived yet, but even when they did, her military would still be much smaller than her uncle's.

The thing that worried her most of all, however, was her friends. Was Mahdi safe? Was his ruse still working? Had Astrid and Desiderio encountered death riders at the Qanikkaaq? What had happened to Becca and Ava? Sera had heard nothing from either of them since she'd warned them that Vallerio's troops were heading for Cape Horn and the Mississippi. The goblin fighters she'd sent to protect them couldn't cast convocas, so Sera had no idea if they'd been able to carry out their task.

And then there was Ling. Sera's heart ached when she thought of her. She was still optimistic that the others were okay and were making their ways to the Karg, but her hopes for Ling were fading.

Ling was an incredible communicator. If she were still alive, she would have found a way of letting Sera know. Sera told herself, a hundred times a day, that it was time she faced the fact that Ling was gone. But deep in her heart, she couldn't let go. *We're bloodbound, aren't we?* she told herself. *If Ling died, part of me would die with her. Surely I'd feel it?*

The sound of singing pulled her out of her thoughts.

She'd led the hunting party of about a hundred Meerteufel out in the early evening when sea creatures rose to the surface to feed. The party had moved north of the camp to Skuld's Rise, then divided itself into groups of three, fanning out over the hills and shallows. They'd agreed to meet back at the rise two hours later. A goblin named Dreck led the party Sera was hunting with. The goblins Totschläger and Garstig led the other groups. Totschläger's band was returning now, singing as they trudged along. Some of them carried thick kelp stalks, the ends balanced on their shoulders. From the stalks hung their kills.

'Well done,' Sera said approvingly.

Totschläger smiled at her praise, revealing his stumpy, broken teeth, and then the goblins from both groups admired each other's kills and discussed how best to prepare them. Sera, meanwhile, wondered where the third group was. The dusk was deepening. It was time to return to camp. She didn't like to be in the open waters after dark.

'Totschläger, Dreck . . . where's Garstig?' she asked.

The goblin leaders looked at each other. Their smiles turned to frowns.

'He should've been back by now,' Dreck said.

'He might've been ambushed,' Totschläger said. 'He's stupid enough.'

Sera's fins prickled. She gathered everyone and swam off after Garstig. 'Keep your weapons raised,' she ordered.

After only a few minutes, Totschläger picked up the trail. 'They came this way,' he said, pointing to footprints in the silt.

They followed the tracks to the edge of a kelp forest and were just about to enter it when they heard voices. Sera quickly signalled the goblins to fall back. They hid behind rocks or flattened themselves in ditches, their weapons ready.

The noises grew louder. Kelp fronds cracked and snapped as whatever was in the forest moved through it. Sera held up a hand and the soldiers raised their weapons. Sera heard goblin voices coming from the kelp, and mer voices, too. Had death riders captured Garstig?

The stalks at the edge of the forest shuddered, and then Garstig burst out of them, followed by his troops.

At Sera's command, Totschläger and the others lowered their weapons.

'Garstig, where *were* you?' she shouted, angry and relieved at the same time. She swam up to him. 'We thought you'd been ambushed!'

'Garstig ambushed?' the goblin growled, insulted. '*Never*. Garstig did the ambushing and caught more than eels. We caught spies – three of them. Bring the sea scum here!' he bellowed.

Three mer, their hands behind their backs, were roughly pushed forward.

'Wow. This is some welcome, Sera,' said one of the spies. She was tall and blonde, wearing a sealskin parka and a furious expression.

'Hey, Sera,' said the second spy, a mermaid with red hair and glasses.

'Sera? Is that *you*?' said the third spy, a merman with green eyes and copper-coloured hair.

Sera shook her head, so overjoyed she could barely speak. She rushed to her brother and, half-laughing, half-crying, threw her arms around his neck.

'I hardly recognize you. Where's the gown and the jewellery, little sister? Where are the conchs you always carried around? Where's your *hair*?' Desiderio asked.

'Gone, Des. It's gone. Everything's gone. Cerulea. The palace. Mum and Dad—' Her voice broke.

'Shh, Sera. I know, I know,' said Des. 'Astrid told me everything.'

Sera held on to her brother for a long moment, eyes closed, their sorrow too deep for words. Then she let him go.

'Astrid . . . Becca . . .' Sera said. 'I'm so glad you're safe. So glad you're *here*.' She pulled both mermaids into a tight embrace.

'Me, too, Sera,' Becca said, emotion in her voice.

'Okay, that's good. We're good. I'm good,' Astrid said, clearly unused to public displays of affection.

Sera kissed her cheek. Astrid grimaced. When Sera kissed Becca, she realized their hands were bound. Desiderio's, too.

'Garstig, cut them loose!' she ordered.

Garstig looked crestfallen. 'They're *not* spies?' he said.

'No, this is my brother, Desiderio. And these are my friends, Astrid Kolfinnsdottir and Becca Quickfin. Des, Astrid, Becca . . . meet Garstig, Totschläger, Dreck, and their fellow Meerteufel.'

A collective sigh of unhappiness moved through the goblin troops as Garstig cut the ties around his prisoners' wrists.

'What's the matter?' Sera asked, confused.

'Spies are very delicious stuffed with beach plums and roasted,' Garstig explained.

'Sorry to disappoint you,' Astrid said.

'Totschläger and Dreck caught over thirty conger eels between them,' Sera said. 'The Meerteufel will feast tonight.'

Garstig's eyes lit up. 'Eels are also delicious stuffed with beach plums,' he said.

Totschläger snorted. 'They're better wrapped with ribbon worms and basted with squid ink.'

As the goblins argued, Sera turned back to her friends. 'How did you get here?' she asked.

'Some friends gave me a lift,' Becca said, glancing around. 'That part's a long story. I'll explain later.' Sera nodded and Becca continued. 'They dropped me off a few leagues west of here. I had to swim down from the surface, and as I did, I saw two other mer swimming towards the camp. I recognized Astrid and caught up with them.'

Sera had to ask them. She had to know.

'Becca, did you . . .'

She didn't finish, but she didn't need to.

'It's in my pocket,' Becca said, smiling.

Sera almost whooped for joy. 'Becs, you're amazing! That makes three out of six!' she whispered.

She looked at Astrid next, hoping against hope, but Astrid shook her head.

'We got to the maelstrom, Des and I, about eight centuries too late,' she said. 'It's not there any more.'

Sera's heart fell. Her feelings must've shown on her face,

because Astrid brusquely said, 'Sorry to let you down.'

'You *didn't* let me down,' Sera said fiercely, taking her by her shoulders. 'You're here with us, Astrid. We're the Six now, just like we were meant to be. And that means the world to me.'

Astrid looked at Sera sceptically. 'But I didn't get the talisman. We don't have it,' she said.

'*Yet,*' Sera said. 'Maybe there's still a way. Once you've rested up you can tell me what happened, then we'll figure out the next stroke together. Has anyone heard from Ava or Ling?'

'No,' Becca said, worry creasing her brow. 'We were hoping you had.'

Their conversation was interrupted by Garstig shouting at Totschläger. The argument over the best way to cook conger eel had escalated.

'I'd better see to this,' Sera said.

Desiderio's eyes widened in alarm. 'Don't, Sera. Goblins get nasty when they fight. You might get hurt.'

Sera laughed. 'Yes, I might,' she said. Then she swam between them, placing a hand on each goblin's chest. 'Stop,' she said. 'You need to sort that out with Antonio at the mess hall. We shouldn't be out here. It's not safe. Let's get everyone back to camp.'

The two goblins grumbled, but they followed her orders.

Desiderio looked at her, obviously impressed. 'Guess I shouldn't call you little sister any more,' he said. 'I know grown mermen who won't get between two angry goblins.

I can't wait to see the camp.'

'I can't wait to lie down in a soft bed,' Becca said.

'I could use a hot meal,' Astrid added.

'You'll see most of the camp on our way back in through the north hills. As for the rest . . . how about a nice *hard* bed and some roasted conger eel?' Sera asked sardonically.

There were few comforts to be had at camp, but suddenly that didn't seem to matter. Her brother was here. Her two friends were, too. Vrăja said they were more powerful when they were together. Sera had sensed that back in the Iele's caves. She sensed it again now. She felt stronger and more hopeful now than she had in many months.

Maybe the tide was finally beginning to turn.

SIXTY-ONE

SERA HAD FORGOTTEN what an excellent waterfire caster Becca was.

She had conjured some crackling flames in the centre of the command cave and they were all sitting around them now – Sera, Astrid, Becca, Yazeed, Des, Sophia, and Neela.

Sera smiled as she passed around a bowl of reef olives, remembering Neela's reaction when Des, Astrid, and Becca had swum into the cave. She'd screamed at the top of her lungs, hugged all three of them until they could barely breathe and turned the most bright, beautiful shade of blue. She was still glowing now, an hour later.

While Becca had cast the waterfire, everyone else helped scrape together a meal. The goblins were still arguing over the best way to prepare conger eel and Sera predicted it would be quite some time before the issue was settled. All Sera, Neela and Yaz had to contribute were reef olives and walrus cheese, but Becca had water apples, a marsh melon and whelk eggs, and Astrid and Des had salted tube worms and silt cherries.

To Sera, it felt like a feast. As they ate, Astrid, Des and Becca told their stories, and Sera and Neela recounted theirs.

Becca described her trip to Cape Horn, and how she found her talisman and tried to escape the Williwaw – only to have it toss her into some rocks. She said that she had the new duca di Venezia and his sister to thank for saving her.

Sera asked what Marco was like. Her heart still hurt when she thought about Armando, Marco's father, and how he'd been killed by Rafe Mfeme.

'He and Elisabetta are very kind. And very brave,' Becca said, with gratitude in her voice – and something else. Something Sera couldn't name at first, but then recognized – love.

It was an odd emotion to feel for a terragogg, but Sera understood. She herself had loved the old duca for his kindness and bravery. Becca, she reasoned, probably had similar feelings for the new duca and his sister.

Then Becca gave her Pyrrha's gold coin. Sera held it in her hand, feeling its power, and then passed it around. When it was handed back to her, she rose and put it in a strongbox together with Merrow's blue diamond and Navi's moonstone. She placed the strongbox in a niche in the command cave's wall, then cast a camo songspell that made it look as if there was no niche, only smooth cave wall.

As Sera sat down again, Astrid informed them about the death of her father and Commodora Rylka's treachery. Desiderio described his imprisonment and how Ludo had helped him and Astrid escape on an orca named Elskan.

Astrid actually sounded a little sad when she described how she'd had to command Elskan to go back home once they'd hit the east Atlantic. The waters there were too warm for the orca, but Elskan hadn't wanted to go. She'd nosed Astrid and cried in her whale language.

Des said, 'Elskan wasn't the only one who cried.'

Astrid scowled. 'You're *so* wrong; I just had something in my eye.'

Then Astrid and Des related their trip to the maelstrom and how a Viking chieftain named Feimor Fa Eaemor had come to possess the pearl. Sera leaned forward as they spoke, eager to hear every word.

When they finished, she asked, 'What happened to the black pearl after Feimor died?'

'The maelstrom didn't say,' Astrid said. 'It was too busy trying to kill us.'

Sera nodded thoughtfully, remembering how Vallerio and Portia had spoken of the shadowy *he* who, they claimed, had the pearl. 'If only we could find out for certain. Maybe someone knows who became chieftain after Feimor, and if he inherited the pearl,' she said.

'Um, Sera,' Astrid began, 'I know you're Little Miss Optimistic, but this whole thing has gone from pretty impossible to totally impossible. Feimor was a Viking. He would've been buried with the pearl. And even if he wasn't, even if he passed it down to a relative, that relative was human. Humans live on *land*. And we don't have feet.'

A silence descended in the cave. Becca broke it. 'Lots of things are impossible,' she said softly. 'Until they're not.'

'That's true,' Neela said. '*We're* not human – but Marco and Elisabetta are. They might be able to find out if the pearl was passed down and if a living human now has it.'

'How, Neela?' Astrid asked. 'Marco and Elisabetta . . . they can only cover so much ground. The pearl could be *anywhere* on land. With *any* human. There are hundreds of *millions* of them.'

'Forget that,' said a voice from behind them.

The mermaid leaning on Garstig's arm, in the cave's mouth, was frighteningly thin. She had dark circles under her weary eyes and a pale, haggard face.

'I know who has the pearl,' she said. 'And he's definitely not human.'

SIXTY-TWO

'*LING*!' SERAFINA CRIED.

She swam to her friend and embraced her. It was like hugging a bundle of reeds. Ling started to cough as Sera released her, and couldn't stop. Her face took on a bluish cast. Just as Sera started to panic, the cough stopped and Ling inhaled a lungful of water.

'Depth sickness,' she said. 'And sea wasp poisoning.'

Neela, Becca and Astrid had swum over, too.

'Some of my fighters found her on the south side of the camp,' said Garstig. 'She collapsed there. They brought her to me. Is she a spy?' he asked hopefully.

'No, Garstig, she's not. Thank you for bringing her here,' Sera said.

Disappointed, the goblin stalked off. Astrid and Becca got Ling to the waterfire and eased her down. Neela brought her a cup of hot sargasso tea. Ling took it gratefully.

'Let me find you some food,' Neela said.

Ling held up a hand, stopping her. 'Thank you, Neela,

but I need to talk to you all first. Just in case I start coughing again and can't stop.'

Ling's eyes, wary and untrusting, took in the unfamiliar faces in the cave. Sera saw her doubt. 'They know everything, Ling,' she said. 'I trust them completely.'

Ling nodded. She slipped off her backpack, dug inside it, and pulled out the puzzle ball. 'Here you go,' she said, handing it to Sera. 'Sycorax's talisman.'

Sera gasped, astonished. She couldn't believe she was holding yet another of the precious objects. As she'd done with Pyrrha's coin, she passed it to the others, then put it safely away in her strongbox.

'How did you get it?' she asked, sitting down again.

'I'll tell you, but before I do, you need to know something.'

Another bout of coughing shook her emaciated frame. She had to sit for a moment after it was over to gather strength before she could continue.

'Ling, do you need to lie down?' Sera asked, scared for her friend.

'No, Sera, I need to *speak*,' Ling insisted. 'What I've got to tell you is very important. Rafe Mfeme has the black pearl.'

The brutal terragogg flashed into Sera's mind. She saw him aboard his ship, the *Bedrieër*, trying to haul Ling up in a net.

'Great Neria, *he* has Morsa's pearl?' she said.

'Wait, Ling,' Astrid cut in. 'I thought you said that the one who has the black pearl *isn't* human.'

Ling laughed wearily. 'I did.'

'But how can that be?' Astrid asked. 'Rafe Mfeme's definitely a terragogg.'

Ling shook her head. 'We had no idea who we were dealing with. Duca Armando didn't know. Even Vrăja didn't.'

Sera's fins prickled. 'Ling, what exactly are you saying?' she asked.

Ling looked at them all in turn. 'Rafe Mfeme *isn't* human. He's not even Rafe Mfeme. He's the most powerful mage who ever lived. *Orfeo*.'

SIXTY-THREE

A SHOCKED SILENCE DESCENDED.

Sera was reeling. From the looks on her companions' faces, they were, too.

'Orfeo's here. And he's very much alive,' Ling said. 'He's the man Sera and I saw in the mirror in Atlantis.'

Sera remembered that horrible face. 'I saw him in my room, too, in the palace,' she said quietly.

'He's the one who wants to free Abbadon,' Ling added. 'He's trying to find the talismans before we do.'

Astrid sat forward. 'How do you know this?' she asked, an intensity to her voice that Sera hadn't heard before. She wondered at it.

Ling smiled bitterly. 'Because I had the not-so-great pleasure of being a guest aboard his trawler.'

'What happened?' Neela asked.

Ling told them everything, starting with the interrogation aboard the *Bedrieër*. She recounted how Mfeme spelled out his full name, RAFE IAORO MFEME, with her letter tiles, then used magic to rearrange them into I AM ORFEO FEAR ME. She described the prison camp, and informed them about the weapons shipments. They were riveted by her reunion with her father, her search for the talisman and her journey to the Kargjord.

'I planned to go to Miromara,' she said. 'But I knew I didn't have the energy to swim the entire way. So I decided to go through the mirror realm.'

'That was *very* risky,' Sera scolded.

'It was also very lucky,' Ling said. 'Rorrim was busy upsetting a terragogg so I was able to slip down the Hall of Sighs without his seeing me. I found a mirror that led to a room in Cerulea's palace. A vitrina lived in it. I knew you wouldn't be in the palace, Sera, but I thought the vitrina might've overheard something about where you'd gone.'

'Good thinking,' Becca said.

'I had to flatter her like mad,' Ling continued, 'but she finally told me some gossip about Lucia Volnero – I gather she thinks she's the new regina?'

'*Thinks* being the operative word,' said Sera, her fins flaring.

Ling nodded. 'The vitrina overheard a very unpleasant man named Baco Goga tell Lucia and her mother about your activities. He said he has a spy in your midst.'

Sera looked at Yazeed. 'You were right,' she said.

'As soon as I learned that you were in the Karg, I started searching for a mirror that would get me close to it. The vitrina—'

Here Ling started coughing again. Sera told her to take

a break and just listen to the others for a while. Ling was happy to hear that Neela had indeed recovered Navi's moonstone and that Pyrrha's gold coin had been found, but she was puzzled when Sera told her that they had Merrow's diamond, too.

'Orfeo told me *he* has it,' Ling whispered hoarsely.

'He only thinks he does,' said Sera. 'The infanta wore a fake in case it was ever stolen from her. That's what Orfeo has.'

Ling sat back, a smile spreading across her face.

'I still can't believe he's alive. *How?*' Neela asked. 'Orfeo died *four thousand years ago*! How did he just – *poof!* – reappear?'

Ling shook her head. She took another sip of tea before speaking. 'I don't think he just reappeared. After hearing your stories, I think he's been around for a very long time.'

'What do you mean?' Sera asked.

'Remember how I told you that Mfeme's full name – Rafe Iaoro Mfeme – is an anagram for I AM ORFEO FEAR ME?' Ling asked.

There were nods all around.

'So is Feimor Fa Eaemor,' Ling said.

Sera's heart lurched. 'Oh, my gods,' she said in a hushed voice. 'Amarrefe Mei Foo . . .'

'Who's that?' Becca asked.

'He's the pirate who tried to get Merrow's blue diamond from Maria Theresa, the infanta of Spain. *His* name's an anagram, too.'

'Holy silt,' Becca said. 'So's Maffeio Aermore. The sea captain who tried to sail into the Williwaw's cave.'

'There were probably others. Way before Feimor,' Astrid said. 'Names that are lost to time.'

'Orfeo *never* died. He's been here ever since Atlantis fell, hunting for the talismans,' Sera said, chilled to her very soul.

'But all the histories, all the accounts – they all say he *did* die. Merrow and the other mages *saw* him die. They killed him themselves! I'm asking you again, merl . . . *how?*' Neela demanded.

'He used the black pearl somehow, together with the secrets of immortality Morsa gleaned from her necromancing,' Ling offered.

'But that still doesn't answer Neela's question,' Desiderio said. 'It still doesn't tell us how.'

'The black pearl was the container. It *had* to be,' Astrid said.

'*Container?* What do you mean?' Desiderio asked.

'What remains when the body dies?' Astrid asked.

'The soul,' Yazeed said. 'Horok carries it to the underworld.'

Astrid nodded. 'In what?'

Desiderio snapped his fingers. 'A pearl!'

'Exactly,' said Astrid. 'Morsa knew how to capture a soul, too, in her black pearl. Isn't that what Thalia said?'

'That's correct,' Sera said.

'Orfeo used the goddess's pearl to hold a soul, too – his own,' Astrid said.

'I think I see where you're going with this,' Sera said excitedly, impressed that Astrid had put it all together.

'Merrow and the other mages killed Orfeo,' Astrid ventured. 'Or so they thought. But as the life ebbed from his body, his soul entered the black pearl. He probably wore it around his neck then, just as he does now.'

'And Merrow had no idea,' Sera said.

'Not a clue,' Astrid said. 'She took the pearl from his body, never knowing his soul was inside it, and chucked it into the Qaanikaaq. Then the tuna swam into the maelstrom and ate the pearl. The fisherman caught it, found the pearl, and sold it to the Viking warrior, who wore it on his body. As he did, Orfeo's soul flowed into him, possessing him. That's why he changed his name. And how he became so formidable so quickly.'

'Because he wasn't a simple warrior any more, he was the most powerful mage who'd ever lived,' Becca said.

'And when *his* body wore out, Orfeo's soul flowed back into the pearl, only to be worn by a different host, and so on,' said Ling.

'He would've had to know when his host body was dying, and make sure he had another host in place,' Neela said.

'Which isn't impossible,' Ling added. 'I've seen Orfeo's tactics. He'd think nothing of having his thugs string the pearl around a new victim's neck.'

It was perfectly quiet in the cave as the mer digested this.

Sera was the first to speak. 'If we're right, it explains everything,' she said. 'It explains how Traho was always one stroke ahead of us. How he knew what the talismans were when even the Iele didn't. Because Orfeo told him. It explains who the mysterious *he* is that Vallerio and Portia talked about after Lucia's Dokimí, the *he* who helped fund Vallerio's army, who wanted the talismans.'

'We *are* right, Sera,' said Astrid. 'Orfeo said he would do it, didn't he?'

Sera nodded. 'He did. Thalia said he vowed to take Alma back from the underworld if it took him a thousand lifetimes.'

Sophia, who'd been quietly listening this whole time, spoke up now. 'We've got to get the black pearl.'

Becca raised an eyebrow. 'And how will we do that? Just ask Orfeo politely? Astrid's right. This *is* impossible. There's no way to get it.'

Astrid stared into the waterfire, as if gazing at something only she could see. 'No, I was wrong. There is a way,' she said solemnly.

'What is it?'

'We kill Orfeo for real this time.'

'*How*, Astrid?' Ling asked.

She didn't answer.

Ling turned away, sighing with frustration. Neela made a plate of food for her, and as she ate, the others' conversation became even more animated.

But Astrid, Sera noticed, didn't join in. She just kept staring into the waterfire, wearing a grim, and determined, expression.

SIXTY-FOUR

'REGINA SERAFINA!' a harsh voice shouted. 'Wake up! There's trouble.'

Astrid's eyes flew open. In a heartbeat, she was up off the cave floor and reaching for her sword. Sera, one stroke ahead of her, was already rushing to the cave's entrance.

Three goblins stood there, illuminated by lava torches. As Astrid's eyes adjusted, she realized she knew two of them: Dreck and Totschläger. They were supporting another goblin between them – a young female. She had a ragged bandage on one leg, another on her head. Blood stained her uniform.

'This is Mulmig,' Totschläger explained to Sera. 'She was part of the force you sent to the Mississippi to look for the mermaid Ava.'

Astrid joined Sera, the better to hear the goblins. Neela, Ling and Becca did the same. The five mermaids had only bedded down for the night about an hour ago. They'd stayed up so late talking, they'd decided it was easier to just sleep in the cave where they were, on patches of seaweed. The other

Black Fins had left for their barracks, with Des joining Yazeed in his.

'We made it into the swamps,' Mulmig said wearily. 'We picked up Ava's trail.'

'You found her? Is she okay?' Sera asked urgently.

Mulmig shook her head. 'We *didn't* find her. The death riders found us. It—' Her voice broke. She tried again. 'It was a bloodbath. We fought hard, but they outnumbered us four to one. I took a spear to my leg. And then I got knocked out. When I came to, it was like I was lying in a cemetery. Everyone in my unit was dead. And the death riders were gone.'

Sera looked as if she'd been gutted. 'How did you get back here?' she asked.

'A bull shark, a dolphin and a basking shark,' Mulmig replied. 'Each carried me part of the way. I owe them my life.'

'Thank you for what you've done,' Sera said, taking the goblin's hands in hers. 'I count myself lucky to have you fighting with us.' She turned to Dreck and Totschläger. 'Take her to the infirmary.'

As the goblins left the cave, Becca cast some fresh waterfire. Sera turned to the others, the heels of her hands against her forehead. 'An entire unit wiped out, death riders in the swamps and no Ava,' she said. She took a deep breath and lowered her hands. 'We've got to convoca her. Now. Ling, do you feel up to it?'

Ling nodded. Becca and Neela took each other's hands.

And Astrid's stomach dropped.

This was the moment she'd been dreading. She'd known it would come, but she hadn't thought it would come so soon. She wasn't ready.

'Maybe it would be better if I helped out with Mulmig,' she said, panicking. 'I'm good with bandages. You don't need me for the convoca.'

Astrid felt Becca's eyes on her. She glanced over at her. *Tell them*, Becca mouthed. *It's okay*. Astrid shook her head.

'We *do* need you,' Ling said. 'Vrăja told us that our magic is strongest when it's combined. We'll have a better chance of getting Ava if we cast together.' She reached for Astrid's hand.

'I . . . uh, I'm really tired,' Astrid said, desperate. 'I think I need some sleep.'

Becca couldn't contain herself any longer. 'You need to tell them,' she said. 'This can't go on forever.'

'Tell us what?' Ling asked.

Astrid glared at Becca. 'Thanks,' she said. 'Thanks a lot.'

'Is something wrong? Maybe we can help you,' Sera said.

Astrid heaved a deep sigh. They were kind and concerned now, but would they still be when she told them the truth?

Becca swam up to Astrid and put a gentle hand on her back. 'When you keep a secret, the secret keeps you,' she said. 'Haven't you figured that out yet?'

Astrid *had* to tell them now. There was no getting out of it. 'I can't songcast,' she blurted out. 'I lost my singing voice when I was little.'

'You have no magic?' Sera asked. 'None at all?'

Astrid listened for any sound of derision or contempt in her voice, but she didn't hear any. Only compassion.

'I have *some* magic,' she said. 'Remnants, I guess. I didn't even know it until Becca made me a whalebone pipe. I've learned to play a few basic songspells on it.'

'And this is a problem why?' Ling asked impatiently. 'We haven't got all night here, merls. Neither does Ava.' She held out her hand to Astrid again.

But Astrid shook her head. 'I. Can't. *Songcast*. You don't want me with you. You really don't. When you get into Abbadon's prison you'll need everyone to be at the top of her game. I'm *not* at the top of my game and I never will be.'

'*We*,' Ling said simply. 'When we get into Abbadon's prison. Need I remind you, Astrid, who saved the day back in the Iele's caves? I'd be very happy for you to have my back in the Incarceron whether you were at the top of your game, the bottom or anywhere in between.'

Becca crossed her arms over her chest. 'That's what *I* told her,' she said. 'She doesn't listen.'

'Maybe she will now,' Sera said, pulling her dagger out of its sheath.

'Whoa! What are you *doing*?' Astrid asked, her eyes wide.

'Bringing you into the bloodbind,' Sera replied, drawing the blade across her own palm. 'We swore an oath to each other in the Iele's caves after you left, and sealed it in blood.'

'A bloodbind is darksong,' Astrid said, remembering that Becca had told her about the pact they'd made in the Iele's caves. 'You break a blood oath, you die.'

'Yes, you do. Maybe now you'll believe that we mean it. We want you with us, Astrid. Vrăja summoned six of us. Not five. We can't do this without you.'

Sera handed the dagger to Ling, who made a small slit in her palm, too. Becca followed suit, then Neela. When Neela finished, she gave the blade to Astrid.

Astrid took it and stared at it. She was trembling. The EisGeist, the Qanikkaaq, even Rylka – none of them had made her feel as afraid as she did right now. What these four mermaids were asking was so hard. They were asking her to join them, to trust them, to let them be her friends.

Voices echoed in her head again. Even though she'd tried to forget them.

Her father's. *Who wants a mermaid without magic?*

Tauno's. *She's a freaky freakin' freak!*

And the mirror man's. *Where are you going, Astrid? To your friends? Do you really think it will be different with them?*

At that moment, Astrid realized there would *always* be voices telling her she wasn't good enough. Old voices. New voices. And she knew that she'd never be able to silence them.

But here, surrounded by friends who wanted her, she recognized for the first time that there was only one voice that truly mattered. Only one she had to listen to. Her own.

She took a deep breath, and cut her palm.

As her blood swirled in the water with the blood of her friends, Sera sang the words to a bloodbind. The others joined her. Astrid did, too, surprised to find that she somehow knew the words.

At last all six are joined together
And bonds of blood cannot be severed.
One mind, one heart, one soul are we,
Our vows as deathless as the seas.
My heart, my sister, and my friend,
Our ties no mer can ever rend.
Now the circle is complete
And Abbadon we will defeat.

The blood of the five mermaids combined, then spiralled back down into the wounds on their hands. Their flesh closed and instantly healed, leaving a thin, livid scar. Astrid knew she had the blood of her five friends in her now. Ava's too, because her blood had mixed with the others' in the first bloodbind. Astrid felt stronger than ever before.

'Okay,' she said, looking at each of her blood sisters in turn. 'Enough touchy-feely stuff for one night. Can we get on with the convoca now? Ava needs us.'

The other four mermaids looked at each other, trying not to smile, then all five joined hands.

SIXTY-FIVE

'*OLÁ, GATINHAS!*' Ava called out. '*Como vai?*'

'Ava, are you crazy? Keep it *down*!' Sera hissed. 'The death riders are in the swamps now. They could be close!'

Ava nodded and held a finger to her lips. Baby circled her protectively. The spell had worked – Ava had answered them almost immediately.

'It's good to talk to you!' she said in a quieter voice. 'Astrid, is that *you*?'

'Hi, Ava,' Astrid said. 'Wow. That is one creepy swamp you're in.' Her mind's eye took in the black water; the long, twining tree roots, and the alligator floating overhead.

'I know!' Ava said. 'It's smelly, too! You're all together . . . does that mean your talismans are together too?'

'All but the black pearl,' Becca said.

Ava whisper-cheered, and was about to congratulate them, but Sera cut her off.

'Ava, *listen* to me. We didn't convoca you to chat. This is urgent,' she said. 'After I found out my uncle's troops were headed to the swamps, I sent a unit of goblin fighters there to protect you. The death riders killed all of them except one. She made it back here and told us that they're closing in on you. You've *got* to get out of there. Forget about the talisman and make wake for the Kargjord!'

Ava shook her head. 'No,' she said.

'*No?*' Sera echoed, dumbfounded. 'Didn't you hear what I just said?'

'I did, but I'm not leaving the swamp. Not without the ring. I can get it, I know I can. I talked to some swamp mer a few days ago. They say the Okwa Naholo are so terrifying that just the sight of them is enough to kill a mer instantly.'

'*What?* Ava, don't you go near them!' Neela shrilled.

Ava laughed. 'Aren't you forgetting something? I'm *blind*! It doesn't *matter* how scary the spirits are – I can't see them!'

'You also can't see the death riders coming!' Sera said frantically.

'I'm not leaving. Not without my talisman,' Ava insisted. 'Don't you understand? The gods chose *me* to go into the swamps and deal with the Okwa Naholo. Me and no one else. I'll succeed because I can't see the spirits. The gods knew that. They're going to answer my question.'

Sera shook her head, speechless with frustration.

'What question? What are you talking about, Ava?' Ling asked.

'I never told any of you how I lost my sight.'

'Ava?' Sera said, struggling to keep her voice level. 'I'm

not sure we have time for *stories* right now. Death riders could be close and they *can* hurt you. You need to get *out of there*!'

'Vrăja said stories tell us who we are. My story tells who *I* am. You need to know that. You need to know why I won't leave.'

'*Ava* . . .' Sera said through gritted teeth.

'Let her speak,' Ling said.

'I live in a *favela*, a poor part of town,' Ava began. 'When I was six, I came down with a fever. There was no money for a doctor. My parents tried to break the fever with home remedies, but nothing worked. The fever took my sight. My papi cried so hard when I recovered. He was happy I was alive, but very sad I'd lost my sight. He took my hand and told me the gods dimmed my eyes for a reason. His words were all I've had to hang on to. Growing up in a favela is hard. Growing up there blind . . . well, if it hadn't been for Baby, who knows if I would have grown up at all?' She chuckled, then added, 'There's more than one *bandido* back home with a chunk missing from his *bumbum*.'

'Ava, I understand, but this . . . this is a *suicide* mission,' Sera said.

'It's not, Sera. You have to trust me. I'm here because I *still* believe what my father said – that the gods dimmed my eyes for a reason. I need to find out what that reason is, and nothing's going to stop me – not alligators, or death riders, or slimy swamp spirits. I'm going to get the ring, and then I'm coming to the Karg. So make sure you get the black pearl by the time I get there!'

The convoca began to weaken. The six mermaids said their goodbyes.

'Don't *worry*,' Ava said. 'I'll be fine. I'll be with you all soon . . .'

And then she was gone.

Becca dimmed the waterfire so they could get back to sleep. Ling and Neela returned to their seaweed beds. Sera remained where she was, distraught. Astrid stayed by her side.

'She'll never make it out alive,' Sera said. 'One frail mermaid against gods-know-how-many death riders. Did you see how thin she looks? I should have been truthful with her. Maybe *then* she would have left the swamp.'

'What do you mean?' Astrid asked.

'I didn't have the heart to tell her that Orfeo has the black pearl,' Sera replied.

'It's good you didn't tell her, Sera. She needs hope,' Astrid said, returning to her bed.

Sera laughed bitterly. 'Hope isn't going to get us that pearl,' she said.

No, it isn't, Astrid agreed silently as she curled up in the seaweed.

But I am.

SIXTY-SIX

LUCIA CIRCLED THE MALIGNO, the skirts of her gown swirling around her.

It was after midnight. She'd led the creature out of Alítheia's den and into the ruins of Merrow's reggia by the light of a weak illuminata spell.

'You're so beautiful,' she whispered, running a hand across the maligno's back. She marvelled again at the cheekbones, the strong jaw, the broad shoulders, the powerful blue tail – all exactly the same as Mahdi's. The only difference was in the creature's eyes. They had no light. But that didn't matter. By the time Sera looked into them, it would be too late.

Lucia stopped in front of the maligno. She held up a small conch. 'Speak the words exactly as I told them to you,' she said.

The maligno opened its mouth and in Mahdi's voice said, 'Sera, it's Mahdi. I'm near the Karg, in the Darktide Shallows. I couldn't send this news with Allegra. We've got big trouble.

Vallerio's heading for the Karg. He's got twenty thousand soldiers with him and is going to attack. There's more to tell you, but I can't come into the camp. There's a spy in your midst and I don't want to be seen. Come to the Shallows. Hurry, Sera. *Please.*'

The maligno spoke with urgency and fear, but all the while, his eyes remained empty and cold.

'Very good,' Lucia said when he finished.

She tucked the conch into the breast pocket of his jacket, then she held something else out to him – Sera's jacket.

The maligno took it in both hands and pressed it to his face, scenting it for traces of its owner, as a shark scents the water for blood.

Lucia unbuttoned the maligno's jacket, tucked Sera's inside, then fastened the creature's jacket again.

She snapped her fingers, and a huge, ugly black sea scorpion crawed out from under a toppled pillar. Its sting would cause instant paralysis, but it didn't sting the maligno. It climbed its tail, crawled up the back of its jacket, and settled on its shoulder.

'Go to the Darktide Shallows. Send the conch to the mermaid Serafina, then wait for her. When you've captured her, bring her to me,' Lucia said. She smiled, her eyes glittering darkly, and added, 'Alive.'

SIXTY-SEVEN

THE FIRST LIGHT of morning broke across the Kargjord, stealing into the command cave's entrance and waking Serafina. She was exhausted. Worried about Ava, she'd barely slept a wink.

As she opened her eyes, she realized she wasn't the only one who was up. Someone else was making small, hushed noises, as if trying not to wake the others.

Sera raised her head and saw that it was Astrid. She was sitting up in her bed, quietly putting things into her backpack.

As Sera watched, Astrid put on her coat, picked up her backpack, and left the cave. It was barely dawn.

Where's she going at this hour? Sera wondered.

She followed, being careful not to disturb Becca, Neela, and Ling, and found Astrid sitting on a rock. She was softly playing the notes of an illuminata songspell on her whalebone pipe. A light, drawn from the sun's first rays, formed near her. Sera swam over and sat down next to her.

'Cool trick,' she said.

'Thanks.'

'Leaving us again?' Sera asked.

Astrid snorted. 'I've been trying to leave you ever since I met you. I never seem to get very far.'

Sera smiled at that.

Having made a good illuminata, Astrid put her pipe down. 'You've changed. A lot. You've become an amazing leader,' she said.

Sera was surprised, and pleased, by Astrid's praise. Compliments were not something Astrid Kolfinnsdottir lavishly bestowed.

'I don't know about that,' Sera said.

'I do.'

'Thanks. I'm trying. I keep hearing Vrăja's words in my head. After you left the Iele's caves, I sat down with her.'

'Let me guess . . . to complain about me,' Astrid said.

'Pretty much,' Sera admitted. 'While I was with her, Vrăja told me that to lead, I needed to help the others. I needed to bring out the best in them. She said I have to help Ling break through silences, and help Neela believe that her greatest power comes from within, not without. I have to help Becca believe that the warmest fire is the one that's shared, and help Ava believe that the gods did know what they were doing when they took her sight.'

'You're doing all that, Sera. The others . . . they're different now, too. I can see it.'

'I hope so,' Sera said. 'Neela's changed for sure. Her power really does come from within now. She hasn't demanded any zee-zees or worried about her hair ever since we've been here.'

Astrid laughed.

'But Becca and Ling? I have no idea. They only just arrived. Ava?' She shook her head. 'I only hope I get the chance to find out.'

'And Astrid?' Astrid asked. 'What about her?'

'I'm not sure,' Sera said, meeting her frank gaze. 'I told Vrăja you were scared.'

'What did she say?'

'She said *I* was scared,' Sera confessed.

'You both were right,' Astrid said. 'I *am* scared, Sera.'

Sera was pretty sure she knew why. 'You've seen him, too, haven't you? Orfeo. You didn't say so, but I saw the expression on your face last night when we were talking about him,' she said. 'Has he come to you in a mirror?'

Astrid nodded. 'I didn't tell you everything. I *have* seen him. He wants me to go to him. He knows I can't songcast, and he wants to fix me. I'm his descendant. Which means I have his blood in my veins, the blood of the most powerful mage who ever lived. He wants to make me powerful, too.'

'So you can help him unlock Abbadon,' Sera said. Dread filled her heart. She knew what Astrid was going to say next.

'I'm going to him, Sera. I'll make him think he's won me over, and somehow, some way, I will get the black pearl.'

'No, Astrid, you *can't*,' Sera said vehemently. 'It's way too dangerous.'

'It's the only way. No one else can get close to him. He'll

kill anyone who tries. I can do this. I can bluff him.'

'Maybe you *can* bluff him,' Sera said. 'But can you resist him?'

Astrid cocked her head. 'What do you mean?' she asked.

'He's powerful, Astrid. So powerful that he cheated death. He's going to focus those powers on you. He's going to try to make you his own. What if he succeeds?'

'He won't.'

'Astrid—' Sera said.

'I'm going.'

Sera, furious with her friend, rose and slapped the rock she'd been sitting on with her tail.

'Hey, *that's* mature,' Astrid said.

'I *just* got us back together,' Sera said angrily. 'All of us except Ava. I *need* you, Astrid.'

'Yes, you do. You need me to get the pearl. I'm the only chance we've got, and you know it.'

Sera heaved a sigh. As painful as it was to admit it, Astrid was right.

'Find Ava. Get the remaining talisman,' Astrid said. 'Then go down to the Southern Ocean with them. I'll meet you there.'

'When?'

'I don't know. I'll get word to you. You may have to wait for me, but I'll be there, Sera. With the black pearl. I promise.'

'Wherever you're going, you're not going alone,' Sera said. 'You have us with you now. Me, Neela, Ling, Ava, and Becca . . . your friends, your sisters.'

Astrid nodded and Sera thought she saw a shimmer of tears in her blue eyes.

'Tell the others goodbye for me,' Astrid said. 'And tell Desiderio . . . tell him I . . . just tell him thank you.'

'I will,' Sera said.

Astrid turned and swam away. Sera watched her move through the camp as the first rays of sun struggled to penetrate the North Sea gloom. Past caves and tents she swam, getting smaller and smaller, until she reached the north gate, and was gone.

Sera waited for a while, not wanting to return to the cave just yet. If the others were up, they'd ask where Astrid was. They might try to follow her, to stop her. Sera knew that wasn't what Astrid wanted.

From her perch on the rock, Sera watched the camp come to life. She saw the guards change their shifts and Antonio make his way to the mess hall. She wondered how they would find enough food to feed everyone in the coming days. She wondered where she would find medicine to make Ling and Mulmig better. She wondered if Ava would make it through the day. She wondered where she'd find the strength she needed to get up off the rock and lead the resistance.

Then she looked at the fresh scar on her hand, and smiled. She had her answer.

As the waters brightened, Sera rose.

'Good luck, Astrid Kolfinnsdottir,' she whispered.

Then she swam back to the cave to rejoin the others.

SIXTY-EIGHT

HIGH ABOVE THE Black Fins' camp, on a lonely, current-swept bluff, the maligno floated.

Tireless, dead-eyed, implacable, it coldly surveyed the ragtag group spread out far away in the distance.

The sea scorpion chittered from its perch on the maligno's shoulder, its venomous tail lashing, its black eyes hateful and bright.

The maligno reached into its pocket, pulled out the small conch its mistress had given it, and wordlessly handed it to the scorpion.

The creature took the conch in its pincers and crawled down the maligno's back. It scuttled off over the bluff, heading towards the camp.

The maligno watched it go.

Then it smiled and headed for the Darktide Shallows.

ACKNOWLEDGEMENTS

CAN A DRESS change your life?

If it was made by the late Alexander McQueen, then quite possibly yes.

I'll explain.

Some time ago, I was casting about for a new idea for a novel. Ghosts from the past had inspired all my stories, but I needed to get away from them. Ghosts are beguiling creatures. They give you their stories but take pieces of your heart in return.

Looking for inspiration, I went to the Metropolitan Museum in New York City. The museum was staging a retrospective of Alexander McQueen's work. As you may know, McQueen was a clothing designer – and a brilliant and troubled man.

His collections were shown in dusky jewel-box rooms; walking through them felt like walking through a dark fairy tale. The dresses were so fierce. They were made of cloth and thread, but of other things, too. Of antlers and skulls. Thorns, flowers, feathers.

And emotion. Love, longing, desire, regret – these things were bound into every stitch. I could feel them. I could feel *him*. McQueen was there, moving through those rooms.

I came to the last rooms, to collections inspired by the sea, and they blew me away. One dress looked as if it was cut from white waves, another like it was fashioned from seaweed. And overhead, on a large screen, was an image of a young woman sinking slowly through water, her dress billowing around her.

Who was she? I didn't know. All I knew is that I was spellbound by McQueen's vision of the sea – a sea that was beautiful, but also treacherous and dark. I knew then that I had to write a story about it.

I thought I was done with ghosts, but it turns out they weren't done with me. Because to this day, I believe that Alexander McQueen sent me a gift. *Dark Tide* is for him, wherever he may be, with gratitude for things rich and strange.

GLOSSARY

Abbadon an immense monster, created by Orfeo, then defeated and caged in the Antarctic waters

Achilles a brigantine, captained by Maffeio Aermore, that went down in 1793 near Cape Horn; now a shipwreck full of ghosts that protect the Williwaw's lair

Alítheia a twelve-foot, venomous sea spider made out of bronze combined with drops of Merrow's blood. Bellogrim, the blacksmith god, forged her, and the sea goddess, Neria, breathed life into her to protect the throne of Miromara from any pretenders.

Alma the woman Orfeo loved; when she died, he went mad with grief

Amarrefe Mei Foo a pirate who attacked the *Demeter*, looking to steal the infanta's blue diamond

Armando Contorini the late duca di Venezia, leader of the Praedatori (aka Karkharias, the Shark)

Artemesia Sera's grandmother, a regina of Miromara who considered the Volnero family tainted and decreed that there would be no alliance with their bloodline

Astrid Kolfinnsdottir teenage daughter of Kolfinn, ruler of Ondalina

Atlantica the mer domain in the Atlantic Ocean; Becca's home

Atlantis an ancient island paradise in the Mediterranean peopled with the ancestors of the mer. Six mages ruled the island wisely and well: Orfeo, Merrow, Sycorax, Navi, Pyrrha and Nyx. When the island was destroyed, Merrow saved the Atlanteans by calling on Neria to give them fins and tails.

Ava teenage mermaid from the Amazon River; she is blind but able to sense things

Baba Vrăja the elder leader – or obârsie – of the Iele, river witches

Baby Ava's guide piranha

Baco Goga an eel-like merman; spy for Vallerio and Portia Volnero

Bastiaan, Principe Consorte Regina Isabella's husband and Serafina's father

Becca Quickfin a teenage mermaid from Atlantica

Bedrieër one of three trawlers that Rafe Mfeme owns

Bianca di Remora one of Lucia's ladies-in-waiting

Black Fins members of a Cerulean resistance group

Black Pearl Orfeo's talisman; given to him by Morsa

Blackclaw Dragon one of the many types of dragons that breed in Matali and are the main source of the realm's wealth; huge and powerful and used by the military

Bloodbind a spell in which blood from different mages is combined to form an unbreakable bond and allow them to share abilities

Bloodsong blood drawn from one's heart that contains memories and allows them to become visible to others

Britannia a luxury ocean liner that went down in a storm in the Adriatic Sea; now a ghost ship

Camo a songspell used to change appearance

Canta malus darksong, a poisonous gift to the mer from Morsa, in mockery of Neria's gifts

Canta prax a plainsong spell

Canta sangua blood magic, an even more heinous violation than canta malus

Carceron the prison on Atlantis. The lock could only be opened by all six talismans. It is now located somewhere in the Southern Sea.

Cassio the sky god

Cerulea the royal city in Miromara, where Serafina lived before it was attacked

Cirrian the language spoken by barnacles

Citadel a city carved out of an iceberg in which Ondalina's admirals live with their families and top members of government

Commodora second-in-command to Ondalina's admiral; spymaster and in charge of the realm's military

Commoveo a songspell that can be used to push objects

Conch a shell in which recorded information is stored

Convoca a songspell that can be used for summoning and communicating with people

Currensea mer money; gold trocii (trocus, sing.), silver drupes, copper cowries; gold doubloons are black market currensea

Daímonas tis Morsa demon of Morsa

Darksong a powerful canta malus spell that causes harm, legal to use against enemies during wartime

Death Riders Traho's soldiers, who ride on black hippokamps

Demeter the ship that Maria Theresa, an infanta of Spain, was sailing on when it was lost in 1582 en route to France

Depth Sickness a dangerous and occasionally lethal condition caused by diving too deep; symptoms include headache, nausea, disorientation, hallucinations, asphyxiation and brain bleeding

Desiderio Serafina's older brother

Dokimí Greek for *trial*; a ceremony in which the heir to the Miromaran throne has to prove that she is a true descendant of Merrow by spilling blood for Alítheia, the sea spider. She must then songcast, make her betrothal vows and swear to one day give the realm a daughter.

Duchi di Venezia created by Merrow to protect the seas and its creatures from terragoggs

EisGeists murderous spirits that dwell in cold water; created by Morsa, they are neither alive nor dead; they drag their victims behind them until the flesh rots away and then eat the bones

Ekelshmutz one of the four goblin tribes

Elisabetta Contorini sister of Marco Contorini, the current duca di Venezia

Elskan an orca that Kolfinn bought for his wife Eyvör to ride

Elysia capital of Atlantis

Eveksion the god of healing

Eyvör wife of Admiral Kolfinn and mother to Ragnar and Astrid

Feimor Fa Eaemor a Viking chieftain who bought Orfeo's black pearl from a fisherman

Feuerkumpel goblin miners, one of the Kobold tribes, who channel magma from deep seams under the North Sea in order to obtain lava for lighting and heating

Fragor lux a songspell to cast a light bomb (frag, abbreviation)

Freshwaters the mer domain that encompasses rivers, lakes and ponds

Fryst a clan of giant ice trolls that protects Ondalina's Citadel

Gândac a bug that is planted near a person or thing that a songcaster wants to observe; it catches and holds the ochi spell

Ghost ship a shipwreck entwined with the life force of a human who died onboard; it does not rot or rust

Gold coin Pyrrha's talisman, with an image of Neria on it

Great Abyss a deep chasm in Qin where Sycorax's talisman is believed to be located, and where Ling's father disappeared while exploring

Guldemar the Meerteufel sea goblin tribe's chieftain

Hafgufa the kraken; according to legend, Meerteufel chieftains can call the creature forth in times of trouble

Hagarla queen of the Razormouth dragons

Hall of Sighs a long corridor in Vadus, the mirror realm, whose walls are covered in mirrors; every mirror has a corresponding one in the terragogg world

Hippokamps creatures that are half horse, half serpent, with snakelike eyes

Höllerbläser goblin glassblowers, one of the Kobold tribes

Horok the great coelacanth, Keeper of Souls, who takes the dead to the underworld, holding each soul in a white pearl

Iele river witches

Illuminata a songspell to create light

Illusio a spell to create a disguise

Incantarium the room where the incanta – river witches – keep Abbadon at bay through chanting and waterfire

Iron repels magic

Isabella, La Serenissima Regina Miromara's former ruler; Serafina's mother

Kargjord a hilly, desolate barrens at the northernmost reaches of the Meerteufel's realm; the Black Fins' military training ground

Kharis priestess of the death goddess Morsa

Kobold North Sea goblin tribes

Kolfinn Admiral of the Artic region, Ondalina; Astrid's father

Kolisseo a huge open-water stone theatre in Miromara that dates back to Merrow's time

Lagoon the waters off the human city of Venice, forbidden to merfolk

Lava globe a light source, lit by magma mined and refined into white lava by the Feuerkumpel

Ling a teenage mermaid from the realm of Qin; she is an omnivoxa

Lucia Volnero once one of Serafina's ladies-in-waiting, now a pretender to the Miromaran throne; a member of the Volnero, a noble family as old – and nearly as powerful – as the Merrovingia

Ludovico di Merrovingia, Principe younger brother to both Vallerio and Isabella; a Miromaran exchanged with Kolfinn's sister as part of the permutavi; breeder of hippokamps and trainer of orcas used by Ondalina's military

Macapá Ava's home village in the Freshwaters realm

Maelstrom a powerful whirlpool in the sea

Maffeio Aermore captain of the *Achilles*, a brigantine that went down in 1793 near Cape Horn

Mahdi crown prince of Matali; Serafina's betrothed; cousin of Yazeed and Neela

Maligno a creature made out of clay and animated by blood magic

Månenhonnør Ondalina's moon festival

Månenkager a cake, eaten during Månenhonnør, made of pressed krill and iced with ground mother-of-pearl, so it shines like the moon; baked with a silver drupe coin in it for good luck

Marco Contorini the current duca di Venezia; brother of Elisabetta

Maria Theresa an infanta of Spain who was sailing to France on the *Demeter* in 1582 when it was attacked by a pirate, Amarrefe Mei Foo

Markus Traho, Captain leader of the death riders

Marlin a Wave Warrior boat fitted with a saltwater tank to transport sick and wounded sea creatures

Matali the mer realm in the Indian Ocean; Neela's home

Matalin from Matali

Medica magus mer equivalent of doctor

Meerteufel one of four goblin tribes

Merl Mermish equivalent of girl

Mermaid's Tear another name for Neria's Stone, the blue diamond, which Neria gave to Merrow

Mermish the common language of the sea people

Merrovingia descendants of Merrow

Merrow a great mage, one of the six rulers of Atlantis, and Serafina's ancestor. First ruler of the merpeople; songspell originated with her, and she decreed the Dokimí.

Merrow's Progress Ten years after the destruction of Atlantis, Merrow made a journey to all of the waters of the world, scouting out safe places for the merfolk to colonize.

Miromara the realm Serafina comes from; an empire that spans the Mediterranean Sea, the Adriatic, Aegean, Baltic, Black, Ionian, Ligurian, and Tyrrhenean Seas, the Seas of Azov and Marmara, the Straits of Gibraltar, the

Dardanelles and the Bosphorus

Moon jelly a bioluminescent jellyfish

Moonstone Navi's talisman; silvery blue and the size of an albatross's egg, with an inner glow

Morsa an ancient scavenger goddess, whose job it was to take away the bodies of the dead. She angered Neria by practising necromancy. Neria punished her by giving her the face of death and the body of a serpent and banishing her.

Moses Potion a liquid from the Moses sole in the Red Sea that puts people to sleep

Navi one of the six mages who ruled Atlantis; Neela's ancestor

Neela a Matalin princess; Serafina's best friend; Yazeed's sister; Mahdi's cousin. She is a bioluminescent.

Neféli a cloud nymph

Neria the sea goddess

Neria's Stone a blue, tear-shaped diamond that Neria gave to Merrow for saving Kyr, her youngest son, from a shark attack

Nyx one of the six mages who ruled Atlantis; Ava's ancestor

Ochi a powerful spying spell in which the songcaster plants a gândac, or bug, near the person or thing being observed

Okwa Naholo water spirits in the swamps of the Mississippi that guard Nyx's talisman

Omnivoxa (omni) mer who have the natural ability to speak every dialect of Mermish and communicate with sea creatures

Ondalina the mer realm in the Arctic waters; Astrid's home

Orfeo one of the six mages who ruled Atlantis; Astrid's ancestor

Ostrokon the mer version of a library

Palazzo Italian for palace

Permutavi a pact between Miromara and Ondalina, enacted after the War of Reykjanes Ridge, that decreed the exchange of the rulers' children

Portia Volnero mother of Lucia and a powerful duchessa of Miromara; wanted to marry Vallerio, Serafina's uncle

Praedatori soldiers who defend the sea and its creatures against terragoggs; known as Wave Warriors on land

Praesidio Duca Contorini's home in Venice

Prax practical magic that helps the mer survive, such as camouflage spells, echolocation spells, spells to improve speed or darken an ink cloud. Even those with little magical ability can cast them.

Principessa Italian for princess

Promising an exchange of betrothal vows that, once spoken, cannot be broken until death

Puzzle Ball Sycorax's talisman; a small, ornately carved white ball containing spheres within spheres, with the image of a phoenix on the outside

Pyrrha one of the six rulers of Atlantis; Becca's ancestor

Qanikkaaq a giant maelstrom in the Greenland Sea; believed to be the location of Orfeo's talisman

Qin the mer realm in the Pacific Ocean; Ling's home

Rafe Iaoro Mfeme worst of the terragoggs; he runs a fleet of dredgers and super trawlers that threaten to pull every last fish out of the sea

Ragnar Astrid's older brother

Raysay the language spoken by manta rays

Razormouth dragon one of the many types of dragons that breed in Matali and are the main source of the realm's wealth; they are feral and murderous and prevent invaders from getting past the Madagascar Basin

Reggia Merrow's ancient palace

Regina Italian for queen

River Olt the Freshwater region where the Iele's cave is located

Rorrim Drol lord of Vadus, the mirror realm

Ruby Ring Nyx's talisman; a large stone, with many facets, in a gold setting

Rylka Kolfinn's commodora, the second most powerful mer in Ondalina

Scaghaufen capital of the Meerteufel sea goblin tribe

Sea Wasp the most deadly jellyfish in the world

Sejanus Adro Portia Volnero's husband, who died a year after Lucia's birth

Selection the death riders' daily process of choosing which of their captives will dive into the Great Abyss to search for Sycorax's talisman

Serafina regina di Miromara and leader of the Black Fin Resistance

Shan Lu Chi Ling's father, an archeologist

Shayú Amarrefe Mei Foo's pirate ship

Shipwreck ghosts hungry for life, their touch – if prolonged – can be lethal

Somna potion a sleeping draft

Sophia a Black Fin; she saves Serafina's life during the raid on Miromara's treasury

Stickstoff head of the Meerteufel's military

Svikari one of the trawlers that Rafe Mfeme owns

Sycorax one of the six rulers of Atlantis; Ling's ancestor

Talisman object with magical properties

Tauno Rylka's son; a major in the Ondalinian military

Terragoggs (goggs) humans

Thalia, Lady a vitrina who knows what the six talismans are

Traitors' Gate the entrance to the dungeons underneath Miromara's royal palace

Transparensea pearl a pearl that contains a songspell of invisibility; Transparensea pebbles are not as strong as transparensea pearls

Trykel and Spume twin gods of the tides

Vadus the mirror realm

Vallerio, Principe del Sangue Regina Isabella's brother; Miromara's high commander; Serafina's uncle, Lucia's father

Vitrina souls of beautiful, vain humans who spent so much time admiring themselves in mirrors that they are now trapped inside

Vortex a songspell used to create a whirl

Waterfire magical fire used to enclose or contain

Wave Warriors humans who fight for the sea and its creatures

Whalefall the hallowed ground where the remains of dead whales lie; some magic remains in their bones after death

Williwaw a wind spirit at Cape Horn; possessor of Pyrrha's talisman

Yazeed Neela's brother; Mahdi's cousin; Sera's second-in-command

Zee-zee a Matalin candy

Zeno Piscor traitor to Serafina and Neela, in league with Traho

Zephyros god of the wind; son of Cassio, the sky god

the Freshwaters
the Freshwaters
THE GREAT ABYSS
QIN
Okwo Naholo